W9-CQP-893

THE IRISH ROGUE

Judith E. French

IVY BOOKS • NEW YORK

An Ivy Book
Published by The Ballantine Publishing Group
Copyright © 2000 by Judith E. French

Ivy Books and colophon are trademarks of Random House, Inc.

ISBN 0-7394-1121-7

Manufactured in the United States of America

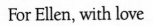

For Ellen, with love

Fortune aids the brave.
—TERENCE

Chapter 1

St. John's Churchyard
April 1820

The earth seemed to crumble beneath Anne's feet. She staggered back, unconsciously protecting with a gloved hand the new life inside her. She stared at her betrothed in disbelief, as stunned as if he'd struck her with a clenched fist.

"You said you loved me," she stammered as the solid chill of a marble tombstone halted her retreat. "You promised to marry me. . . ."

His cool tone smothered her remaining hopes. "You are such an innocent. You should thank me, you know. Not many women have the benefit of expertise such as mine in their first alliance."

Rain dripped from the overhanging trees, soaking Anne's cloak and hair. The night was raw and damp. Puddles of water seeped up through her kidskin boots, but her mouth felt almost too dry to answer. "You call yourself a gentleman," she whispered. "I believed you. I brought my things because you told me that we were going to New Jersey to be wed." Her throat constricted with emotion. "I'm carrying your child, Stephen. Doesn't that mean anything? What am I supposed to do?"

1

In the dark, Stephen was little more than a shadowy outline of a broad-brimmed hat and greatcoat against the deeper blackness of the wooded churchyard. His mocking voice seemed to come from a distance to echo off the mossy stones and swirl around her. "Are you certain that it's mine?"

"You can ask me that? After I defied my father to come here? After all your vows of love and—"

"Spare me your pitiful whining. You were willing enough to be bedded. Mayhap you found someone else to keep you warm after I left Maryland."

Anger replaced terror and Anne stiffened. "We've made a child between us. Can you turn your back on that?"

He shrugged. "That's your problem. Get rid of it, or have your father buy you a red-cheeked farmer boy too stupid to realize that his fields have already been plowed and planted."

"If I were a man, I would call you out on a field of honor and—"

Stephen chuckled. "If you were a man, you'd not be in this unfortunate condition, and I'd never have been attracted to your charms."

"My father will come for you."

"If you're stupid enough to let that happen. He might try. But I'm an excellent shot. I killed a man in Bristol in a duel over a woman. That's why my family sent me to America. Naturally, his wife's reputation was ruined. So send Papa after me with hounds in full cry, but he could end up in a grave. As for you, Anne, let us agree that a gentleman can be forgiven many slips, a lady none."

Anne had never hated anyone before, never wanted to hit and keep hitting until she drew blood—not until this moment. "Why? Why me?"

"Don't be a fool. I thought you gullible but never stupid."

"My father's money?"

"Of course. I have needs that require somewhat more than my family allowance provides for."

A vile taste flooded Anne's mouth. "You admit that you're nothing but a fortune hunter?"

He laughed. "Don't take it so to heart. You've a pretty figure and a talent for pleasing a man. I would have married you if I hadn't met a better prospect. But it would have been a mistake for both of us. I'm really not cut out to be a Maryland farmer. Philadelphia is more my style. My plump Quaker heiress is too well bred to object to my personal life, and her father is much wealthier than yours."

"Burn in hell, Stephen Preston!" Sickened, ashamed, Anne turned and fled down the crumbling brick walkway out of the walled cemetery to a waiting carriage.

A wavering circle of lantern light illuminated her sister Mary's pale face. "Anne! Is that you? Hurry. Get in, out of the weather."

Bells on the leather harness jingled, and the horse moved restlessly between the shafts. Mist enveloped the high-wheeled chaise as Anne climbed onto the damp seat beside Mary. Icy droplets ran down Anne's face, and she clenched her teeth to keep them from chattering.

"What's wrong?" Mary clutched at Anne's arm. "I thought I heard voices. Where's Mr. Preston? Isn't he coming for your trunk?"

Anne shook her head, so overcome by loathing for Stephen that she found it hard to speak. "I've been such a fool."

"You're not calling off the elopement?" Mary's tone took on an edge of hysteria. "You can't go home to Papa without a husband. You've got to—"

"It's over. Finished." Anne's eyelids prickled. She wouldn't cry for the likes of Stephen Preston. Not now. Not ever. "Papa was right. Stephen is a lying, despicable swine."

"Oh, oh dear." Mary covered her mouth with her hand. "What will you do? What will we do? If anyone finds out, the family will be ruined."

"Stop blubbering and give me the reins." Anne took the lines and slapped them over the horse's back. "We're going back to your house. It's late. We don't want George to find us gone." Mary's husband was a self-righteous man who had strong opinions about proper behavior for ladies. Anne had never liked him, and she knew the feeling was mutual.

"Oh, goodness," Mary fretted. "George will be livid. He'll blame me, Anne. The last time I disappointed him, he cut off my allowance for weeks. And Papa . . . Papa will disown us."

Anne wiped the rain off her face and leaned forward trying to see where the horse was going. "He can't disown you, Mary. You already have your inheritance settlement."

"You don't. You know how Papa can be. He'll cut you off without a dime. Nancy Swift's family struck her name from the Bible when she . . ."

"Had a baby. Surely you can say the word. You've given birth twice yourself."

Mary bit her lower lip. "But my girls were legitimate," she whispered. "If you . . . If you don't marry Mr. Preston at once, I shudder to think what people will say about us. Lucy and Margaret may never find husbands in Philadelphia."

"Or Baltimore." Rage seethed in Anne's breast. She wanted to scream, to kick something. But tantrums were Mary's domain. Anne had spent nearly a quarter of a century being the practical sister, the reasonable one. And it was too late to change. She could only vent her anger by poking fun at Mary's irrational fancies.

"Sarcasm doesn't become you, Anne. George would hardly condone a prospective bridegroom from Baltimore. His family has been an important one in Penn's town since—"

"Since Noah built the ark." The gelding's iron-shod hooves thudded against the wet cobblestones. "And the girls are what? Two and four? Surely George will be seeking good matches for them by Christmas."

"This is serious," Mary persisted, wringing her hands. "I don't think you realize how serious this is. I should never have let you talk me into being a partner to your deception. You are the eldest. You're not supposed to lead me into wrongdoing."

"You thought it was great sport until now. Hiding the meetings from Papa, sending me Stephen's letters hidden in yours. Romantic, you said."

"It was. Mr. Preston was so handsome, so English. And he seemed to be of such good breeding." Mary clutched Anne's arm. "What are we going to do?"

"Do?" The horse slowed. Anne peered through the fog. She wasn't familiar with these streets at night, but she had a pretty good sense of direction. She reined the horse left.

"Not that way," Mary corrected. "We can't get through that way. The workmen are digging some sort of hole in the street. We have to go around the cemetery. Take a right here, then left, down two blocks, then left again."

"Are you sure?"

"I've lived here for five years, haven't I?" She began to fret again as Anne reluctantly turned the horse's head to the right. "I should never have let you come to visit. If you'd stayed at Gentleman's Folly, none of this would have happened and your innocence would still be intact."

"Stop it, Mary. Don't make things worse than they are. All I need to do is find a husband."

"But Mr. Preston—"

"Forget Stephen. I'm lucky to have escaped him. I wouldn't have him now if it cost me my immortal soul."

"But you must have a husband."

"Of course I must. But at this point, any other God-fearing man without foul breath or nasty habits will serve." They were alone in the narrow lane. Here and there a light glowed, but most houses were dark. Mist blanketed the city, distorting sounds eerily.

"You don't mean that."

"Don't I? I'll do what many women before me have done." Anne made her plans as she spoke. "I'll make a marriage of convenience. I'll trade Papa's fortune for a man's name and protection. He'll gain the plantation, silver, and slaves, and my baby's name will be saved from the brand of—"

"Don't you dare say it," Mary warned. "Such words are best not thought of by a lady, let alone uttered. And how will you find a gentleman willing to trade his honor for your acres? Especially since the . . . the child must be claimed as his own and come first in all future inheritances."

"Leave that to me, little sister," Anne replied, trying to ignore the hollow ache in her chest. "I will find a proper husband."

"You'd best do it soon, then. Within a month at least. Any more and everyone will guess. Besides, having an early birth is nearly as bad as having one without a father." She pointed. "There, turn there."

"What's that?"

"Mercy save us!" Mary cried as a burly sailor lurched in front of the carriage.

"Watch where yer goin'!" he warned.

Anne yanked on the reins as a second drunk staggered from a recessed doorway. Through the opening, she could hear curses and raucous male laughter. "Where are we?" she hissed to her sister. "We didn't come this way."

The horse tossed its head as the two swaying seamen delivered a volley of blistering oaths. Anne seized the whip and cracked it over the gelding's head. "Get up!"

The blasphemers dived for the safety of the gutter as horse and carriage jolted past. Mary clung to the seat, wide-eyed. A block later, Anne slowed the horse to a trot, unwilling to risk the animal's safety on the slick cobblestones.

"Look at that, would ya," a man with long dirty-blond hair said to his companions from the interior of the tavern. Swinging a crutch under one arm, he heaved himself up and pointed to the chaise rattling away through the fog. "What do ya make of 'em?" His two companions shouldered their way through the regulars onto the street.

"Rich doxies out for a thrill," the skinny one said.

"Headed toward the docks, they was." Cove drained the dregs from his mug and tossed it into the gutter, then repositioned his padded crutch. "I didn't hear no gent in that carriage, did you, Shannie?"

"Easy pickin's?"

"Easy pickin's," the third agreed as they turned to follow.

Across the way, a couple stood watching from the shadowy entrance of a tall brick house with shuttered windows. "What makes me think those three are up to mischief?" An Irish lilt sweetened the deep timbre of the tall man's voice.

"No good, 'tis certain." The scantly clad woman gripped his arm. "Stay here with me tonight, O'Ryan. Haven't you enough trouble of your own? You know how you are when it comes to the ladies."

"How am I?" He flashed a devilish grin as he touched her rouged cheek.

"You don't need me to tell you," she purred. "You've a soft spot for the lasses." She stood on tiptoes to rub her voluptuous body suggestively against him. "Those three wharf rats are a bad lot. Why risk steel in your gut for rich nobs when you could be taking your pleasure between my sheets."

He sighed with regret as he toyed with a rose-scented

silken curl. Peg was a sweet broth of a wench who knew how to please a man. He couldn't see the shape of her talented mouth in the darkness, but he could feel it on his skin. Her musky scent lingered in his head, and his loins ached to take her up on her offer.

Why, just once, couldn't he think of his own best interests? Forget his father's admonition that a man's duty was to protect the weak and never abandon a woman in trouble. "Old habits die hard," he muttered.

"What's that, love?"

He drew in a deep breath. "Nothing, Peggy, just remembering someone. Those three who followed the carriage, footpads, are they?" he asked lightly, knowing he wouldn't be content to leave well enough alone.

"Worse than thieves. The bogtrotter with the yellow hair and the crutch is Ty Cove. Not meanin' to give offense," she added. "Them being Irish as yourself."

"None taken," he assured her.

"A rare devil with a knife is Cove. Word on the dock is he's responsible for the floaters found Sabbath mornings with pockets and throats slit. They say one of his victims fought back and smashed Cove's leg before he died." She caressed his burgeoning arousal. "Come back inside. 'Tis your lucky night, me great boyo."

"Ah, Peggy, you'd tempt a saint. But you worry too much." The big Irishman kissed the crown of her head as he cupped her rounded bottom with his hand. "I heard a lass cry out from that gig. I've a mind to follow and see what Master Cove and his mates are up to."

"You'll not listen to good advice?"

He laughed. "When have I ever?"

Anne knew they'd made a terrible mistake when the cobblestones turned to gravel and the horse's hooves clattered against wooden planks. "This isn't right. Smell the rotting fish? I think we're going toward the docks." Spits of rain peppered her cheeks and dripped off her lashes. The light from the single carriage lantern only accentuated the ghostly white mist around them.

The way was narrow. Windowless buildings crowded close on either side of the alley. They'd not passed a lit doorway in the last two blocks.

Far off a dog barked; Mary slid across the seat until she was practically sitting on Anne's lap. "George has forbidden me to come to the harbor, even in daylight. So many undesirables about. Ruffians everywhere. We have to turn around."

"I am." Anne wished she could see how close they were to the water, but fog draped like a curtain beyond the gelding's head. "There seem to be crates and rope heaped along the sides of the lane. I don't want to risk breaking a wheel and overturning the chaise. I'd best get out and lead the horse." She passed the reins to her sister. "Hold these."

"Do be careful."

A sharp retort rose on Anne's tongue, and she suppressed it. What worse could possibly happen tonight? Anne tried not to think of Stephen's betrayal as she climbed down and felt along the carriage wheel, then down the shaft to take hold of the bridle. "Come on, boy," she murmured as she carefully turned the horse and carriage away from the dock.

"What's yer hurry?"

Anne gasped as a hulking figure with stringy yellow hair materialized out of the mist. The apparition's gait was uneven, and he seemed to be leaning on a staff.

"Whatcha got in this trunk here?" another harsh voice came from behind them, the direction of the harbor. That one was Irish, too, his brogue so thick Anne could barely make out his words.

Mary screamed.

Anne leaped for the buggy whip near the right wheel. The trunk contained her best clothing, the trousseau she'd packed for her elopement with Stephen, and she had no intention of handing it over to a skulking thief. "Stay away from my luggage!" She plucked the whip from the holder as she scrambled to find the iron step to climb back into the carriage.

"Get the goods!" the yellow-haired thug ordered. Hard-faced and quick, he closed in on the far side of the chaise. Anne saw that his stick was really a padded crutch.

Mary shrieked and flung her purse at his face.

"Take my money!" she cried. "Don't hurt us!"

The horse shied and snorted. Anne found her balance on the step and used the dash to lever herself up onto the seat. Behind her, she could hear the Irishman tearing at the straps that held her luggage. "Get away!" she shouted. "They hang thieves in this city!"

"Hear that? The bitch means to see us swing." The bully with the crutch reached for Mary. Anne lashed out at him with the whip.

The lead-weighted tip tore a furrow down his cheek, and he staggered back, howling in pain. Then a third man grabbed Anne's arm and tried to yank her from the carriage.

She didn't hesitate. She cracked the whip across the horse's rump as hard as she could and yelled, "Get up!"

The gelding bolted ahead, but the man hung on, half in and half out of the chaise. Anne struck at his face with her fist, but the far wheel hit something and the vehicle tilted and bounced.

Both Anne and her attacker fell. He tried to keep his footing, but he tripped and she landed in the lane on top of him. Her right palm skidded across splintery boards, sending pain shooting up her arm. For an instant, the wind was knocked out of her.

Then rough hands encircled her waist and yanked her up. "Sure and that's no way to be friendly," the Irishman hissed into her ear. His unshaven jaw scraped against her cheek, and she caught the sour smells of old sweat and unwashed clothing.

The man who had pulled her from the chaise got to his feet and laughed, exchanging foul jests with his comrade. Then he began to paw her as well.

"Anne! Anne!" Mary's strident cries echoed above the din of the galloping horse and speeding carriage.

Heat flared through Anne's body, and her knees went weak as milk. Her heart hammered wildly, and she bit her lip to keep from crying out.

She was going to die.

Her unborn child would die with her.

"No!" She drove the palm of her hand up and caught the Irish villain squarely under his nose. He yelped and let go, blubbering curses. She hoped she'd broken his nose.

The leader uttered a foul oath. "You've lost the carriage, you witless arseholes." The *thump-thump* of the crutch approached. In his free hand, the thief carried the twisted lantern that had hung on Mary's chaise.

"Lost the other'n, but got this'n. And she smell good enough to eat." The third robber, the drunkest of the lot, snickered stupidly.

Anne took a hesitant step back, careful not to look directly into their faces. If they weren't afraid for her to see them . . . The thought was chilling. "My father will pay you well to let me go unharmed," she stammered, trying to hide her fear. She'd lost her bonnet when she fell from the chaise. Her torn cloak and muslin dress gave little protection against the raw night or the pawing hands of her tormentors.

Bony fingers tangled in her hair, pulling her head back. "Singin' a different tune now, ain't ya? We all know ya came to the docks lookin' fer action."

She gritted her teeth against the pain. Tears stung her eyes, but she would not give in to her terror. Instinctively she sensed that any show of weakness would mean her end. There was no pity to be found in these men, only greed. "We were lost. My family is wealthy. You've done nothing irrevocable yet. Will you lose all that money and risk your necks . . . for . . . for . . ." The awful words died in her throat.

"I say we cut our losses," the Irishman said. "Swive the wench then wring her neck."

Anne sucked in a deep breath and screamed, "Help! Help me!"

"Shut up!" The man with the crutch slapped her, and she tasted the coppery bite of blood in her mouth. The other two crowded close, and the big man handed the lantern to the drunk. Anne tried to run, but the brigand was on her in an instant, shaking her until her teeth rattled.

"Be still," Cove rasped. "This can go easy or this can go hard."

"Quit talking and get to the swiving," the drunk urged. "Less you want me to show ya how."

The yellow-haired brute seized hold of her collar and ripped the neckline of her gown. "Be nice. You might like what I got fer ya."

"No! Stop!" He gripped her wrist, twisting her right arm behind her back. She screamed again, beating at his head with her free fist as foul whiskey breath scorched her face. He slobbered at her throat and she gagged as his wet tongue rasped her skin.

"She's too much for ye!"

"Let me show ya how it's done."

Anne fought back with every ounce of her strength. Cove shoved her and she fell, landing on a heap of rope. Instantly, he was on her, pinning her thrashing body and groping her leg with a filthy hand.

A pistol shot shattered the night.

Chapter 2

Anne's attacker swore and released his grip. Stomach churning, she scrambled out of his reach and crawled on hands and knees until a solid wall blocked her way.

"Stand away, lads," the stranger called.

Another Irishman. Anne's hope of rescue plummeted. Numb with fright, she got to her feet and braced her back against the crumbling bricks. She clenched her fists, preparing to sell her life dearly.

"Ease off, paddy," the Irish thief said. "Nob or nay, that's Limerick Town I hear in yer words. That makes us brothers."

"Not kin to you, by the grace of God." The newcomer moved closer. "I've no wish to shed your blood. Crawl down your rat holes, and I'll let you live."

Anne's heart thudded. Irish he might be, but he spoke with the cultured authority of a gentleman.

"There's three of us and only one of you!" The drunk laughed. "Not good odds fer a bloody gent."

"True enough. But I'll put a ball through your heart before you get close enough to make use of the advantage."

Anne's knees were weak. She didn't think she had the strength to run, but she began to inch slowly down the wall, closer to the shadow with the pistol. He might be as wicked as the others, but one devil was better than three.

"What's the trull to you?" demanded Cove.

"Bitch worth getting yer throat cut for?" The bubbling, distorted voice could only have come from the man with the smashed nose.

The reply rang with quiet confidence. "I'll ask you the same."

"Rush him before he reloads!" The lantern went out.

"He can't get all of us!"

"Gutter wisdom." The gentleman's scornful laughter echoed through the dark alley. "Your captain seems willing to allow one of you to take my second bullet."

Anne froze. She hadn't heard footsteps, but the gunman was directly in front of her, an arm's length away.

"Shhh," he whispered. "I've come to help."

Yes, she thought. But whom does he mean to help? She drew in a ragged breath as his coat brushed her hand. It was too dark to make out his features, but he was taller than the footpad with the crutch and had broader shoulders.

"I've no need to reload, lads. I've a single shot left. Who feels lucky?"

A bulky figure rushed out of the swirling fog. Anne stuffed her hand in her mouth to suppress a cry of fear as the men slammed together and scuffled. Fists and knees collided. Then came the thud of a dull blow, a groan, and a body slumped to the ground.

Anne shuddered.

"For shame." If her rescuer was out of breath, his mocking sarcasm gave no evidence of it. "One down, and I didn't need to waste my powder and shot. Who's next?" The metallic click of a pistol hammer echoed through the mist.

"If he had another bullet, he'd have used it!" the yellow-haired ruffian exclaimed.

Anne waited for what seemed an eternity. Then the silence was broken by receding footfalls as one thief fled back toward the water.

"Another time, Shannon." A crutch tapped away across the worn planks.

"Aye, Ty Cove. Another time."

Seconds passed.

"Are you all right?" Anne's rescuer's words were accented, but pleasant. He sounded like a man she could trust.

"Than—thank you, sir." Her tongue felt thick, her mouth dry. "I'll be on . . . on my way."

"Did they hurt you?" Hard steel lurked just beneath the surface of that lilting Irish veneer.

"No . . . not . . . No." She was bruised and shaken, her palms scraped and bleeding, but that wasn't what he meant. He was asking if she'd been violated. The thought made her stomach pitch.

Anne took a step. Something scurried beneath her foot. She yelped, stumbled back, and would have fallen if he hadn't caught her in powerful arms.

"Easy, colleen."

He smelled slightly of tobacco, oiled leather, and brandy. She could detect no hint of body odor on him or on his clothing. His touch was oddly reassuring. Still, she began to shiver violently.

"Hist, hist," he soothed, removing his coat and wrapping it around her quaking shoulders. "You're safe."

"Am I?" She didn't feel safe. The air around her seemed charged with electricity. "I don't know you. I don't even know your name."

Little flashes of exploding light sparked behind her eyes. She'd never fainted in her life, but she feared this might be a first. Once, when she was small, she and her father had been caught on the Chesapeake in a storm. Wind and water had churned a maelstrom, tossing the sailboat, making her certain she was going to die. She had closed her eyes and clung to her father.

She wanted to do that now.

"I'm Michael O'Ryan, late of Dublin."

A single tear welled up and spilled down her cheek. "I . . . I am Anne Davis of Gentleman's Folly." The words were no sooner out of her mouth than she realized how foolish she sounded. "On the Chesapeake—in Maryland," she finished lamely.

"You're a long way from the Chesapeake." He released her and she heard the scrape and click of a pistol being loaded.

"You—you were bluffing," she managed. "You didn't have a second shot."

"No."

The thief on the ground stirred and began to moan.

"You faced them down without any bullets in your gun." His bravery made even more tears spill from her eyes. This man, a total stranger, had risked his life for her.

He gave a small sound of amusement. "I've had a fair run of cards this night. I hoped luck was still with me."

"But if they hadn't believed . . ." She couldn't complete the thought. Her mind was jumbled—wild. She knew she had to get away from this awful place before her terror got the best of her—before she shamed herself by begging him to hold her again. "My sister," she said. "I'm visiting my sister."

"She lives near here?" He sounded doubtful.

"No. We were— She lives on Spruce. If you'd just point the way to St. John's Churchyard, I could find the house from there." O'Ryan's greatcoat slipped off one of her shoulders. "I'm grateful for your help, but I'm perfectly capable of—"

He cut her off brusquely. "What were you doing on the docks at this hour?"

"I—we—went to St. John's to meet . . . Sweet hope of heaven! Mary! My sister! She was still in the carriage when the horse ran away. She may have been injured. She may be dead!" The thought that she had been so concerned with her own welfare that she'd forgotten Mary cut through her like a whip. "I've got to find Mary."

"Like as not the horse has carried her safely home. At least she didn't have to contend with these dock scum."

"Do you think she's really all right?"

"I'll wager she gained control of the animal before the chaise tipped over. You'd have heard the carriage smash if she'd not rounded the corner safely." Then his voice dropped even lower. "You went to the churchyard to meet someone—a lover?"

"No!" The lie made her cheeks flame. "Yes," she whispered. "He was my betrothed. We were running away to be married. This was supposed to be my wedding ni—night." Her tears became a torrent as she dissolved in racking sobs.

Muscular arms enfolded her, and his act of compassion washed away her last reserves of caution. Shamelessly she pressed her face against his chest and told him how Stephen had seduced and betrayed her.

"Shh, shh," he crooned.

"He swore he loved me. I believed him, and now . . . now I'm lost. My father will disown me."

Anne's fresh burst of weeping pierced O'Ryan's reserve, and he was filled with the urge to protect her and kiss away her tears. Peggy was right. The ladies were his undoing.

What is stronger than a sword? demanded the lyrics of an old Irish ballad. And the answering refrain, *A woman's tears are stronger than a sword,* was as true today as it had been in the ancient days of Irish kings.

"I'll see you safely home, Annie Davis."

'Sblood, but his jaw ached where the river swine had landed a solid left before he'd rapped him on the skull with his pistol barrel. The blackguard's knife had sliced through his best pants and nicked his thigh deep enough to draw blood. The wound wasn't serious. He'd suffered far worse and lived to tell the tale, but a few inches to the right and he'd have lost something far dearer to him than a pair of good wool trousers. And broken saucy Peggy's heart, no doubt, he mused with black humor.

". . . I can't let you—"

What was it the lass was saying? O'Ryan shook his head, impatient to be out of here before the thieves came back with reinforcements. "They may be out there in the dark, waiting for you. I'd not sleep this night if I didn't take you safely to your family."

"But—"

"Enough," he answered firmly. "By now your sister should have raised the alarm. We must get you back before the city is up in arms."

When horse and carriage clattered into the side courtyard, George Whitfield, Mary's husband, rushed out of the house, swearing so fiercely that she could barely explain what had happened.

"The ruffians have Anne," she sobbed hysterically. "They've murdered her—I know they have." Mary rocked back and forth, hands over her face. "It was awful. I didn't mean to leave her. The horse bolted—"

"And what purpose would have been served had you been kidnapped as well?" George waved her toward the house. "Go inside and leave this to me."

"We made a wrong turn in the fog. I didn't—"

"Not another word!" His mouth tightened. "I've been patient with you, Mary, more so because of your youth and childish nature. But this stupidity is beyond belief." He scowled. "A less patient husband would have taken you in hand well before this."

"Don't—"

"Well you might weep, wife. If we find your sister alive, she will never be the same. And you must share the blame for her ruin."

Mary's maids followed her into the house as George shouted commands. Menservants milled about, lighting torches, saddling horses, and arming themselves with staves.

Brandishing a musket in his left hand, George led his employees out the back gate and down a side alley. They turned onto Spruce, the main street that ran in front of the town house, just as O'Ryan and Anne rounded the corner.

"Step away from that woman!" George bellowed. "Reach for a weapon and I'll send you to your grave."

"No!" Anne called as they paused under a circle of lantern light. "I'm unhurt. This brave gentleman came to my assistance. Is Mary all right?"

"Unharmed, praise God," George replied. "No thanks to you!"

O'Ryan glanced down at Anne. "Your brother-in-law?"

"I'm afraid so." She laid her hand on his arm. "Thank you for saving my life. I hope you'll forgive me for behaving like—"

"You have nothing to be ashamed of. And you have my word that what you've told me will go no further," O'Ryan said. "I'll bid you a good night."

Still yelling, George jogged toward them.

"But you must come back to the house," Anne insisted. "My father will insist on rewarding you for your courage. He—"

O'Ryan's back stiffened. "Do you think I did it in hope of reward?"

"I didn't mean to insult you."

She tilted her face up to his in the lantern light, and he found her striking despite her disheveled hair and tear-swollen eyes. In the time it had taken them to walk from the docks, Anne had regained much of her composure. She was, he decided, a rare woman of pluck and good sense, despite her naïveté about gentlemen who promised marriage in exchange for favors.

"I will ask you for one thing," he said.

"Of course. Anything. I—" She gasped as he pulled her into his arms and kissed her full on the mouth. Her protest died unspoken, and her lips molded to his, so warm and tender that his teasing caress became something more.

O'Ryan's heart slammed into his chest and excitement spilled through his limbs, making his toes curl in his boots. Vaguely, he was aware of her brother-in-law's cry of outrage.

Trembling, Anne pulled back. "Go," she urged. "Quickly, before . . ."

For an instant, their eyes met. Then he touched the brim of his hat in salute. "Good luck to you, Annie Davis," he murmured. "And try to stay away from dockside without an escort."

"How dare you!" George bellowed. "Stop!"

O'Ryan ignored the outcry. Thrusting broad hands into his pockets, he sauntered into the shadows, cut down a lane between two houses, and headed back toward Irishtown near the river. He had no wish to speak with Anne's brother-in-law tonight or to give further explanations as to why he had been near enough to the docks to come to her rescue.

He needed to think.

O'Ryan wasn't a man who believed in coincidence. Maybe stumbling into Anne's predicament was evidence that his luck had turned for the better. He'd not survived an English prison, cheated the executioner's noose, and escaped Ireland by ignoring his instincts.

By the time he climbed the stairs to the third-floor rooms he shared with wheelwright Sean Cleary, Sean's wife Nora, and their three small children, O'Ryan had reached a decision. It would take a greater fool than his mother had cradled to let fair Annie and her fortune slip through his hands.

He knew enough of society's ways to realize that she must wed someone and soon. Why not him? A smile creased the corners of his mouth. Marriage was a business arrangement after all—an alignment of families to ensure property and the protection of children. Nothing more.

Let poets and balladeers babble about true love between a husband and wife. He was no romantic. He'd seen enough of the trouble that following your heart could bring you. A sensible man depended on reason.

If a kiss was any measure, Anne Davis was a woman of fire and spirit, one that any sensible bridegroom would welcome to his bed. If giving his name to her fatherless babe would save her from disgrace and gain him the means to protect Kathleen . . .

"Is that you, Michael?" Sean called sleepily when O'Ryan pushed open the sagging door.

"Aye, it's me. Sorry to wake you. Go back to sleep." O'Ryan stepped carefully over a coughing child rolled in a blanket, felt his way around a table, and went into the narrow cell that served as a bedchamber. He didn't bother to light a candle but undressed in the dark and—still deep in thought—slipped into bed.

On the far side of the crumbling plaster wall, the Flynn baby was shrieking, and Joseph Flynn was cursing his wife. Grateful that the bully was too far in his cups to resort to anything worse than words, O'Ryan turned his back and tried to shut out the racket.

His sheet blankets were clean and the bare floor scrubbed spotless, thanks to Nora Cleary. But nothing could hide the odors that permeated the house, of urine, dampness, and humans packed too tightly together.

Seven families lived in a dwelling that his father wouldn't have considered fit to stable his hounds in. And that wasn't counting himself or the daft old man who slept in the attic without heat or a place to cook.

At home in County Clare, men said the streets of America were lined with gold. They boasted that any jack willing to work could become rich. Here, in the New World, he could hold his head high, own land, educate his children, and practice his religion beholden to none.

O'Ryan flopped onto his belly and tried to shut out the baby's wailing with his blanket. He hadn't come here by choice; he'd landed in this port because the ship he'd stowed away on was bound for America.

But honest Sean Cleary had sacrificed all he owned to make the journey. He'd left behind aging parents and grandparents, his job, a house and forge. And after six months in the City of Brotherly Love, all he'd gained was the taunts of little men who judged him by his accent and the place where he'd been born.

Sean was an artist with wood. He'd learned his craft as boy and man, but no shop would hire him. These pious Quakers claimed to be men of God, but they had small charity for those who spoke differently or worshipped in a different church. Sean was one of a flood of Irish immigrants looking for work—any work at all. And what little he earned unloading an occasional ship or knocking together coffins for potter's field barely kept his family fed and a roof over their heads. His good wife Nora was far gone with child, but when her time came she'd have to depend on the charity of a neighbor or Sean's strong hands to bring her babe into the world. For even if they managed to scrape together the money for a midwife, none would venture to this part of town.

In Ireland, O'Ryan—a gentleman's son—and Sean Cleary the tradesman would have passed each other in the streets with barely a word exchanged. But twelve weeks on the Atlantic aboard a pest-ridden ship had changed all that. Sean Cleary had saved O'Ryan's life and become the brother that he'd never had.

Taking comely Annie Davis to wife might offer an opportunity to help Sean and his family. And it could be the only hope of bringing Kathleen and her babe to America before it was too late.

The problem now was how to convince the lady Anne that an Irish adventurer with a price on his head was the answer to her prayers.

Chapter 3

A uniformed maid drew back the velvet bed hangings, and sunshine flooded over Anne's face. "Time you vere up, miss."

"Ohh," Anne groaned. She buried her face in the pillow and tried to block out the smell of lamb sausage and coddled eggs. "Take the tray back to the kitchen," she mumbled. "I'm not hungry."

"Mistress Mary said you should eat hearty." Gerda left the bed, filled the washbowl from a waiting pitcher, and threw open a window. "Fresh air vill do you good." Her German accent was as thick as corn pudding, her attitude almost too cheerful for Anne to bear.

Outside on a branch, a Carolina wren scolded. Horses and carriages rolled noisily past the front of the house, and a fishwoman shouted her wares. "Oysters, mussels, fresh herring!"

The sounds vibrated in Anne's head. Why had she ever left the bay country? How she wished that she were at home in her own bedchamber on Gentleman's Folly, as innocent as she had been three months ago. She'd been a reasonably attractive woman of marriageable age with a good fortune, a prize many suitors would fight for. Now . . . Now she was a liability, a shameful daughter who might well be thrown out of her home and forced to fend for herself and a fatherless child.

And she suspected that she was suffering from morning sickness.

"Miss," Gerda insisted. "Best you eat before your breakfast gets cold."

"Just the tea." Anne's stomach felt as though she'd swallowed a live frog. Her lacerated knees and the battered palms of her hands stung. Every bone in her body seemed about to come unhinged, and the bright sunlight made her head throb. "Close the curtains."

She and Mary had barely had time to hug and whisper endearments last night while George hustled her into the house. Each had been grateful that the other had survived, but Anne had seen the uneasiness in her sister's eyes. Mary could never be counted on to hold firm in cases of adversity. Any moment she might cave in and tell her husband everything. And if George learned of Anne's pregnancy, he would race to inform Papa.

Her father had always been fair, even indulgent, but he did have the Davis temper. Papa would be furious with her. He could be very stern when his children disobeyed his orders. And whatever punishment he decreed in anger, he would stand by to his grave. Papa might well disown her, and George knew it.

She and Mary's husband tolerated each other at best. George thought that Papa spoiled her and that it wasn't fair that she, as the eldest, would inherit all his property.

She felt that George treated Mary like a pretty object, pleasant to show off, suitable to provide him with heirs, but not his equal. Anne would never settle for such a match. Correction, she thought with a start. At one time, she had never intended to wed such a man. Now she was hardly in a position to be particular.

Why hadn't she accepted young Nathaniel Greensboro's proposal of marriage the summer before last? She liked Nate, even if he did have a shrew for a mother and they talked about nothing but horses and fox hunting. Nathaniel's land bordered Gentleman's Folly. They had known each other since they were children, and they shared many of the same friends. Everyone had assumed she would eventually become Mrs. Greensboro. That would have been the sensible thing to do.

No, she had to be particular. She had to wait for her true love to come along, someone who could send goosebumps running up and down her spine, someone who would devote himself to her as Papa had to her mother.

Mama had been in her grave for almost twelve years, but her father had never even looked at another woman. He kept Mama's bedchamber exactly as it had been on the last morning of her life, and he put flowers on her grave every Sunday. He still wrote her love letters, for pity's sake.

It was too late to marry Nathaniel. He'd wed redheaded Susannah Steele from Chestertown at Christmas. At this moment Susannah was probably sitting in the parlor planning a Sunday picnic and listening to her mother-in-law brag about breeding her prize hound bitch. Anne doubted that Susannah's stomach was tumbling like a cow on ice.

"Miss." The serving woman cleared her throat patiently and lifted the painted teapot from its quilted cozy. Her broad, placid face beamed as she gently swished the steaming brew, poured, then added two lumps of sugar and stirred them in.

Tea might not kill her, Anne decided. Or maybe it would.

She closed her eyes and visualized a cup of Assam, the dark golden liquid rolling, pitching. Her determination to fight the sickness wavered. If she died, Mary could bury her at once. No one, least of all Papa, need ever know that she had disgraced the family by letting Stephen have his lustful way with her and by becoming enceinte.

"Poor t'ing," Gerda fussed. "God vas vith you last night. Food vill give you strength. Coddled eggs, bread, eel pie, lamb sausage . . ."

Greasy links intertwined with writhing eels danced behind Anne's swollen eyelids. She could imagine the fat pooling on the flowered porcelain plate and spilling over the rim to drip onto the red Turkey carpet, visualize headless eels wiggling across the floor toward her.

"No!" Flinging herself from the high four-poster, Anne dashed to the closestool and hung her head over the chamber pot. She heaved, but nothing came up. "Go away." She motioned weakly to Gerda. "Take the food out of here."

The maid fisted broad hands on broader hips and winked knowingly. "Toast and tea. That vill ease the belly." Gerda nodded. "Touch of ague, you got, maybe. And no vonder, out in fog and rain getting soak to bone."

Anne licked dry lips and tried to still the buzzing in her head. "Please, just the tea."

"Vill you vant help in dressing?"

"No, thank you. Just take that food out of here."

Gerda shrugged. "As you vish, miss. And this?" She pointed to the forest green coat draped carelessly over the back of a chair. "It may be that the gentleman vill send a servant to collect his—"

"Leave it." She waited until the door closed behind Gerda's ample form, then fingered the folds of O'Ryan's garment thoughtfully. The cloth and the cut were fine; the buttons were good silver. But the garment had seen much wear, and it was far from the latest fashion. If Michael O'Ryan was a gentleman, he was not a wealthy one. She caught a hint of the Irishman's scent and lifted the coat to her face.

Anne reeled as an intense flood of vivid memories engulfed her senses. Instantly, she felt herself wrapped in O'Ryan's muscular arms. Once again, as if in a dream, she tasted his demanding kiss, heard the strength in his deep Irish laughter, thrilled to the powerful thud of his heart beating close to hers.

Startled, she dropped the coat. Her breath came in short, quick gasps as she stared down at the palms of her trembling hands, half expecting that they would blister from the heat.

When her fingers did not redden, and the odd notion faded, she scoffed at her own foolishness. Pregnancy must do strange things to a woman's mind, she decided, if a stolen kiss from a mysterious stranger could unnerve her so. Absently, Anne rubbed the nape of her neck, dispelling the odd prickling sensations, and chuckled aloud. Doubtless, she would never see her mysterious knight again.

The thought was strangely disconcerting. What was wrong with her? This should have been the first day of her marriage to Stephen Preston. Where were her tears for him? How could she have been so convinced that she loved Stephen and then dismiss him from her heart so easily? Was she as shallow as George insinuated?

How could she possibly wish for further contact with O'Ryan after her shameful behavior? She'd not only admitted her sin with Stephen, she'd allowed O'Ryan liberties, even participated in them, kissing him in full view of George and the servants. She'd given Michael O'Ryan every reason to think her a lewd and common trollop.

"It proves what Papa said," Anne murmured softly into the empty room. She was a foolhardy woman, ready to spin fancies over any rogue who glanced her way.

A dizzy spell swept over her again, and she stepped away from the forest green coat and made her way back to the tea table. A few swallows of the strong Assam tea did help. She slowly drained the cup, then poured herself another and took it back to the bed.

She finished the last drop and stretched back against the

pillow, wondering if she would bother to get dressed. She didn't want to listen to more of George's scolding, and her brother-in-law would hardly intrude on her in her dressing gown.

"Auntie Anne!" The bedroom door flew open and a small freckle-faced girl rushed in, the ties of her spotted muslin gown flying loosely behind her. "There's a big man. On the front step. He talks funny."

Anne's heart skipped a beat.

"Miss Margaret!" The children's nanny appeared, breathing hard. "Sorry, miss," Jane said as she bobbed a curtsy in Anne's direction, then reached for the four-year-old.

Giggling, Margaret scrambled under Anne's bed.

"Come out of there, you little scamp. You know your mother told you that you were not to trouble your aunt this morning."

"I'm not! The big man wants Auntie Anne." Margaret came out the far side and climbed up on the bed. She bounced several times and then cuddled against Anne.

"I am sorry," the red-cheeked nanny said. "I was changing Miss Lucy's nappy and—"

"And Margie escaped again." Smiling to cover her nervousness, Anne rose from the bed, bringing the little girl with her. "It's all right, Margie's never a bother. She's my shadow, aren't you, dumpling?"

Margaret nodded and giggled again.

A bubble of hope made Anne almost giddy. "Is there a gentleman at the door for me?"

"Yes'm," said Jane. "Somebody askin' for you, he was, but Mrs. Troyer wouldn't let him in. She told him to come back at a proper hour. Doubt he's a gentleman. What gentleman would come calling in hat and waistcoat? Some tradesman, no doubt, one that don't know his—"

Michael O'Ryan. It had to be him. "Was he tall with an Irish accent?" Anne asked, feeling her cheeks grow warm.

"Didn't see him, miss. But I heard him. Yes, I do say he was Irish. No need to fret yourself. Mrs. Troyer's not the kind to let just anyone in this house, not with the master away." Jane stopped long enough to take a breath and scoop up the little girl. "Back to the nursery with you, sweet."

"Only if I can have a gingerbread," the child bargained.

When the nursemaid nodded, Margaret clasped her arms around Jane's neck.

"Send someone after him," Anne said. "That's the brave man who risked his life to save Mary and me from those ruffians last night. I must speak with him. Hurry, before he gets away."

Jane nodded again. "I will, miss."

"And send Gerda back. I need someone to help me dress. I cannot receive him in my dressing gown." Hastily, Anne threw open her wardrobe, took out a robin's-egg-blue muslin, scrutinized it, then tossed it aside and chose another dress. "Gerda," she called. "Where are you?"

"Comin', miss."

Minutes later, dressed and hair arranged to her satisfaction, Anne descended the front stairs in time to see the grumbling housekeeper admitting a tall, fair-haired man.

Anne had almost reached the middle landing when the gentleman looked up. For an instant their gazes locked, and her breath caught in her throat as the slow fluttering began in her chest once more.

O'Ryan's eyes were a startling, clear blue, as vivid as a Chesapeake summer sky. His forehead was broad, his nose straight, and his chin square. He smiled at her, a slow, brilliant flash that revealed white, perfectly formed teeth and a dimple on one cleanly shaven cheek.

She swallowed, trying to ignore her hammering pulse and the gooseflesh that rose on her arms.

He was bigger than she remembered, with shoulders that

filled the doorway, close-fitting fawn trousers, and high leather boots that covered a horseman's long, shapely legs. His thick hair was the color of ripe wheat and slightly curly. He could be anywhere in his thirties, but no matter his age, he had a face that would make an old maid weep with regret.

"Is this a bad time?" he asked.

"No." Her voice was throaty. "It's . . . it's not a bad time." What was it about him that made her suddenly at a loss for words? "You've come for your coat?"

She noted that he wore a matching waistcoat with a spotless stock tied at his throat. His arms were lean, and his biceps strained against the seams of his starched white shirt. Worn silver buttons gleamed at his cuffs and down the front of his old-fashioned double-breasted waistcoat.

O'Ryan smiled, and she felt a fluttering sensation in her chest. Her lips tingled as she remembered the pressure of those sensual lips slanting across her own.

"I wanted to be certain you'd recovered from your adventure," he said as he passed his hat to George's scowling footman.

Ignoring the obvious disapproval of the servants, Anne led the way into the east parlor and closed the door securely behind them. She was determined to be firm with Michael O'Ryan, no matter how devilishly attractive she found him to be. If he made a single reference to their shared kiss or made one suggestive statement, she'd have the servants toss him out on his ear.

"How—how did you find me?" she asked, handing him his coat. "We parted at the corner last night." She hoped he hadn't noticed that her palms were damp, that her hands trembled ever so slightly.

He smiled again, and his blue eyes sparkled merrily. "I asked your neighbor's gardener where the bold and lovely Annie Davis was visiting."

Sweet heaven, the man could charm the leaves from the trees. Using her first name was a total breach of etiquette, and she certainly had never been called *Annie*. But how could she complain without seeming ungrateful? "Forgive me my attire, sir," she stammered. "I wasn't expecting—"

"Had I known you'd receive me alone, I would have come sooner."

She averted her eyes. "George and Mary are at services. Please, have a seat. Can I offer you refreshment? Tea?"

"Coffee?"

"Yes, of course." She pulled the bell cord, gave her instructions to the maid, and sat across from him. He'd shrugged into his coat, settled into a high-backed chair, and crossed his ankles. Whatever his fortune, it was obvious to Anne that O'Ryan wasn't impressed by George's wealth.

"I trust you slept well," he said.

"Yes. And you? You had no problems after you left—"

She stopped in midsentence as Mrs. Troyer knocked then pushed into the room with a tray and an assortment of cakes. Gerda followed with a pot of coffee and another of Oolong tea, Mary's favorite.

"Anything else?" The housekeeper's small eyes peered suspiciously at O'Ryan.

"No, thank you," Anne said. "I'll pour." When they were gone, she served O'Ryan. "Have you reconsidered my offer of a reward?" she blurted out as he added cream to his coffee.

His eyes twinkled.

Her cheeks felt as though they were on fire.

"Other than the one I took last night?" he teased.

Anne didn't think she'd ever seen a man with eyes so vividly blue. He seemed to be looking through her rather than at her.

"Do you believe I've come for a reward?" he asked.

"No." She busied herself with her own cup. "Then what . . ."

She raised her gaze to meet his. "I'm not sure why you—
That is, I was overwrought. I never intended to—"

He cut her off. "I want to make you a business proposition."

"What?" Her hand trembled and drops splashed over the
side of her cup as she set it on the tray. Anne forced herself to
hide the disappointment she felt. He had come to demand a
reward for saving her. The man she thought of as a knight in
shining armor had all-too-human failings. "Yes, well, you
certainly deserve financial compensation. But I'm not the
one to apply to. My father takes care of all the plantation's—"

"I want to marry you, Anne Davis."

Her eyes widened. She opened her mouth to speak and
nothing came out but a tiny squeak. She drew in a ragged
breath and swallowed, trying to regain her composure.

"I'm offering you my name and protection," he continued.
"I believe the term is a 'marriage of convenience.' "

Tears welled up to cloud her vision, but she would die before she'd let one fall. "Marry you?"

"Let's be honest with one another," he said quietly. "You
need a husband, Anne. You need a father for your child."

She looked down at her clenched hands. "I don't know
you," she murmured.

"I am thirty-six, born within sight of the River Shannon,
and I am of sound mind and body. I have never been married.
I ride well, dance tolerably, and play a fair hand of cards. I've
never struck a woman, and I think I could be a decent father."

"And what . . ." She searched for the right words. "You
said, 'Let's be honest with one another.' What do you get
from such an alliance?"

He shook his head. "Annie, Annie. You've a good head on
your shoulders. Do I look like a man of wealth?"

"You're a fortune hunter—no better than Stephen."

He chuckled. "Far better. I've never lied to you."

"No." She sighed and glanced away. What was wrong with

her? Wasn't this exactly what she had told Mary she would do? Why did it sound so cold coming from O'Ryan's mouth? Had she secretly hoped for some romantic declaration from this golden stranger?

"You have Stephen to thank for your problem. I'm offering you an honorable way out of it."

"Yes." She studied his handsome face. "You are not . . . I mean . . ." She felt lightheaded. "My father—"

"Your father can have no objections to your marriage to me that he would not dismiss if he knew the circumstances."

"Which he can never know," she said. "He expects me to marry a gentleman of means."

O'Ryan shrugged. "I imagine he does. I can pass as a gentleman. I am, in fact, the grandson of an earl. But the means . . ." He gestured hopelessly with broad hands.

His nails, she noticed, were neatly cut and clean. They were strong hands, seemingly too hard and callused for a gentleman of leisure. The backs of two lean sun-bronzed fingers bore the thin white traces of a deep scar.

"You do not seem the type of woman to deceive a man," he continued, jerking her from her reverie and drawing her attention back to his eyes. "I know you are carrying Stephen's child, and I don't care."

If I marry him, I'll feel those virile hands on me every day, she thought. Still, she could not speak the words that would bind her to him, perhaps for the rest of her life. It was all too soon, too frightening. She'd never known a man who could cause her to summon up such notions.

"Would another suitor be as accepting?" he asked.

"You could never reveal that the baby is—"

"If we marry at once, there won't be any lies. There can be no question of legitimacy. Even in America some babes must be born early. We have a saying in County Clare: 'A second child takes nine months; a first can be born in two.' "

Anne covered her face with her hands. The room was suddenly too warm, the fire in the hearth unbearable. Waves of heat rushed under her skin, and her stomach began to protest again. "Stephen knows I'm with child. As does my sister. I told her last night."

"Stephen will be silent as the grave. Your sister I cannot be so sure of. Is she to be trusted?"

"I think so. Yes. Once I am married, I can secure Mary's oath. If she swears on our mother's grave, she will never tell." She had used that ploy a dozen times on Mary when they were children. "But I have not agreed to this . . . business—"

"Partnership," he supplied.

"Of the mind only. At least until the baby comes. I couldn't—"

He laughed and stretched out his long horseman's legs. "I am a man of good humor, Anne, not a saint. I would expect the usual rights of a husband."

"Oh." She nibbled her lower lip. She wasn't sure if that part was good or bad. "I thought that with a baby . . ."

"You are an innocent," he answered. "Your child will come to no harm by normal pleasures of the bedchamber."

She shook her head, unable to meet his eyes. How could he speak of such intimate matters when . . . No, she must preserve some semblance of proper behavior. She must have safeguards against her own carnal nature. If a mere kiss could confuse her so, what would happen if they carried lovemaking to its natural conclusion? She might do anything.

"No. I can't agree to those terms. That would make it a true marriage, not one arranged solely for profit, and—"

"Why don't we see what happens?" He leaned toward her. "I am not a man to use force against a woman. If we can share a chamber and you choose to remain chaste . . ." He left the rest unsaid.

She glanced down at her restless hands, and then back to

O'Ryan's amused features. She was unsure what to do. What he'd suggested was crazy, but it might work. If he really was the grandson of an earl, even being Irish wouldn't keep him from being accepted by Tidewater society.

"You're afraid," he dared her.

"No, I'm not afraid of you," she lied.

"Then prove it, Annie, and say you'll be my wife."

"All right. I mean—I'll think about it." What they were proposing would satisfy society's rules, but what of her own? Stephen had made promises that he never intended to keep. Why wouldn't O'Ryan do worse once he had control of her future?

"I could have joined with that river scum last night, Annie. I didn't. That should tell you what I am."

She swallowed. He did seem to be a good man. Who was she to say that a blessed angel hadn't sent him to rescue her from this mess as well as the brigands?

"If, and I say *if*, I go along with this," she said, "it must be for a specific length of time, until after my confinement and the christening. I have money from my grandmother. I could give you that. You could return to your native country for a visit and never return."

"And then?" His jaw tightened, and the steely gaze was suddenly shrewd. "I would abandon you and my child?"

"Oh no. You're much too honorable for such action. You would have . . . an unfortunate accident. A dear friend—a relative perhaps—would send a letter telling of your fall from a horse."

"I die?"

She smiled. "Instantly."

"Without pain, I hope." Mischief glinted in his eyes.

"Oh yes," she agreed. "On your way home from church."

"And I said that you weren't deceptive."

"I'm not, about important things."

"Just killing off an unwanted husband."

"You could have the marriage annulled. Say that I'm crazy, that we're cousins. I don't care. Just treat me kindly until after the child comes, then take the money and get out of my life."

"Leaving you free to marry again," he answered.

She stood. "If you'd care to think about the matter. I'll give you until tomorrow to—"

"How much money are we talking about?"

"Nine thousand dollars."

"Cash?"

The room had become stifling. If she didn't open a door or window, she'd faint. "American silver," she replied. "And I'll throw in several building lots in Baltimore city. Grandmama left me those as well. I'm of age. Once we're married, it will be natural that I would want to put the land in your name."

"Annie, Annie, you're a clever woman."

"Don't call me Annie. My name is Anne, and I never gave you leave to call me by it." She offered him her hand. "Can I expect your answer by the morrow, Mr. O'Ryan?"

He laughed. "You may have it—" He broke off as a loud male voice sounded from the entranceway.

"That's George," Anne said. "He—"

The parlor door crashed open, and her brother-in-law charged into the room. "What's amiss here?" he demanded. "How dare you entertain this upstart Irishman in my absence! I'll have—"

"We haven't been introduced," O'Ryan said, standing and giving George the slightest civil nod. "I am Michael O'Ryan of Belfast. And I must ask you to keep a civil tongue in your head when addressing Miss Davis."

"How dare you?" George blustered. "This is my house and—"

"So I've gathered, sir. But that gives you no right to be disrespectful to Anne."

"My wife's sister? How dare you refer to her by her given—"

"You obviously haven't heard, sir," O'Ryan replied calmly. "I am pleased to tell you that Anne, *Miss Davis,* has just done me the honor of accepting my proposal of marriage."

Chapter 4

Gentleman's Folly Plantation
Eastern Shore of the Chesapeake Bay

Anne stood nervously on the deck of the sloop *Bay Belle* and watched as her father's landing came into sight. On her left hand, she wore her grandmother's wedding ring, and her marriage lines were securely tucked into her silk reticule.

Her sister Mary and Sean Cleary had been the only witnesses when she and Michael O'Ryan exchanged vows before a Methodist minister. The ceremony took place a week after O'Ryan proposed to her in George's parlor. The Irishman had wanted them to be wed at once, but she had insisted that he be fitted for a suitable wardrobe, and she paid for his fine new clothing with her ruby earrings. If they were to pass her bridegroom off as a gentleman, he had to dress like one.

Anne wasn't sure what Papa's reaction would be. Certainly, he would be angry and hurt that she had married without his knowledge. But since he and her mother had eloped against the wishes of both sets of parents, she hoped that he would forgive her in time.

George had been so enraged that she hadn't wished to return to Mary's house after the brief ceremony. Instead, she had stayed with a widowed friend of her sister's until O'Ryan could arrange passage to Maryland for them. She hadn't asked where he'd slept, hadn't cared. She'd known only that they hadn't been alone together since he'd given her a wedding kiss on the church steps. And that suited her fine.

Being near her new husband was unnerving. Anne couldn't deny her physical attraction to him, and that terrified her. Her sexual involvement with Stephen had proved that she possessed a reckless nature when it came to matters of the heart. And if she allowed her new husband physical intimacies, she might become as entangled emotionally as she had with Stephen. She simply could not trust her own judgment.

She must rely on reason rather than fall prey to feminine weakness. She had done what she had to do. She'd secured a husband and saved herself from ruin. Now all she had to do was to maintain the deception, to convince Papa and the others that this was a real marriage and that she loved O'Ryan.

So far he'd played the part of devoted bridegroom well. He'd acted the perfect gentleman on the journey, giving her privacy and seeing to her welfare. She continued to experience stomach discomfort at midmorning, but otherwise the trip had been a pleasant one. The weather had favored them with clear skies, enough wind to fill the canvas, and calm seas.

The first day's sailing had taken them down the Delaware River to the small town of Lewes, where they'd found a sloop bound for Baltimore. From that bustling town, it had been easy to hire a captain to cross the bay to the Eastern Shore and Gentleman's Folly.

Now only a few hundred yards from their destination, Anne disregarded fashion by removing her straw bonnet, closing her eyes, and tilting her face up to enjoy the sensations of sun and breeze on her face. How she loved the mingling scents of fresh-turned earth and bay. She didn't have to see the huge oaks that divided green tobacco fields from marsh or the brown cattails rising out of the shallows to feel their timeless peace.

A red-winged blackbird's cry, the lapping of waves against the hull of the sloop, and the taste of salt on her tongue were as familiar to her as her own reflection in a mirror. They were the threads that wove the tapestry of home, of Papa and the redbrick mansion house that she'd lived in since the day she was born.

"It's a fair sight," O'Ryan said, coming up behind her.

Startled from her reverie, Anne glanced at him. "Yes, it is." When she looked, the scene was much as she had imagined in her mind: a long wooden dock resting on cedar posts, a to-bacco packing house not far from the water's edge, and a dirt lane leading up the hill into a grove of chestnut trees.

Such an ordinary sight, she thought. So ordinary and yet so precious. Her heartbeat quickened as she thought of home.

"Wait until you see the house," she said with almost childish excitement. "Grandfather built it after the English troops burned the old one during the Revolution."

"You colonials have had your share of troubles with the Sassenach, true enough." He draped an arm around her with the ease of a man who was used to having his way with women.

Anne inhaled sharply and stepped back to put distance between them. Her fingers trembled as she replaced her bonnet and tied the wide lavender ribbon under her chin.

"You're as flighty as a yearling colt," he teased.

"I'm not flighty." It did make her uneasy when he touched her or stood too close. His shoulders were too wide, his gaze too volatile. No matter his charm, she had the feeling that beneath that impeccable attire and easy humor lurked more of a pirate than an earl's grandson. And she had no wish to allow him inside her outer line of defenses.

"In 1814 they burned Washington and attacked Fort

McHenry across the bay," she continued hastily, trying to cover her nervousness with chatter. "Papa was with the militia and thought we might lose the house again. He sent word for Grandmother to take Mary and me and flee inland to friends in Delaware. But she wouldn't. Instead, she flew a British flag from the dock, and invited the enemy to dinner. They stole our poultry and pigs and went away without destroying anything."

O'Ryan scanned the shore, taking in—she was certain—the wide fields and rich brown soil. "Was she an English sympathizer?"

"No, she was a Baptist."

O'Ryan's blue eyes clouded with puzzlement.

"It's a family joke," she explained. "Whenever Grandmother was unreasonable, Papa said it was because she was a Baptist." Anne spread her gloved hands, palms up. "Grandmother said that she didn't have any cannon, so she stitched up a flag and used that to defend Gentleman's Folly."

"Your neighbors didn't object?"

"The ones who lost their homes did, but she answered that they were sorry they hadn't thought of it first. Besides, she had Jacob and Jonah serve the meal. They were twelve and just coming down with mumps. Grandmother said that if God was listening to her prayers, half the British navy would come down with mumps before they got home to England."

"It's good to hear you laugh, Annie. You're much too serious for a bride." He removed a spotless handkerchief from his pocket and brushed her cheek with it. "Stand still," he ordered. "You've got a smudge on your chin."

"I do not." Again she retreated, uncertain if he was teasing or simply making an excuse to touch her. "You haven't seen me at my best," she replied quickly. "I haven't had much to be happy about in the last week."

"I'll keep my bargain, fair Annie," he promised. "See that

you do the same, and we'll both get what we want out of this—"

"Arrangement," she finished, trying not to take up the challenge she read in his eyes. It was ridiculous. He wasn't doing anything that she could reasonably protest, but Michael O'Ryan was altogether too masculine, too intense for them to share the close quarters of a sloop without coming into intimate contact. It would all be different once they reached home. There, she would be on familiar ground. She could be in control of her actions, and of his.

"Aye, it's a good place." He smiled and looked back at the rich, green land. "Nearly as beautiful as County Clare."

"Just don't get too fond of it," she reminded him. "You'll only be here until—"

"Until you don't need me anymore?" His amused glance became a wicked grin.

She turned her face away from him and watched as the mate furled the sail and the sloop drifted the last few yards to the mooring post. The lean young waterman leaped onto the dock with a heavy line and snubbed the boat securely.

O'Ryan was in the process of unloading her luggage when Anne noticed that some of the dock's decking was scorched black. A dinghy lay submerged in the shallows on the far side of the dock.

A flash of uneasiness washed through her. "Something's happened here—" she began, then broke off as she saw a man galloping pell-mell down the slope on a bay hunter.

"Miss Anne! Miss Anne!" he called. "Thanks be! You must come up to the house right away." Reining in the spirited horse, he dismounted, dropped the reins, and hurried toward her.

"Abraham, what's wrong?" she demanded.

Sweat ran down the slave's ebony-colored face as he

jerked off his hat. "Master James is taken bad with his heart. That island scum attacked us last night and—"

Anne went all hollow inside. "The bay pirates?"

Abraham nodded. "They brought two boats in to this dock just before dusk. Must have been nine or ten of them. Master James shot one, and I ran one through with a pitchfork. They burned the cow barn and killed two of our hounds. Master James—"

Her heart hammered in her chest. "Was my father hurt in the raid?"

"No." Abraham's heavy-lidded eyes were full of concern. "Aunt Kessie's having a hard time keeping him in the bed, but she thinks it's serious. You'd best hurry, Miss Anne. He's been callin' for you."

Minutes later, Anne sat on the edge of her father's bed, clutching his callused hands in hers. "Papa, Papa, I should have been here with you."

"Nonsense, girl. What would you have done? Hit one of the beggars over the head with your bonnet?" He forced a grim smile. "Truth to tell, it was rare good fun. Things were too dull around here with you away." Raising her hand, he tugged at her white glove. "What's this I feel on your finger? And who is your tall companion?"

"Sir." O'Ryan stepped into the room. "I'm Michael—"

"O'Ryan, Papa," Anne supplied. She didn't know whether to laugh or cry. Papa didn't look as bad as she had feared. His weather-tanned face was pale, but his sinewy hands lacked none of their customary strength. "We met in Philadelphia."

"Met and married," O'Ryan said. "It is my honor, Mr. Davis, to be Anne's husband."

"God's teeth! You've wed my girl without my leave?" He flung off his nightcap and halfheartedly tried to climb out of bed. "I should teach you a lesson or two about—"

"No, no, you must not," Anne said, pushing him back. "Please stay where you are." It seemed so strange to see her father lying in bed in his nightshirt in broad daylight. She studied him, looking for some outward sign of weakness. His dark eyes had circles under them but that was normal for him after a late night. His chestnut hair was thinning, and gray streaked his temples, but he was ageless. He looked no different than he ever had.

"Blast and damn, stop fussing over me," Papa grumbled, but he surprised her by sinking back against the heaped pillows.

"I didn't know you were ill," she soothed. "I'm so sorry to shock you like this by—"

"You should be sorry. You disobeyed me when you ran off to Mary's without my permission after I put the fear of the Lord in that no-good . . ." He trailed off, rubbing his right shoulder. "I should have come for you at once. Would have, if plantation matters hadn't kept me here."

"It was very wrong of me, Papa," Anne said contritely.

He scowled at O'Ryan. "Irish, are you?"

"Aye, late of Belfast."

"No notion of taking my Anne back across the water, have you? I warn you, I'll not permit it."

"No, sir."

"I would have preferred she chose one of her own kind, a Marylander rather than a foreign fop." When O'Ryan remained silent, her father added, "James will do. James I was christened. We stand on little ceremony here."

"James it will be, sir."

"Married, are you? Legally? By a man of God, no civil servant?"

"Yes, Papa," Anne said. "A proper Methodist minister. You can see the paper if you like."

"Damned well will want to see it!" He glared at O'Ryan. "Not a pauper, are you?" he demanded. "Some trumped-up manservant aping his better and seeking a wife with a good piece of land?"

"No," Anne said. "Michael isn't like that. He is the grandson of an earl."

"English or Irish?" her father demanded. "I've little use for the English. Greedy—"

"Irish. My mother's father was Lord Bessborough of County Clare."

"Irish is not so bad as English, I'll grant you. But there were Irish troops among the redcoats we drove off this land not ten years past."

"None of my family, I assure you," O'Ryan replied. "Lord Bessborough was the father of six girls, and my own father was more of a scholar than a military man."

"Papa." Anne hesitated, finding it hard to put the lie into words. She'd rarely been dishonest with anyone, let alone the father she adored. It made her feel sick inside. "Michael and I love each other."

"Love a man you haven't known six months?"

"Please, give him a chance. He's not a man of great wealth, but he's . . . comfortable."

"Aye," her bridegroom agreed. "Comfortable."

Her father cleared his throat and frowned. "Not a farmer, I suppose."

"I can learn."

"That's to be seen." Her father adjusted his nightcap and looked back at her. "What does George think of your Irishman?"

O'Ryan chuckled. "He can't bear the sight of me."

"First good thing I've heard. George is no judge of men. Stupidest thing I ever did, let him have my Mary. He's rich enough, I suppose, but sour as four-day milk." He patted Anne's hand. "You've a bit of me in you after all. Forgetting common sense to follow your heart."

She blinked back a tear. "You're not angry with me?"

"Angry? Of course, I'm angry." His eyes narrowed. "Some rascal waltzes in and snatches my daughter without a by-your-leave. Why shouldn't I toss the both of you into the bay to sink or swim?" He uttered a sound of disgust. "But I suppose you could have done worse, girl. I could have had the likes of Stephen Preston at my table."

"Please, Papa. I'd rather we didn't talk about him."

Her father didn't appear to notice her distress. "Preston was an English fortune hunter," he said to O'Ryan. "Took one look at my Anne and thought he'd use her to get his hands on Gentleman's Folly. I saw through him at once. Worthless as a dead crow. I took the cad aside and told him to stay away from my daughter or pay the consequences, if you take my meaning."

"I do," O'Ryan replied.

"I suppose if you're truly wed with book and ring, we'll try to make the best of it. But you're both here on trial. I want that understood."

Anne nodded, wanting more than anything to throw herself into his arms and confess everything. But she couldn't. The risk was too great. She had never doubted her father's love, but neither had she doubted his temper or his stubbornness. She couldn't bear to lose him or the home she loved. "Yes, Papa," she replied, falling back into her girlhood practice of pretending to agree with whatever he said.

"Perfectly understood," O'Ryan agreed.

"Do you ride, at least?" James asked. "Shoot?"

"I do."

"Then all's not lost, and my daughter's not the world's silliest wench. A man who can't sit a horse or bring down a game bird isn't worth his salt." He cleared his throat again. "Away with the both of you, while I get dressed. Enough time's been wasted today, and we've much to tell each other, I'll venture, Mr. O'Ryan."

"But, Papa, you're not well enough to get up."

"Out!" he bellowed. "I'll be the judge of how I am and how I'm not. Not a girl not yet dry behind her ears." He glanced at O'Ryan. "I'll give you a piece of advice, boy. Although I doubt you're smart enough to heed it. Start your wife the way you mean to go. I've spoiled her and coddled her for love of her dead mother until she's near impossible to live with. See that you don't make the same mistake."

There was a faint knock, and then a petite black woman wearing a shapeless, brightly patterned dress and turban entered the bedchamber. "Master James, I've brought your warm milk and bread." She smiled at Anne. "Good to have you home, precious," she said. "He's difficult to handle without you being here."

Anne rose and kissed the older woman's cheek. "I've missed all of you, too, Aunt Kessie." She glanced at O'Ryan. "Aunt Kessie is part of our family."

The black woman nodded regally. "I'm the housekeeper here."

"She's more than that," Anne insisted. "Aunt Kessie raised Mary and me from babies. And since Mama . . ." She trailed off, knowing how even a mention of her mother would trigger her father's grieving.

Aunt Kessie filled the gap. "We would have given you better welcome to this house if Master James wasn't under the weather. I've asked the girls to ready the west rooms for you."

Anne averted her eyes. She'd known, naturally, that the family would expect her and O'Ryan to share a bedroom and the adjoining dressing area. But somehow she'd thought of herself alone in the chamber she'd slept in since she was born. "Thank you," she murmured. "The west rooms will be—"

"Best view in the house," her father said. "You can see the bay from there, watch the sun going down over the water. Closest sight to heaven you'll see in this life."

Aunt Kessie motioned toward the door. "You'll want to freshen up after the journey, Miss Anne. I'll tend your father. Dr. McNeal will be here directly. Daniel saw the dust from the doctor's dogcart on the road. You go along. No sense in Master James wasting good cash by paying for a doctor and not staying put until he's looked at."

Anne took the hint. Squeezing her father's hand once more, she and O'Ryan left the room. "Aunt Kessie can manage Papa better than anyone," she said when they were far enough down the hall to be certain that he wouldn't hear her.

"You do have slaves on Gentleman's Folly?"

"Some. Aunt Kessie is free. She was born in the islands." She stopped to look directly into his face. "No one thinks of her as a servant. I told you, she's part of our family."

"One slave is too many in my opinion. I may as well be honest with you. I don't believe in the practice of enslaving other humans."

Anne sighed. "Neither do I, not really. But slavery has been a way of life in America for generations. Here on Gentleman's Folly, we've always treated our people kindly. We never break up families or—"

"You say that, but I wonder how they must feel. To be owned by another . . ."

"We didn't invent the practice. Even the ancient Celts kept slaves."

"You're well read for a woman," he replied. "You're right. The ancient Irish did have slaves, but it was a cruel custom then as it is today. Mayhap you'd agree with me if you'd ever spent a day wearing chains."

She looked at him in amazement. "Surely you don't believe my father would put irons on our people? He isn't like that. They are well cared for, given good food and good lodging."

"I'm not judging you or your family, Anne. I only wanted you to know exactly how I feel."

"That's fair."

Turning, she continued on into the oldest section of the house, past another set of stairs and through a low doorway to a newer passage. "Papa built this addition when he and Mama were married," she explained. "I think he expected to father a half-dozen brawny sons."

"There are only you and your sister?"

"Yes. There were two little boys, but both died at birth. They had all but given up hope when I was born healthy. I suppose it's why Papa doted on us." She pushed open a paneled door into a spacious corner room with four windows, high ceilings, and lovely old cherry furniture.

The oversize four-poster bed was hung with white gauze mosquito netting and piled high with pillows. A bouquet of flowers stood on the cold hearth, and two high-backed chairs flanked the brick fireplace. A small antique breakfast table with a window view of both water and pastureland provided an area for private dining.

O'Ryan grinned. "Our bed, I presume?"

Prickles of apprehension ran over her skin. "My bed," she corrected. "There's another in the dressing room that you can use." She indicated an interior door. "It's quite private. There's a bathing tub and—"

"You expect me to sleep in a closet?"

"It's not a closet," she said. "There are books and a writing desk. You'll be quite comfortable."

"I'm sure."

She felt a flush creep up her throat and cheeks. "I told you that this would be a marriage in name only."

"But you intend to let your father and the household staff believe that ours is a real marriage . . . in every sense?"

"Of course. I—" Anne gasped in surprise as O'Ryan gathered her in his arms and carried her across the threshold. "Put me down!"

"Tish, tish," he soothed. He bent his head so that she could feel the heat of his breath on her face.

"Please . . ." she managed, but when his lips brushed hers, she closed her eyes and welcomed the kiss.

He tasted of wild mint.

A rush of forbidden yearning swept over her. His tongue touched hers and she groaned in pleasure. Then, as quickly as it had begun, it was over, and she found herself standing unsteadily in the center of her bedroom.

O'Ryan's blue eyes gleamed with self-satisfaction. "An old custom in my country," he said. "And it must be here as well."

She swayed, feeling the flush of heat spread up her throat to set her cheeks aflame. "You shouldn't have done that," she managed. "I—"

"It was your idea that we should present the picture of happy newlyweds," he reminded her. "Besides, you seemed to enjoy it as much as I did." He caught her hand and lifted her fingers for a light kiss. "This Aunt Kessie of yours. Does she have a last name?"

Anne took a breath, trying to regain her composure. "Her grandfather was Ashanti from the Gold Coast of Africa. He was a slave, but when Aunt Kessie's father won his freedom, he took the surname Africa. She's widowed, but she still goes by Kessie Africa."

"So she's not really your aunt."

"You know perfectly well that 'aunt' is a title of respect. In many ways she's been like a mother to us. Even when Mama was alive, it was Aunt Kessie who looked after us."

He folded his muscular arms across his chest. "For me, it was a country lass named Edana. She could not read or write her name, but she was a merry soul who filled my head with stories and listened to all my secrets. I loved her with all my heart. Mother sent her away when I was ten because Edana began walking out with our coachman."

The room no longer seemed as large as it had. "Speaking of secrets," she said, "why did you tell me that you were from County Clare and tell Papa that you were from Belfast? I may not have ever been to Ireland, but I know that they are far apart. Which is true? And why can't you keep your stories straight?"

"Miss Anne?" A chubby girl in white cap and apron appeared in the hall doorway. "Dr. McNeal is come."

"Good. Grace, this is my husband, Mr. O'Ryan."

"Please t' make your 'quaintance, sir." She pushed a lock of carrot-orange hair back under her cap and dropped an awkward curtsy. "Glad to have ya home, Miss Anne."

"I hope your mother's well," Anne said. "And the new babe?"

Grace grinned. "Oh yes, miss. Another boy, as red and freckled as the rest of us."

"I brought a gift for him from Philadelphia. As soon as I unpack, I'll call you. That way you can take it home with you tonight."

"Yes'm. And Miss Kessie wants to know will you be wanting hot water for a bath."

Anne nodded. "As soon as I've talked with Dr. McNeal."

Grace bustled off and Anne looked back at O'Ryan. "She's indentured until she comes of legal age. Then Papa will give her a cow and a dowry. Her parents have fourteen children— no, fifteen, including the new one. Grace is the oldest. She's been with us since she was twelve, learning how to cook and sew and manage a household. Perhaps you find some fault with this arrangement as well?"

"No, not at all. She isn't a slave. Her bond will be up when she's twenty and one."

"Of course." Anne wasn't sure what he was getting at.

"It is slavery that troubles me," he said with quiet passion. "I ask only that you consider my concern. If Grace's skin was brown instead of white, would she be less deserving of that freedom on her twenty-first birthday?"

Chapter 5

Anne glanced up at him through a fringe of dark, thick lashes. "You have a lot to learn about me, Irish," she said, "and a lot to learn about our ways. Dinner is promptly at one. Any of the servants can show you to the dining room. If you'll excuse me, I must talk to Papa's doctor."

Saucy, he thought as she left the room. He'd always liked that in a woman. A female with a brain in her head and a tongue to share it was like salt on a man's porridge. It made life more interesting.

He smiled. The sway of Anne's hips as she walked was enough to give a man a fever. Perhaps his brief stay on the Chesapeake would be memorable.

He whistled a few bars of "Fair Lady of London" as he unpacked his few belongings and went to the nearest window. Throwing it open, he gazed out at the lush fields and green forests that spread out from the manor house in multicolored splendor and considered his change in fortune.

He'd never expected to come so far when he decided to follow those three footpads that evening on the dock. Annie Davis—Annie O'Ryan, he supposed he should consider her—was not only a lovely armful, but she was endearing.

Anne might not be a great beauty by society standards, which asked a gentlewoman to be as soft and sweet as meringue and as delicate in coloring as a pink-and-white porcelain shepherdess, but to his eye, she was a woman meant to warm a man's heart. Her hair was a shiny auburn mass that curled in ringlets around her heart-shaped face, tempting him to loosen the pins and let it fall around her shoulders. Her brown eyes were large and spirited, framed by those dark lashes that she used to such effect, and despite the light sprinkling of freckles over her high cheekbones, her fair complexion would have done justice to any Irish colleen.

Anne's mouth was a delight, prettily curved and sensual, a mouth that demanded kissing. And her body . . . her shape was as lush and fruitful as these Maryland acres.

Some men never found a pregnant woman appealing. He was not one of them. Although Anne's condition was still hidden from view, her cheeks were rosy and her lips the color of ripe cherries. He was certain that she would carry her child with grace.

As Kathleen had done . . .

The familiar pain knifed through him, and he cursed himself for the hundredth time for not being man enough to do what should have been done. He supposed it was why he had agreed so readily to give his name to Anne's unborn child. Kathleen had begged him to marry her, but he had refused her. And she'd had to bear the shame of giving birth to an illegitimate child alone.

O'Ryan gritted his teeth and studied the broad acres of Gentleman's Folly. It was truly a bountiful land, without rocks or wasteland as far as he could see. Briefly he considered what it might be like to remain here on the plantation instead of taking his payment and leaving as he'd promised. It had been a long time since he'd called Cuchulainn home . . . a long time since he'd had any home at all.

The life of a wild rover was all well and good in the light of day or the bright lanterns of a raucous pub. But in the dark hours of the night, he was often lonely. Women there were aplenty, but none except Kathleen honestly cared if he lived or died. He wearied of being always alert for a knife in the back and of knowing that every man he met would the next day be a stranger.

He'd never considered himself a greedy man, but here within his reach was a new Eden. He thought of Kathleen at home in the old country, struggling to put food on her table. And he remembered Sean Cleary's hollow-cheeked children. He could provide for them—bring them here to Maryland, perhaps even to the plantation. If he were master here, he could do that and more. Surely he could fulfill his obligations to Kathleen and her babe without hurting Anne.

Yet, he had given his word that he would take the nine thousand dollars and go. And whatever else he'd done to regret in this life, he'd never been a liar. If Anne still wanted to be rid of him after her child was born, he'd have to go. Nine thousand would go a long way toward easing Kathleen's plight.

"You cannot change the world. Why can't you be content with what you have?" his father had asked his mother many times in the midst of one of their bitter quarrels.

She'd never had an answer for that question, and it was a fault that she had passed on to her only child. And that lack of acceptance of the way things were had remained in his character to this day.

"Take the money and be grateful," his father would have advised. But he was Isabel's son, and he recognized the ache in the core of his soul. He wanted to be a part of this new land with a fierce yearning that would only grow more insistent.

The question was, what price was he willing to pay to get it?

Against Dr. McNeal's orders, Anne's father insisted on joining the newlyweds for dinner. Garbed in an old-fashioned dressing robe, James Davis took his place at the head of the massive teakwood table and rang a small bell to signal the servants to start serving.

The meal began with crab bisque and a hardtack that James referred to as beaten biscuits. To O'Ryan's taste, the bread could have stood more beating or more yeast. The small white lumps were as hard as those served aboard the *Providence*, the ship that had brought him from Ireland. These, however, seemed free of weevils, which was a small blessing.

Anne sat on one side, across from him. The table seemed ridiculously large for three people, the amount of food scandalous. The servants carried around platters of roasted pork, fried chicken, and a roast of beef large enough to serve a platoon of soldiers, followed by bowl after bowl of vegetables. What he tasted was delicious, but the quantity of the feast was enough to dull his appetite. Once he would have enjoyed the rich dishes, but he'd missed too many meals and seen too many hungry people to appreciate them now.

There was little need to do much talking. Anne's father was more than able to fill the silence, retelling the tale of the pirate attack with gusto. "Cheeky bastards!" he said, with an apology to Anne for his swearwords. "We'll have to gather a band of stout men and burn out their nests one of these days."

"You say that, Papa, but no one ever does," Anne said. "And that's a task for the authorities, not you and Nathaniel and the other landowners. Criminals shouldn't be allowed to hide out on the islands and rob honest folk as they please."

James scoffed. "What should be done and what is are cats of different colors. When have the authorities—British or American—ever been willing to risk their necks for the taxpayers?"

"Who are these pirates?" O'Ryan asked. "Are they a real threat to the area?"

"Scum," Anne's father replied. "Runaway slaves, half-breeds, deserters from the British navy, Irish outlaws, and a handful of inbred, godless riffraff. The Chesapeake islanders have always been a lawless bunch. Don't doubt there may be a few real pirates among them, but they fight among themselves too much to be any real threat."

"Papa makes too light of the problem," Anne insisted. "These marauders are a real danger to honest folk."

"Nothing for a pretty girl to worry her head about," James proclaimed loftily. "And certainly not a proper topic for dinner conversation," he added, completely forgetting that he had been the one to bring it up. "This is men's business. The thrashing we gave them will keep them clear of Gentleman's Folly, you can count on it."

"But, Papa—"

"Enough. Now tell me about Mary and the children."

"You can't ignore these criminals," Anne said. "I don't think—"

"Leave the thinking to me," James replied sternly. "I've spoiled her, I admit it, Michael. Had her mother lived, bless her soul, my Anne would have learned when a lady should hold her tongue." He reached over and patted his daughter's hand. "There, there, girl. Don't glower so. You know you've a tongue on you. Smile, dear, Papa loves you. Now, where's that wench with the French wine I wanted served?"

Clearly mortified by her father's words, Anne stared into her lap, back ramrod straight and mouth taut.

A maid produced the wine. That was followed by another course, and then yet another wine, all of which the master of Gentleman's Folly proceeded to sample without showing any ill effects.

"Just as I told you," James said as they finished the meal with an assortment of sweets. "McNeal couldn't find a thing wrong with me. Indigestion, nothing more. The man's a quack, getting rich off inventing illnesses for his patients."

"Stuff and nonsense, Papa," Anne replied. Small spots of red still stained her cheeks. "Dr. McNeal's no more a charlatan than you are."

"Fresh air is what I need," her father grumbled. He motioned to the serving girl. "A slice of that pecan pie, and don't spare the cream." He nodded as she slid a large piece onto his dessert plate. "Yes, that's fine. And tell Daniel to saddle Greyboy and the new black." He glanced back at O'Ryan. "I mean to show you around Gentleman's Folly," he said.

"Abraham can do that," Anne suggested. "I'd feel better if you'd go back to bed, at least until tomorrow."

"Listen to her," James said good-naturedly. "The ladies are all alike. They'd love to run a man's life if he'd let them. No, I'll take your upstart Irishman myself. I mean to see for myself how well he can sit a Maryland steed."

O'Ryan saw no more of Anne until supper. James and he explored the plantation, visited the slave quarters and the plantation mill. They watched as boys checked crab traps in the river, and paused to admire the thoroughbred stallion James had bought from a breeder on the James River in Virginia. The two men walked the length of a tobacco field shoulder to shoulder and cut through a virgin hardwood forest where oaks and chestnuts grew in undisturbed splendor.

"Your new husband likes Gentleman's Folly," James told his daughter over the light evening meal. "And so he should. This is some of the finest land on the peninsula."

Anne nibbled at her crabcake and took a few bites of the garden greens. "I would feel better if you would rest more, Papa," she said.

"I'm fit as a fiddle, girl. Fit as a man half my age."

After they had eaten, the men retired to the library for a glass of port. James offered O'Ryan a pouch of tobacco. He accepted, drawing a pipe from his coat pocket and filling the bowl with the sweet-smelling leaves.

"Oronoco, son, the lifeblood of this state. A man who won't smoke his own tobacco is in the wrong business," James said as he passed O'Ryan a light. "What do you think of the taste?"

O'Ryan took a puff and nodded.

"Good climate for tobacco, here on the Tidewater." James settled into an easy chair with his wineglass in one hand, his pipe in the other. "Of course, the land's growing poorer every year. Tobacco sucks the life out of the soil. I've seen it. Every year the fields produce less."

O'Ryan smoked his pipe. A clock ticked on the mantel. A faint sound of drumming drifted in through an open window.

Finally, James broke the silence. "I can't let you think I've forgiven you for marrying my Anne without my permission. You needn't think I'm an old fool. This was all too hastily done to be proper. I'll be watching you. Her husband you may be, but no man lays a hand in anger on either of my two chicks and lives to tell about it. Am I making myself clear? You will treat her at all times as the lady she is."

O'Ryan nodded. "Aye, on that we are agreed. I've never struck a woman, and I don't intend to start."

"And one more thing." The lines around the older man's mouth grew taut. "No dallying with the serving wenches, white or black. I won't stand for it. I've a rule here on Gentleman's Folly, ten lashes for lustful mischief, hanging for rape. Our women have always felt free to walk where they would, day or night, without fear of being molested."

O'Ryan's muscles tensed as anger flared in his chest. "Do I look the kind of man to—?"

"No, you do not," James answered. "But I am a plain-spoken man. I say what I expect of you so that there will be no misunderstanding. Conduct yourself as a gentleman, treat my Anne right, and we'll have no quarrel between us."

"Fair enough. I like you, James Davis. I see no reason why we shouldn't become friends."

"We've one thing in common," James said heartily. "We are Anne's protectors. If you love her as I do, it will count for more with me than you being an Irishman with foreign ways." He puffed slowly on his pipe and took a sip of port. "My two girls are my greatest treasure. God knows I valued their mother more than my own life. They're all I have left of her."

"I'll do what I can to make Anne happy," O'Ryan said. "If it's in my power."

"That's all I can ask of any man." James raised his glass in a toast. "To your marriage," he said, "and a grandson in my arms within the year."

O'Ryan accepted the toast with a smile, wondering if Anne's father had any inkling of how close his wish was to being fulfilled.

Hours later, O'Ryan threw off the linen sheet and tossed restlessly on the narrow bed. The small room was stifling. Somewhere over his head, a mosquito droned angrily. He'd already killed two; one had left a welt on his shoulder that itched incessantly.

"Some honeymoon," he grumbled.

The problem with this closet was that there was no cross-ventilation. It reminded him of the cramped quarters aboard the *Providence*.

He beat the pillow into shape and turned onto his back. Of course, he'd shared a space this size with four other families and there'd been no window at all. No window . . . and no feather tick to lie on.

He tried to push thoughts of the ocean voyage away. That bleak time was over, and there was no profit in remembering the vermin, the smell of vomit and spilled bowels, or the incessant wail of dying children in steerage. The *Providence* had been at best a leaking, rat-infested tub and at worst a plague ship. If the captain hadn't bribed port authorities, the boat would never have been permitted to drop what remained of its human cargo in Philadelphia.

And the *Providence* had been better than prison.

He chuckled with black humor. "I must be coming up in the world to sleep in a water closet." The mosquito attacked and he swatted it, feeling satisfaction as the insect was squashed under his palm.

"Damn." He sat up and ran fingers through his damp, tangled hair. What kind of fool was he? Anne's father had said it, hadn't he? "Start out the way you mean to go."

If he let Anne treat him like a hireling in the first week of their marriage, things could only get worse. Why was he sleeping on a maid's cot when she was a few feet away in a high bed in a room with four windows?

"Cross-ventilation," he muttered. By moonlight, he located the short flannel drawers he'd taken off earlier. He thrust his legs into them, jerked the garment up, and buttoned the waist.

He stubbed a bare toe against the bedstead as he approached the passageway between his room and the larger chamber. "Ouch!" he swore quietly, then turned the knob and found the door locked.

He tapped firmly. "Anne. Open up."

Nothing.

"Annie O'Ryan, you have one minute to unlock this, or I'll break it in." He took a breath. "One, two, three, four . . ."

Bare feet padded on the floorboards. "Hush! You'll wake the servants."

"I'll wake Old Scratch himself. Let me in."

"You knew my rules," she insisted, trying to sound as if

she'd been asleep. But she hadn't. She'd been lying awake, thinking of him in the next room, wondering what it would be like to curl against his hard, masculine chest and feel his arms around her.

Even now, her body betrayed her. With every step she could feel the texture of her linen nightgown rubbing against her sensitive breasts. Waves of heat fluttered down her belly to the damp forbidden spot between her thighs.

Every sound seemed magnified—the hoot of an owl in the garden, the rustle of leaves outside her window. Fear, she told herself, it was only fear that made her so uneasy. Husband or not, he was a stranger.

"Annie, listen to me. I've no designs on your body, as desirable as it may be. It's hot in here. If I'm to act your husband for the next year, I want to sleep in your room."

"No." If she opened the door for him, he would surely expect more. And if she did, how could she be certain she wouldn't give it to him?

"We're not going to argue about this. Either let me in quietly, or I'll do it the hard way."

"I don't trust you." It was easier to believe that it was Michael O'Ryan she didn't trust, rather than her own will. What if she was the weak one? Wasn't she the one who couldn't forget the heat of his big hands on her? Didn't her heart race when he spoke her name in that soft, almost musical Irish that made *Annie* sound like a caress?

"You've no need to fear me," he said. "If I'd wanted to do you harm, I had plenty of chance to do it the night we met."

Her mouth was as dry as last year's tobacco leaf. Her skin felt all prickly. "You swear? On your mother's grave?"

"How do you know she's dead?"

"All right, just be quiet. And if you do lay a hand on me, I'll scream loud enough to bring the servants running."

She turned the key and fled back to the bed.

"That's more like it."

A cool breeze off the bay stirred the curtains as he strode across the room with almost catlike grace to where she lay with the sheet pulled up around her neck. A lady would have closed her eyes to avoid seeing him, but she had lost all modesty.

O'Ryan was all bare, ridged chest, wide shoulders, and craggy features in the moonlight. His curling hair gleamed silver-gold, and she caught a glimpse of his flat, taut belly. Her pulse bucked and raced as he approached the bed. He's beautiful, she thought. My beautiful husband.

But not really her husband, she told herself. Theirs was a marriage in name only, a relationship that could only be complicated by sharing this bed.

"You smell like lavender," he said

His words were as sweet as honey, but she knew she had to be strong. "I allowed you in the room," she whispered coldly. "I didn't say you could come into my bed." She didn't know if she could stand to have him so close without having him closer.

He chuckled.

"You could sleep on the floor." She wondered if he was naked below the waist.

"Not likely. But you're free to do so if you wish."

"I am with child. No gentleman would ask a lady to—"

"I am no mooncalf, Annie. Are you so enamored of my good looks that you cannot sleep beside me without being overcome by lust?"

"That's nonsense. And stop calling me Annie! My name is Anne. Anne, do you understand?"

"You are a bit of a scold, aren't you," he chided. "And you act so meek in front of your father. 'Yes, Papa, no, Papa.' "

She didn't answer. It had never been something she was proud of, just the way things had to be.

"Which side of the bed is mine?"

"Please, take a quilt and a pillow and make your bed on the floor."

"Not a chance."

"I warn you, I've got a weapon. Touch me and—"

"I thought you were going to scream. Now you say you mean to attack me."

"Not this side. The other side." The mattress sagged under his weight. "Stay on your half if you know what's good for you," she warned, trying not to think about how much she wanted to go into his embrace.

He laughed. "So you can't bear to leave me."

"I'll not be driven from my own bed by a . . . a Patrick-come-lately." She turned away, drew her knees up tightly, and covered her head with the sheet.

He stretched out. "This is much better."

"Go to sleep," she snapped. "You weren't satisfied until you got in here. Now you're here. Stop talking and go to sleep."

She lay motionless, listening to the sound of his breathing.

"What is it?" he ventured after a few minutes.

She started. "What? What's what?"

"What kind of weapon do you mean to use against me? A pistol? Saber?"

She didn't reply.

"A butcher knife?"

"No."

"Pitchfork?"

"I've a candlestick, if you must know, but it's brass and heavy enough to split your skull."

He chuckled softly. "Go to sleep, wife. On my mother's grave, I vow I will not lay a finger on you tonight."

"Good."

"Tomorrow you may wish to renegotiate."

Her answer was one that no lady should utter.

He laughed. "Whatever the next year brings, Annie, it won't be dull, I promise you."

No, she thought. It won't be dull.

Chapter 6

The first streaks of dawn were beginning to color the sky when a rooster crowed outside the window. O'Ryan came instantly awake. He sat bolt upright and looked around, then realized where he was and glanced over at his bride, sleeping just beyond a wall of pillows.

Anne, clad primly in a long-sleeved white nightgown, lay curled on her side, facing him. Her left hand clutched the sheet, pressing it tightly against her breast. Her right arm was flung over her head. One slim ankle and high-arched bare foot peeked out from under the covers at the far edge of the bed.

Her hair had been twisted into a single plait and tied with a ribbon. The thick braid spilled over her face, hiding most of her features. Her tresses were dark in the shadowy confines of the big bed, but he could still smell her faint lavender scent.

He raised himself on one elbow and gently moved the braid aside. She stirred slightly and sighed, but her eyes remained closed and her breathing told him that she was still wrapped in deep slumber.

He resisted an urge to touch her face, to run his fingers through the wild tendrils that had escaped the braid and curled around the sides of her cheeks and over her temple. He tried not to think of what it might be like to kiss her eyelids and feel the tickle of those winglike brows against his skin.

Anne's hair felt like strands of silk against his fingertips, and he longed to tug the ribbon free and spread her tresses like an auburn curtain against the pillow. But he didn't. He merely studied her heart-shaped face as the gray light turned to gold and sunlight poured through the open windows.

She sighed again and drew her knees up.

O'Ryan felt an odd sense of loss when he could no longer see her exposed ankle. Despite the soft mattress under him and his utter contentment, he felt himself growing hard.

The curtains on the windows facing the bay puffed inward as a breeze shifted, washing away the heat of the night. The draft was sweet and clean, bringing images of whitecaps and wheeling gulls. He would have sworn he could taste the bite of salt on his tongue.

The bedroom should have been cooler with the movement of air, but O'Ryan felt beads of moisture gather at the nape of his neck and trickle slowly down his back.

He was suddenly restless. He knew he should get up, go to the far chamber, and dress. He'd always been an early riser. No matter what time he went to sleep—and it was often after midnight—it was his custom not to lie abed after daybreak.

This morning was different.

He enjoyed the view from his spot very much, and had no wish to leave before Annie did. He wondered if she had any idea how lovely she was when she was asleep . . . how desirable to a man.

Her nose was small and slightly turned up at the end, her mouth full, and her chin just right for a determined woman. Her ears were delicately shaped and lay close to her head, perfect for whispering secrets into or . . . Sensual thoughts crowded into his mind, making the heat in his body more intense, until even the palms of his hands seemed overly hot. He shifted on the mattress, trying to ignore a growing tension in the length of his body.

Devil take him! Hadn't he promised her that he'd act the gentleman? What kind of man was he that he could spy on her in her sleep and make love to her in his mind?

She's your wife, isn't she? came a treacherous voice from deep in his head. *Who has a better right to look?*

Anne rolled onto her stomach, still holding the tangled sheet in her fist. As she turned, she twisted the pillow, and he saw the base of the brass candlestick tucked under it.

"Damned if you didn't mean to brain me with it," he murmured half under his breath.

It had definitely been too long since he'd shared bed-sport with a lady. He was a man who enjoyed the pleasures of the opposite sex, but he had never seduced a virgin or paid a whore.

The woman beside you is neither.

Nay, it is too soon, he answered firmly, and slid his feet over the bed. He'd not taken two steps toward the antechamber when someone rapped on the door. O'Ryan barely had time to dive back under the sheet and hide his burgeoning erection before the knob turned and Kessie's voice came through the opening crack.

"Miss Anne, make yourself decent. Your papa's coming."

Anne, still half-asleep, struggled to a sitting position. "Kessie? What . . ." She glanced over at O'Ryan and her eyes widened in alarm.

"Sorry, precious," the housekeeper called. "I told him not to disturb you two so early, but you know how he is."

"Papa?" Anne mumbled. "Why is he—?" O'Ryan slid over beside her and slipped an arm around her. Anne gasped, snatched the coverlet up to her throat, and kicked his leg. "Get over on your side!"

A man's spurs clanked in the passageway.

O'Ryan leaned down and laid his hand on her midriff just as her father appeared in the doorway.

"Morning!" James declared. "Time you two were up and about. I had my breakfast an hour ago." He rubbed his stomach. "Milk toast and cornbread, but enough to hold body and soul together."

James was dressed for riding in a wide-brimmed hat, hunting coat, and boots. In one hand he carried a leather crop, in the other a mug of ale. O'Ryan could smell the yeasty odor of the hearty brew.

"I mean to go to Greensboro Hall and invite young Nate and his family to join us for supper. I hear his wife's brothers are visiting from Chestertown. With Sibyl—that's Nathaniel's mother," he explained, "that will make eight at the table. A good number, don't you think?"

"Yes, Papa," Anne agreed without much enthusiasm. "But why tonight, when we've only just arrived home and you've been under the weather? Wouldn't it be better to—?"

"Lord, no!" James replied. "Don't know how long Graham and Miles Steele mean to stay. Good cardplayers, both of them. I took them for eighteen dollars last Christmas. More jingle in their pockets than good sense. Nate's little Susannah is in the family way. She'll be delighted to come and hear about the latest fashions in Philadelphia. Sibyl knows her horseflesh, but she's bound to be a bore to live with day in and day out. A little of Sibyl Greensboro goes a long way." He shook his head and looked at O'Ryan. "She's a widow, and she's set her cap for me, but she'll never catch this old fox. One good wife is all a man needs."

O'Ryan hugged Anne tighter. She smiled up at him and reached under the sheet and jabbed him in the ribs. He cut off a yelp of surprise and covered his distress with a cough.

Her father didn't seem to notice. "You'll do well, both of you, to be pleasant to Sibyl," he advised. "If she approves of the match, you'll have no trouble. But if she doesn't, she's bound to spread gossip about your hasty marriage."

Anne elbowed O'Ryan. "Since when do you care about women's gossip, Papa?"

O'Ryan wondered how long James intended to stay in the room.

"The Davis name is a respectable one," Anne's father said sternly. "The Eastern Shore is a small place. I'd be less than responsible if I let you behave recklessly and cut yourself off from proper society. We're informal here, with none of the fancy manners you'll see on the Continent or in Philadelphia. But Anne comes of good stock, as I hope you do. And there's no reason the two of you can't be received in the best homes."

"Give me a few minutes to dress," O'Ryan said. "I'll be glad to ride out with you again."

"Anne can come with us," he replied. "She's quite the rider herself. What do you say, my girl? Will you join us?"

"Not today," Anne answered. "If we're entertaining tonight, I should be helping Aunt Kessie with the preparations. You two go."

"Right. That we shall." He looked back at O'Ryan. "Downstairs in a quarter hour, or I'll come back to fetch you."

As the door closed behind him, Anne twisted free of O'Ryan's grasp. "I'll thank you to keep your hands to yourself," she whispered urgently.

O'Ryan grimaced. "First you bruise my flesh and now you accuse me? Next you'll be thumping me with this." He retrieved the candlestick and hefted it dramatically. "I'm lucky I wasn't murdered in my sleep."

"Because I felt sorry for you and let you in here doesn't mean I intend you to take liberties." She retreated to the far side of the bed and pulled the sheets up to her chin. "Go back into your own room and don't come out until you're decent."

"Are you planning on getting dressed?"

"Not until you're downstairs and I can lock the door."

He was tempted to tease her further, but her rosy complexion had taken on a distinctly green hue. "Are you unwell?" he asked. "Morning sickness?"

"No," she protested weakly. "Yes, I . . . think so." She took a deep breath. "Just get out of my bed."

He nodded. He rose, noticing that the evidence of his earlier excitement no longer stood at attention. He crossed the room, then stopped when he heard her gasp. "What's wrong?"

"Your back."

The room, which had seemed so comfortable before suddenly became cooler. O'Ryan became acutely aware of the smooth floorboards under his bare feet and the acrid taste in his mouth. "You've never seen a man's naked back before?"

"Those—those scars. What happened to you?" The sting was gone from her tone. Her brown eyes brimmed with compassion.

O'Ryan braced himself inwardly, trying not to let the bad memories flood back. "Cat tracks," he answered lightly. "A cat-o'-nine-tails."

"You were beaten?"

He stiffened, certain he could feel the leather whip slicing through his flesh and hear the jeers of the onlookers. "My past is my own affair."

"Even when my child will carry your name?" Her face paled to the color of buttermilk. "Who are you, Michael O'Ryan?"

"You said it yourself. Just a fortune hunter."

"Fortune hunter or not, I mean to keep you to our bargain."

"Aye. And so do I. For I'll not be cheated of what's due me, Annie."

She wilted under his hard gaze, lowering her head and clapping a hand over her mouth. "I—I . . . ," she stammered.

"Are you sick?" He returned to the side of the bed. "Lie back against the pillow." She obeyed, eyelashes fluttering.

"Tish, tish," he soothed. "It will pass, lass. It's only the morning sickness." He went to the washbowl and pitcher and poured cool water onto a towel. Wringing out the cloth, he carried it back and placed it on her forehead.

"Thank you," she murmured. "That feels good."

Her skin was nearly translucent; even her lips seemed to have lost their color. "You're likely carrying a boy," he said. "The old women say that it's the boys that bring the most rough weather for a mother."

She grasped his hand, opening her eyes to look directly into his. "You're very kind, Michael O'Ryan, too kind for a fortune hunter."

"Only with ladies in distress."

"You always seem to be coming to my rescue."

"I'll try not to make a habit of it."

She gave him a half smile. "You'd best go. Papa will be looking for you."

"Shall I send up your maid? Do you want anything?"

"Just for the room to stop spinning. No, I'll be fine. Hurry or my father will be back up here insisting we both ride with him."

O'Ryan nodded. He wanted to be away from Anne, to shed this overwhelming feeling that he had to protect her. He needed to be outside in the fresh air, where he could remember his priorities. "All right," he agreed. But as he opened the door to the smaller bedroom she called after him.

"You can't fool me," she said. "You're not as tough as you pretend. And for a bachelor, you seem to know a lot about having babies."

An hour later, when she came down the wide front staircase, Anne had to admit that O'Ryan had been right. The queasiness had passed, and she felt clear-headed and happy. In fact, she was hungry—ravenous to be exact.

O'Ryan and Papa were nowhere to be seen, so she assumed that O'Ryan had eaten and they had ridden off to Greensboro Hall. The table was still set for one. Heavy silver serving dishes rested on the mahogany hunt board, and a pitcher of rich cream stood nestled in a bed of ice beside her plate.

The pairs of tall windows on the bay side of the house and at the back had been thrown open, and a breeze played through the dining room. Servants had rolled the rugs and packed them in the attic so that the wooden floor was bare and cool underfoot for summer.

Anne helped herself to fresh strawberries and biscuits still warm from the oven. She turned up her nose at the boiled eggs, but chose a few strips of bacon, two pancakes, and an oyster fritter. Balancing her heaped plate in one hand and a cup of tea in the other, she pushed open the door to the winter kitchen.

Two identical young black women were polishing silver. Aunt Kessie stood at a writing desk checking her ledger. "Morning, Miss Anne," the twins said in unison.

Anne greeted all three cheerfully and carried her breakfast over to a battered old table near the brick fireplace. The hearth was wide enough to roast a full-grown sow on the spit, but it contained no fire today. The iron pulleys and wheels, the blackened three-legged spiders, and the Dutch ovens were cold. In warm weather, all the cooking was done in the summer kitchen, a whitewashed brick building that stood a dozen yards behind the house; this room was used for preparation.

Aunt Kessie glanced at Anne's plate and smiled enigmatically. "Didn't they feed you in Philadelphia, child?" The twins giggled, but one serious look from the older woman sent them back to work with renewed vigor.

"Nobody cooks like Toby," Anne said. "Mary's food is good, but it doesn't taste like home." Between bites, she asked a dozen questions about the health and well-being of people and animals on Gentleman's Folly. "Did you see the pirates? Was anyone hurt? When—?"

"One at a time, if you please, miss," Aunt Kessie replied. She clapped her hands twice. "Afi, Afua, you can leave that until later. Send one of the children to gather the eggs, see if the wash is dry, and start on a new batch of butter. Hurry, now. We want everything right for Miss Anne's supper party tonight."

"Yes, ma'am." The two maids wiped their hands on their aprons and hurried out the door onto the back porch.

Aunt Kessie poured herself a cup of tea and drew a chair over to sit near Anne. "Your new husband may not like you coming into the kitchen to eat with us."

"He won't mind." Anne finished the last strawberry and wiped her mouth with a napkin. "Oh, they're lovely this year, aren't they? Delicious."

"Is he a good man?"

"O'Ryan?" Anne got up to find honey for her tea. "Yes, I think so. I think Papa likes him, although he'll pretend he doesn't for a while."

"What's important is that you like him." Aunt Kessie's sloe-black eyes grew anxious. "Mr. Preston was not right for you. I knew that. I could feel his evil. But this Irishman is different. He worries me. I cannot see into his heart. I cannot feel what he thinks."

"Did you look into a candle flame? Ask the old people spirits?"

Creases formed at the corners of Aunt Kessie's mouth.

"What kind of talk is that? You've been listening to these silly girls. If I see something, I just see it. I don't ask, sometimes the voices tell me things about a man or a woman. But Kessie Africa doesn't mess with black magic. You should know better."

"Mr. O'Ryan—Michael, his name is Michael. He risked his life for me. Footpads attacked Mary's carriage. One of them pulled me out onto the street. Michael came to my rescue. That must prove what kind of person he is."

Aunt Kessie nodded. "Maybe so. Maybe not. My voices see danger around him." She took Anne's hands in hers. "You should have waited. You should have brought him here to meet Master James. Marriage is a big step. You are still young. Maybe too young to pick a man you must spend the rest of your life with."

"I couldn't wait."

"Ah." The black woman nodded again. "I thought so." She laid gentle fingers over Anne's womb. "Is a girl child in this cradle. That was the small voice I heard crying."

"A girl? Are you sure?"

"Definitely a female life."

"A little girl. Somehow, I thought of it as a boy, but I'd love a daughter. Promise me you won't say anything to Papa, not yet. He would be angry with me."

Aunt Kessie's dark eyes dilated and became glassy as she breathed slow, deep breaths. "I feel something . . ."

"The baby?" Anne shivered despite the warmth of the kitchen.

The older woman stood up suddenly. "Pay no attention to me," she said. "I am getting old, foolish, maybe even hard of hearing. There's no reason you and your husband should not have many healthy sons and daughters."

Anne's mouth went dry, and a tiny frisson of fear slid down

her spine. "Tell me," she begged. "If something's wrong, I want to know. What—?"

"You surprised me, nothing more," Aunt Kessie said in a voice that told Anne that the discussion was over. "I was disappointed to miss your wedding. I always thought that when the right man came, you would marry here at Gentleman's Folly. Now . . ." She sighed and shrugged. "What's passed is past. We must worry about tonight. You know I want only the best for you, child."

"I wish I could have waited," Anne agreed, trying to push back her uneasiness. "But sometimes we just don't have the choice." She cupped a palm over her still-flat belly. "I want to try to be a good mother to this baby."

Aunt Kessie nodded. "I know you do."

"Even if it's coming sooner than I wanted, it's still mine. And I'll love her more than any little girl has ever been loved."

"Children come when God is ready to send them."

"A little girl," Anne murmured. "She'll grow up here on Gentleman's Folly, and she'll have you to tell her secrets to, just as I always have."

"Perhaps."

"Papa will adore having a granddaughter, once he gets used to the idea."

"Yes, they will have each other, I think."

"If it really is a girl, I'll name her after Mother. Papa will like that, won't he?"

Aunt Kessie gave her another long, thoughtful look. "Enjoy each day as it comes. It may be that your father's days here are not long."

"Don't say that!" Anne shook her head. "Papa's going to be fine. I know he will. O'Ryan can take over some of his work, and I'll make certain that he rests more. I need him, Aunt Kessie. I need him, and this baby will need him, and I don't intend to let anything happen to him. Not until he's an old, old man."

"May the Lord grant it so."

"He will. I know He will." Anne rose and brushed Aunt Kessie's smooth cheek with a kiss. "I'm home now, and everything will work out. It simply must."

Chapter 7

Anne curled up on her bed and pulled the coverlet over her shoulders. It was late afternoon, and she had a dozen things to do before their guests arrived at six, but she was unbearably sleepy. She would just catch a quick nap, a few minutes' rest before she called one of the girls to help her dress and do her hair in the fashionable coiffure Mary's friends were wearing in Philadelphia.

One garden window was open a crack, and she could smell the heavenly scent of lilacs. Her eyelids felt as though they weighed a pound each. She never took to her bed in the daytime, but she knew she'd feel much better after a few moments of total relaxation. Yawning, she let her eyes drift closed and listened to the muffled clatter of servants' shoes on the stairs.

The kiss began as lightly as falling corn pollen. It teased her bottom lip and then her top. She sighed as the sweet pressure became slowly and exquisitely more intriguing.

His mouth slanted perfectly to hers. His touch was warm and mischievous, yet it promised more. She uttered a tiny sound of pleasure as he continued to kiss her.

She stirred restlessly, feeling the swell of her breasts, the eager heat rising in the pit of her belly. It was impossible to lie still when he was kissing her like this . . . impossible to keep from . . .

The click of the door latch brought her wide awake. Startled, she looked around the empty room. Then, she blinked and rubbed her eyes, struggling to shed the memories of her dream. The smell of lilacs seemed stronger than ever.

Anne moistened her lips with the tip of her tongue and smiled lazily as fancies of her phantom lover faded. She glanced at the closed door, and then back to the pool of sunlight that draped her bed in gilded splendor. No more than a quarter hour could have passed since she'd nestled in the soft folds of the featherbed. She chuckled at the foolish notion that the kiss had been more than a dream.

Until she found the single spray of purple lilac lying on her pillow.

Several hours later, O'Ryan set his full wineglass on the Irish hunt table and wandered through the open doorway into the formal garden behind the house. The music and laughter of the merrymakers faded as he strolled under an arch of lilacs that framed the gateway to a high boxwood maze.

The moon was full, the brick pathways illuminated with a pearly glow. Here and there, fireflies sparkled like tiny flittering fairies. The air smelled of lilacs and apple blossoms.

"Annie?"

"I'm here," she answered from the shadows.

He ducked his head to avoid the overhanging foliage and moved to her side. "It's very warm for April," he said. "At home, peat fires would still burn on the hearths." He trailed a finger intimately down her bare arm.

Trembling, she pulled away. "Here, too—usually. We had an early spring." Her words came in short rushes. "But it's nearly May." Retreating a safe distance, she sank gracefully onto a bench.

He sat beside her, close enough to feel a fold of her silk

gown brush against his hand. "Why are you out here instead of enjoying the dancing?" He wanted her where he could see her . . . where he could watch the sway of her skirts and the tilt of her head.

"Did you kiss me earlier? In the bedroom, this afternoon?"

"Kiss you?" he teased. She intrigued him, this wife of his. She was so different from Kathleen, fair where Kathleen was dark, but every bit as high-spirited. And Anne affected him in ways that Kathleen never could.

"I think you did."

He laughed. "Perhaps you were dreaming."

She didn't answer, but the silence between them was affable rather than strained. He liked sitting here beside her and gazing back at the manor with the moon shining off the roof and candlelight spilling through the multipaned windows.

Gentleman's Folly wasn't nearly as grand as Cuchulainn, where he had grown up, but it was a gracious house, and O'Ryan felt instantly at home here. It had been a long time since he'd been accepted so easily by strangers. As an Irishman, he hadn't expected to be welcomed by Anne's friends and neighbors. Their courtesy and openness was a shock after the reception he'd had in Philadelphia. Most Americans he'd met before he came here acted as though they despised the Irish immigrants.

"Someone left lilacs on my pillow," she murmured.

"Do you like to be kissed, Annie? I think you do."

"What do you think of our neighbors?" Anne asked, ignoring his question.

"You have a mouth made for kissing."

Her soft, slow Maryland voice was throaty. It made him want to take off his coat and lay it on the ground. It made him wonder what she would do if he pushed her back against the thick green grass and covered her with his body. He wanted to feel her under him, feel her silky skin against his, free her breasts and taste them to see if they were as sweet as her lips.

"Our friends like you," she continued. "You're quite charming when you want to be, even if you are extraordinarily lucky at whist."

"I've always been very lucky at cards and unlucky in love." Moonlight dusted the curve of her chin and the crown of her head with silver. Her high-waisted silk dress was cut simply with a deep vee neck that showed off her shapely bosom and tiny, puffed sleeves that revealed more of her arms than they concealed.

He caught her hand and lifted it, turning her palm to kiss the throbbing pulse at her wrist and the underside of her elbow.

"Michael. Don't," she protested. But she didn't pull away, and he took her in his arms.

She placed her hands against his chest. "This will only complicate things between us," she murmured. "Neither of us need that, considering our bargain. There's no reason why we shouldn't make the best of this time together."

"My feelings exactly," he replied as he kissed her.

She drew back as if his mouth was a burning coal. "I didn't mean that way," she stammered. "As friends."

Every instinct screamed for him to continue his assault on her shaky defenses. Her words told him *no*, but her body . . .

He fought to keep his emotions under control. "We are husband and wife under God. Why shouldn't we—?"

"No." She shook her head, and he could feel her alarm. "It's all happened too fast. I— There's the baby to think of, and . . . Please, Michael, cannot we be friends?"

"Michael, is it?" He wanted her, God, how he wanted her, but it was too soon. She was no lightskirts to be wooed and won on a whim. If she came to him willingly, something told him it would be worth the wait.

"O'Ryan, then."

"I like the sound of my name on your lips, Annie. And if we are friends, I suppose that's more than most married couples achieve in a lifetime."

"Not so for my parents," she said. "Theirs was a love match. They never argued."

"Are you certain, or are you seeing them through a child's eyes? Mine never went a day without exchanging bitter words."

"I'm sorry for that."

O'Ryan shrugged. "My mother was a great lady and very beautiful. Wherever she went, heads turned. She had her choice of husbands, some of them titled."

"Didn't your parents care for each other when they married?"

"Yes . . . at first. Or they thought they did. The trouble came when my father lost his money in an ill-fated investment venture. She never forgave him for it."

"It must have been difficult for her."

"It was. She began as the pampered bride of a well-to-do man and ended her life . . . in much-reduced circumstances."

"I'm sorry," Anne said. "Is your father still living?"

"No, he died shortly before she did." He wouldn't tell her how his father had taken his own life rather than face debts he couldn't pay. It was one more thing in his past O'Ryan didn't care to dwell on. "The music is beginning again. Shall we go back inside?"

"You're right," she agreed. "I will be happy to dance with you, Mr. O'Ryan."

He could hear the amusement in her voice. "Is there something wrong with Michael?"

"No. Actually, I was wondering how I could—"

"Make a nickname of it, as I do Annie?"

"Exactly." They laughed together.

"You should always laugh," he said as he took her arm and led her under the lilac arch. "And you should always wear green. It's your color."

Anne didn't intend to dance more than a set or two. It felt very strange to be led through the steps of a country reel by O'Ryan. She had always loved to dance, and they moved through the steps as though they had had many years' experience as partners.

The warm night—or was it O'Ryan's hand on her waist, or thoughts of that mysterious kiss?—soon had her giddy with excitement. As bright notes filled the room and echoed through the hall, she passed from partner to partner, always returning to the big Irishman.

After nearly an hour, she paused to catch her breath while O'Ryan went in search of a cup of sweet cider to quench her thirst.

Her father joined her. "You're having a good time, puss," he said, giving her fingers a squeeze. "I'm glad. I only wish your mother could be here to celebrate with us."

"It is odd," she replied. "I couldn't wait to get to Philadelphia. Gentleman's Folly seemed so dull. But I missed it terribly, and I missed you." Now the thought that she had risked everything for the likes of Stephen Preston was repugnant to her. She couldn't understand her attraction for the cad or why she had allowed him the liberties she had. Her involvement with Stephen had happened an eternity ago, as though she had been another woman . . . a much younger and sillier woman. "Gentleman's Folly is the most beautiful place on earth, Papa," she said. "I love it, almost as much as I love you. And I'll never leave either of you again. I promise."

"Your mother loved this land, pet. God, but I miss her."

O'Ryan returned with her drink, and he and her father fell into easy conversation. ". . . a talented woodworker," her husband was saying. "Cleary is both carpenter and wheelwright, and he possesses the skill to fashion plain furniture. I notice you employ many workmen here on Gentleman's Folly. Do you have need of another craftsman?"

Her father shook his head. "No, I'm afraid not. Abraham does all our carpentry."

"Abraham is the man who met us at the dock on our arrival," Anne explained.

"I'll ask around to see if any of my neighbors need a wheelwright," her father said. "And there's always Talbot Courthouse—Easton some are calling it. The town's growing. Your man may find work there."

"Cleary is honest and skilled at his trade."

"It is a pity," Anne said, "that there are so many immigrants and so few here that wish to hire them. Mr. Cleary seemed a decent man. I understand he has a family to provide for."

"You met him, Anne?" Her father pursed his lips. "It's true that there are scarce jobs for the Irish. Most on the Eastern Shore would rather have people they know working for them."

"Slaves, you mean?" O'Ryan said. He was standing behind her so that she was able to nudge him without letting Papa see. She hoped he wasn't about to start an argument about the use of slaves on Gentleman's Folly. "I was impressed with Abraham," he continued. "He seems intelligent."

"He is," her father agreed. "He's one of the few slaves not born on the plantation. I bought him along with three field hands at an auction downstate about five years ago."

"We all like Abraham," Anne put in. "He's one of our best

workers. And Papa treats him very well. He even allowed him to marry a woman from Greensboro Hall."

"His wife is a slave as well?" O'Ryan asked.

Her father nodded. "Ivy's a house servant."

"Here?"

"No," Anne explained. "Ivy belongs to Nathaniel's mother. But Papa allows Abraham to visit her on Sundays, and sometimes she's permitted to come here on holidays."

"I see," O'Ryan replied.

Anne could tell that he didn't, but she didn't want to begin another fuss with him. Instead, she half turned and touched his arm. "The music's beginning again," she said. "Shall we—?"

O'Ryan took the hint. "Yes, if you'll excuse us, James," he said.

They danced the next two sets together. The parlor was a swirl of candlelight, bright gowns, laughter, and brighter music. For a little while Anne could forget what she'd done in Philadelphia, forget the lies, forget her worries about Papa's health, and pretend that all was as it should be.

The musicians finished the tune with a flourish and everyone clapped. Servants passed among the guests with trays of wine, ale, and cider. "I thought Irishmen were staunch drinkers," she whispered to O'Ryan when he refused anything stronger than cider.

"Don't believe all you hear of us," he said. "And I promise not to believe that all Americans paint their faces like Indians and eat their beef raw."

She laughed. "If I had to find a husband on the dock," she murmured. "I could have done worse than you."

"You might have," he agreed, then nodded his head politely as Sibyl Greensboro swooped down on them with her daughter-in-law Susannah in tow.

"I must know more about your mystery man," cried the old woman. "Where exactly in Ireland are you from? And who is your family?"

"I will be delighted to tell you all, madam," O'Ryan said, "if you will do me the honor of this next dance." He winked at Anne. "With your permission?"

"Of course," Anne replied.

Sibyl sputtered with delight as O'Ryan took her hand and led her into the next set. Susannah raised an ivory lace fan to her lips and stifled a giggle. "I don't know where you found him," she whispered to Anne, "but I wish he'd keep her occupied all evening."

James Davis joined the two young ladies. "Do you think I might have one dance with my daughter?" he asked.

"You've been dancing all evening, Papa," Anne hedged. "I'm feeling a little—"

"Nonsense, I'm fit as I ever was, and this is your wedding celebration." He lifted Anne's gloved hand to his lips. "Be happy, child. It's all I ever wanted for you."

"I am happy, Papa."

"Then indulge an old man and let him dance with the most beautiful lady in Maryland."

Knowing defeat when she saw it, Anne sighed and let her father guide her to join the others.

Ivy replenished the pitchers of sweet cider and lemonade, then cleared away the dirty glasses. She carried them to the kitchen and put them on the table near the dry sink. One of the twins was washing dishes and silverware while Grace arranged tiny pastries on a silver platter. Ivy wiped her clean hands on her apron and was preparing to slice a pan of gingerbread when Aunt Kessie motioned her to the back door.

"Someone out there wants to see you," the housekeeper said.

Ivy looked hesitant.

"It's all right, I've plenty of hands to help. You go and spend an hour with your man."

Ivy whisked off her apron, ran fingers through her close-cropped hair, and murmured a quick thank-you as she hurried outside. She'd taken only a few steps across the back porch when strong hands grasped her around the waist and lifted her high.

"Abraham!" she cried. "Stop such nonsense. You—"

He cut off her token protests with a kiss. "Missed you fierce," he said thickly, then kissed her again.

She hugged him, inhaling deeply of his familiar scent, feeling the smooth texture of his skin. "I missed you, too. I thought Miss Sibyl meant to stay a month visiting her sister in Chestertown."

"There's dancing at the quarters." Abraham eased his grip enough so that she could draw breath. "There's a bonfire and a pig roasting on the spit. Do you—?"

"Are you hungry?" she asked him softly. "Or would you rather—?"

"How long have we got?"

"Miss Kessie said an hour." She slipped him three coins from her skirt pocket. "I earned that by selling fish I caught in the Chester River last Sunday. Put it in the jar."

"I will." He kissed her neck, soft moth-wing caresses that made her heart beat faster.

"How much do we have now?" It was hard to think about the freedom savings, with Abraham's big hands on her and her breath coming quick.

Afua came from the well with a bucket of water. "You best stop this foolin' around and get busy."

"I've a right," Ivy protested. "Miss Kessie gave me leave."

"Leave, is it? Leavin' us to do all the work." Afua set the

bucket on the floor. "Guess I'd rather be doin' such instead of fetchin' water."

Ignoring Afua, Ivy followed Abraham off the porch and down the brick path past the summer kitchen and the smokehouse.

The tinkle of the harpsichord and the rhythmic beat of a drum mingled in the night air as the two ran to Abraham's shop. Inside, a ladder led to a single room on the second floor. Ivy waited impatiently as Abraham lit a candle.

His room was as neat as always, with a small, sturdy table, two chairs, wooden pegs along one wall for his two changes of clothing, a chest of tools, and a bed covered with a patched and faded coverlet. A leather-covered Bible lay at the center of the table. A pair of old riding boots stood beneath the clothes pegs. Beside the low bed a brightly colored rag rug— the one she'd made for him—adorned the spotless floorboards.

"Welcome home, wife," he said to her, and opened his arms.

Shyly, she went to him, part of her bitter that they had so little time together, most of her wanting to make the most of this precious hour. "Will it always be like this?" she asked him. "Will we ever have a place when I can cook your breakfast and sew your clothes? Where we can watch our babies sleep in that cradle you're goin' to make for me?"

"Shhh," he said, shaking his head. "Not tonight, Ivy. No talk of babies tonight."

She swallowed the lump in her throat, thinking how badly she wanted to give him a son with skin the color of ripe blackberries and lion eyes. Wondering if they could hold to his plan of not having children so long as they were slaves . . . "Oh, Abraham," she whispered.

Then he kissed away the tears and led her to the bed. "I want you," he said. "Want you so bad."

"Blow out the candle," she begged him. "You know I like

it best without the light." Silently, he left her, padding to the table to please her. And then he was back and it was just the two of them with the clean sheets beneath and heaven above. And for a little while, Ivy could forget everything but how lucky she was to have him for her husband.

Chapter 8

The following day was overcast, with a promise of rain from the west. O'Ryan yawned as Abraham led two horses to the gate. He'd gotten little sleep in the hours between the end of the party and dawn. Most of the guests had remained for the night, and Anne had shared their bedchamber with Susannah Greensboro and a maid. O'Ryan had slept in an attic room with Nathaniel and his brothers-in-law.

This morning, O'Ryan was riding to Oxford to send a letter to Sean and another to Kathleen in Ireland. He'd written both before breakfast, assuring them that he'd not forgotten his promises. Each envelope contained money that he'd won at cards the night before. He would have preferred sending bank notes or letters of credit, but he didn't have enough to open an account. He hoped the cash would arrive safely.

A few drops of rain fell as O'Ryan and Abraham rode down the lane and turned north onto the Oxford road. "Sorry to have to drag you out on a day like this," O'Ryan said, turning in the saddle to look back at the slave.

"No trouble, sir." Abraham kept his eyes lowered, but his spine was straight, his strong fingers tight on the reins.

"My name's O'Ryan, and since I've never been knighted, I'd just as soon you called me that."

The black man glanced up with guarded eyes. "Reckon

not, Mr. O'Ryan. There's ways and then there's ways. Maybe you don't have too many of my kind where you come from."

"Craftsmen?" O'Ryan nodded. "I know what you mean. Slaves. We do have them in Ireland, I'm ashamed to say. I don't approve of slavery."

"Different for you, meaning no disrespect. But I know my place."

"Do you?" O'Ryan reined in his mount, looked around to be sure there were not witnesses, and offered his hand to Abraham. "Let's start again. I'm Michael O'Ryan. And you are?"

Abraham hesitated. "Abraham Washington." He didn't accept the hand.

O'Ryan withdrew his offer. "I understand you're a carpenter?"

"I can make most anything out of wood."

"I've heard as much. What about farming? Planting? I don't know wheat from oats, but I'd like to learn. I'd appreciate it if you'd help me."

Abraham studied him suspiciously. "If I can," he said finally.

"Good." O'Ryan nudged his horse and fell in beside the woodworker. "You can start by telling me what this is in this field."

"Horses."

O'Ryan winced. "I can see that they are horses—two, a bay mare and a chestnut stallion."

"Master James's prize stud, Isle of Jersey's Scarlet Earl. Master James calls him Jersey."

"And the mare?"

"Belongs to Mr. Payne Voshell in Oxford. Master James charges forty dollars breedin' fee with Jersey. The mare's not in season till next month. They put them together so they can get to know each other before the gunpowder goes off."

"Gunpowder?"

"You'd think a barrel of black powder had gone off if you tried to get into Jersey's paddock when he gets the smell of a mare in heat. Any other time, Jersey's as gentle as a kitten, but not when he's got lovin' on his mind."

O'Ryan nodded. "I understand perfectly. And what's planted in that field across the road?"

"Tobacco."

"I thought as much. How do you start it? From seed? In the field, or in beds someplace? Where do . . ."

By the time they returned from Oxford in early evening, O'Ryan's respect for Abraham had increased threefold. In other circumstances, O'Ryan suspected they could have become close friends. But the gap between the mistress's husband and her slave was too wide. And Abraham had lived too long as a possession to try and breach it.

Anne watched through the parlor window as O'Ryan dismounted and handed the gelding's reins to Abraham. For a big man, her husband moved with a flowing grace that made her breath catch in her throat whenever she caught sight of him. She could well believe that he was descended from Irish nobility, as he claimed. Surely no one could behave with such elegant assurance unless they were to the manor born.

He'd left the house early, before she came down for breakfast, so she hadn't seen him all day. But his absence hadn't kept her from thinking about him, from wondering if she'd done the right thing in marrying him or in lying to her father.

She'd been so sure of herself when she told Mary that a union of convenience would be the answer to her problem. She hadn't counted on the sting of her conscience, or the possibility that dealing with a flesh-and-blood bridegroom would be so difficult.

Anne had to keep reminding herself that O'Ryan had

given her his name for money. He cared nothing for her, and once he had her grandmother's inheritance in his hand, he'd never think of her or her child again. And that was best for all of them—wasn't it?

"Anne?" He was standing in the entrance hall, hat in hand. A short-waisted, sky-blue coat stretched dangerously tight across O'Ryan's broad shoulders and his buff doeskin breeches fitted his lean, long horseman's thighs and calves like a second skin.

Dangerous. That was the right word to describe him, she thought. "Michael." She managed a half smile. "We've eaten, but the girls have kept your supper warm."

Those blue eyes seemed to read her soul. Was it possible he knew what she was thinking?

"Will you join me?" he asked.

She should refuse. But when she opened her mouth, "All right" slipped out.

"If you'll give me a few minutes to—"

"Of course," she answered graciously, falling into the familiar role of hostess. "You must be dusty from your long ride. I'll be in the dining room."

Her father and most of the servants had already retired. Anne had thought about going up to her room, but she hadn't wanted to be waiting in bed when O'Ryan came in. She didn't know what she would do if he insisted on sleeping in her bed again. That arrangement simply wouldn't work. Having him beside her at night was impossible. Who knew what liberties he would take next, or how far she could trust herself? She would sit with him while he ate, and they could discuss the matter calmly. Theirs was a business arrangement, so that made them partners, albeit in an unconventional manner. O'Ryan obviously valued frankness, and that's what she would give him.

She went into the dining room, checked the serving dishes

to be certain the food was of proper temperature, then dismissed Grace. She didn't want anything she and O'Ryan discussed to be overheard. Servants were notorious gossips, and what one suspected the whole Tidewater would claim as gospel in a matter of days.

Anne rubbed the small of her back as she eased into her own chair at the long table. The Greensboro family hadn't departed until midafternoon, and she'd helped Aunt Kessie and the staff slide the parlor furniture back into place and re-lay the rugs that had been removed for the dancing.

The party had gone well, and Anne was certain her guests had enjoyed themselves as much as she had. Still, it had been tiring. Susannah might be the perfect wife for Nathaniel, but she was terrible to share a bed with. Susannah had talked and talked, then when she finally dozed off, she'd snored. The good thing was that this morning's bout of sickness had been brief and easily hidden.

O'Ryan came downstairs without his waistcoat or stock, wearing a clean, wide-sleeved linen shirt, open at the collar. His wheat-colored hair was damp and stray tendrils framed his face. His throat was tanned and as smoothly muscled as his sinewy arms.

"You didn't have to do this," he said to her. "I could have found something to eat in the kitchen."

"And shock Aunt Kessie?" Anne chuckled. "You don't know her yet. She has a rigid sense of what's proper and sees that we stand by it or suffer the consequences."

A smile tugged at the corner of his sensual mouth. "I suppose we're lucky she's gone to bed. There'd be the devil to pay if she caught me taking supper in my shirtsleeves."

Anne laughed. "Amen to that. But we're lucky to have her. My grandfather found Aunt Kessie selling plantains in Barbados before I was born. They liked each other immediately, and he could see that she was an educated woman who had fallen on hard times. He brought her and her children back to the Tidewater, and she's worked for us ever since."

He reached for a biscuit. "Does her family work here as well?"

Anne shook her head. "Her oldest daughter is a midwife across the bay, and one son is a brewer in Baltimore. Her youngest daughter died, but there are grandchildren, some in Baltimore, others here on the Eastern Shore."

"And none are slaves?"

Anne removed the serving lid and passed a plate of fried chicken to O'Ryan. "No. I told you, Aunt Kessie is a free woman."

"My first husband was a Creole," said an amused voice from the hall, "and my father was Alexandre Gautier, a French merchant."

Anne glanced up. "Aunt Kessie?"

The housekeeper's mouth was a thin line, but her dark eyes showed amusement. "If there is anything else Mr. O'Ryan would care to know about me, he can ask."

"No disrespect meant." O'Ryan said.

"Good." Aunt Kessie nodded graciously. "Is there anything else that I can do for the two of you before I go to bed?"

"Nothing, thank you," Anne replied. She busied herself with a napkin as Aunt Kessie's footsteps receded, then looked at O'Ryan.

"I think I've been put in my place," he said.

Both chuckled. "Me, too," Anne replied. "I told you how she is."

The shared feeling of being scolded eased the tension between them, and Anne found herself enjoying her husband's company as they chatted easily about Oxford and last night's frolic. When O'Ryan finished eating, she was reluctant to end the pleasant conversation.

"Would you care to stroll in the gardens?" she asked. "It won't be dark for nearly an hour."

"I'd like that."

She let him take her hand, and they walked side by side. She showed him the herb garden and the fountain with the Greek statue of a boy and a dolphin at the center.

"Spray used to come from the dolphin's mouth when I was a child," Anne explained, "but something broke, and Papa hasn't found anyone who could fix it. Now it just collects rainwater and fallen leaves."

"I might be able to do something with it." He didn't tell her that the fountains had been his favorite place to play when he was too young to venture out without his nurse, or that he had watched the head gardener at Cuchulainn clean and repair the fountains many times.

Together, they explored the maze and the orchard beside the kitchen garden. Then, as the light faded and stars winked on, one by one, they walked down the hill to the dock, where the plantation sloop lay at anchor.

"Turn your head, please," Anne asked him.

"Why?"

"Can't you just do it?"

When she gave him permission to look again, he found that she'd removed her shoes and stockings and laid them neatly on a patch of grass.

"Good thinking," he said, pulling off his boots.

"It's a holdover from my infancy," Anne teased. "I can't get near the bay without wanting to wade in it." She raised her skirts to reveal a lovely flash of pale ankle and splashed into the water.

"No fair," he said. "My breeches are too tight to roll far."

"Watch out for the crabs," she warned. "They grow to the size of wagon wheels here."

A few minutes later, they sat on the edge of the dock and

dangled their feet in the cool water. "This land should have been named Eden," O'Ryan said.

"I've heard that Ireland is very beautiful."

"It is, with a different beauty." Like yours, he thought. He wanted to take her in his arms, to kiss her as he had before in the garden, but he sensed that this wasn't the right time. Like a wild rose in the bright sunshine, she was opening a petal at a time to reveal her inner secrets.

"Tell me about it." She crossed her arms and rubbed them as a crisp, salty breeze played over their faces.

"I wouldn't know where to start."

"How about the River Shannon? What does it look like?"

"Wide, ever changing. Always the same." Memories of County Clare flooded over him. "Rocky shores, green pastures running down to—"

She broke in. "Why did you tell my father that you were from Belfast?"

"I lived there for a time. Studied there." He looked into her face. "Why? Did you think I was lying?"

"I think you prefer to be a gentleman of mystery," she replied. "You evaded that question the last time I asked."

"Did I? It seemed to me that we were interrupted by Grace."

"If you say so." She smoothed her skirts. "Tell me more. I want to know what peat smells like when it burns and why you came to America and—"

"One thing at a time." He stared out over the water, thinking that she was very clever and that he would need to watch what he said. It wouldn't do to give Anne more information than she needed. "Peat is the blessing of Ireland," he said. "It burns with a blue smoke and . . ."

The moon was halfway over the trees when he paused to catch his breath. Anne was a good listener, a rare gift in a woman and one that made her even more dangerous. He'd bed her if he could, but he wouldn't let himself become emotionally involved with his wife. True love and marriage were pretty words for ballads. Anne had wed him for his name. Once her child was born, she would pay him off, and he could begin to build a new life.

"It's time we went back," he said, getting to his feet and offering her a hand.

"Yes," she agreed. "Morning comes early on Gentleman's Folly." She took a few steps, then stopped. Her expression reflected her sudden discomfort.

"What's wrong?" he asked.

"Nothing. I . . ." She clasped her midsection. "A sudden cramp. Oh." Her eyes clenched shut and she drew her breath in sharply. She swayed and he put an arm around her shoulders to steady her.

"Sit down," he ordered.

"No!" She shook her head. "I must get to the house. I must—"

He picked her up in his arms and carried her up the hill, flinching inwardly as she tensed with each contraction. By the time he reached the house, trickles of blood stained her legs.

"Am I to have no say in this matter?" O'Ryan thundered at the housekeeper. "Is she not worth the silver it will cost to fetch the doctor?"

Aunt Kessie didn't retreat a step down the hall. Instead, she drew herself up to her full height in front of Anne's bedroom door and crossed her arms stubbornly. "I cannot stop you from calling him, but know that by doing so you condemn her to death as surely as if you plunged a knife into her heart."

"Damn you, woman! Can't you see? She's bleeding!" He wheeled on Anne's father. "Will you stand there and let her die?"

James's brow furrowed. "This is women's business. If Kessie says that McNeal will kill her—"

"You're mad, both of you." O'Ryan shouldered past his father-in-law. "I'll go for the physician myself."

Kessie grabbed his arm. When he glared into her face, it seemed to him as smooth and dark as polished walnut.

"Listen to me, Irishman!" she said fiercely. "It be as Master James says. This is women's sorrow, and women have the knowing to tend to it. The last babe that Dr. McNeal brought into the world was a fine, fat boy child. His mother—Agnes Walker—was young and strong. It was her third child. She should have lived to see him have sons of his own. But two days after the doctor caught the babe, she took the birthing sickness. Fever ran through Agnes Walker's blood. It burned hotter and hotter until it burned her up."

"You called McNeal before," O'Ryan argued. "Anne said he was a friend."

"We called him to see to Master James's heart," Kessie answered. "Not for slipping a babe. That's different." She made a clicking sound with her tongue, and her sloe-black eyes narrowed. "You listen to me," she repeated, then released his arm. "This Dr. McNeal is a good man, but he has bad luck with mothers. I won't see him touch Miss Anne."

A fragrant scent of sandalwood lingered in the air as Kessie shifted her gaze from his face to Anne's father. "You trusted me with her all her life, trust me with this. I've given her herbs to make her sleep, and I've washed her body in salt water. The bleeding is not bad. It is nature's way. It will stop in its own time."

"Kessie's right about McNeal," James rasped. He looked as though he had aged ten years since the party the night before. "I know of three other mothers that McNeal lost in the past five years. I don't want my Anne to be the fourth. I trust Kessie. If she says Anne will be all right, she will."

Kessie's features softened. "You wait here. I need to be in there with Miss Anne. She needs to grieve for this lost baby child."

"You don't think there's a chance—" O'Ryan began.

The black woman shook her head sadly. "There is no more baby. But you will have more children. Miss Anne is healthy and has good hips to be a mother. It wasn't her fault that this baby girl had a spirit too weak for this world."

"But how could you know that it was a girl?" O'Ryan asked. "She couldn't have been more than . . ." He stopped, suddenly aware that Anne's father was glaring at him.

"Is that why you two married so hastily?" James demanded. "Did you take advantage of my girl?" He swore through clenched teeth. "I'll disown her! By God, I will. I'll take a horsewhip to you both!"

"Hold your tongue, man," O'Ryan warned. "Curse me all you want. But mind how you speak of my wife."

"She's my daughter!"

O'Ryan's eyes narrowed. "I swear on my mother's grave that I had no improper knowledge of Anne before we were wed."

"You'd best be telling the truth!" James's face purpled in anger. "I didn't raise my daughter to be a harlot."

O'Ryan took a step toward his father-in-law. "Are you questioning my word?"

"Yes. No." Rage drained from James's features. "If I've spoken out of turn, you have my apology. But I draw the line at immorality."

"For shame," Kessie admonished. "Miss Anne will hear. Will you add to her heartbreak by scrapping like banty roosters? Now let me go and see to her." With a shooing motion, the housekeeper slipped into Anne's chamber.

O'Ryan caught a glimpse of Anne's pale face against

heaped pillows, and an icy hand gripped his heart. He turned away, silently offering an urgent prayer for her safe recovery.

"She's right," James said. "I've let the Davis temper get the best of me again. This is no place for us. Come downstairs and join me in the library for a glass of—"

"No," O'Ryan gestured impatiently. "I'm not leaving until she's out of danger."

"Forgive my words. I love Anne. I know she wouldn't do anything—"

O'Ryan gritted his teeth, in no mood to be pacified.

"Women often lose a first child." James ran a hand through his sleep-tangled hair. "My wife and I lost several children, but we were blessed with Anne and later Mary. I always thought I'd have sons to carry on after me, but it wasn't meant to be. Sometimes you just have to accept things."

"My mother died in childbirth," O'Ryan said softly. "I was there. She bled and bled. I didn't know there could be so much blood."

"I'm sorry," James replied. "I know what it's like to lose a mother and a wife. Anne's mother . . ." His voice grew thick and trailed off. "I'm going down for that drink now. If you change your mind—"

"I won't."

"And if I was wrong about . . . what I said . . ." The older man's face reddened. "I'm upset. I should have known that Anne would never disgrace the family name."

"I will say this one more time and never again," O'Ryan said. "Your daughter and I did nothing dishonorable before the vows were taken. Anyone who suggests otherwise will have me to answer to."

"Anne's a good girl, raised right. And I can see that you are a gentleman. I should have known better."

"I know little of these matters," O'Ryan said. "But doesn't

it seem reasonable that even an early miscarriage can bring on an alarming flow in a delicate lady?"

"Exactly so," James agreed. "Right. And we shall never speak of this again. You have my word on it."

O'Ryan continued to pace the hallway for what seemed an eternity until the door opened and the housekeeper came out, accompanied by the twins.

"You two girls go on to bed," Kessie said.

"Is Anne all right?" O'Ryan asked. "I want to see her."

"She's sleeping," Aunt Kessie said. "The bleeding has almost stopped. I'll stay with her until morning."

"I'll sit with her." Without waiting for a reply, O'Ryan entered the room and went to Anne's side. She looked small and fragile. Someone had braided her hair into two thick plaits.

He swallowed and blinked away a speck of dust in his eye.

Anne sighed and murmured something he couldn't make out. Her complexion seemed translucent, but her breathing came slow and steady.

"I'm sorry, Annie," he whispered. "So sorry about the child." Strangely, he was. The loss of another man's child had left an empty ache in the pit of his stomach.

It was impossible to forget that she'd married him to give this lost babe a name. Now, she didn't need him. She didn't need him at all.

Chapter 9

Anne didn't want to open her eyes. Instinctively, she turned away from O'Ryan and curled up on her side. She felt no pain other than a dull throbbing in her womb. Strange, she thought. It should hurt more. She had suffered spasms during the night. This morning, she was left with a dry mouth, a headache, and a feeling of acute loss.

She didn't want to look into O'Ryan's face, didn't want to remember how she'd felt when she first suspected she was pregnant. She should be happy. The child that would have been such a problem in her life was no more. Her womb was empty, her body her own.

She wouldn't have to keep up the pretense that this baby was O'Ryan's. She'd never have to listen to well-meaning friends tell her how much the baby looked like him, and she wouldn't watch her son or daughter for some hint of Stephen Preston's lack of character.

Now that there was no coming child, she wondered if she'd been too hasty. She'd rushed into a marriage with a mysterious stranger who didn't love her—a man who'd wanted only her grandmother's legacy—when all she'd had to do was wait a few weeks for nature to take its course.

"Anne."

She didn't answer.

"You're awake. I know you're awake," O'Ryan said. "How are you?"

His voice sounded tired, like that of a man who'd sat beside his beloved all night, like someone who cared. She steeled herself against his false compassion.

"Go away," she whispered.

He took her hand and gripped it tenderly. "It's a hard thing . . . losing a babe." He leaned down and kissed the backs of her fingers.

She opened her eyes and looked at him in confusion. "How can you say that? You know how I got pregnant—how can you have any respect for me?"

"I'm the last one to condemn you for being human, Anne."

"I never wanted this baby."

"You were afraid."

There was no contempt in the deep Irish voice. "I couldn't even do this right, could I?" She sat up, holding the sheet modestly over her breasts.

"Don't blame yourself for the miscarriage. It happens."

"What do you know of women and childbearing?" The room was bathed in half-light, his face barely visible. "I mean . . . It's not an area where most men—"

"My mother lost six. She died a little with each one."

Gooseflesh rose on Anne's arms as, almost too low for her to hear, he continued, "Even after she'd left my father for another man."

She was shocked that he would reveal such a private thing about his life when he'd been so secretive. "I—I'm sorry."

He shook his head. "It was a long time ago."

O'Ryan didn't sound as if it was long ago. She could hear the ache in his voice. She wanted to weep for all those lost children—for her lost child. "You must have loved her very deeply . . . your mother."

"Aye. I still do."

It was something they had in common, being motherless. It said something about O'Ryan that he could harbor such feeling for a woman who had broken society's rules, and she liked him the better for it.

But her own guilt cut deep and the thoughts she had been mulling over slipped out. "My—my miscarriage makes our bargain one-sided, doesn't it?"

"Tish, Annie, don't say things you'll regret. It's the pain of your loss that makes you angry."

"What do you know about me?" she asked softly. "We're still strangers, despite this ring on my finger." Tears welled in her eyes, but she would not give in to them. "For that matter, what do I know about you?"

"The less the better. You've troubles enough. You don't need mine."

"I don't, do I?" She'd made such a fool of herself, woven such a snarled web that there was no way to undo it. "Have I put my family in danger by bringing you here?"

"I'll not lie to you. I've done things . . ." His voice hardened. "I've broken man's laws and God's, but I swear by all that's holy, you and yours have naught to fear from me."

She shivered with apprehension, wondering if she would ever know truth from lies where he was concerned. "You'd not be stupid enough to tell me if you meant us harm, would you?"

"Nay."

She swallowed, heart hammering against her ribs. "I want to believe you," she murmured. "But . . ."

"We'll talk about it another time." He rose to his feet, then leaned down, brushed a lock of damp hair off her forehead, and kissed her gently. "Be well, sweet," he said.

"I—I must ask you to move to another room . . . just until—"

"Until you recover." He nodded. "Of course. Rest now. I'll be here if you need anything."

"Thank you." Anne watched as he retreated to a chair near the open window. Oddly, she felt no thrill at regaining her privacy. She'd never wanted him in her bed, but she hadn't wished her victory to come at such a cost. Her eyes clouded with moisture as she closed them and turned away.

Anne woke in midmorning to find O'Ryan gone and Aunt Kessie sitting beside her. "Good morning, child," the black woman said. "How do you feel?"

"Sore. I need to—"

"You'll not leave this room today. You need to heal." Aunt Kessie went to the cupboard for a china container. "I'll leave you a little privacy while I get those girls to bring up some hot water, a nice breakfast, and my special herb tea. There are fresh cloths here. Don't worry if you're still bleeding a little. It's natural after losing a babe."

"I'm all right. I—"

"You scared us half to death, especially that new husband of yours. He did right by you. Many a man would make himself scarce, but he didn't. It says something about him."

Anne had little appetite that day despite the delicacies the servants brought to her chamber. Her father and Aunt Kessie each spent several hours sitting with her. Her husband made only a brief appearance at noon and again at mid-afternoon to ask if he could get her anything. Both times, she'd told him that she was fine.

Just before supper, he knocked at her door again. "Do you want company now?" he asked.

She didn't answer, pretending sleep. She waited, hoping he would come in anyway. And when he didn't, she wept again.

The following morning, she rose and dressed, and went down to join the family for breakfast. When she went to the dining room she found a small handful of wildflowers next to her plate.

"Don't you remember what day this is?" Aunt Kessie said. "It's the first of May."

She glanced up to find O'Ryan studying her face. "I thought you'd like them," he said. "At home, we always—"

"Glad to see you up and about." Her father patted the crown of her head. "You take it easy now. Feet up, lots of Kessie's abominable tea. That will set you right as rain."

Anne barely nibbled at the food in front of her. She noticed that O'Ryan appeared to have little appetite as well. "Perhaps we could invite Mary and the girls to visit us," she suggested. Her sister's company would be a blessing. With Mary here, she would have no time for feeling sorry for herself. Mary would fill the house with chatter.

"Of course," her father said. "Write to her and ask her to come. She's welcome to stay as long as she likes."

"I will."

There was a strained silence.

"Your husband intends to put his day to good use."

Anne laid her fork down and glanced at O'Ryan expectantly.

"Abraham and Silas are taking me fishing."

"If you catch any, Kessie will want fillets for tomorrow's breakfast," her father said.

O'Ryan finished his meal and excused himself. He couldn't wait to get out of the house. For the first time since he arrived at Gentleman's Folly, he wished he were back in Philadelphia. He wished he'd taken Anne Davis home safely to her sister and walked away without ever asking her to become his wife.

In the days since he'd saved her from being assaulted, he'd come to admire her, and he'd forgotten a rule he'd tried to live by since he was eighteen: he'd confused sexual attraction for something more. He'd let himself begin to imagine living here with her as his true wife.

His first concern had to be Kathleen. Anne had promised him nine thousand dollars. It wouldn't take a tenth of that to bring Kathleen and her son out of Ireland before the authorities traced him to her and arrested her as his accomplice to murder.

He couldn't let her down a second time.

When O'Ryan returned to the house after a successful morning of fishing, he found an invitation waiting for him. Nathaniel and his guests wanted him to accompany them to Swan's Nest plantation for an evening of cards and billiards.

"You're going, of course," James said heartily.

O'Ryan hesitated. He welcomed the opportunity to add a little more money to his nest egg, but he didn't want to be insensitive to his bride's condition. "I thought I should stay with Anne—"

"Nonsense," her father replied. "Rest and time will fix what ails her. Last thing she needs now is a husband knocking about the house. Go on and enjoy yourself. Get to know the locals. Ashton Swan is a damned sharp cardplayer, even if he is topping seventy. He'll trim your pockets, my boy."

"You must go, of course," Anne agreed. "Just don't count on your luck holding at Swan's Nest." She threw him a meaningful look. "As Papa says, Mr. Swan is a skilled player. Doubtless he'll pick you clean."

Not that that would require much, O'Ryan thought. He'd kept little enough of his last winnings, and he'd brought almost nothing with him from Philadelphia. He wondered how long he could decently wait before asking Anne for his nine thousand dollars. He wanted to make this as easy on her as possible, but as she'd already realized there was no need to prolong the charade of their marriage. The sooner he was out of her life, the better it would be for both of them.

Early that evening, halfway between Greensboro Hall and Swan's Nest, he, Abraham, Nathaniel, and the Steele brothers were crossing a creek when O'Ryan noticed a rough canvas cloth bobbing in the current downstream.

Curiosity aroused, he urged his horse to the far side of the low bridge and down the bank into the shallows. Water had risen to soak his boots before he was able to snag the object. When he opened the drawstring, he stared into the frightened eyes of a half-drowned puppy. The tiny bitch was a tangle of long, matted black-and-white fur, huge feet, and vermin.

"Best knock it in the head," Miles Steele suggested. "You don't want to walk into Swan's parlor covered in fleas."

Ignoring him, O'Ryan guided his mount back to shore, dismounted, and stood the pup on her feet. She uttered a plaintive yip and promptly tumbled over, too weak to stand. He knelt and ran his fingers over the dog, cautiously feeling for broken or deformed bones. The animal was pitifully thin, but he could find no injuries.

"Let me take him, sir," Abraham offered, sliding down from his mule. "Master James is partial to dogs. He won't mind another on Gentleman's Folly."

Nathaniel laughed. "What James doesn't need is a mongrel bitch in his kennel. That thing looks like it's half wolfhound and half bear."

O'Ryan offered the hungry animal his index finger. The pup sniffed it, then began to suck frantically. "What do you think, Abraham?" he asked the slave. "Does my wife like dogs as well as her father does?"

"Yes, sir, she does." Abraham nodded. "She'd love this one. Let me clean her up for you."

"This pup might be just thing to cheer her up," he said,

more to himself than to the black man. O'Ryan handed the animal to Abraham, washed his hands, and gathered up his horse's reins.

It was two hours past midnight when he rode away from Greensboro Hall with his pockets heavy with silver and his arms full of squirming puppy. He'd left Abraham behind so that he could spend a few hours with his wife.

"It's good of you to give me leave. Me and Ivy, we don't get many nights together. But Master James might not like it," Abraham had said.

"If he asks for you, I'll tell him it was my orders," O'Ryan had answered. "Be back in time for that morning tide. I want to try my luck at those rockfish again."

Abraham had thanked him, then hurried off to Ivy's cabin.

Again, O'Ryan felt disgust at a system that would require a man like Abraham Washington to live apart from his wife. "I've never met a man less suited to slavery," he murmured aloud. If Abraham's skin were a different color, O'Ryan had no doubt he would quickly rise in the world.

Abraham had worked miracles on the pup—on Shannon, as O'Ryan had decided to call her. The small belly was taut with milk, the filth and fleas had been washed from her hair, and she'd been brushed until her fur shone.

O'Ryan had begged a red ribbon from his host. The length of silk was snug in his pocket, ready to tie around Shannon's neck before he presented her to Anne.

"You have to look your best," O'Ryan warned the pup. "If the lady doesn't like you, you're stuck with me."

Every window in the house was dark when he finally let himself in by the kitchen door and walked quietly through the downstairs and up the center staircase.

It was too dark inside to see, but O'Ryan prided himself on

his good memory. He navigated the hallways until he reached his bedroom, across and down from the one he'd previously shared with Anne.

He made a bed on the floor with his shirt for Shannon, but being female, she had other ideas. He'd no sooner laid his head on the pillow than the little dog began to whine. "Shhh," he warned. He didn't want to wake Anne or the rest of the household.

In the end, he was forced to take Shannon under the covers and let her curl up next to him. "A fine turn of events," he grumbled in Gaelic. "The first woman who's voluntarily come to my bed in months and she's a hound."

Sometime before dawn, O'Ryan awakened to a warm wetness on his chest. Only half awake, he rose, pulled on a pair of trousers, gathered up the dog and the damp sheet, and made his way downstairs to the back porch. The sheet went into a basket of dirty laundry; the dog went to the lawn, somewhat late, to continue her housebreaking training.

After a quick swim in the bay and a stop at the barn to secure a little milk for Shannon's breakfast, O'Ryan returned to the house. Brushed and presentable, they knocked on Anne's door a few hours later.

"Go away," she answered when she found out who was there.

"I've brought you something," O'Ryan replied. Despite Shannon's brief fall from grace in the semidawn, he was pleased with the pup's appearance. The scarlet ribbon made a fine touch, and he wanted Anne to see the little dog before she chewed the ends to shreds.

"I'm getting up," Anne said. "I'll see you at breakfast. You can give it to me then."

"All right, have it your way, Annie," he said. Kneeling, he opened the door and pushed Shannon inside.

"Don't you dare—" Anne broke off and gave a brief exclamation that might have been either delight or exasperation. "A puppy!" she cried.

Seconds later she flung open the door. Shannon was clasped tightly against her breast, and her eyes brimmed with tears. O'Ryan thought her a fair sight with the sunlight frosting her auburn hair.

"I did not mean to make you cry," he said, hugging woman and pup in one embrace.

She laughed, and he bent his head to kiss her lightly on the lips before releasing her and stepping away. Her eyes widened and she touched her mouth with a fingertip. "Oh," she murmured. Her breath came in quick, excited gasps. "It—it's all right."

He used his handkerchief to brush away a tear from the corner of her eye. "The dog's name is Shannon," he said. "I thought you might—"

"Thank you." Anne rubbed her face against the curly fur, heedless of the pup's darting red tongue and squirming body. "I love her." She smiled at him.

"It was worth soaking my good boots to see that smile on your face."

"Just don't stand there. Come in," she said shyly. She motioned to the small table where a tea tray stood. "Now that you've seen me at my worst, you may as well join me."

"I don't suppose you have coffee in that pot," he said.

"Tea, a blend of orange pekoe."

"I've drank worse." Smiling at her, he entered and closed the door behind him.

Shannon couldn't take away the sadness of Anne's miscarriage, but the puppy did make her laugh. Feeding her and trying to remember to take her out kept Anne from hiding in her room. And cuddling the soft, warm body eased the ache in her heart.

O'Ryan's kindness in saving the puppy and then in bringing it home for her said more about his character than any words. His kiss . . . That had surprised her. She wouldn't think about that just now, perhaps later.

He needn't think that she would let him kiss her whenever he pleased. If he tried . . . Well, if he did, she'd make it plain that his attentions weren't welcome.

But he didn't try to kiss her again, and gradually she let herself begin to relax in his company. In the weeks that followed, they often walked together or sailed the skiff along the shores of the bay. During these bright days and soft spring nights, thanks partly to O'Ryan's devilish charm, her body and spirit healed.

She could not forget the child that came and left so quickly. She didn't want to. But she could learn to live with her loss and look forward to tomorrow.

O'Ryan continued to ride the lengths of the Eastern Shore with Nathaniel and his friends for the gentleman's pastimes of gambling, horse racing, and other sporting events. Occasionally, her father accompanied them, and when he did, he brought home tales of O'Ryan's lucky streaks at cards.

"He's a hard man to beat," Papa had said admiringly.

"You don't think he cheats, do you?" Anne had asked. There was much about O'Ryan that caused her apprehension. He harbored too many secrets to be entirely safe. Was that part of his attraction for her? Was she destined to be always drawn to handsome rogues?

"No, I think that he's simply lucky. Of course, I knew he must be when he persuaded you to marry him."

On the evenings that O'Ryan remained at home, he, she, and Papa would gather in the parlor after supper. There O'Ryan played the violin and she accompanied him on the pianoforte. Sometimes, O'Ryan and her father joined together in singing an old ballad or popular song. She had always loved to hear Papa sing, but her husband's Irish voice was so rich and pure that she was certain he could have won fame in the music halls of great cities.

As May passed into June and then July, her father's health seemed to take a turn for the better, and he would often stay up past ten o'clock, sipping port and regaling them with stories of his boyhood. As always, after he'd bid them good night, he would walk to the far end of the formal garden and follow the brick path to the small family cemetery where her mother and brothers were buried. There, he would lay a flower on Mama's grave and read her a letter that he'd written during the day.

"He misses her terribly," Anne said to O'Ryan as they started up the stairs to bed. O'Ryan was still occupying a guest room, and the knowledge that he was content to sleep apart from her made her more comfortable with him.

"My father loved my mother as well," O'Ryan answered. "But he'd have been better off had he never met her."

"What a terrible thing to say about your parents!"

"Aye, but true. She was the death of him."

She did not question him, knowing from experience that he would tell her only what he wished about his past. Instead, she'd gone alone to her chamber and pushed open the casement windows to stare out at the bay. Moonlight played across the dark water in an endless variety of sparkling patterns, and the salt breeze carried a hundred memories of childhood and her mother.

"I don't care," she murmured. "I wish I had what Papa and Mama had . . . even for a little while."

* * *

In the second week of July, O'Ryan had the servants hitch a horse to the gig and drove Anne to Oxford for the afternoon. While she shopped in the various merchants, he mailed a thick packet to Kathleen in Ireland and collected a letter addressed to him, in care of Gentleman's Folly.

Outside, he walked down by the water to open his message in private. A letter had been painstakingly inscribed in ink on the back of a torn broadsheet offering a reward for information leading to the arrest and conviction of one Cormac Payne, Irishman, thief, and mutineer, who did most foully murder bosun's mate Thomas Dyce, late of Philadelphia. The crude sketch of a bearded man's face could have been anyone, but the fugitive was described as a gentleman, blue-eyed, over six feet and muscular. Known to be skilled at games of chance.

O'Ryan scanned the warrant a second time then flipped the page to read the unsigned message, penned in rough Gaelic.

Friend. The money was a godsend. Do not put yourself in danger by sending more. You have a bad enemy on the dock, a Belfast man with a crutch. A certain lady warns me that authorities are asking questions about you. Taking my family to Irish settlement in Baltimore. Hoping to find work. You can reach me in care of Father Joseph at Our Lady of Sorrows that city.

O'Ryan swore an unprintable oath as he shredded the paper and scattered it on the incoming tide. His earlier instincts had been right. It was time to collect his wages and move on before he put Anne in danger.

She was just coming out of the milliner's with a large parcel when he arrived back at the carriage. "Are you finished?" he asked, taking her purchases and putting them in the back of the gig.

"Yes, I think so." She nodded. "Yes, I am. I found the most adorable hat. Absolutely the latest in fashion. Copied after one made in London that came in just a month ago. It's a fine straw with a high crown and . . ." She stopped and chuckled. "You don't care, do you?"

He shrugged.

"Heaven help me. I sound like Mary." She laughed. "I never thought I was a vain woman, but I suppose I'm as foolish as the rest."

O'Ryan didn't think she was vain or foolish. He tried not to think how appealing she looked with sunshine filtering through the trees to catch the highlights in her auburn hair. She'd lost a little weight since the miscarriage, honing her features and making her dark eyes look larger and more luminous than ever.

"Do you have family in Ireland?" Anne asked, breaking into his reverie.

"What?"

"Family. Mrs. Parsons, the milliner, said that her cousin Amos told her that you frequently send letters to Ireland. I thought your parents were dead. Do you have other relatives there?"

"My father's ward."

"A child?"

"Hardly. Kathleen was six years my junior. We were raised together."

"Oh. What's she like, your Kathleen?"

"Beautiful. Funny. Wise."

"Did you live in—?"

He put his finger to his lips. "No more questions, Annie. My past is my own."

"You needn't always be so mysterious," she said as he helped her up into the carriage. His hands were strong as they tightened around her waist, and the familiarity both intrigued and frightened her. "Papa has mail as well, but I'm sure it's just a bill. Mr. Moore asked me to deliver it." She held a sealed envelope up and peered at it but was unable to read what was inside. "Papa's so forgetful. He's probably forgotten to pay again. I've offered to take over the plantation house accounts, but he won't hear of it. Mama never interfered in his business affairs, and he won't let me ask him anything about financial matters. He says it's unwomanly of me to ask. Do you think it is?"

O'Ryan raised one eyebrow quizzically as he untied the horse and climbed into the gig beside her. "You are the sole heiress to Gentleman's Folly, aren't you?"

"Yes. Papa gave Mary her share when she married," she answered. "Everything, land, ships, houses, slaves, comes to me at his death."

"Mrs. Reed. Miss Reed." O'Ryan tipped his hat to Martha and her mother—the worst gossip in Oxford. "And don't the two of you look fine this afternoon."

They smiled thinly and called a greeting. "Good day, Anne. Mr. O'Ryan."

Anne forced an equally insincere reply.

O'Ryan nodded, flicked the reins, and the horse broke into a high-stepping trot. "Then he's a fool not to teach you to manage the plantation," he continued as they left the last of the shops behind and began to pass private homes.

Anne's eyes narrowed. "My father's no fool. He's an excellent farmer, and he breeds the finest riding horses on the Eastern Shore."

"Yet he raises his daughters to be at the mercy of any man they marry."

"You should know," she accused only half in jest.

"Aye." He turned and looked full into her face. "And that's something I've wished to discuss with you."

She swallowed. "And that is?"

"Make whatever arrangements you must. It's time."

Her heart sank. "You want your money."

"I do." He fixed her with a shrewd gaze. "You don't need me, Anne. Pay me off and send me on my way. Hell, I'll be fair with you. I'll settle for five thousand. Give me the cash, I'll leave, and you can get on with the rest of your life."

"Fine," she said, stinging from the inevitable rejection. "I accept your offer. You can take your money and go back to Ireland and your little Kathleen, and I'll—"

"Be the rich widow," he finished.

Anne looked away. He was right, she thought. The game had never been anything but a farce, and now it was over. The sooner she got on with her real life, the happier she'd be.

Chapter 10

Anne heard the tolling of the plantation bell long before they reached the manor house. "Something's wrong." She leaned forward on the carriage seat. "Hurry."

O'Ryan's grip tightened on the reins. "The bay raiders?"

"No, it can't be. The daylight warning signal for raiders is a column of black smoke. Papa keeps an oily brush pile ready to fire at the back of the kitchen garden. So do all of the other plantations within miles. At night we would send riders to Greensboro Hall, but in the daytime the field workers can see the smoke and set off a similar blaze at Nathaniel's."

O'Ryan snapped the whip in the air over the horse's back, and the carriage bumped and rolled up the back lane, past the stables and outbuildings. Chickens squawked and scattered in all directions. Hounds raced barking after the gig.

Everywhere the servants stood idle, staring empty-handed toward the mansion. Anne clung to O'Ryan's arm and urged him to go faster while terrifying possibilities crowded her mind.

Something awful had occurred in her absence. Anne could feel it in her bones. Papa had suffered another heart attack. Mary had had an accident on her way to Gentleman's Folly.

She was out of the carriage and running toward the front door before the dust from the wheels settled. Aunt Kessie stepped out on the porch steps, her face contorted with grief, her eyes puffy with tears.

"What is it?" Anne cried. "What's wrong? Is it Papa?" Her voice sounded shrill in her ears, but inside she was numb. O'Ryan's muscular arm tightened protectively around her shoulders.

"He's gone, child," Aunt Kessie said.

"Gone? Gone where?" She tried to push past her foster mother, but the black woman was an immovable wall.

"He's dead?" O'Ryan asked the question that Anne's lips wouldn't form.

Aunt Kessie nodded.

"Oh no. No . . . not Papa. Not yet." Anne drew in a strangled breath while black spots pinwheeled behind her eyelids. "No, you must be wrong!"

O'Ryan pulled her against his chest. "How?" Anne heard him ask. "His heart?"

"No, sir. That big stallion of Master James's, Jersey. The horse had a swelling on his neck and Master James went to take a look at it. There must have been a nest of ground wasps in the stall, and he stepped on them."

"The horse killed him?" O'Ryan asked.

"No," Aunt Kessie said. "Jersey got stung, too, but he never hurt Master James. Your daddy got stung over and over. It was the poison from those bites. Master James came up to the house looking sick, right after you left for Oxford. He said his head hurt him fierce. His breathing got bad, and finally it just stopped."

"No." Anne bit her lip and tried to stop the waves of pain from enveloping her.

"There, there," O'Ryan soothed as he rocked her against him. "It's a sad, great sorrow to lose a father. But so long as you keep him in your heart, he'll never be far from you."

She pulled away and looked up with haunted eyes. "Do you believe that?"

"Aye." He gazed back, his features full of compassion. "For I've been where you stand. I buried both my parents."

"I loved him so much," Anne whispered.

"Then know that by grieving for him, you've taken the harder part," O'Ryan replied. "When the souls of two people touch, one has to go first and the other must mourn. You must be strong enough to bear up under that grief and take comfort in knowing that he didn't have to weep over you as he did his lost sons."

Anne sent a message to her sister, giving her the tragic news. But as much as she wanted Mary with her, there was no question of waiting for her to come from Philadelphia. Because of the July heat, the service was held the following day. Anne buried her father next to her mother in the small brick-walled cemetery on Gentleman's Folly.

She didn't know how she would have managed without O'Ryan. He took control, instructed Abraham to build a coffin, calmed the other servants, sent word to friends and neighbors, and made arrangements to feed the mourners. And at the end of the funeral, at her request, O'Ryan played Mozart one final time for her father as they lowered the casket into the earth.

Anne didn't weep until the poignant notes of the violin drifted through the warm misty rain and she had to scatter a handful of Tidewater dirt over the pine box. Then her composure crumbled, and a flood of tears blinded her.

O'Ryan handed the instrument to Nathaniel Greensboro and put his arm around her. "Remember you're a Davis," he whispered. "Make him proud."

Anne nodded.

He offered her a clean handkerchief. "He's with your mother now."

"Yes," she agreed as she wiped her eyes.

The certainty that her parents were in each other's arms kept Anne from breaking down again that day and the following one as she listened to the words of sympathy and advice from friends.

"He's gone to a better place," Sibyl Greensboro declared as she polished off a huge slice of cake. "The good die young. The rest of us suffer the torments of this world until—"

O'Ryan appeared at Anne's side and tucked his arm through hers. "True words, madam, true but sorrowful," he murmured piously. "Please excuse us. Reverend Nichols is leaving and wants a few words with Anne."

She followed him without question as he led her out of the parlor, down the hall, and out the back door. "Where are we—?"

He winked at her. "The minister can wait." He motioned for her to follow, and they dashed through the light rain to Aunt Kessie's cabin.

Inside the cozy room, a small fire took the damp off the air. Anne's puppy, Shannon, lay sprawled on her back on a faded rag rug. The puppy's feet were in the air, her red tongue lolling. As soon as the dog spied Anne, she leaped up and ran in circles barking joyously.

Anne knelt, and Shannon jumped into her arms and covered her face with doggy kisses.

"I thought you might be ready for a few minutes of quiet," O'Ryan said. "A little less hereafter, and a little more relaxation. Are you hungry? Kessie sent a plate—"

"No," Anne answered as she hugged the squirming puppy. "I'm sick of the smell of funeral ham and hard-boiled eggs.

And I'm sick of people telling me that the Lord needed Papa in heaven. Maybe He did, but I didn't want to give him up, not even to heaven."

"Aye," O'Ryan agreed. "Hide here awhile. I'll make your excuses."

"Would it be awful if I did?" she asked.

"Awful," he teased with a boyish wink. "Leave them to me. If an Irishman cannot bluff a few farmers, who can?"

The last visitor didn't depart until the third day after the funeral. Anne watched the lane for Mary, knowing it was too soon for her to come, but wanting her just the same.

A dry-eyed woman who looked like Anne moved through the house and conversed with O'Ryan and the others. The shadow Anne wrote letters to friends and distant relatives. She carried fresh flowers to the grave, prayed for her father's soul, and kept up the pretense that she wasn't numb inside.

She told herself that Papa had lived a good life, that she was lucky to have had such a loving father, and that it was natural for children to outlive both parents.

Vaguely, she was aware of O'Ryan's kindness and concern, and that he and Aunt Kessie continued to manage the day-to-day affairs of Gentleman's Folly. Anne knew that she should rouse herself and take over her responsibilities as plantation mistress, but somehow, almost as if she were in a trance, the days piled one upon another.

Then two weeks after the funeral, Aunt Kessie came to Anne's chamber early one morning before she had gotten out of bed. "Did you sleep, child?" the housekeeper asked as she pulled back the curtains and let in the sunshine.

Anne nodded. She still felt exhausted. Each night, she fell into bed, slept like one drugged, then awakened at dawn with the sensation that she'd lost something.

Oddly, it always took several seconds before she remembered that it was Papa. He wasn't waiting downstairs to share breakfast with her and tell her about his plans for the day; he would never be there again.

Aunt Kessie put a tea tray on the table and poured two cups, one for each of them. Through the years, they'd often shared a pot in the privacy of the kitchen or Anne's bedroom, where there was no one to complain of the familiarity between the housekeeper and the daughter of the house.

Anne sat down in one chair and motioned the older woman to take the other. For a few minutes they sipped the hot Darjeeling in silence, then Aunt Kessie set down her cup and took Anne's hand. "It's time to get on with living, child," she said. "Don't let your sorrow tear you apart."

"Losing him hurts so much," Anne said. "I don't know what I'll do without him."

"You'll grow up and be the strong woman your mother was. Time will soften your wounds. You won't forget him. You shouldn't. But you have to go on living."

Anne felt stung by the reprimand. "You think I'm acting like a child?"

"It's natural. Master James was a good father, but he protected you too much." She sighed. "Now, it's all come down on you at once. You've got to shoulder your burdens and go on or turn into a wilting flower like Mary. And I'm afraid I have something to tell you that will add to your problems."

Anne felt a sudden chill. "Not Mary? Is Mary—?"

"Nothing like that. No word has come from Philadelphia yet, and no news is always good. Bad news will find you quick enough."

"Then what?"

"I'm going to leave Gentleman's Folly."

"For a visit?"

"No, for good."

"What do you mean? I don't understand! Why would you leave? Is it something to do with O'Ryan?"

"Not at all. It is something I want, child. I discussed this with Master James right before you lost your baby. He agreed, but he wanted me to wait until you'd recovered your strength. He said that I'd looked after you and Mary for a lot of years, now it was time I looked after my other young ones."

Anne rose to her feet, twisting her napkin in her hands, no longer able to sit still. "But you can't go! I need you here more than ever."

Kessie laid a heavy set of iron keys by Anne's cup. "You've got a good husband to help you. And you'll never truly be mistress here until you take the keys to this house."

"But—"

"Sit and finish your tea. Think about this. You're twenty and four, a woman grown. It's time you thought about what I want, not just what's easiest for you." She motioned with strong, lean hands. "Now you sit down and finish your tea. Lord knows when you'll get another quiet minute today."

"But where are you going? And why?"

"You know my granddaughter Abigail up in Delaware was widowed last year. She's got two little boys, not much more than babies. She wants me to come and help her with the children. Abigail's a midwife, and she gets called out all hours of the night. If I'm there with her, she can go to her patients without the worry of finding someone to stay with them. I've decided that I'm going to live with her."

"I love you, Aunt Kessie," Anne protested. "This is your home. Can't you bring Abigail here?"

The wise brown face grew serious. "No, that wouldn't do. My Abigail's strong for the Methodist church just down the road. She lives near Dover in a settlement of free folk called

Moortown." She smiled up at Anne. "You know I've loved you since you were knee-high to a duck, but I love the ones born of my flesh and blood as well. It's right I spend my last years with those that need me most."

"I'll miss you terribly."

"It's better that I go. The busier you are, the easier this grieving time will be for you."

"I don't understand . . . but if it's what you must do . . ." Anne paused. "You know you would have had a home here in your old age. Do you have enough money to take care of yourself?"

Aunt Kessie nodded. "Don't worry about that. Your daddy was good to me. He gave me a Christmas gift every year, even though I hold more with the old African ways than his. I've put that silver and most of my wages away. I'm not going to Abigail empty-handed, and I'm aching to get my arms around those little boys of hers."

"Nothing I can say will change your mind?"

"I'm a free woman, darlin'. I came here from the islands on my own two feet and I'm going away the same."

It was on the tip of Anne's tongue to tell her that she wouldn't have O'Ryan's help, that he was leaving. But she didn't. Instead, she swallowed the lump in her throat. "You deserve to do what will make you happy, Aunt Kessie. When—when are you going?"

"Today. I didn't tell you before because of Master James passing. Now it's said, the sooner I go, the easier it will be. Ivy Washington will be coming from Greensboro Hall to be housekeeper here. Least she will if you want her. Ivy has a good head on her shoulders. You could do a lot worse than to put her in charge."

"But Ivy Washington belongs to Nathaniel's mother. I doubt that she'll part with Ivy."

"Already did. Master James, he signed the papers last week. She'll be coming here this afternoon."

"But why didn't you tell me any of this? Why keep it—"

"Your daddy said he wanted to see the grin on Abraham's face when Ivy moved into the housekeeper's cabin. Then, after the accident, I didn't want to burden you. You'll like Ivy, and she'll be grateful to come to Gentleman's Folly. It's only right a husband and wife live together, even if they do be slaves."

"Yes," Anne agreed. "It is only right. But she won't be you, Aunt Kessie. No one can take your place."

"Doubt if she'd try to. Ivy's got her own ways. She's honest and clean, and she's smart. Just treat her like you've treated me." Aunt Kessie finished the last of her tea, then rose and kissed Anne on her cheek. "You have your mother's good sense, Miss Anne, but you worry too much about what other folks say. You're a woman, and it's harder for us. Don't let any man—not even that good-looking Irishman you married—think for you."

"I'll try," Anne promised.

"That's all a body can do. Listening to my own heart got me through a lifetime of trouble, and it will do the same for you."

Aunt Kessie left before noon, driving a good mare and riding in a wagon loaded with gifts from Anne: clothing, household items, and furniture. Tied at the back of the sturdy vehicle were a three-year-old cow and a pair of fine work mules.

"If there's ever anything you need, you must write," Anne insisted as she pressed a velvet-covered jewelry box into the black woman's hands. "These were my mother's. She would want you to have them. I only wish I had more to give you."

"Think of me kindly, that's all I ask," Kessie said after they had embraced a final time. "Don't worry so much about tomorrow that you forget to live today."

That night, alone in her bedchamber, Anne sipped a glass of wine as she mulled over Aunt Kessie's words in her mind. Follow your heart, her foster mother had advised. But how?

Anne was so empty inside, it felt as though she didn't have a heart. How could she know what she wanted?

With both Aunt Kessie and Papa gone, the whole weight of running the manor house and maintaining the plantation rested on her shoulders. All she had was O'Ryan. He had been her rock since her father died, and soon he'd be leaving her as well.

She flung herself across the bed, making no protest when Shannon jumped up and snuggled in the crook of her arm. She stroked the dog and laid her cheek against the warm, silky fur, but tonight, not even Shannon could fill the hollow ache inside.

If only my baby had lived . . .

The mantel clock ticked. The house seemed much too quiet. Anne sat up and poured herself a second glass of wine. It seemed to go right to her head; she wondered why, then remembered that she hadn't been hungry at supper.

What did she want? She put down the empty glass and went to the window. She couldn't see the bay in the darkness, but she could sense the ebb and flow of the tide. What did she want?

Papa, alive and hearty, looking up at her and laughing . . . Her lost child growing inside her . . . O'Ryan's arms around her . . . his strong body pressed against hers and his hands caressing her.

Anne's crushing despair lifted as she thought of Michael—

her husband, sleeping down the hall . . . so close and yet so far away. Her pulse quickened as she remembered how his mouth felt on hers.

"I want him," she whispered aloud. "Just for tonight, I want to be his wife."

Downing a third glass of wine for courage, she went to his bed. When the knob turned and the door hinges squeaked, O'Ryan lunged up, a pistol in his hand. "Don't shoot," she managed breathlessly. "It's me."

"Annie." He lowered the gun. "I'm sorry. I was asleep. I didn't—"

"Expecting pirates?"

Moonlight streamed through the windows. She could see him clearly.

"You startled me." He was naked, his hard-muscled body luminous and fluid as he lowered the weapon and eased down the hammer.

Her heart raced. Her palms felt moist and tingly, her fingers clumsy as she fumbled with the tie of her dressing gown. The ribbons came undone, and the silken folds fell around her bare ankles.

Anne felt the bay breeze lick her breasts and thighs. She trembled from head to foot, wishing it weren't too late to turn back. But she knew it was.

"Why are you here?" O'Ryan asked. The sound of his deep, lilting voice made her giddy.

She wanted to explain, to tell him why she'd had to come, but she couldn't find the words. Instead she took a hesitant step toward him.

"I can't stay with you, Annie."

She nodded. How could she feel so terrified and so thrilled at the same instant? This wasn't about tomorrow or the day after that. Her coming had nothing to do with keeping him at Gentleman's Folly.

"I have to go."

Was that regret she heard? Was he as torn between reason and hope as she was? "It's all right," she answered.

The room seemed to sway as he crossed to take her in his arms. She could smell the sweet fragrance of new-mown hay and hear the haunting call of a loon through the open window. Then O'Ryan's powerful hands were on her, touching, stroking, and molding his flesh to hers.

Heat flashed under her skin.

She moaned softly and tilted her chin to meet his kiss. His mouth slanted against hers, hot and demanding. His fingers tangled in her unbound hair, and his long, sinewy legs pressed against hers.

The taste of him was intoxicating—maddening. He filled her with his tongue, and she drank him in savagely, needing more, wanting more.

He tore free from their embrace and stared into her face. "Are you certain? I won't lie to you, Annie. I want you. But this doesn't change our bargain. I can't stay—"

"Damn it, O'Ryan! I don't care! Just this once—just tonight—I want you to . . ." Words failed her. She touched his cheek and traced the line of his jaw and the cords of his throat with her fingertips. She closed her eyes and let her last doubts fall away as she moved her hand lower to caress his chest and brush the contours of a hardening male nipple.

"Devil take me." He groaned. "We'll both regret this later."

"I won't." Tremors of excitement darted over the surface of her fevered skin. She felt her own nipples tighten as he reached an exploring hand to cup her right breast.

He squeezed her gently, lowering his head to take her quivering flesh into his mouth. Her eyes widened with shock as his fiery tongue laved the eager bud and sucked until she cried out with sudden pleasure.

O'Ryan's hands were all over her, kneading, crushing her against him. His groin thrust against her and she felt the heat of his swollen organ.

Then, without her realizing just how it had happened, he was pressing her down against the braided rug, straddling her with long, lean legs. His fierce kisses drove all reason from her mind, and her own desire flared. She arched her back and wrapped herself around him, reveling in the ripples of his muscles, the curve of his lean buttocks, the weight of his male body claiming hers.

The scent of his skin and hair, the feel of their sweat-sheened limbs intertwined wrenched hungry whimpers from deep in her throat. A warm flood of moisture pooled between her thighs, and she strained beneath him.

She found his hand and wantonly pushed it between her legs. He groaned again and nipped her throat with quick, sharp love bites. Shudders of need ripped though her as he delved deep inside her wet folds.

"Please," she begged him, "I want . . ."

She gasped as he slid down her thrashing body and parted her legs then buried his face in her heat. The room spun as her body spasmed with pleasure. Wave after wave rocked her to the core. She clung to him, calling his name, losing all sense of time and space.

And when she thought that she could never move again, she sighed and looked into his eyes.

"Now, Annie," he murmured hoarsely. "Now I'll love you."

He plunged into her, pounding deep and hard, filling her with his passion. For an instant, she was stunned, unprepared for his size and power. But then her body responded. To her astonishment, her exhaustion fled before a renewed passion.

Laughing, she spread her legs wider, taking the length of him. She met frenzied stroke for stroke with joyous abandon as each thrust brought them closer and closer to a shared rapture.

They climaxed, one after another, in two heartbeats, and Anne felt the surge of his release as she stopped thinking and surrendered to the glory of their joining.

Chapter 11

O'Ryan lay with Anne wrapped in his arms for a long time before he kissed her hair and spoke. "Annie, Annie, we've opened a box of trouble now, haven't we?"

She murmured, "Um-hmm."

"You're completely unrepentant."

She snuggled closer, utterly content, and sighed.

He swallowed and wrapped a lock of her auburn hair around his finger. He couldn't see the color in the dark bedroom, but he could feel it in the same way that he could feel the sensual intensity of her gaze. "You were the one who said we should keep this all business," he reminded her.

"Yes, I did."

Her slow, soft Tidewater accent flowed over him like warm honey. The silken texture of her skin, the feel of her breasts and thigh pressing against his body, made it hard for him to think. Already he felt a growing need to have her again.

"You've bewitched me, you shameless wench." He tried to keep his words light to hide the depths of his emotion, but her only response was to utter a sound of contentment and lift his hand to her lips. One by one, she kissed his knuckles and teased them with the tip of her tongue.

He groaned and kissed her. He'd enjoyed bed-sport with many women in his lifetime, some beautiful, some not. But he'd never known one whose mouth fitted his so perfectly, who made love with such unabashed passion or who awakened such yearning in his own heart.

Ah, sweeting, he thought. *Another few days and I'd have been clean away without a broken heart.*

"I've put you in danger," he said, trying to salvage reason from an experience he couldn't explain. "I should have protected you. There could be—"

"A child?" She slipped her arms around his neck and brought her mouth up to his. "Don't worry," she whispered when they broke apart. "We are husband and wife. If you leave me with a babe, it won't matter."

"It would matter to me." That was one thing he didn't want to do. If he ever fathered a child, he wanted to be part of the babe's life. It would be easy to deceive himself that this marriage could work, that he could have the love of one woman forever . . . that they could build a life together.

But he knew better. He had seen firsthand the pain that loving a wife could bring. Hell, even Sean's Nora had cursed her husband for bringing her to America. If Sean couldn't hold his marriage together, who could?

Anne pulled him back into the present by massaging his neck and shoulders with slow, steady circular motions. Her fingers were surprisingly strong and very warm. He could feel his cock growing hard as she tilted her head back and he nuzzled the damp hollow of her throat and inhaled her natural fragrance.

"I didn't mean for this to happen." He brushed the curve of her breast and her nipple puckered into a hard peak under his caress. "Annie, Annie." Every instinct for self-preservation told him to get up off this floor and go—to flee the Eastern Shore and not stop running until he reached the Pacific Ocean.

The charge of murder against him in Philadelphia, the peril of being sent back to Ireland to hang, were not nearly as threatening as the touch of this one small woman. But he could have sprouted wings and flown out the window easier than refuse what she was offering.

Anne shifted her weight so that she lay on top of him. "I don't care about tomorrow," she whispered. "Only tonight."

"But I—"

She put her fingers over his lips. "Don't speak about tomorrow," she said. "Don't think about it."

He traced the line of her back and the hollow of her waist, cupping her round, firm bottom before slipping his fingers lower. She was still slick and wet, and the knowledge inflamed him.

He found her nipple with his mouth and drew in the sweet bud of flesh, sucking until she groaned with pleasure, writhing against him. The taste of her was intoxicating, and before he could stop himself, he seized her hips and lifted her onto his swollen member.

This time he held back, savoring each movement, making each deep thrust slow and exquisite torture. He used every ounce of self-control, forcing himself to wait until his body screamed for release and her urgent pleas echoed through the room.

Moonlight glistened over her sweat-sheened body and her glorious hair brushed his face and chest. "Is this what you want?" he demanded.

"Yes . . . yes . . ."

He slammed into her, plunging faster and faster, until he thought he would die if he couldn't bury himself inside her.

"Ohhhh."

He knew when she'd reached the peak and slipped over. He gave one final stroke and he was with her, falling into an abyss of mutual exultation that left him totally exhausted, unable to lift his head or move from the spot where they lay, half on and half off the rug. His last thought before sleep claimed him was that he still wanted her and that he would never let her go.

"Michael."

He opened his eyes and felt Anne's warm breath on his face. Damn, but she even smelled sweet after a hot bout of bump and tickle. "You'll be the ruination of me, woman." He groaned. "My manhood is worn to a nub."

She sighed.

"What time is it?"

"Late."

"Too early for breakfast, I suppose." He rather liked the feel of her stretched out on him, even if he was too satiated for anything more than words. "Has anyone ever told you how beautiful you are? As fair as sunrise over the banks of the Shannon."

"It's dark. You can't see what I look like."

"Aye, that's true, but I have the Celtic gift of *sight*."

"And you called me a witch."

"There's nothing of the devil in the *gift*." He cupped her cheek in his hand. "You've a talent for loving, Mrs. O'Ryan."

"Let me loose." She tried to wiggle free.

"That's what got you in trouble the second time."

"I need to . . ." She sighed, impatiently this time. "I need to go out, to the necessary."

"Ah, that." He sat up, turning her so that she fitted nicely into his lap. He kept his arms around her so that she could not escape. Hadn't she said that they shouldn't think about to-morrow? Tonight was what mattered, and he wasn't ready to have it all end yet.

"Michael. Be reasonable. A woman has certain—"

"Needs." He chuckled. "So I noticed."

"You didn't fight very hard."

"A sensible man knows when he's outflanked." He wondered if she could hear the thump of his heart or know just how deeply she'd gotten inside his defenses.

She laughed. "I really do have to—"

"All right. I'll give you that. But if you're going to the garden, I'll come along."

She turned her face away, and he had the feeling that she'd suddenly turned shy. "I'd prefer privacy for—"

"To protect you. Who knows? There might be pirates in the maze." He released her and got up. Pale moonlight was still filtering through the open window, filling the air with the scents of honeysuckle and wild roses. He knew he'd never smell either again without thinking of Anne and this moment.

"You don't think me a harlot?"

He found her dressing gown on the floor and wrapped it gently around her shoulders. "Nay, sweeting. I think you a rare woman, one who isn't afraid to say what she wants."

"My father hasn't been dead a month," she murmured. "What kind of woman could think of—of this when she should be mourning?"

"A heart can only take so much. You've had your share of troubles and more. Not even the angels could find fault with easing your sorrow in a husband's arms."

"Not really a husband."

"In the eyes of the law and in your church, we are married."

"But not your church. You're a Catholic, aren't you?"

"My father was, but my mother was Protestant. What I am is between me and my maker."

"Please, do this one thing for me." Her words were a bare whisper. "Tomorrow, we go on as we were before. And we never speak of what happened tonight."

"I can't stay with you even if I wanted to," he said. Better to leave it as it was, a good memory for both of them, before the sweetness turned cloying and she found out what kind of a man she'd let into her bed.

"What makes you think I want you to?" Her heart thudded. She wasn't sorry she'd come to him. She'd never be sorry. What had happened between them was—was more than she'd ever expected, more than she'd guessed could ever be between a man and woman. But she'd not beg him to stay with her. She'd done that with Stephen and he'd scoffed at her and denied the child they'd made together.

One rejection from a man she thought she loved was enough to last a lifetime. She hadn't guessed what a scoundrel Stephen was, but O'Ryan had been honest with her from the beginning. What she needed was an ordinary man like Nate Greensboro, someone of her own kind and definitely not another fortune hunter with the marks of a criminal on his back.

Her heart had gotten her into the worst trouble of her life. Now, without Papa to guide her, she needed to govern her life by reason. And there was nothing reasonable about Michael O'Ryan.

She pulled her gown tight around her. She was shivering, despite the July heat. "We have a bargain," she said softly. "I'll keep my promise if you'll keep yours."

"Aye, our bargain." He gave an enigmatic chuckle. "I suppose no harm can come of tonight so long as we both understand the rules of the game."

She left the room and walked down the hall to her own chamber, opening and closing the door hard enough for the sound to carry. Then, without going in, she crept away on bare feet. She went silently down the stairs and out through the front entrance.

Not allowing herself to run, she strode purposefully through the garden, past the graveyard, and down a hidden path to the water's edge. There she dropped her garment and waded out into the bay, letting the cool water caress her naked body.

Anne was an excellent swimmer. She'd learned to swim almost before she could walk, and the bay had never failed to comfort her. This time she wanted to commit to memory each kiss, each touch, each sensation that she and O'Ryan had shared. She wanted to fix these hours in her mind so that she would never forget the one night she had thrown aside all thought of who she was and what she should do. And she suspected that even when she was old and gray and toothless, thinking of this night with Michael would still bring a smile to her lips.

He found her early the next morning in her father's library. The puppy lay curled at her feet in a wicker basket, and Anne was poring over the plantation journals. "Good morning, Annie," he said.

She glanced up, felt her cheeks go hot, then picked up the little dog and cuddled her against her breast.

"So that's the way it's to be, is it?" he asked. "Last night's heat and this morning's chill?"

She pretended to ignore his question and made a show of inspecting the journal on the desk. "I told you, I don't want to talk about that." She sighed. "I'm afraid I can make little of Papa's accounting." Her voice trembled only slightly. "There's a little cash in the strongbox, but I'm afraid we must go to Annapolis and see his lawyer."

"Did your father leave a will?"

She nodded, obviously eager to be on more impersonal ground. "Yes. He did. There's a copy here. You needn't worry. Everything is as I said. I have the deed to Gentleman's Folly and his will leaving everything to me. Mr. Sawyer, that's our lawyer, has copies of everything."

"But you don't know where any of your money actually is?"

Anne rose to her feet. Shannon squirmed in her arms, and she put him on the floor. "My father's only just buried. Decency would require that you wait until—"

"He should have shared the information with you. How

did he expect you to manage Gentleman's Folly if he kept his finances a secret?"

"Papa was a wealthy man," she protested. "Would you have expected him to keep his money here? How safe would that have been?"

"Don't get excited. I didn't mean to upset you. We'll go to Annapolis and see this Mr. Sawyer. A will must be probated, but—"

"I should be able to take control of the money my grandmother left me," she replied. "I'm sure you want what was promised you."

"That isn't what I said." He reached for her, but she moved back. "I'm only thinking of you and what's best for—"

"Were you? Or were you wondering when I would fulfill my part of the bargain? Before Papa died, we'd decided that it was time to settle things between us." She tried not to let the hurt show in her words. Last night she'd lain in his arms, given herself to him, body and soul. And today . . . Today, the reality of her marriage of convenience had reared up to face her squarely.

"Hist, honey, you mustn't think that I don't care about you. I do, but things are more complicated than—"

"You're anxious to be rid of me."

"Anne, don't say that."

"It's true. We never intended this to be a permanent arrangement. And I know you have expenses . . . your gambling."

"I don't lose at cards," he reminded her.

"You expect me to believe that you always win?"

"I usually do." He frowned. "I don't want to argue with you. That's the last thing I want. We both agreed that our marriage was best ended quickly and cleanly. I want none of what your father left you."

"Grandmother's money is there. Why shouldn't you have it

at once?" she answered sharply. "Ask Abraham to prepare the sloop for sailing. We'll leave within the hour."

"Anne . . . I want us to part as friends. Can we do that?"

"We can try."

An early afternoon storm rolled and cracked over Joshua Sawyer's office. Rain sheeted against the windows and drummed on the shingled roof. Lightning flashed, striking the earth nearby, sending a sudden white light through the dim room that smelled of musty papers and old leather.

Anne blinked, shielding her eyes with a hand, certain that the crash of thunder had prevented her from hearing Mr. Sawyer correctly. "I'm sorry," she apologized. "What did you say?"

The lawyer removed his glasses, wiped away an imaginary smudge on the lens, and repositioned the spectacles on his wide nose. Sawyer was a large man of ample girth, but his voice was surprisingly soft, almost lisping. "As I said before, this is not a discussion for a lady. If you would just wait in the outer office, I can explain the situation to your husband."

O'Ryan shook his head. "My wife is heiress to Gentleman's Folly and all her father's estate. Explain your *situation* to her."

Sawyer cleared his throat. "Your father and I were friends for many years, Mrs. O'Ryan. I would have spared you this, but—"

"But what?" she insisted.

"It is my unpleasant task to inform you, Mrs. O'Ryan, that your father's untimely death leaves you in a difficult position." He pursed his lips and went on as Anne's world dropped away. "As you may be aware, Mr. O'Ryan, tobacco planters all over Maryland are in dire straits. Many have already lost their land. These acres have been put in tobacco for nearly two hundred years, and the tobacco is a greedy master. It robs the soil, yielding poorer grades and lower crops each season."

O'Ryan glanced at Anne. He'd heard similar grumbling from Nate and his friends, but since they all seemed prosperous, he hadn't taken their complaining too seriously. "Did you know about any of this?" he asked her.

She nodded. "A little, but nothing so serious. My grandfather always bragged about the quality of leaf he grew before the Revolution, but—"

"Exactly my point," Sawyer said, cutting her short. "Gentleman's Folly is heavily mortgaged to the banking house of Rawlings and Rawlings."

Anne clenched her hands together. "But Papa told me that I never had to worry, that he'd provided for us and—"

The lawyer shook his head. "The expenses of your sister's wedding and dowry were exorbitant. I've heard rumors that certain merchants in town, even those in Oxford, had been refusing him credit."

O'Ryan swore a French oath.

Anne drew in a deep breath. "But I do have monies of my own, an inheritance from my grandmother, the lots in Baltimore. Surely that will—"

"Gone, Mrs. O'Ryan. Everything." His brow furrowed. "Your father was your executor until your marriage. The property in Baltimore city was sold two years ago. I handled the deeds myself."

"What do I have?"

"A husband who will look after you. As I said, this really isn't something a lady should concern herself with. Your father, I'm afraid, was admirable, but a poor businessman. He made shipping investments that . . . Frankly, Mrs. O'Ryan, I advised him to put his money in the slave trade. That's where fortunes are being made. But he wouldn't listen. He bought a half interest in the *Mary Kincaid*, a coastal trader, not a slaver. Unfortunately, that ship went down off Bermuda last winter with a total loss of cargo and crew. I can give you other examples, but—"

Anne felt sick. It was suddenly stifling in here. She wanted to be outside, even if it was pouring rain. "You're telling me that Papa left nothing but debts?"

Sawyer stood and leaned forward over his desk, sympathy etched on his poxed face. "The only thing clear of debt are your slaves and personal belongings. Even this year's tobacco crop is pledged for interest on the mortgage." He made eye contact with O'Ryan. "Sir, I would advise you to contact your own bankers and your solicitors. Naturally, I would be happy to represent you in these matters, but if you already have—"

"Thank you for your time, Mr. Sawyer," O'Ryan answered tightly. "I will consult my own advisers. Be assured that I appreciate your efforts on behalf of my wife."

"I know this comes as a shock," Sawyer said. "James never intended to be remiss in his duties to his family. It's the times and the tobacco market. Many of his neighbors are in the same state. But you must act quickly. Obediah Rawlings isn't a man to delay the unpleasant. Expect to hear from him very soon. With Mr. Davis's death, he will want full payment or he will foreclose on the plantation. Be certain of it."

"There isn't any damned money." O'Ryan pulled Anne into the shelter of an enclosed well house a half block from the lawyer's office. They'd left Sawyer's intending to make a run for the sloop, but torrents of wind and rain had battered them so fiercely that they'd taken shelter here.

O'Ryan was so angry he wanted to curse the whole damned Chesapeake. He wanted to drive his fist through the oaken latticework wall. Twice in his life, he'd put his fate into the hands of a woman. And both times, he'd been skewered, skinned, and spread over a fire to roast.

He gritted his teeth and muttered the foulest dockside oath he could summon. The loss of the money he'd expected was a blow, but that wasn't what twisted like a knife in his gut. He couldn't help wondering if Anne had known the truth when she'd accepted his offer of marriage.

"Don't swear at me!" she shouted above the downpour.

"I'm not swearing at you."

"And I'll not have you curse Papa."

What would he do about Kathleen? She depended on him. And now Anne's fate rested in his hands as well.

"You think I deliberately cheated you, don't you?" Anne said.

"What am I supposed to think?"

Normally, the three-sided well house at the edge of the public sidewalk would have been in full view of passersby. But with the thunderstorm the street was deserted, and the window shutters were closed on the brick houses on either side of the small structure.

He wiped a dripping lock of hair out of his face. "All that land, the house . . . How the hell could there be only debts?"

Anne pushed at his chest with both hands. "Keep a civil tongue in your head. None of this is my fault."

"Well, it's sure as hell not mine!" He didn't want to fight with her. He needed time to reason this out.

Rain pounded the tin roof and poured in through the latticed walls to soak Anne's skirts. Her shoes were already sodden, the ribbons on her hat dripping blue onto her cream-colored pelisse. His own clothes were as wet as if he'd gone swimming in them, but he didn't care.

The thought came to him that she might have deceived him as she'd deceived her father about their marriage. "Anne, I need to know the truth. When you promised me the money, did you believe it was there?"

She didn't answer.

He'd been so sure that Anne was different from the woman who'd sold his neck to the English soldiers . . . different from his mother. "Were you laughing inside . . . that day I proposed to you in your sister's parlor?"

"No, I wasn't." She shoved him again, and he took a step back. "What's wrong with you, Michael? I've lost everything and all you can think of is your blasted agreement."

He swore again. Damn, what *was* wrong with him? Didn't he know she couldn't do such a thing, that she wasn't capable of such a lie? And regardless of whether she had known or hadn't known, she was in terrible trouble.

"We built a house of cards, and it's come tumbling down around us," he said. He wanted to believe her—God, he wanted to believe her. But nothing could erase the doubt that he'd been duped again by a beautiful woman.

"You know how Papa was," she argued. "He didn't believe it was a woman's place to concern herself with such matters."

"How the hell could he live like a gentleman without money?"

"Stop cursing at me."

"I'm not . . ." Guilt curled in the pit of his belly. "Damn it to hell!" He couldn't walk away now. He was as responsible for Anne's welfare as he was for Kathleen's. Feeling the way he did about Anne, it would have been hard enough to leave her when he thought she was rich. He couldn't leave her now. "I'm not going anywhere."

"You heard Mr. Sawyer. I don't have any money. I may not even have a roof over my head. Just go back to Ireland, you greedy blackguard. Forget you ever laid eyes on me."

"Not likely!" He was the injured party here, so why did he feel like dog vomit? Why did he want to put his arms around

Anne and tell her that he'd take care of her, that he'd make everything all right?

"Maybe Mr. Rawlings will give me an extension on the mortgage. This year's crop looks like a good one. Perhaps—"

O'Ryan folded his arms over his chest. It was the only way he could keep his hands off her. She looked as if she was going to burst into tears. Damn, but he hated it when a woman cried. "Weren't you listening? Sawyer said that this year's crop is already promised. And what are the chances that you can make a success of the plantation when your father couldn't?"

"I can try."

"You're an expert on agriculture, I suppose." His sarcasm was thick enough to block out the rain.

"Stop it. Stop being negative. I'm trying to think of a solution. I won't let them take my land without a fight."

"You can't win this alone." He wouldn't let her try.

"Can't I?" She stiffened. "I'm a Davis."

Her steely resolve turned his tenderness to desire. Memories of the night before rushed through him. He wanted to unbutton the bodice of her dress and bury his face between her breasts. He wanted to slide his fingers up her leg and inner thigh until he felt her moist warmth.

He felt himself growing hard, and he groaned. What would she do if he pressed her back against the well and made love to her here with the thunder and lightning cracking around them and the steady cadence of the rain? Would she refuse him or would she ride him as wildly as she had on his bedroom floor? Would she scream with pleasure when he entered her?

"Annie." He put a hand on her arm.

"Go away."

"I'm not leaving you."

"Why not? It was always the money that kept you here."

Her scorn cut him like a whip. He wanted to tell her that she was the reason he was staying, but the words wouldn't come. "You'll not be rid of me so easily," he answered. "I'm staying until you keep your half of the bargain."

"It may take months. Are we to go on with our pretense of marriage for so long?"

"Think, Anne. It's impossible for me to go now. Your creditors will surely fall on you and pick you clean. They won't deal with a woman. I may be able to negotiate with them. Everyone seems to assume I have money."

"They should. Wasn't that our scheme? To pass you off as a wealthy gentleman?"

"Has it been so bad? Having me beside you?" Not for him. For him, these last months had been the happiest he'd ever known.

She met his gaze directly. "No, not so bad," she granted. "So long as we both remember that this is a business relationship. That way—"

"Neither of us get hurt," he finished for her. *Least of all you.*

"And what gratitude am I supposed to show for your generosity?"

"I'm sure I'll think of something."

Chapter 12

"The least I can do is to lend you my man Taylor," Nathaniel Greensboro said. "Without James, neither you nor Anne has the experience to keep the field crews working. If you don't keep after the tobacco worms, you'll lose your crop." He leaned forward in the saddle and rested his hands on the gray horse's withers.

O'Ryan stood beside the gate just outside the front entrance of the manor house. Nate had ridden by to ask if there was anything that he and Susannah could do for Anne.

"I appreciate your concern," O'Ryan said. "But no thanks. We've a good man in Abraham."

"I know him, and you're right. He's savvy about working the land, but you've got a mixed labor crew. The free men won't take orders from him because he's a slave, and the other slaves . . . Well . . ." Nathaniel shrugged. "You really need Taylor."

"If Abraham knows what's needed, I can give the orders," O'Ryan replied. "I suppose you've heard that the plantation is in financial trouble."

The younger man nodded. "It's common knowledge. Everyone knew Anne's father was living beyond his means."

"Everyone but us."

"James worried so much about providing an adequate dowry for Mary. When he told me what he gave her as a wedding gift, I was shocked. With tobacco prices falling and the competition from Virginia, most of us are land poor. Farming is always a gamble, but James was an optimist. He took chances, thinking he'd make the money back."

A horsefly buzzed around the gelding's head. The animal snorted and pawed the grass, arching his neck as Nate curbed his urge to bolt. Despite his thickening middle, Nathaniel Greensboro was a superb horseman with a firm but gentle hand on the reins. O'Ryan thought that you could tell a man's character by the way he rode, and he liked Nate immensely.

"I'm serious about loaning you Taylor," the younger man continued. "He'd be invaluable under the circumstances."

"I can't argue that your overseer would know more than I do, but Anne and I are cutting expenses until my funds from Ireland arrive. We appreciate your concern, but we'll make do."

"You're the best judge of what's right for Gentleman's Folly," Nate said. "Just remember, we're here for you if you need help." Nathaniel shook O'Ryan's hand and turned his mount for home.

O'Ryan went back into the house. When they'd come back from Annapolis late yesterday, he'd slept in his separate room. He fully intended to put an end to that nonsense tonight.

If he and Anne were going to survive, they needed a united front. He wanted her in his bed. He didn't feel whole without her.

He hoped she felt the same.

He found Anne in the dining room discussing the coming week's meals with Ivy. Abraham's light-skinned wife seemed shy. O'Ryan hadn't heard her string three words together. He hoped that she would be up to the job of running a large household.

"I've asked Ivy to take an inventory of all the foodstuffs,"

Anne explained as the new housekeeper retreated to the kitchen. "Aunt Kessie managed all the supplies for the staff and outside help as well as the family. I'm going to do that myself as soon as I find out what's here. Obviously, we'll have to live on what we have. I can't make any more purchases on credit, and I want to save what hard cash we have."

Anne was garbed all in black. The mourning dress should have made her stiff and doleful. Instead, the stark color brought out the flush of her cheeks and made him ache to peel away her bodice and nestle against her sweet bare skin. He wanted desperately to throw her back across the breakfast table and make passionate love to her amid the fine linen and silver plate. Instead, he ground his teeth together, drew in a shallow breath, and shifted to ease the pressure on his loins. "Ivy seems terrified of me," he ventured, torturing himself by attempting normal conversation. "Did I do something to—?"

"No." Anne moved closer and lowered her voice.

O'Ryan's mouth went dry. He could smell her, all clean and lavender. God, but he wanted her!

"I don't know how the servants know that Papa spent all the money, but they do." She shrugged and gestured hopelessly.

Only a few nights ago, those soft hands had stroked him, cupped his sack, and teased his cock to swollen need.

"Ivy asked me if I was going to sell her and Abraham together."

"What?" What had she said about selling?

"Ivy asked if I meant to sell her and Abraham to the same buyer," she repeated.

That tore him from his lustful daydreaming. "Sell them?" O'Ryan felt his ire rising as he stared at her in disbelief. "We're not selling anybody. I hope you told her that that was ridiculous."

Anne sank into a chair, her dark eyes haunted, her features a mask of grief. "How could I tell her that? I don't know what's going to happen. If we lose the plantation, our creditors will sell our people to the highest bidder."

"We're not going to let that happen."

She covered her mouth with her hand and made a small sound of distress. He went to her and put his arm around her. "I'm not a monster," she murmured. "I care about Ivy and Abraham and young Daniel. I care about all of them. Most were born here. I can't bear the thought that families might be separated."

"The hell they will!"

Her eyes teared up, and she worried at a thumbnail already chewed to the quick. "What can we do, Michael?" She picked restlessly at the folds of her gown. "I suppose I can try to borrow money from my brother-in-law if he and Mary ever get here. Lord knows, George is rich as Croesus. But I'm not his favorite person. He might refuse me."

"We don't need George's money. I'll find a way, Anne. You have to trust me. I'll protect you and your people." He'd do it if he had to turn highwayman, he thought. She'd had enough heartbreak. He didn't intend to see her lose her home as well.

"Don't you have any assets of your own?" she asked.

"No. I sent the last of what I had to Kathleen. I'm bringing her to America."

Anne gasped in surprise. "Your father's ward? You've asked her here?"

"No, not here, Baltimore. And she'll be traveling with her small son and a companion, Blanche Tully." He gripped Anne's shoulders with both hands. "I should have told you. I didn't think I'd be here when she—"

"I see." Her back straightened and her chin went up. The hurt look in her eyes made his gut clench, but he released her and stepped back, giving her space.

"And her husband? Will he be coming too?"

O'Ryan folded his arms across his chest. "Kathleen has never been married."

"Oh." Anne steepled her hands thoughtfully. "I see."

"No, you don't." He gestured impatiently. "Please, don't judge her. Kathleen means a great deal to me. We are as close as any brother and sister."

"I'm hardly in a position to condemn another woman for a folly I was guilty of, am I?" Anne asked softly. "But why bring her to Baltimore? Why didn't you invite her here to Gentleman's Folly?"

"I sent the passage money before your father died. I thought . . . You have to understand about Kathleen," he said. "I feel responsible for her. I am responsible. She has no one else."

Anne's jaw tightened. For brief seconds he studied her face, but it was impossible to read what she was thinking.

Anne got to her feet. It was obvious to him that she was disturbed by the news, but he couldn't guess the reason. Surely not jealousy?

"Why did you come to America without her if she depends on you?"

"It was impossible to bring Kathleen and the child then. I wanted to establish myself, to have a home to bring them to." And there was the small matter of my being pursued by the king's army, he thought wryly. His departure from the Emerald Isle had been irregular, to say the least.

"What if we still have no money when they arrive in Baltimore?" Anne asked. "How will you support them?"

"I haven't thought that far yet. I suppose I could bring them here, if you wouldn't object to extending your hospitality."

Anne nibbled at her bottom lip. "Is there any reason why I shouldn't?"

Damn, but he did detect jealousy beneath those auburn curls. He touched her arm. "You've no need to worry about

Kathleen," he assured her. "I love her, true enough, but it's a brother's affection, nothing more or less."

"Why would I be concerned?" She frowned. "If she means so much to you—"

"Then you don't mind if they come here?"

"Of course not." She averted her gaze and stepped away briskly. "Your family is welcome here so long as we are— business partners. It was just the money I was concerned about. When I'm terrified that I won't be able to hold on to our people . . ."

"I give you my word. No matter what happens, I won't let anyone sell your slaves or split up their families."

"I wish I could believe that, Michael."

"You can. And you'll like Kathleen. Everyone does. And Blanche looks after the child. He'll be no trouble for you."

"Then you must bring them here," she said. "A perfect solution for everyone." But the expression in her eyes told him that she thought otherwise.

Ivy pushed open the heavy wooden door to the smokehouse and stepped inside, pulling the leather tie behind her. It took a minute for her eyes to adjust to the darkness in the windowless cabin. The dirt floor was hard-packed and cool under her bare feet, and the air was heavy with the pungent scents of sage and brown sugar and smoked meat.

Carefully, she circled the pit in the center of the structure. The ashes were cold. There had been no fire here for years, but the old hearth might contain nails. Ivy didn't want to put one through her foot like she had last fall, or get herself so dirty that she'd have to wash before she went back into the big house.

It was quiet here. The thick hand-hewn walls shut out the sounds of chickens, dogs, and children. She couldn't hear that red-and-white heifer—the one that was dropping her first calf in the barnyard—lowing. And she could barely feel the rhythms of old Henry's drum.

Ivy had been so excited when she found out that Miz Greensboro had sold her to Master James that she'd near burst with joy. Seeing Abraham every day, sleeping in his bed at night, seemed the answer to all her prayers. Coming to Gentleman's Folly hadn't been like leaving home, even though she'd been born on Greensboro Hall and had two sisters there. She was close enough to walk over and visit on Sundays, and if she went to the top of the house and looked out an attic window, she could see the roof of her old home.

No, being sent here was the best thing that had ever happened to her, next to being the lawful wife of Abraham Washington. Her heart swelled as she remembered the young priest who'd said the words over them. No jumping the broom for her and Abraham. Master James had been that set on having his people married by a man of God. When the Methodist minister had put up a fuss, Master James had taken the two of them to the Catholics at Chestertown. She even had a ring that Abraham had hammered out of an old horseshoe nail, and to Ivy's way of thinking, it was as pretty as the gold one on Miss Anne's finger.

Ivy had been certain she'd be happy at Gentleman's Folly, but she'd no sooner got here than she'd heard whispers that the Davis slaves were going to be auctioned off to pay the mortgage on the land. She and Abraham had set up half the night talking about what might happen, and he'd been so angry that she hadn't wanted to tell him her news.

How could a thing be good and bad at the same time? She'd known how Abraham felt. She had never agreed to what he said, but she hadn't wanted to fight with him, especially not when they got to see so little of each other. Now he had to be told, and she was scared to do it.

"Ivy?"

Hearing Abraham's voice when she was thinking about him so hard nearly made her heart jump out of her chest. "I'm here," she whispered.

There was a quick crack of light when the door opened. She caught a glimpse of her husband's broad shoulders and close-cropped hair. Then he stepped inside, and the smoke-house was dark again.

"Ivy."

She flung herself into his arms. She'd seen him just before dawn, when she'd cooked up a mess of johnnycakes and sausage for his breakfast, but it didn't matter. She was too crazy for him not to wrap herself around him every time they were alone.

Abraham made a sound that might have been her name and crushed her against him. He kissed the top of her head, then her face, and finally her mouth. "Did she say anything to you?" he asked breathlessly, when they stopped kissing to breathe.

He smelled as though he'd been working hard, a good smell that always made her feel proud inside. She swallowed the lump in her throat and ran exploring fingers up his throat and over his clean-shaven face. Abraham wasn't a hairy man, but what whiskers he had were steely. She loved the way his bristling cheeks felt against her naked skin.

"Miss Anne," he urged. "Did she say anything?"

Ivy drew in a ragged breath. Her heart was thumping fast. She didn't want to talk about Miss Anne or her new husband. She wanted to tell Abraham what had been laying heavy on her mind for weeks.

"I got a little Abraham growin' in my belly," she said, all in one gulp before she lost her nerve. "I know you won't like it that I'm caught, but I don't care. I want your child. And I want you to want it like I do."

"Sweet Jesus."

For a few seconds, he let her go, and she was standing there all alone in the dark. "Please be glad," she said. Tears welled up in her eyes. If he blamed her, she didn't know what she'd do.

"It's all right, sugar." He drew her back into his embrace, and suddenly it was all right. They were hugging and kissing and both talking at the same time. "I'll make it all right," he promised.

"It's a boy, I know it's a boy."

"Boy or girl, it don't matter."

"Boy first, that's what the old ones say. A black boy's life is a hard row, but a girl child's is harder."

He hugged her until she could hardly get air, rocking her, making her feel safe and protected with his strong body standing between her and worry.

"Now tell me what you heard," he said after a while.

"How do you know I heard them say anything?"

"I need to know, Ivy. I've got to get back to the shop. I'm fixing a wheel for the gig. If Mr. O'Ryan comes looking for it, I'd best be there."

"Well, I was talking to the missus, and he come in. I went in the kitchen, but I listened at the door. She said, 'How do they know?' And then something about how I was afraid of being sold apart from you."

"And what did he say?"

"He said he wasn't lettin' anybody get sold, but she said maybe they couldn't stop it. She said that if they take the plantation, we're all gonna be sold off anyway."

"We're not staying here long enough for that to happen." Abraham's voice was so deep and low, it might have been the rush of the river.

"What you saying?" she demanded.

"I won't have my child a slave, and I won't lose you. We're

going north, sugar, north to Canada, where we can start over free."

"Run away?" She went cold inside. "They'll send men after us. They'll catch us, and then—"

"They won't catch us," he said softly. "One way or another, we're going to be free, you, me, and our child you're carrying."

"This looks wonderful." O'Ryan replied as he pulled out a chair for Anne to sit down. The dining-room table was set with a simple dinner for two, fresh vegetables, steamed fish, hot biscuits, and crab cakes. He sat across from her and unfolded his napkin.

Anne motioned to one of the twins to pour drinks, apple cider for her and ale for O'Ryan. "That will be all," she said. "I'll call if I want anything more before dessert."

She offered a simple grace, and then smiled at O'Ryan as he passed her the bread. "How do the fields look?"

"Abraham says it will be a good crop if the worms don't get it or the weather doesn't turn on us. It looks fine and green to me, but I'm a poor judge of tobacco. Until a few months ago, I didn't know a tobacco plant from a shock of corn."

She laughed. How natural it felt to be sitting here with him, talking over plantation matters like any husband and wife. If only there weren't so many unknowns about Michael O'Ryan, so many reasons to be suspicious. She genuinely liked him, and what had happened between them in his bedchamber had been exhilarating. If only she could trust her own judgment. Unfortunately, she couldn't.

"Anne?"

"Oh yes, sorry," she murmured. "I was thinking of something. What did you say?"

He smiled at her, and her pulse quickened. Sweet salvation, but he was handsome. The slight dent in the bridge of his nose, the tiny scar on his chin only made him more masculine, more attractive to her way of thinking.

"There's something I wanted to ask you about. I'd like to take the sloop to Baltimore later this week. I want to look for Sean Cleary and his family. They're supposed to be in Baltimore. I want to bring them here to live."

"More guests?" Anne looked doubtful. "I'm not certain this is the right time. We have limited supplies, and I don't know when we can restock our foodstuffs. Mary and her husband will surely be arriving any day and—"

"Sean Cleary won't be a guest. I intend on giving him a job here. He's a skilled carpenter and woodwright. He and his wife Nora are both hard workers."

She put down her fork. "We simply don't have the funds to hire—"

"Sean will work for a roof over his head and food. Conditions are bad for newcomers in the cities. If I'm staying indefinitely, I want to find something for him here. I noticed that there's an empty cottage on the far side of the orchard. We can fix that up for him."

"But that place hasn't been lived in for years. There are holes in the floor and the roof is in shambles."

"Aye, but the walls are solid brick. I told you, Sean's a carpenter. A few days under his hammer and you won't know the place."

"I wish you'd discuss these things with me before you make up your mind," she said. She felt as though O'Ryan was taking plantation matters out of her hands. First his Kathleen, and now the Clearys.

"I didn't ask you about Kathleen because I didn't think it was any of your concern. But I'm asking now. Sean came over from Ireland on the same ship as I did. It was a voyage cursed with storms and sickness. Sean and Nora saved my life."

"So, what you're telling me is, I have no say in whether you hire them or not?"

"You do have a say. I wouldn't bring them here if I thought they'd be more of a burden to you." He looked into her eyes. "I don't blame you for being cautious, Annie. I haven't given you a lot of reason to trust me. But Sean is a decent man. He deserves a chance."

"All right." She took a sip of the cider and gave in gracefully. "Since you put it that way. I don't mean to be miserly. It's just that I'm afraid. I've never been without money before."

Catching her hand he held it for long seconds. Then he lifted and turned her palm to tenderly kiss the pulse at the underside of her wrist. "Fortunately, Mrs. O'Ryan, this is an area about which I know much. You might say that I'm an expert."

Her heart seemed to swell. She knew he was making a deliberate effort to charm her, and it was a mistake to let him get away with it. "And do you have any wonderful ideas for making money, sir?" she replied, pulling back her hand. "Or just in spending it?" It was hard to sit here and talk to him as if they were no more than business partners when she kept thinking of what they had done together in darkness . . . of how it had made her feel.

"As a matter of fact, I'm intending to enter a horse race at Talbot Courthouse on Saturday."

"With Jersey?"

O'Ryan nodded.

"Do you think your luck at cards will extend to a horse race?" she asked.

He smiled impishly. "It always has before."

She looked pensive. "It could work. Jersey nearly won last

year. Papa rode him. But the prize is a silver cup. It can't be worth more than twenty dollars. That won't—"

"It's not the prize money I'm after, Annie."

"It's not? What then? Not more of your gambling?"

"Me? Gamble?" His Chesapeake-blue eyes danced with humor. "I'd never think of it."

Chapter 13

O'Ryan found young Daniel playing with another slave boy near the barn and asked the two of them to begin clearing the leaves and rubbish around the cottage. Then O'Ryan mounted a horse and rode to the tobacco fields. Abraham wasn't in the first one, but men and women were moving up and down the rows pulling weeds and picking worms from the growing plants under the bright Tidewater sun.

The Maryland heat was vastly different from Irish weather. It seemed that the summers here were hotter and the winters colder, but O'Ryan didn't mind. His grandmother had always told him that hell wasn't fire and simmering cauldrons, it was ice and blast-force winds that sucked the life from a man's bones.

His stint in prison had confirmed her wisdom. O'Ryan doubted that he'd ever be warm enough to forget the constant drip of water inside a bitterly damp and airless cell. Without a single blanket, amid Stygian darkness and the constant rustle of hungry rats, he'd prayed for a glimpse of moonlight.

No, the temperature here on the Eastern Shore would have to soar before he'd find cause to complain of heat. And as for humidity . . . O'Ryan scoffed. Until a man slept in fetid bilge-water in the hold of a plague ship, he could well hold his tongue.

O'Ryan found Abraham on the small acreage near the

river. O'Ryan didn't interfere with the work crews. He simply reined in the gelding and watched long enough to see that there appeared to be no problems.

Two teenage girls paused in pulling up a crab trap and waved at O'Ryan from a rowboat anchored in the river. O'Ryan recognized Grace. He'd seen the other lass working in the dairy, but he didn't know her name.

"Having any luck?" he called out.

They grinned and lifted a basket half full of blueclaws.

Riding on, he followed a back lane that led through the old-growth forest. Three older men were trimming the limbs from a newly felled oak. A team of oxen stood patiently nearby, waiting to drag the massive log to a sawmill near the river. The air was heady with the scents of woodchips, old leaves, and the ever-present tang of bay air.

O'Ryan had accompanied James on this same route, but it seemed different now that Anne's father was dead. At this moment, the plantation was O'Ryan's responsibility. A farm this big was much like a town. The inhabitants needed food and fuel. Most of what was used on Gentleman's Folly was grown or constructed here. There was a dairy, a weaving house, a potter, a smithy, and a brick kiln.

If the land were sold, the lives of every man, woman, and child who made their home here would be changed, perhaps for the worse. For Anne, the blow would be devastating.

No matter how O'Ryan told himself that this wasn't his problem, that his authority here was temporary, he could not shed the heavy mantle of responsibility. He found himself thinking *what if*. What if there were no slaves but only free men and women working the plantation? What if some of the tobacco lands were put into wheat or pastureland to raise beef animals? Surely the growing port of Baltimore must have a market for salted meat. Ships from all over the world delivered cargo to the Chesapeake Bay. They would need supplies for their crews.

At home in Ireland, he'd seen what too great a dependence on one crop could do. When the yield of potatoes was down, people went hungry. Here, the Eastern Shore's fortunes rose and fell with the price of tobacco. If he could diversify . . .

The horse stopped short as a doe bounded across the track in front of him. For an instant, she stopped and stared at him wide-eyed. The animal was so close he could see the quiver of her nostrils and the texture of her buff-colored hair. Then, abruptly, her white tail flagged in alarm. She leaped once, twice, and vanished into the thicket as silently as a dream.

O'Ryan swore under his breath, not at the deer but at his fancies. Perhaps if things had been different, he and Anne might have had a chance, but his past was littered with the bones of poor choices. He had Kathleen and the boy to think of, and he didn't want to endanger either of his women.

"Damn me," he muttered aloud. "When did I start thinking of sweet Annie as mine?" Regardless, she didn't deserve more hurt. He'd help her as long as he was here. Hell, he'd even enjoy her bed if she'd let him, but he had to stop thinking of anything more. The last thing she needed was a husband with a price on his head.

His resolve lasted through the afternoon and early evening, until the tall case clock on the hall landing of the manor house struck ten.

O'Ryan had gone to bed as the red-and-gold sunset shimmered over the rippling waves of the Chesapeake. He had lain restless as the doves ceased to call and the last song of the Carolina wren faded into dusk.

Gradually, the plantation slipped into tranquillity. The dogs stopped barking, voices hushed, and the last door squeaked shut. The only sounds were frogs, the chirping of crickets, and the buzzing of a single mosquito.

O'Ryan swatted the mosquito.

Now his breathing sounded loud in the room. He flattened the feather pillow with a fist and tried to remember the details of an article he'd read in one of James's agricultural texts. His mental images should have been of heads of wheat. Instead, he found himself thinking how soft Anne's skin was and the way her head fit into the hollow of his shoulder.

"Madness," he muttered. "Two adults, married in the eyes of society and the church, sleeping apart because . . ." Because of what? Because he was afraid of falling in love with his wife?

She was willing, even eager to bed him. So long as they remembered who they were and why they were together, what harm could come of giving each other a little human comfort?

Anne strained to hear a footstep in the hall. It seemed to her that her bedchamber was overly warm, that the breeze off the water carried only heat. She had told O'Ryan that they could never repeat what had happened that night. She'd said it and meant the words when she'd said them. But now . . .

She had too much pride to go to him again. If he didn't want her enough to dispute the point, then she could live with her memories. Lazily, she trailed a hand over her belly and down her bare thigh.

Stephen Preston had taken her virginity, but he hadn't taught her what it meant to be a woman. His lovemaking had been quick and awkward, leaving her confused and restless. Until O'Ryan had taken her in his arms, until he'd filled her with his passion, she had been innocent of desire.

A smile played over her lips. She'd given that innocence to Michael O'Ryan, and had received far more than she'd expected.

Was that a scrape outside her door? She closed her eyes and counted to fifty. Nothing. Fifty more.

A horse whinnied. Odd: it sounded to her as if the animal was below in the garden. Rising, she crossed to the window just as something light struck the glass. Anne jumped back, startled.

Three pebbles clattered across the plank floor. From the box at the foot of the bed, the puppy whined and yawned sleepily.

"Annie!"

"What are you doing?" She looked out the open window.

Below were two saddled horses. O'Ryan lounged in the saddle of the nearest and commented, "It's a hot night."

"What do you want?"

He grinned.

She realized that the neckline of her nightgown was gaping and clutched it together. "Why are you throwing things at my window?" Shannon chewed on Anne's ankle, and she bent and lifted the little dog in her arms.

"Come down, Mrs. O'Ryan. It's a grand night for a ride."

"You must be out of your mind." Shannon squirmed and licked her wrist.

"There's a hunter's moon," O'Ryan called. " 'Tis a night for ghosts and sprites and all manner of fairy folk to be abroad. I don't blame you for being frightened."

She laughed and hugged the pup.

"Come down and ride with me," he coaxed. "It will be fun. When's the last time you did something just for fun?"

Nearly half an hour later, they rode down the back lane and took a path through the woods. Dressing alone without the help of a maid hadn't been easy, and then Shannon had cried to go out. Getting away from the house without being discovered had required a great deal of stealth and several trips up and down the staircase with the puppy. But now, in the shadows of the forest with her favorite mare beneath her, Anne was glad she'd come.

"I don't know if we have any fairies on Gentleman's Folly," she said to O'Ryan, "but there is at least one ghost. It's a white doe that some say is the spirit of an Indian princess."

"I saw a doe today, but it was rusty-red, not white," he answered.

"Sorry, not our ghost."

"So you say, but spirits and wee folk are tricky. It could well have been your native princess in her summer gown."

Anne chuckled. Funny how the sound of O'Ryan's speech had become familiar. Here, with only the breeze rustling the leaves and the rhythmic thud of the horses' hooves, the rich timbre of his voice sent chills running up and down her back.

O'Ryan was a man unlike any she'd ever known. He was a total mystery. She knew practically nothing about him, yet in some ways she felt that he was a vital part of her life.

She had hoped that he would come to her bed tonight, but she'd never suspected he'd want her to come riding with him when all sensible people were sleeping.

"Are you still planning on going for your friends in Baltimore in a few days?" she asked.

"Yes, I am. You can't imagine the poverty I've seen among the immigrants. At home, Sean was a man of property, respected in the community. Here, he's perceived as another shiftless paddy among hundreds. He deserves better."

"Why did he leave Ireland?"

"Opportunity for his children. He wants them to have an education, to live in a place where they don't have to tug their forelocks and step out of the path when an Englishman rides by."

"Is it so bad for you there? In Ireland?"

"Worse than you could imagine. Not for me—I grew up sheltered by wealth and privilege. But terrible for those who have only what they can earn with their two hands, and for the women and children unable to care for themselves."

"I'm sorry," she said. "I didn't know."

"Nor I, Annie. Not until I was wounded and hunted by English soldiers one rainy night. A farmer found me and risked his life and that of his family by giving me shelter through the storm. Supper for my host, his good wife, and their seven children was a single bowl of boiled potatoes without salt or butter."

They rode in silence for a while, leaving the woods and riding through a meadow. O'Ryan offered to open the gate, but she touched her mare's rump with her quirt and the little bay leaped ahead.

Anne seated herself firmly in the sidesaddle, leaned forward, and guided her mount easily over the three-rail fence. O'Ryan was just behind her. His horse galloped past, heading toward the far side of the field and the river.

She urged her mare faster, reaching the sandy bank just a length behind O'Ryan. "No fair!" she cried. "Cheater! You never told me that it was a race."

"Never give your opponent the edge," he answered as he swung down out of the saddle and placed his hands on her waist.

She stared full into his luminous eyes, and her heart began to race.

Her throat and cheeks felt hot. Her riding coat was summer weight, of the lightest wool, but suddenly it seemed to smother her. "Am I your enemy?" she asked breathlessly.

"Nay, Annie, never." He lifted her out of the saddle and set her lightly on the ground. But his hands remained around her middle, and he bent to find her mouth with his. Their lips brushed, and she felt a jolt of lightning pass between them.

She sighed, and he slid callused fingers up to cup her breast.

"O'Ryan . . ."

"Yes . . . say yes."

She put her arms around his neck and kissed him again. Slowly, tantalizingly, tenderly they blended lips and tongues. She felt his fingers fumble the top button of her coat and then the next.

She didn't care. She wanted to get closer to him. She wanted to feel his bare skin against hers. She tugged off one kid glove and dropped it.

"Oh, sweeting."

Another button parted from its loop.

His lips were on her throat. He nipped her gently through the thin fabric of her lace collar with his teeth. His hand tangled in her veil, dislodging her hat so that it tumbled onto the sand.

Buttons flew as she tore away her second glove.

"Help me with this damned coat," he murmured between kisses.

Her coat followed the hat. Anne shivered as the cool night air embraced her. One by one, he removed her garments until she stood shameless, clad in nothing but her linen shift and the moonlight.

"Am I to be the only brazen one?" she whispered.

He laughed. "Not if I can help it." He wore no coat or waistcoat, only a white shirt and buckskin breeches. Off came his high leather boots and stockings. Between more kisses, she untied the stock at his throat and helped him pull his shirt off over his head.

O'Ryan, she found, was not a man who troubled himself with drawers. And once he shed his tight pants, his intentions toward her were quite clear.

"Satisfied?" he demanded, then kissed her until she struggled for breath.

"Not yet." She closed her eyes and sighed as he drew off her shift.

Two fingers touched her naked breast, gently exploring, trailing down over her belly to tease the triangle of curls below. Arousal flared through her, heightening her senses as he leaned and nuzzled her breasts, drawing her nipples one after the other into his hot mouth and suckling until she cried out with anticipation.

But even as desire coursed through her, her own hands skimmed over his broad chest and caressed the nape of his neck as she whispered his name. "What are you doing to me?" she asked.

"Loving you."

A sweet aching curled between her thighs, and her breath came faster. From across the river, she could hear the hoot of an owl, and closer, the creak of a rowboat rocking against a mooring post. Clouds passed over the face of the moon, turning the silver light to palest gray.

Anne had never felt so alive, so conscious of the blood pulsing through her veins or the sound of her own heartbeat.

Tendrils of his hair brushed her skin as he traced the curve of her belly with moth-wing kisses. She could feel his hard fingers massaging the small of her back and stroking her buttocks.

"I want you, Annie. I need you."

He raised his head and his mouth plundered hers. The fire within whipped higher, threatening to consume her. She found the hard length of him and stroked it until he groaned and arched against her, corded muscles straining to possess her.

Then they were on the ground and mating in a wild frenzy of raw heat and sweat-sheened limbs. Their passion seemed to go on forever. Anne lost track of earth and sky. And when she was swept over the edge and tumbled weightlessly into a velvet expanse of exploding stars, the only reality she knew was that O'Ryan was there to catch her as she drifted back to earth.

They lay together for long minutes, while he whispered sweet endearments. Then he kissed her bruised lower lip and nibbled at her ear. She laughed, and he laughed with her.

"Come, swim with me," he said, getting to his feet and pulling her up with him.

"Now?"

"Why not now?" He chuckled. "If the parson happens by, he will think the worst of you anyway."

She tried to protest, but not in earnest. And her heart skipped a beat as he swept her up in his powerful arms.

"Last chance, woman," he teased. "Will you go willingly or nay?"

"Yes."

"Good, because, yea or nay, I'm not going in alone."

She giggled and held on to him as he waded into the river. The water felt heavenly as it washed over her fevered body. She locked her hands behind his neck, prepared for him to drop her. Instead, he stopped, chest-deep, and kissed her again.

"I'll not let you go so easily," he said.

For the barest moment, she wondered if he meant to tell her that he would never leave her, that he would stay on Gentleman's Folly forever and be a true husband to her. And she wondered, in that brief space, what she would answer if he ever said such a thing.

She loved his touch. She could not get enough of his body. But physical need was not enough to make a marriage. She needed trust, and Michael O'Ryan, for all his charm and passion, had not earned that. Not yet.

Then, as quickly as it had come, her mood passed. O'Ryan released her and dived under. When he came up, he laughed again and splashed her. She dunked him, and they played like children until the touch of his lean hands kindled the spark of lust within her again. Quickly, their kisses turned from teasing to something more.

There in the river, rocked by the gentle blue-green tide, with a ceiling of scattered diamonds and soft sand under their feet, he made slow, sensual love to her. And once again, her ardor rose to equal his. And in the quiet lull of peace that followed, Anne was utterly content.

In the dark hour before dawn, O'Ryan helped her to dress. The pins that had bound up her hair were hopelessly lost, so she plaited her tangled tresses into one thick braid and tucked it under her riding hat.

They rode home and slipped into the house as the first rooster stretched his wings and uttered a feeble crow. And Anne held tight to O'Ryan's hand when he walked her to her bedroom door.

"You may as well sleep here," she whispered.

"If I do, is there any chance we may be able to make love in a bed?"

She giggled softly. "A chance, perhaps."

She undressed, too weary to be shy. And it seemed quite natural to snuggle up against O'Ryan's chest and close her eyes for a few hours' sleep before it was time to rise and begin the day.

His hand on her bare shoulder woke her when the sun was high. "Anne. Wake up," he said. "We have company."

"Who?" She sat upright in bed and blinked. Memories of the night's mischief flooded her senses, and she stretched and smiled at him. "Who's here?" she said. "Is it my sister? Is Mary here at last?"

O'Ryan bent and kissed the crown of her head. "No. It's those damned bankers. Two of them are downstairs in the parlor with the sheriff. They're demanding money—today."

A hard look passed over his chiseled features. "They say that if we don't pay them, they will foreclose on the plantation and take our slaves and our livestock."

"So soon? Surely not so soon!" She rubbed her eyes. "You'll have to stall them until I can get dressed. I can't go down looking any less than my best." She dug Shannon out from her warm nest under the sheets and handed the pup to him. "She needs to go out."

Anne yawned again. "Feed our guests, or lock them in the wine cellar. You're the adventurer. Surely you can think of something until my maid can have me presentable."

The hard line of his mouth softened into a grin. "You have a devious mind, woman. Are you certain your blessed mother wasn't Irish?" He turned toward the door with the squirming pup tucked under his arm. "I'll send one of the girls in. But hurry. The less I have to do with the law, the better pleased I'll be."

Chapter 14

O'Ryan passed the puppy to a maid, returned to the parlor, and delivered a disarming smile. "Stoddard, Obediah," he greeted the bankers. He nodded to the Talbot County sheriff. "Gentlemen, I apologize for the delay. Mrs. O'Ryan—as you may suppose—is greatly aggrieved by her father's demise. She is not herself. Please, come into the dining room. It's early, and you cannot have had your breakfast yet."

"We didn't come here to eat," the younger Mr. Rawlings said. "If Mrs. O'Ryan isn't receiving visitors, we will conduct our business with you. We want—"

"Hold on, Stoddard," Sheriff John Clough interrupted. "I for one am hungry. Mr. O'Ryan, here, seems disposed to behave like a gentleman. You could do the same. I've known James Davis since we were boys, and I intend to see that his daughter receives the proper respect due her."

"Exactly." O'Ryan ushered the three men back into the center hall and into the spacious dining room. The table was set for breakfast, but no food, hot or cold, was in view. "If you'll permit me to give instructions to our staff."

Ignoring the Rawlings's grumbling, O'Ryan entered the kitchen and shut the door firmly behind him. The twin maids Afi and Afua stood motionless near the hearth, their identical brown faces inscrutable. "Where is breakfast?" O'Ryan asked.

He saw a flash of rebellion before Afi averted her eyes.

175

"What's wrong?" O'Ryan demanded quietly. "Where's Ivy?"

Afua covered her face with her hands and whispered something he couldn't understand. Afi elbowed her sister sharply.

"There's more to this than cold eggs," said O'Ryan. He walked out onto the back porch and surveyed the service area. Smoke drifted from the chimney of the summer kitchen, but otherwise the yard was deserted. No children played on the steps. No chickens scratched around the dependencies, and no women gathered at the well to gossip. Old Henry's African drum was silent.

"Ivy?" O'Ryan called.

No answer.

O'Ryan glanced back at the whitewashed summer kitchen. "Toby?"

"A-ah?" The cook, a bald, moonfaced man with a neatly trimmed beard, pushed open a shuttered window and leaned against the sill. As always, Toby wore a white apron over a blue homespun shirt, and his hands were dusty with flour.

"What's happened to our breakfast?" O'Ryan asked. "We have guests. I need food for three extra, eggs, ham, fish, biscuits, whatever you have."

The cook tugged at his neatly trimmed beard.

O'Ryan noted that Toby's florid complexion was the color of old wax and he was far too affable. "Have you seen Ivy Washington?"

Toby's pale gray eyes narrowed suspiciously as he turned his floury hands palm up in a gesture of total ignorance of the housekeeper's whereabouts.

O'Ryan knew that Ivy was normally at her post before dawn. If she wasn't here, this was serious. "Is Ivy sick? Did you send someone to look for her?"

Toby shook his head.

"Why not?"

The cook mumbled something in Welsh that O'Ryan couldn't quite make out. "What did you say?" He was fast losing his patience.

Toby spat onto the grass. "Gone."

"Gone? Gone where? Is she at Abraham's shop? He must know—"

"Both gone," the little man proclaimed sagely. "Nobody knows where, or if they do, they ain't be telling me."

"No doubt you can venture a guess." Toby could cook as well as any chef in the great houses across the water; he held opinions worthy of his lofty status and was never reluctant to express them loudly.

The Welshman glowered. "They followed the drinking gourd."

O'Ryan shook his head. "I don't understand."

"Gone North, Irish sir. They have run away."

O'Ryan muttered an oath and turned back toward the house. "Breakfast!" he ordered. "The best we can offer and plenty of it."

In the kitchen, he gave instructions to the servants, put Afi in charge, and returned to take a seat at the head of the table. "I apologize for the delay," he said as Afua entered with a silver coffeepot. "We are always pleased to have guests at Gentleman's Folly, but I'm afraid you've taken time from your busy schedules for nothing."

Afi began offering cheese, cold slices of smoked ham, and rare roast beef from a huge platter. Grace followed close on the slave's heels with biscuits and apple tarts. In less time than it took to saddle a horse, the women delivered a feast to the table.

"Please, have some of these oysters on the half shell,"

O'Ryan offered. "The clam fritters are excellent, and I know you'll enjoy the pickled eel."

The sheriff, known throughout the Eastern Shore as a mighty trencherman, ate slowly but solidly, while Obediah picked and nibbled at the delicacies on his plate. Stoddard barely tasted the offerings.

"We did not come here to eat," he reminded O'Ryan. "We came for payment of a debt incurred by James Davis, now deceased. We have no arrangement with you or Mrs. O'Ryan. Either produce the funds, or we will takes steps to claim your—"

"My funds?" O'Ryan drew himself up stiffly. His expression turned haughty. "You are questioning my ability to pay a few thousand dollars?"

"More than a few," Obediah said. He named a sum somewhat greater than that the lawyer had given. "It is never pleasant to—"

O'Ryan cleared his throat, rubbed at an invisible crumb on his lower lip, and fixed the banker with a frosty stare. "My wife's debts are now mine, sir. It is not my policy to discuss financial matters in my home. If you wish to settle accounts, I suggest you contact my solicitors in London."

"London is a good distance from here, Mr. O'Ryan," Stoddard Rawlings answered. "Our policy is—"

O'Ryan flung his napkin onto his plate and stood abruptly. "This is hardly the time or place. My wife is of delicate constitution. She has suffered the loss of our . . ." He turned his head and swallowed, conveying great emotion. "Pardon me. That is a private tragedy, too personal to speak of. It is unseemly of me to mention it. Let me say only that Mrs. O'Ryan has sustained two great losses in a month's time. I refuse to allow her to be troubled by any . . ." O'Ryan pressed his lips together, as if he had tasted something unpleasant. "In all decency, I would expect you to postpone your inquiries until a proper period of mourning has—"

"Rawlings and Rawlings is truly sorry for your wife's loss . . . losses," Obediah put in. "But we'll have our money, sir. Our money or—"

"Slaves, personal goods, livestock, title to—" Stoddard completed the thought.

"Money!" O'Ryan cut him off with a roar. "Money? For the love of God, man, are you a fool? I'm an O'Ryan of Cuchulainn. I could buy and sell your banking house." He shrugged. "I still might."

John Clough paused in sipping his coffee. "Calm down, Mr. O'Ryan. I'm sure they meant no insult. It's just that you're a stranger here, and—"

"Sheriff Clough!" Anne made her entrance, garbed in mourning black from head to toe. "Oh, sheriff, how good . . . how very good of you to come. I've been so worried. We had word just last night of a sighting of those terrible pirates. One of our men saw them butchering a steer."

She rushed around the table and flung her arms around his neck. "Dear, dear Sheriff Clough. My father . . ." Here she broke down, covered her face with her hands, and sobbed pitifully.

O'Ryan went to her and helped her into a chair beside him. He motioned to a servant, who poured her a goblet of water.

Anne took a sip, then wiped her eyes beneath the veil. "Thank you," she whispered weakly. "Forgive me, sheriff. You must think me a foolish woman, but I loved Papa so much. He depended on you. I cannot tell you what a relief it is to see your kind face. It eases my heart to know that you'll be here for Mr. O'Ryan and me."

The sheriff blew his nose on his napkin and cleared his throat loudly. "There, there, Miss Anne," he blustered. "Things will come right. You'll see."

"I don't understand," she replied meekly. "Mr. O'Ryan is . . ." She inclined her head modestly. "Well, let me say only that Papa was exceedingly pleased by the marriage."

"What my wife is trying to say," O'Ryan put in, "is that Rawlings and Rawlings have no need to worry about their debt. It will be taken care of in good time."

"And what exactly is good time?" Obediah demanded.

"Please." Anne fluttered her hands. "A few months only. Foreclosure on Gentleman's Folly would be—"

"Premature and foolish," O'Ryan said. "An embarrassment, not to mention a financial loss to your investors."

The sheriff finished his third biscuit and glanced meaningfully at Stoddard Rawlings. "Well?"

"We'll hold off on the land," the banker replied, "but must have five thousand dollars, hard money. Mind you, we'll accept no notes drawn on foreign banks. By the first of October. If not, every slave, every head of livestock, and all boats will be auctioned to the highest bidder in Annapolis on October second. Is that clear?"

"That sounds fair to me," Clough said, reaching for the platter of cold ham. "Will that satisfy you, Mr. O'Ryan?"

He saw Anne stiffen, and he laid his hand over hers. Her skin was cold, her bones small and fragile under his touch. "We are agreed," he said. "I'll send to Philadelphia for the cash."

"But we will advertise the auction," Stoddard said. "Just in case your funds go astray between Penn's town and Annapolis."

"Naturally you must do as your conscience dictates," O'Ryan answered quietly. "As behooves us all."

"Five thousand dollars! Where will we get five thousand by the first of October?" Anne ripped off her mourning veil and tossed it onto the bed. They had retreated to the seclusion of her chamber as soon as Sheriff Clough and the Rawlings brothers had departed.

O'Ryan took her hand and squeezed it reassuringly. "Don't worry. It will be all right. We'll get the money somewhere."

"Don't. Don't treat me like a child. You don't have it, and I don't have it. Unless we dig up a chest of pirate gold in the garden, it's hopeless." She pulled away, crossed to a window, and gazed out at the fields. They needed rain, but even in late summer, amid the dust and heat, she thought her home the most beautiful spot on earth. "What will we do?" she whispered. "I can't let them auction off our people."

He followed her and slipped a strong arm around her shoulder. "Courage, Annie. At least we're on the same side this time." Moving so that he still held her but could look directly into her face, he said, "I'm afraid I've more bad news. Abraham and Ivy have fled."

Anne stared at him in disbelief. "Run away? Not Abraham! He wouldn't—"

O'Ryan placed two fingers across her lips. "Shhh, think. Why wouldn't he? Because he's smart? Because he has a good trade?"

She brushed his hand away. "Papa was always good to him. I liked Ivy. I thought—"

He pulled her against his chest and cradled her head with a broad hand. "They wanted to be free. Can you blame them? If someone wanted to separate your father from your mother, what would he have done?"

"This is awful. Do you know what they do to runaways?"

"I'm afraid I have an idea."

"They'll be whipped, maybe worse."

O'Ryan's features hardened. A frisson of fear flashed through her breast as he stepped back and stripped off his shirt. Instinctively, she backed away. "What are you—?"

"Tell me about floggings, Annie." He twisted so that she could see the ugly ridges of scarred flesh. "Have you ever seen a man lashed? Can you imagine what this would do to a woman's soft flesh?"

"Stop!" She didn't know whether to run or to slap him. "What do you expect me to do? If they hadn't run away, I could protect them, but when word gets out—"

"If they had a little time—a few days—they might pull it off. Hell, why report them missing at all?"

"I wouldn't, but we won't be able to keep it a secret. You have no idea how word travels among the servants. Old Henry's probably sent out the word by drum, and the slaves will tell their white friends. Half the Eastern Shore knows by now."

"It's not right." His eyes blazed with anger.

"No, it isn't, but I didn't make the laws," she said. "If they're caught, they'll be punished, whether I wish it or not." She laid a hand on his arm. "Who whipped you, O'Ryan? Why?"

For seconds she thought he would refuse to answer, as he'd refused each time she asked about his past. She met his steely gaze without flinching and gradually his stance relaxed.

He sighed. "I stowed away aboard a ship in Ireland. Three days out, a crewman discovered my hiding place. The captain gave me a choice: take the place of an ailing sailor and suffer a flogging, or take the flogging and be put ashore in the Canaries."

"They wouldn't let you pay for passage?"

He shrugged. "With what? My smile?" Slowly, he tugged his shirt back on. "Thomas Dyce, the bosun's mate who delivered the sentence, enjoyed his work. They left me, unconscious and bleeding. A bucketful of salt water might have kept the wounds from mortifying, but Dyce forbade anyone to help me. I was spread-eagled on deck for a week without food or drink."

Anne's throat constricted. "That's inhuman. How did you survive?"

"Sean. He and Nora cut me down and carried me below. I was out of my head with fever. They risked their own lives to save me. Nora's salt and vinegar remedy cured the worst of the infection."

"And this bosun, he didn't care?"

"Half the passengers were down with cholera by then. Twenty-two died in a single night. The crew went crazy. After another week, they started throwing the critically ill overboard. The captain locked himself in his cabin, and Thomas Dyce and his henchmen prowled the vessel taking whatever they wanted."

"It sounds like a nightmare."

O'Ryan's eyes reflected the horror of his words. "Sean's wife awakened in the night. Her youngest was burning up and the water bucket was empty. She slipped topside to fetch more. Dyce and another man cornered her."

Anne's fingers knotted into fists at her side. "This bosun ravished her?"

"He meant to. Knowing Dyce, he would have left no witness. She would have gone overboard once they'd had their sport. But I'd heard her crawl from the bunk. I followed. And when Dyce laid hands on her, I flattened the second man with a belaying pin. Dyce and I struggled. He had a knife. I hadn't regained my full strength yet, and he might have gotten the best of me if Nora hadn't rolled an empty water cask at his feet."

"What happened?"

"He went over the railing."

"He drowned?"

"I saw him come up, and I tossed him the keg. I thought about diving in after him." O'Ryan uttered a bitter laugh. "In truth, I didn't think about it long—not after I saw the first fin slice the water."

She covered her ears, not wanting to hear the rest.

"We'd thrown so many dead and dying overboard that sharks were following the ship. Dyce screamed once, and then he vanished under the surface."

Anne's stomach turned over. "Did you tell anyone?"

"No. And nothing more was said about it. Until now. I had a letter from Sean in Philadelphia saying that there was a warrant for my arrest."

"For killing this Dyce?"

O'Ryan nodded. "Among other charges. Nobody saw what happened but me and Nora. She certainly didn't tell anyone but Sean. The story had to come from the sailor I hit over the head."

Suddenly she was afraid. "Will they come here after you?"

"No, I doubt it. I used another name aboard the *Providence*."

"What name?"

He shook his head. "It doesn't matter, just a name."

"Why tell me anything, if you won't be completely honest with me?" She was torn between suspicion and wanting to believe him. She did want to believe him, but she didn't want to be a fool. That was what some women did, wasn't it? They accepted any wild tale a man offered.

As quickly as it had descended, his dark mood lifted. "Because we're partners in crime, Annie. That was quite a performance you put on downstairs."

"What do we do about Ivy and Abraham? And what do we do when October comes and we still don't have the money?"

"I told you." He smiled grimly. "We don't do anything. We give them a head start. And we come up with the cash by the allotted time."

"Just like that?"

"Just like that."

She sank onto the bed. "I'm scared, Michael. I've never been so scared before. I don't know the person I've become."

He chuckled. "I think you'll like her, if you give her a chance."

"Are you always so sure of yourself?"

"Usually. At least where ladies are concerned."

"You are the most conceited man I . . ." On impulse, she seized a pillow and threw it at him. He caught it in midair and hurled it back.

Giggling, Anne dived for another.

O'Ryan took a flying leap and landed on top of her with such force that one leg of the bed gave way and they both slid off the far side in a tangle of arms, legs, and bedding. The pillow that Anne had intended to use as a weapon was trapped beneath them, and it had burst open, showering them in feathers.

"You're mad!" she squeaked. Gasping for breath, she tried to wiggle out from under him. He trapped her in the circle of his arms and kissed her soundly.

"Take that, wench," he teased.

"Michael!"

A feather landed on her nose and she sneezed. "Let me up! The servants will think—"

"Damn the servants," he answered huskily. "I have you where I want you, Annie, and you'll not get away without paying a forfeit." He nibbled at the lobe of her ear and whispered a deliciously wicked suggestion.

"Feathers? What do you take me for?" she demanded between kisses. The length of his leg pressed between hers, and she could feel the heat of him through the thin silk of her gown. Already, a restless hunger stirred in the dampness between her thighs and her bodice seemed too tight to contain her breasts.

"You're all woman," he rasped as his hands stroked and teased and explored.

"In midmorning? In full light of day? Have you no shame?"

"None at all."

And, apparently, neither did she.

Chapter 15

Dawn was an hour away when Abraham spotted what he'd been looking for, a leaning fence post next to a lightning-struck poplar tree. "This way," he said to his wife. "There's an old Quaker preaching house up there in the woods, hasn't been used in years."

"Are you sure you know where we goin'?" Ivy asked anxiously. Fear made her clumsy as she tried to walk while shifting the pack on her back, and she put one foot down wrong, twisting her ankle. She inhaled sharply and clenched her teeth against the pain. It wasn't a serious hurt, just bad enough to remind her that she ought to keep her mind on what she was doing if she didn't want to spoil their chance at getting away.

But she was still terrified. All night she'd listened for the sounds of hoofbeats behind them, certain that their escape had been discovered, positive that they'd be captured, separated forever.

Ivy had never been beaten in her life, not unless you wanted to count the swats her mama had given her on the backside when she sassed or ran off to play without doing her chores. She was afraid of being whipped, but not nearly as afraid as she was of what they might do to Abraham.

Running away was a terrible crime. No one at Greensboro Hall had ever tried, not in her lifetime. She'd heard stories about slaves from other plantations: some had been caught and beaten or sold south; others simply vanished and were never heard of again.

Ivy reckoned Abraham must be worth nigh as much as Miz Anne's fancy stud horse Jersey, maybe more. Common sense should tell a body that white folks ain't gonna waste all that money by whippin' him half to death or feedin' him to the dogs. Coin came too dear on the Tidewater.

If they were caught, she would likely get a lickin' and maybe be sold off. But Abraham . . . heaven only knew what would happen to her man. One thing sure, he'd never lay eyes on her or their baby boy, not in this life. And that scared her worse than anything else.

She'd never thought much about being a slave. It was the way things was, like the sun comin' up in the morning and goin' down at night. Sure, she'd listened to Abraham's dreams about goin' North and livin' free. But she wasn't sure what "free" meant or how much she'd like it. All her days, she hadn't had to worry about where her next meal was comin' from or whether she'd have a sound roof over her head. If she was sick, she could stay in her bed, and once when she was little, Miz Greensboro had called the white doctor to take a fishhook out of her foot.

Old Miz Greensboro had been hard to please. And once in a while, she'd threaten to cuff you. Sometimes she would, but the slaps didn't hurt much, and Ivy could always think of a way to get even without payin' the price. She could accidentally cut some of the seams on Miz Greensboro's new gown so that they'd split wide open when she sat down, or she could spill her good powder and put cornstarch in its place. She could put a dead mouse on the mistress's best shoe and spiders in her soup.

White folks might think they were the bosses, but it wasn't always the truth. Dinners could be burned or oversalted, butter could be left out to sour, and flies could get in the milk. Not that Ivy was mean-hearted. She wasn't. She'd give a good day's work so long as she was treated right.

She liked Miz Anne, and she'd thought Miz Anne would make a fair mistress. She'd made Ivy housekeeper right off. That was hard work but a good job, and that meant lots of people looked up to her. What with Abraham bein' close by and getting to sleep with him every night, things had been lookin' good, real good.

All that had changed when Abraham said they had to run off North. She'd been uneasy about the decision, but she hadn't tried to talk him out of it. He was hers under God. Nobody had said, "Ivy, you take this man." She'd made that choice herself, and she owed it to them to hold up her half of the bargain.

Abraham was the smartest and the best husband any woman ever had. If he asked her to follow him through fire, she'd hitch up her skirts, grit her teeth, and step out. She reckoned that this run for freedom was about the same as walkin' over live coals. It could hurt you bad, but you'd feel blessed if you got to the other side alive.

He took her arm and helped her through the high weeds. Some briars caught at her bare legs, but she paid them no mind. So long as Abraham's hand was on her, she wouldn't complain about anything.

Still, Ivy couldn't help stumbling over a rough spot. She would have kept from falling herself, but Abraham was quick. He steadied her against him.

"You're tired. Let me take that bundle for you," he offered.

"I'm fine," she protested. He was tired, too. She could hear it in the gravelly sound of his voice. And he was carrying his tools and the cooking pot as well as his Bible and a lot of other stuff. She'd wanted to travel light, taking nothin' but hope and a belief that the Lord would see fit to help them through to the Promised Land.

But Abraham wouldn't budge. "I'll not see us starve or have you catch your death on the damp ground," he'd insisted.

She could see where he'd need his carpenter tools to earn a living for them once they got to Canada. But it all added up to a heavy load. And she was strong, in spite of carrying the baby. She'd not ask him to tote her fair share, not so long as she could put one foot in front of the other.

The Quaker meetinghouse was a dark shape against darker trees. Abraham left her while he circled around the building, looking for a way in. He said that the door was nailed shut to keep out varmints, and tearing it open would only leave a plain trail for anyone tracking them.

For a while there was only silence and the thumping of her heart. Then she heard a flapping sound, like wings, and something gray passed close overhead.

Ivy swallowed hard as sweat broke out on her face. She couldn't hear anything but crickets and frogs. She wanted to call out to Abraham, but she didn't dare.

She heard a dull snap and the squeak of rusty iron hinges. There was a soft thump and then nothing for several long minutes. Ivy's arms prickled. Where was he? Where was Abraham? She didn't believe in haunts. At least she didn't think she did.

Thick branches swayed and rustled as a salt breeze blew through her hair. They'd come a long way tonight, but the bay was still on their left, not more than a mile away.

Abraham's whisper from right behind her made her leap half out of her skin, no matter how she had longed to hear it. "I found a rotten shutter along the far side," he whispered. Abraham moved quiet, like an Indian. Old Henry said that Abraham had a lot of the old African ways.

"Put your arms around my neck," he said. "There's a fallen tree. I don't want you to trip over it."

She started to protest, but he lifted her, baggage and all, and carried her around the church.

"Careful," he warned as he approached the window. "It's high. Let yourself down easy."

She wiggled over and reached with her toes for the floor. When she couldn't find anything solid, she shut her eyes and let go. A cloud of dust rose up around her as she landed and backed away from the opening.

Abraham followed close behind, pulling the ruined shutters closed from the inside. Together they cleared some old benches and spread blankets on the floor. Then he stretched out and she lay down beside him.

"You hungry?" she whispered. Her eyelids were scratchy, weighed down by the miles of walking. The roof and the walls felt good around them, and the familiar smell of the blankets made her feel safe inside.

"Later," he said.

Ivy curled in his arms, laid her head on his shoulder, and savored the joy of what they had together. She wouldn't think about tomorrow or even the next hour. For now, she was happy and content with Abraham's steady breathing in her ear and his little'n tucked warm in her belly.

"I'll win us free, Ivy," Abraham promised. "I will."

"We're free now, ain't we?"

"Really free," he insisted. "Free where nobody will ever keep you away from me again."

"Umm-hmm," she murmured as he talked on about how much she'd like Canada and how he'd see their child learn to read and write. Sleep teased at the corners of her mind as she listened. She sighed, not willing to give in just yet, wanting to remember this perfect time . . . this feeling.

"I'll die before I go back," he said.

She wondered if that meant he'd kill to keep from letting it happen, but she didn't want to ask him. Instead, she took his hard hand and slid it inside her blouse to cup her breast.

"Do you know how much I love you, woman?" he said as he caressed her gently.

"About as much as I love you." She smiled in the darkness and gave up the fight to stay awake any longer.

By Friday, word had passed to the neighbors that two of Gentleman's Folly's slaves were missing. First Nate Greensboro and then two other planters had ridden by to ask O'Ryan what they could do to help.

"The longer you wait, the bigger head start they're getting," Roger Council said. Council was an outspoken fellow with a head of oily black curls that spilled out from under his old-fashioned tricorne hat. Married with a large family of equally vocal children, he farmed thirty acres just beyond Greensboro Hall.

Council didn't own any slaves, but he'd told O'Ryan that he was saving to buy two field hands to do the heavy work. Considering the yeoman's ragged appearance and the condition of his swaybacked horse, O'Ryan didn't believe that Council would be purchasing slaves anytime in the foreseeable future.

"I appreciate your concern," O'Ryan said, dismissing the man with as much tact as he could summon. "Neighborly of you."

"Got to stick together," Council replied, offering a battered snuff tin.

O'Ryan declined.

The farmer sniffed and sneezed twice, then wiped his nose on his shirtsleeve. "Wanted you to know that I rode in and informed the sheriff. They'll be caught, don't you fear, Mr. O'Ryan."

"I have no doubt."

O'Ryan sent him on his way with a pork shoulder from yesterday's butchering and went back into the house to find Anne. "The sheriff knows that Abraham and Ivy are missing," he said as he entered the library.

Anne looked up from where she sat at the desk. An odd expression crossed her face, and he noticed a sheet of paper fall from her fingers. Her eyes were red, as though she'd been crying. He knew she'd visited her parents' graves earlier in the day. And he knew there was nothing he could say or do to soften her loss.

She flushed. "I'm sorry. I didn't mean to pry into your . . ." She raised her chin, suddenly defensive. "I'm not a sneak. I came in here to look for something of Papa's and I found . . ." She looked down at the unfinished letter he'd been writing when Grace informed him that Council was in the yard.

"Your point?" he asked.

"Nothing." Anne's flush spread down her throat. "I simply didn't wish you to think that I was reading your private correspondence."

"If it were private, would I have left it in plain view?"

Woodenly, she smoothed a sleeve of her gown. "Did you contact the sheriff?"

"No, our neighbor Council did us the favor."

Anne's lips tightened. "Papa disliked that little man."

"Your father was a good judge of horses and of men."

"Yes, he was." And Papa had liked Michael, she thought. He hadn't wanted to approve of her husband, but the big Irishman had won him over. And if Papa had thought him worth something, just maybe . . .

"Did you see me with Jersey this morning?" O'Ryan asked. "He's in top shape. I think—"

"You think he's fast enough to beat those other horses in tomorrow's race."

"I do."

"He's the fastest animal we've ever had here at Gentleman's Folly. Papa . . ." She paused while the sharp pain of losing her father echoed through her. Each morning she woke thinking about him. The days ahead stretched out so empty for her, knowing she would never hear him laugh again, or offer his advice.

"It's hard," O'Ryan said. "But in time, I promise you, it will get easier."

"You think I'll forget Papa?" she asked in disbelief.

He shook his head. "Nay. You could never do that. But you'll find yourself remembering the good times. His love made you strong, Annie. You'll always carry it with you." He touched the place over her heart lightly. "There."

She hoped he was right.

"It's one advantage a woman has over a man," he added thoughtfully. "She can shed tears for those dear to her that she's lost. A man who did so would be considered weak. So he must bury his hurt."

"You don't think me foolish, forever running to their graves with flowers?"

"I think you a good and loving daughter. It does you credit, so long as you use what your parents gave you to make a life for yourself. They would want that, above all."

"I suppose so," she agreed. "Yes." She exhaled softly and straightened. "Yes, I know so. And it is comforting to know that they are together again." She looked up at him. "Do you believe that?"

"Aye, I do."

"What do you weigh?" she asked suddenly, thinking again of the coming race.

"Upward of thirteen stone. Why?"

"Not all of the horses will be ridden by their owners. At least two that I know of will have jockeys, very small men."

"I'd thought of that. But none of the boys on Gentleman's Folly have the skill to—"

"I do," she said, rising and placing both hands on the desk. She leaned toward him. "You've seen me in the saddle, Michael. You know that I have good hands."

"You're a superb horsewoman. And a good fifty pounds lighter than I am. But a race is no place for a woman. It's dangerous and—"

"Only dangerous if I fall off. And I haven't done that since I was four years old. I can do this, Michael. I can."

"By all that's holy!" He shook his head. "How can you ask me to let you take such a risk when—"

"No. Listen to me. Gentleman's Folly is my home. If we lose it, I lose far more than anyone. We need whatever money you can raise from this race, and we need to win. I think it's common sense to give Jersey every advantage."

A crooked grin spread over his face. "You'll cause a scandal, Mrs. O'Ryan. You'll be the talk of Talbot County."

"And the sheriff auctioning off my plantation wouldn't?" She laughed with him. "No one has ever said that the riders had to be male." She went to him and grasped his forearm. "At least let me ride him today. See if I can handle him."

"You should have been a lawyer, Annie. You never cease to surprise me."

"Good. You need a good setting down now and then, sir."

An hour later, wearing her oldest riding habit, Anne allowed O'Ryan to help her onto Jersey's back.

"Keep a firm hand on the reins," he ordered.

"I've ridden him before. You don't have to tell me." She tightened her knees and clicked softly to the animal. The big chestnut stepped out smoothly, calm as a kitten once the saddle was on his back.

Anne circled the paddock once at a walk, then urged the

animal into a trot. O'Ryan continued to make suggestions. The thought crossed her mind that what they were about to do might be the smallest bit unfair to the other contestants. Might not Nate and some of the others hold back their own horses and try to keep her from coming to harm? She pushed that notion aside. If she could save Gentleman's Folly, she'd have years to atone for her actions.

"Open the gate," she called to O'Ryan. "I want to take him out into the big pasture."

"Wait until I saddle up," he said turning back toward the barn. "I'll come with you."

She waited until he was inside then waved to the boy hanging on the fence. "Daniel! Open the gate!"

The boy glanced from Anne to the doorway where O'Ryan had vanished.

"Now!" Anne said sharply.

Daniel hurried to do as she ordered.

Anne touched her crop to the stallion's rump and gave him his head. The animal leaped forward. Clods of dirt and grass flew up as he galloped away from the farmyard toward the open meadow.

Wind tore at Anne's hat, but she had tied the ribbon securely under her chin and it didn't blow off. She leaned forward in the saddle, taking joy in the sheer beauty and power of the big horse.

Soon the far pasture fence loomed up ahead of them, but Jersey sailed over it without missing a stride. She wanted to get away from O'Ryan, away from the house. She needed to be alone—to try to think.

She rode on, taking a little-used path down toward the beach. There, she reined him in as a great blue heron took flight and winged over her head. They crossed the small strip of sand at a trot, and she urged the horse into the lapping waves of the Chesapeake.

When she was a child, she and her father had ridden here, splashing through the incoming tide, laughing and shouting as though they hadn't a care in the world. She needed those memories now, needed the solidity that had come from knowing who she was and what was expected of her.

Things between her and O'Ryan were becoming too complicated. She wasn't sure what she wanted anymore or what was important.

Damn the man to eternal perdition! She couldn't look at him without feeling his hands on her—without wanting him to push her back and make love to her all over again.

She patted Jersey's spray-dampened neck as water rose over her riding boots and wet the hem of her habit.

O'Ryan was a rogue and a scoundrel, a man who admitted to an unsavory past. She simply would not allow herself to become a fool over him. She knew what he wanted—what he'd wanted from the first day they met. She knew what their arrangement was. Their partnership had never been intended to last beyond their immediate needs.

So why had discovering his letter to Kathleen hurt so much? "My dearest Kathleen," he had begun in a bold, elegant hand. "I think of you and your little son every day. Soon—"

Was this the letter a caring brother might send to his sister, or was it more? Could O'Ryan be her lover and the father of her child?

And then there was the big question. When he'd made love to Anne had he been wishing she was Kathleen?

Chapter 16

O'Ryan's fingers tightened on the fence rail and blood pounded in his head. Dust flew as the lead horse and rider pounded past the beribboned maple tree in the first lap of the annual Talbot County race. Nate Greensboro's gray gelding pressed hard for second place with Swan's piebald and Jersey hot on its heels.

Two more completed the complement of top contenders while a half dozen lesser horses and ponies trailed behind. Men leaped out of their seats, shouting, and cheering for their favorites.

"Nate! Nate!"

"Another twenty on the gray!"

"Give him his head, Josh! Give him his head!"

The morning was clear and bright, the sky a cloudless blue. An hour before noon, the sun was already hot, but no one seemed to mind. Planters, servants, and tradesmen cheered and swore foully in delight amid the frantic barking of hounds and the stamps and whinnies of the onlookers' mounts.

But the raucous clamor was only a dull roar in O'Ryan's ears. His whole being was focused on Anne as she flashed by him. Her expression was grim, her body tensed. And the sight made him curse himself for a coward and a blackguard.

Why had he ever risked her safety in a race against the

best of the Tidewater's riders? She looked like a child on the big chestnut's back. One misstep and Jersey might go down. If Anne fell off, or if the horse stumbled, the horses directly behind her wouldn't be able to avoid colliding with them.

Sweet Mother of God! He'd seen just such an accident in Belfast. A horse had snapped a leg on a tight turn, and three other beasts had crashed into the fallen animal. The jockey's chest had been crushed and both legs mangled. The lad hadn't been lucky enough to die instantly; he had lingered for three days.

This was a race without rules. First rider across the finish line wins, no holds barred. What was he thinking of? Damn the money and the plantation. None of it was worth an English piss if any harm came to Anne. He could have ridden the swiving horse. He should have ridden him.

Why had he let her persuade him to ride in this race? She wasn't even riding sidesaddle. This morning, when the stable boy had led Jersey out of the barn, he'd not been carrying Anne's sidesaddle; a tiny racing saddle sat on the stallion's back.

"You wanted less weight, didn't you?" Anne had said. "And I'll be much safer with two stirrups than on my sidesaddle."

That alone had caused eyes to widen when she first appeared at the starting post. Not that men wouldn't have been staring at her anyway. Anne was stunning in her Lincoln green riding habit and saucy cocked hat.

She'd braided matching green silk ribbons in Jersey's mane and tail. But after the first lap, her silk banners were a dirty gray, as were her skirt and jacket. Even her auburn hair was a dull brown from the churning dust.

He wanted to lunge onto the track and grab Jersey's bridle. He wanted to tell them all that he'd made a terrible mistake.

But he knew that he could never stop the chestnut. And if he tried, she'd never forgive him for shaming her so in front of her friends. Bad enough to defy social custom—but worse to fail in the attempt.

O'Ryan strained to hear the sounds of the returning horses. It was too soon, but he listened anyway. The track ran across an open meadow, down a hill and through a small stream, then uphill through a narrow wood before widening into the hard-packed lane that would carry the racers back to the finish line. The race was two laps, and this was the last.

"Here they come!" cried a black boy from his precarious perch in the top of the maple tree.

"Who's in front?" demanded Swan. The older man's face was red; his hands clenched as he hopped up and down in excitement. "Who is it?"

"Spots! I see spots, Master Swan!"

Tree limbs swayed ominously.

"It's the piebald!" the servant roared. "Damn! Damn! Damn! Here he come!"

Sweat broke out on O'Ryan's face. It should have been him in the saddle, him taking the chances in the mad charge for the finish.

"An' the Jersey horse!" the boy called. "I see the lady! She's on the outside. She's comin'! Damn but she's comin'!"

O'Ryan shoved through the crowd onto the track. Far down the field he could see two animals thundering toward home. The one on the left a half-length ahead was Swan's Choice, but the other . . . It was Anne! And Jersey was eating up the ground, closing fast on the leader.

"Annie! Annie!" he shouted. "Come on!"

Jersey edged closer and closer. The two were neck and neck. Anne was only a green blur on the stallion's back.

"Yes! Yes!" O'Ryan screamed.

The other men were all on their feet. He heard Anne's name burst from a dozen throats as Jersey's powerful legs plunged like pistons, driving him on. The stallion's head thrust ahead of the piebald's.

"Go, Annie!"

Suddenly, Swan's horse veered right and crashed into Jersey's shoulder. The chestnut missed a stride and staggered away.

O'Ryan's world stopped.

"Foul!" the man behind him cried.

"Son of a bitch!"

The piebald streaked ahead. O'Ryan held his breath as he watched, waiting for Anne to go down. But Jersey recovered his balance and lunged ahead, fiercely fighting to catch the spotted horse.

Anne was still in the saddle, clinging to Jersey's mane as they raced past the marker a single length behind Swan's Choice. Boos and curses rose from the crowd. They surged onto the track, converging around the grinning winner.

But Anne wasn't able to rein Jersey in. The big horse galloped on, leaving the track and taking a low fence to race on toward a low swampy area.

O'Ryan didn't hesitate. He vaulted onto a fresh horse and tore after her. He didn't catch up to them until Jersey splashed down a grassy bank and into the cattails.

"Anne! Anne!" he shouted.

She sat, slumped in the saddle, head down, reins still clutched in her gloved hands. She straightened as she heard the sound of his horse.

"Michael." Wearily, she turned the exhausted Jersey back to solid ground. "We lost," she said huskily. "I let him get the best of me. I've failed you."

"Failed me?" He leaped from the saddle and ran to lift her

down. Trembling, she leaned against him. Her hat was gone, her carefully braided and pinned hair undone and hanging. Her heart-shaped face was covered with sweat and dirt.

He pulled a clean handkerchief from his pocket and wiped futilely at her nose and cheeks. "You didn't fail," he said. He wanted to kiss her, but he didn't dare.

Keep it light, he told himself. Bend one inch and you'll crumble.

"I lost the race, didn't I?"

Her eyes were teary but he could feel the strength in her.

"I almost had him though, didn't I?" she said.

"Annie Davis O'Ryan, you're the best woman rider I've ever seen. And he's got more heart than . . ." He trailed off. "You didn't fail. You came in second."

Her eyes widened. "But the bet?"

He laughed. "I never thought you could win. My money was on you coming in second."

"What?" She pushed him away. "You didn't think I'd win, and you let me—" She uttered a sound of pure feminine disgust and placed two balled fists on her hips. "You Irish bastard!"

"But we won close to three thousand dollars."

"Fine!" she snapped. "And what did you use for betting? Did you bet without having the money to cover it if you lost?"

"No. Swan wants to buy your violin for his grandson."

"You sold my grandfather's violin?"

He shrugged. "No, I didn't, but we had the option if our plan went awry. Desperate times, Annie. A man must do what a man must."

"Well, just you remember that that works two ways!" she retorted. Turning her back on him, she gathered Jersey's reins and started to walk him up the bank.

"Leave him," O'Ryan said. "You can hardly stand. Let me put you up on this horse and—"

"Ride with you?" She grimaced. "I'd sooner ride with the devil."

"Don't take this personally," he soothed. "We needed the money, didn't we?"

"Maybe it would be worth losing the plantation to be rid of you," she flung over her shoulder.

Halfway across the meadow, Nate and two friends met them. Nate was riding a fresh horse and brandishing the race trophy. "We took it away from Swan's jockey," he shouted to Anne. "We took a vote, and you win!" He slid down off his horse and covered the space between them in three quick strides. "You're a hero," he declared.

Anne looked into his plain, round face. He was covered in dust and had streaks of sweat smeared across his forehead and chin. "If I look anything like you do, I think I can sneak home with my reputation intact."

He grinned and rubbed at the dirt, making the mess worse.

Anne laughed. "The cup and the race go to Mister Swan's piebald. I knew the rules before I started. It's very gallant of you all to offer me the trophy, but when I beat you, I want to do it on my own."

Nathaniel chuckled. "Suppose you're right, Anne. But Swan feels rotten about the whole incident. I heard him tell his jockey that he'd never ride on the Eastern Shore again, not for anyone who called himself a gentleman."

"Good. The rascal deserves that. He could have injured Jersey." She patted the horse's neck as O'Ryan joined them.

"We tried to make her the winner," Nate explained. "But she won't have it."

"I agree with my wife," O'Ryan said, slipping an arm

familiarly around her waist. "Second place is good enough for us."

Anne flashed him a warning glance, and he winked at her.

"Here, let Walter take your horse," Nate offered. "He needs cooling off. Mrs. Bevins has extended a personal invitation for you. She said to tell you that she'd asked her girls to ready a hot bath. I'm sure she has a dress for—"

"I brought a change of clothing with me," Anne replied. "And my husband can walk Jersey." She tilted her head to offer him her sweetest smile. "He's so particular about his animals. I know he'd worry if he didn't see to the horse himself, wouldn't you, dear?"

"If you won't accept the prize, you'll be the guest of honor at dinner," Walter Irons insisted. "Uncle will want to extend his most sincere apologies for what happened."

"Please tell your uncle—Mr. Swan—that I in no way hold him responsible," Anne said. "But perhaps next year, he'll be willing to give me a rematch. I really thought Jersey had his piebald beaten on the stretch."

Back at the palatial home of their host, Squire Bevins, Anne found herself the center of attention as, one after another, riders and spectators congratulated her. Leaving O'Ryan to look after the stallion, she hurried to bathe and change before the race dinner.

On the whole, Anne was pleased with her showing. The thrill of the race had been wonderful. When she was little, she'd always wished that she were a boy so that she could do exciting things. She'd long given up the desire to be male, but beating the men at their own game was spectacular. And if Michael's lack of confidence in her horsemanship still smarted, at least they had acquired a substantial amount of the much-needed money.

Dinner was a feast of game, seafood, beef roasted over an

open pit, and all manner of hearty delicacies. Anne excused herself after the dessert course and joined Mrs. Bevins in the gazebo on the lawn behind the house. With her were her two married daughters and the few other ladies who had attended the festivities.

"Absolutely outrageous," her hostess proclaimed with a twinkle in her eye. "I'm too old for such tricks, but I do admire you for your courage." She patted Anne's hand. "And I've told the squire that next year, we must have a second race just for the ladies."

"I thought you were wonderful," Jenna Raeur said.

Emma Irons fluttered a delicately painted ivory fan. "Trust Anne to liven up any frolic," she said archly. "But I do say that your new husband is more liberal than my dear Walter. He would never think of allowing me to ride astride, let alone ride against men."

"Mr. O'Ryan is an Irish gentleman," Anne lied smoothly. "In his homeland, riding astride is considered quite the fashion among the titled ladies."

"So soon after your poor father's passing," Emma twittered.

"Yes, it is soon." Anne sighed regretfully. "But I'm sure our hostess would agree that Papa would be the first to encourage me to go on with my life as best I can."

Emma sniffed and reached for a chocolate. "I do hope there's nothing to the rumor that he left you practically penniless."

Anne fixed her with a warning glance. "Nonsense, Emma. You've been listening to servants' gossip again. Mr. O'Ryan is quite—"

"Anne! Anne!"

"Isn't that your husband calling?" Jenna asked.

Anne rose and hurried down to the lawn. "If you'll excuse me," she said hastily, walking quickly toward O'Ryan.

Something was wrong. She could read the tension in his face, hear it in his voice.

He took her arm and turned away from the curious ladies. "A rider has just come from the jail. Abraham and Ivy have been captured. I have to go there right away. Nathaniel's offered to see you home. I—"

"I'm coming with you," Anne said. "They're my people. It's only right that I be present."

"Are you certain? This may be unpleasant."

"They are my responsibility."

"Aye, I suppose you're right."

"You admit it?" She looked at him in surprise.

"I only wanted to protect you, Anne. But maybe it's best if you saw for yourself just how dirty a business slavery can be."

Ivy sat on the ground in the darkened root cellar, arms locked around her bent knees, rocking back and forth in absolute misery. The earth was damp, filled with the scents of stored potatoes, carrots, and turnips. The only light came from the cracks in the board-and-batten door.

No one had hurt her, but she had still wept until she had no tears left. Abraham had put up a fight when the white sheriff came for them. He'd struck one man, knocked him flat before the law put a pistol to her husband's head and cocked it. Cold chills ran through her as she remembered the ugly sound of that metallic click.

"Don't hurt him!" she'd cried. "Please, sir, don't hurt him! He won't be no more trouble. Will you, Abraham? Will you?"

The look Abraham had given her was a haunted, lifeless stare, as if he didn't even see her. She knew that he'd given up for her sake. For his own, he didn't care if they shot him dead. Maybe he'd even wanted it.

Rough hands had shoved and bound him in irons. They

cursed him and locked him in the single cell Talbot Courthouse possessed. Then a stranger had ordered her to come with him.

She'd been near crazy with fear, but he'd only taken her behind a house and shut her behind this thick door. She didn't know how many hours had passed. No one had come, and no one had told her what they were doing to her Abraham.

She'd prayed until she was hoarse. "Please, Lord, don't let them hang him. I can stand anything so long as I know he's alive." That had been her plea, over and over. But she didn't know if she'd been truthful with God. She didn't know if she could live without Abraham—if she could raise her coming child without him.

The silence was broken by the bark of a dog close by. Then Ivy heard the murmur of voices. She recognized Mr. O'Ryan's Irish way of talking and then her mistress's quieter tone.

The door banged open.

"Come out of there."

That was the man who'd locked her in. Blinking, cautious, Ivy crawled out and stood, shielding her eyes from the sudden light.

"Ivy," Miss Anne said. "I'm so sorry this had to happen."

Ivy hung her head. She couldn't meet the lady's eyes, not now. She knew how she was supposed to act, but her fear was fast fading to be replaced with righteous anger.

They expected her to be sorry that she and her man had run off. She was sorry, right enough: sorry they'd been caught. But it wouldn't do to show her thoughts, not if there was any chance of saving Abraham. She muttered a contrite, fragmented apology.

"Follow us," Mr. O'Ryan ordered. He nodded to the man. "We appreciate your help," he said.

"My boys are the ones who spied them sleeping in the old

Quaker meetinghouse," the stranger said. "If there's a re-ward, I reckon they—"

"They will be suitably rewarded," Anne put in. "Ask them to come to Gentleman's Folly on Monday next. I will show them my gratitude—our gratitude—at that time."

"Should I bind this woman's hands?" the man asked. "She may try to run again."

The mistress shook her head. "That won't be necessary. Mr. O'Ryan will see that she does not."

Ivy shuffled after the three of them down an alley and onto the main street. They didn't speak another word to her. But they led her back to where Abraham was still held in the cell.

"You're fortunate," the sheriff said. "If those boys hadn't seen the broken grass and weeds outside the meetinghouse, your slaves might have been miles away by tomorrow morning." He gestured toward Abraham. "This one deserves whatever punishment—"

"I'll see to it," Mr. O'Ryan said.

Ivy inched toward Abraham and put her hand through the bars to clutch his hand. Numbness spread through her, and she tried to shut out what the master was saying.

". . . at least a public whipping," the sheriff insisted. "You've got to set an example for—"

"I agree," O'Ryan said harshly. "That's what I intend to do."

"What?" the mistress asked. "Whip Abraham and Ivy? I told you that Papa never—"

"Leave this to me, Mrs. O'Ryan." The big Irishman glared at Abraham. "I'm taking you back to Gentleman's Folly, where the rest of our people can watch. One hundred lashes for you, and for your wife—"

"You don't need to whip her, Mr. O'Ryan," Abraham said.

"You give them licks to me. My back is strong enough to bear anything you can give."

"No! No!" Ivy cried. "I can take it. Please don't—"

"Have it your way," the master said softly. "One hundred and twenty-five strokes, and I'll deliver every one myself."

Chapter 17

"What are we going to do?" Anne repeated. She followed Michael up the grand staircase of Gentleman's Folly as the tall case clock on the landing was striking eleven. The hall was dark and shadowy; the only light came from a double candlestick on a table beside the clock.

Anne couldn't stop thinking about Abraham's face as the sheriff's men had shoved him, bound hand and foot, into the back of the wagon that would take him and Ivy home. As long as she'd known Abraham, she'd never seen such defiance in his eyes, or such sorrow.

She'd leaned close and asked him, "Why, Abraham? Didn't Papa always treat you well?" And the black man's bitter reply haunted her.

"Respect," he'd hissed, too low for anyone else to hear. "A horse gets good treatment. A man deserves respect." He'd not uttered another word to her or to Michael since.

"Anne. Careful!" Michael caught her as she slipped on the landing step.

"I feel so awful," she said to him. "I won't let anyone whip Abraham, and I didn't believe for a minute that you will, either. But if we don't punish the two of them severely—"

"If we don't, the authorities may come and do the dirty deed for us," he answered. He clasped her hand in his protectively.

"It's inhuman," Anne persisted. "A hundred and twenty-five strokes would kill Abraham."

"Whipping a man or woman is inhuman."

"I agree, and so would my father. He never permitted such a thing on Gentleman's Folly."

"I know that, Annie. You're both too good at heart for such evil."

"I can't get what Abraham said to me out of my head. He said that a man deserves respect. It's the same thing you said about slavery when you first came here. You're right, Michael. You're both right. I didn't want to believe I'd been so blind all my life—that my parents and all our friends had been blind." She hesitated, searching for the right words. "When Aunt Kessie left, it was like losing my mother all over again. Can you understand that? I never thought of her as a black person, only as someone I loved. But I could feel that way about her and not realize that our other people were just as human, just as deserving of—of respect and freedom."

He nodded. "Yes. But you're not the only one who couldn't see what was in front of his own eyes. I was wrong to judge you. It was simply that I felt so strongly about someone owning another that I made assumptions that weren't true. I came to Maryland with certain opinions about your family. I guess we both learned a valuable lesson."

"You were very—sure of yourself," she agreed, smiling up at him. "But what do we do now? How can we save Abraham and Ivy?"

He kissed the crown of her head. "I think that this is something you'd best leave to me." His eyes glittered in the circle of flickering candlelight. "Shout at me, Anne, loud enough for all the servants to hear."

"What?"

He smiled and put his finger to his lips and then bellowed.

"The subject is closed, woman. I mean to retire for the night, and I'll have no more of your nagging! Leave them to me, Anne. I'll do what needs to be done."

Puzzled, she stared at him.

He motioned to her. "Come, sweet," he whispered. "Yell something."

"But why?"

"Trust me. I'll do what needs be done. And if there's blame, it won't fall on you."

"I won't let you!" she shouted before dropping her voice. "Do what? Have you thought of a plan?" When he winked slyly, she snapped. "This is my home, not yours!"

"Excellent," he murmured into her ear. Then he cupped her chin and raised it so that his face was close to hers. "Whatever happens, don't lose faith," he said. "Trust me to do what's best for you and for Abraham and Ivy. Can you do that?"

"Tell me—"

He shook his head. "There are too many chances that it will all go wrong. I'll not have you accused of evading justice or trying to cheat your creditors." He kissed her tenderly, then released her.

"You forget your place, mistress!" he said harshly. "As the master of this house, I have the right to deal with runaways in any way I see fit." He took the last step and strode across the landing and down the hall toward the bedroom they shared.

"My opinions won't be ignored!" she answered, hurrying to keep up with him.

"As you wish." He pushed open the door to a guest chamber. "Feel free to sleep here, Mrs. O'Ryan. I will not force my unwelcome presence on you. It's been a long day, and doubtless tomorrow will be longer. I'm for my bed."

For a few seconds she stared at him, uncertain what game he was playing. "Michael?" she whispered.

"It's best this way," he said quietly. "Trust me." He strode away from her.

"You Irish bastard!"

He didn't look back.

The bedroom was dark except for a few rays of moonlight. She didn't need a lamp; she knew every inch of this house. Desolate, she sank onto a settee, steepled her fingers, and wondered what plot Michael was hatching now.

From the slave quarters came the haunting refrain of old Henry's drum, sounding a different message tonight, one of despair that Anne had never heard before.

Sweet hope of salvation, Michael is right, she thought. No matter what action she took regarding her escaped slaves, it would be wrong. She had to trust him. He was master here at Gentleman's Folly. She had given him that power over her. Now it remained to see what he would do with it.

Thoughts of Abraham and Ivy locked up in separate makeshift cells in the barn made her stomach turn over. Ivy had been terrified by Michael's threat to whip her husband, and neither she nor Michael had dared say otherwise.

A whine and light scratching at the door made her rise and let Shannon in. She knelt in the pale glow of the moon and cradled the squirming dog against her breast.

"What will he do?" she asked the pup. "What has he planned that's too dangerous for me to be a part of?"

The puppy snuggled close and licked Anne's neck and cheek. But for once, the animal's comic antics brought no smile to Anne's lips. All she could think of was the young black couple and their hopeless plight.

She awoke to a strangely silent morning. The sun was already high, but the house remained quiet. No footsteps sounded on the stairs, no giggles, no scrape of dishes. No familiar drumbeat heralded the plantation's traditional day of rest.

Stiff and slightly disoriented, Anne sat up in bed. She rubbed her eyes and looked around. She had fallen asleep fully clothed, and she felt out of sorts. It took her a moment to shake away the cobwebs and remember why she was here in this room instead of her own.

Shannon sprawled beside her on the quilt, gangly legs outstretched, soft white belly exposed, with large paws that seemed to grow bigger every day. Anne leaned over and placed a feather-light kiss on the dog's head.

Brown eyes snapped open. With eager barks, she launched herself into Anne's arms, twisting, licking, and wagging her shaggy tail.

"Not now," Anne cautioned, capturing the overgrown puppy and lowering her carefully to the floor. She got up and went to the open window, looking out to see if anything was wrong.

Cows lowed and horses whinnied. In the garden, a lone chicken plucked at a grub, and a gray cat stalked beneath the rose bushes. Nothing seemed amiss.

She went to a window that overlooked the bay. There was nothing to see but wheeling seagulls, a dory bobbing at anchor, and the sparkling dance of an incoming tide.

Prickles of intuition teased at the base of Anne's skull. Had she overslept? Michael had told everyone that he would deliver the punishment after church services. Surely, it wasn't that late.

But what if he'd changed his mind? What if everyone was witnessing the lashing but her?

Snatching up her shoes, she raced to the room where O'Ryan had slept. The bed was empty, the blankets and coverlet smooth and undisturbed. A note lay on the pillow.

Anne,

 I cannot explain what I must do. I only ask you to trust me. If what we've shared means anything to you, you'll understand this. I will be back soon.

Michael

Where had he gone? And why? Crumbling the letter in her fist, Anne hurried downstairs and into the dining room.

No breakfast waited on the table. No steaming tureens of porridge or pitchers of milk stood on the Irish hunt board. The house seemed utterly deserted.

Shannon's anxious yip reminded her that the pup needed to go out. She called to her, then opened the door into the empty kitchen. "Afua! Afi? Grace?" Puzzled, Anne let the dog out the back.

Puffs of smoke billowed from the summer kitchen, and Anne hurried to investigate. "What's going on?" she demanded as she peered over the bottom half of the Dutch door.

"Oh, Miss Anne!" A tearful Grace coughed and waved her apron at the smoking hearth. "I've been tryin' to cook your breakfast, but I burned the biscuits and—"

"Where is everyone?"

Grace's reddened eyes grew large in her freckled face. "You don't know? Mr. O'Ryan didn't say anything to you before he went?"

Two fat tears rolled down the serving girl's face. "He's gone. He took them all with him—took every slave on the place."

"You're saying that the master took Abraham and Ivy away?" Good, she thought. I hope he's taken them so far that no one will ever find them.

"All the slaves," Grace insisted. "On the big sloop. They sailed on the tide just after midnight. Toby went with them. He and Afua . . ." The girl's freckled face flushed. "Toby and

Afua . . . they're you know . . . He don't care that he's a white man and she's black."

Anne had guessed that the two liked each other, but she hadn't thought that Toby cared so much for Afua that he would run away with her. But Toby wasn't important now. "You're telling me that my husband took all our people away without telling me?" she said to Grace.

"I reckon so, Miss Anne. Even Old Henry's gone. My brother Jasper, he was night-fishing, off the point. He saw the sloop in the moonlight, and he heard African drumming on the deck. It raised the hair on Jasper's head, it did. He said it sounded savage, like nothin' he'd ever heard, like maybe an Injun getting ready for war."

Anne turned away, unwilling for Grace to see the joy in her face. All of her people free. That was what Michael had planned. He'd whisked them all away to freedom. No wonder he hadn't wanted her to know.

Then she thought of the money that they'd won, the money she'd watched him put into Papa's cash box the night before. Fearful, she went into the library. Her hands trembled as she opened the cupboard and took down the metal container. She held her breath and lifted the lid.

The roll of greenbacks was missing.

"How long ago did he take the slaves?" George Whitfield sputtered.

"Three days," Anne replied calmly.

Mary sat down hard in the nearest chair. "Oh, Anne. You poor darling, to be so deceived."

Her sister and brother-in-law had arrived without warning on Tuesday afternoon on the mail boat out of Annapolis, accompanied by a dog, two maids, a nanny, two footmen, and George's personal servant. They had been at Gentleman's Folly less than an hour, and already caused such confusion that

Anne wished Mary were back in Philadelphia and George marooned on the Sandwich Islands.

"You little fool," he sputtered. "What have you done about it?"

Other than pray Michael and her people had made it safely away? And wonder if she'd been completely taken in, first by Stephen and then by O'Ryan? Deceived by two men she'd thought she loved?

George regarded her with what could only be disgust. "Have you notified the authorities? Posted a reward for information?"

"To what end?" Anne's eyes narrowed. "Michael O'Ryan is master of this plantation. Legally—"

"He's a blackguard," Mary cried, breaking into sobs. "He has nothing. He's robbed you of a fortune."

"Your lowborn Irishman will sell your slaves on the nearest block and be gone with every cent." George waved his manicured hands to emphasize his point. "What did I tell you, Mary? Did I not forecast such dire consequences?"

Anne's sister blew her nose and nodded.

"It proves what I said all along," he continued. "No woman should be in charge of her own affairs. The plantation should have been left in my hands."

Anne bit back a hot retort. If George guessed that Michael had taken all her money as well, he'd have her committed as a madwoman. But she'd sooner be torn apart by white mules than betray her husband. Michael had promised her he'd be back. She had to believe that he would keep his word, that he'd taken the money because he needed it more than she did.

"She's ruined. First our dearest Papa and now this," Mary murmured.

Anne studied her sister's high-waisted, pale peach silk dress and matching spencer. Mary's fashionable attire was obviously French, and expensive, but it was overly tight at the bodice. Her unusually plump cheeks and marred complexion made Anne suspect that Mary was again with child.

"Are you well?" Anne asked, ignoring George's ongoing tirade. "You are expecting again, aren't you?"

"Anne Davis!" Mary's eyes widened in astonishment. "Not in front of the servants." A pink stain spread over her face. "Have you no thought for propriety?"

Not particularly, she thought, considering the situation she found herself in. "Mary." She smiled patiently. "Doubtless George and your maids already know that you are with child."

"Yes," her sister replied softly. "It's the reason that we didn't come right away when we received word of Papa's passing. George thought that I should not travel until my morning sickness had stopped. We're hoping so for a son and heir this time."

"No need to make excuses, Mary." He glared. "I'll not have you make a spectacle of my wife, sister," George sputtered. "We know what you did, you know. You couldn't keep such a secret. News is already spreading about your riding James's stallion in the race."

"You heard about that, did you?" Anne straightened her shoulders and smiled. "It was great fun. I'll have to tell you all about it. But I'm sure you are all tired from your journey. Grace will show you to your rooms. And if you will excuse me, I have chores that must be seen to." She smiled with less than genuine warmth. "I hope your maids can cook, Mary. Our Toby seems to have made himself scarce."

"Toby's gone, too?" Mary said. "Whatever will you do?"

"Find another or learn to cook myself, I suppose," Anne answered.

"You must hire someone, immediately," George said. "We can't make do without a proper—"

"Yes, it is a pity," Anne agreed. "Perhaps it might be better if you returned to your affairs and left Mary and the children here with me."

"Not likely," he snapped. "Without a man in the house, God knows what schemes you'd fall prey to. It is my duty to remain here and take charge until the plantation can be sold. Then you will, naturally, come back to Philadelphia with us. I'll make a place for you in our household. Margaret and Lucy will soon be too old for a nanny and will need a governess. You—"

"Will manage my own affairs without your help, George." Anger lent fire to her words. "I will not be belittled or insulted in my own home. May I remind you that you are a guest here. And if you can't show me proper respect, you can catch the next boat north."

"Anne! You didn't mean that," Mary cried. "You can't talk to George like that. He's only—"

"Thinking of his own good, as usual." Anne flung her brother-in-law a defiant look. "Accept my hospitality as you find it or leave, dearest George. The choice is yours." Without waiting for an answer, Anne dismissed him with a curt nod and left the house.

A fool she might be for giving her heart to a handsome Irishman, but she'd not be cowed by the likes of George. She'd sooner live in a hut and crab for a living than accept a penny of his charity. Besides, Michael would be back soon. He'd find a way to deal with her overbearing brother-in-law.

Anne fingered the folded letter in her pocket, the now creased and tear-stained note her husband had left on her pillow. She knew the words by heart, but it helped to have it nearby so she could touch it when she felt anxious.

He has to return, she thought. Rogue or not, she was certain he loved her. But if he didn't come . . . If he didn't, she'd go after him. She'd track him to the ends of the earth and give him such a warm reception that the Devil's bake oven would seem cool in comparison.

Unaware of Anne's visitors, O'Ryan stood in the bow of the plantation sloop and gauged the size of the waves. The single-masted vessel lay low in the water, making it hard for Abraham to steer. Already half of the people were seasick and hanging over the rails.

The boat was sound, made for rough weather on the Chesapeake and an occasional dash up the coast to the Delaware Bay or down to Virginia or the Carolinas. But she was not built to carry so many. O'Ryan had known that taking every slave on Gentleman's Folly would be risky, but he was unwilling to leave any behind.

Abraham stood bare-chested at the wheel; his wife crouched close beside him. Neither Ivy nor Abraham showed any ill effects from the ocean swells, and both wore expressions of hope and continued disbelief.

Abraham had been suspicious when O'Ryan freed him from the tack room in the barn. His big frame had tensed, and O'Ryan sensed that he would explode into violence at the slightest provocation. But when he'd shared his plan with the craftsman, Abraham had moved swiftly and efficiently to locate every slave and get them on board the *Wind Sprite* in absolute silence. And once they'd cast off from the dock, it became evident that the black man knew more about sailing than O'Ryan did.

Ivy touched her husband's leg and whispered. "What if he lyin'? What if Master O'Ryan takin' us someplace to put us all on the block?"

Abraham's features hardened. "He won't."

"How you know he won't?" she persisted.

"Him and Toby are the only white men on this boat. If he's not telling the truth, he won't get off alive."

Her face paled. "You'd kill him?"

Abraham frowned. "Quiet, woman. No need to tell the world. So long as the Irishman's fair with us, he's as safe as if he was in God's hand. But if he's not . . ."

He left the rest unsaid, and Ivy knew that the blood of those old African men did run hot in him. She smiled and patted her belly. "Go on to sleep, little Abraham," she crooned. "Your daddy's here, and your daddy goin' to take good care of us."

"Sail!" a lookout shouted. "Sail there!"

Every eye stared in the direction he pointed. For a long time Ivy didn't see anything but waves and a rocking blue horizon. Then, abruptly, the tall masts of a merchant ship came into view.

Moans and low cries of distress rippled over the deck. "The law," the lookout muttered. "They comin' for us."

One girl, barely thirteen, began to wail and made a lunge for the railing. "I ain't goin' back." Afi seized one arm and her twin the other.

"Hush now," Afua soothed. "No need for that. Likely that old ship just sail right by us."

"She's right," O'Ryan said loudly. "If we're hailed, I've got your papers. There's no reason to panic. If you let on that something's wrong, they'll question us. Otherwise . . ." He shrugged. "I'm a plantation owner taking slaves north to be sold at auction. Nothing illegal about that."

Tears clouded Ivy's eyes. "God, don't let that be so," she prayed aloud. "Let us be goin' all the way to Canada."

"I promised you that, didn't I?" Abraham said. "Come heaven, come hell, my child will be born free."

For several hours, Abraham held the *Wind Sprite* on course, running north, just out of sight of land. The single sail billowed and snapped, pushed along by a gusty breeze. The wave chop increased and clouds thickened overhead. The merchant ship moved on past and eventually vanished from sight.

Once they passed a cattle boat heading south. O'Ryan glanced at Abraham, and the black man turned the wheel, taking them farther from the beach. Old Henry settled in the stern and began to beat his drum in an ancient cadence.

"Weather's turning on us," O'Ryan said to Abraham. "I'm not certain we could stay afloat if this whips into a storm."

"Yonder's the mouth of the Delaware," he answered. "I'll take this boat to hell before I let you land us there."

O'Ryan nodded. "So long as you know the danger."

"If I'm free, I can choose."

"And the others?" O'Ryan shouted to be heard above the wind.

"I'm choosing for them," Abraham declared. "I told them when they climbed aboard. Come or stay. We're not being slaves no more."

Chapter 18

At Gentleman's Folly, Anne began to quietly sell off her livestock to friends and neighbors. If she could find a buyer, she'd part with Jersey, but she didn't want to. According to her father's journal, the chestnut stallion's stud fees had been a dependable source of income for the past four years. It seemed sensible to keep Jersey and dispose of the animals that neither brought in money nor provided food or clothing for the plantation's residents.

On the eighth day after Mary, George, and their noisy brood arrived, Nate called at the house to warn Anne that the bay pirates had attacked a farm on Smith Island, killed Jake Tilghman's hunting dog, and made off with a cow, a rifle, and fifty dollars in cash.

"Are they certain it was the pirates?" she asked. "If it's the same Jake Tilghman Papa used to speak of, the man had a lot of enemies."

"You're right about that," Nate answered. "Men have been killed on Smith Island for far less than fifty dollars." He frowned. "But they've been raiding south of here. A barn was burned in Dames Quarter and slaves stolen in Accomack County."

"I suppose I should feel lucky that there are no slaves left on Gentleman's Folly to steal, shouldn't I?" Anne replied.

"All the same, I want you to be careful."

Anne sighed. "Don't worry about me, Nathaniel. After the thrashing Papa gave them in the spring, I doubt if any of the thieving scum will dare come around here again."

Nate had admitted that she was probably correct, then disclosed his real reason for coming by offering to purchase her pianoforte and the tall case clock.

She suspected that his generous offer was made more out of concern for her well-being than need for either item, but she was in no position to quibble over motives. She accepted with as much grace as possible. Dry-eyed, Anne tucked the cash into her pocket and watched as Nate's workers prepared to remove both clock and pianoforte from the house.

"Disgraceful!" George proclaimed when he realized what was happening. "That pianoforte was worth—"

"It was mine to sell," Anne reminded him. "And no business of yours."

"Have you no pride?" he sputtered. "Mary, can't you talk some sense into your sister?"

"I'll try, George." Mary scowled at Anne. "You must stop this. You can't sell your furniture. What will people think? Next you'll be auctioning off what's left of Mama's jewelry. I know I was promised the ivory bracelet—"

"Take the bracelet and you're welcome." Anne's patience with Mary had run out. She waited until the door closed behind Nate Greensboro, then turned to her sister and brother-in-law. "But if either of you want anything else in the house, it's for sale. I won't lose Gentleman's Folly, not if I have to walk the red lantern district of Baltimore in my shift!"

Two days later George and Mary, accompanied by children, servants, and dog, sailed away on the same mail boat that had brought them. Stowed securely on the deck and wrapped in heavy canvas were Papa's library desk and Mama's best silver.

Mary was weeping, her daughters whining, and George too irate for words. But in George's coat was a bill of sale for most of the west parlor furniture and the six French gilt chairs.

Anne waved at her sister and the little girls. "Come back whenever you can get away without George," she called. "And please write to let me know when the baby is born."

With a lighter heart, she turned away and walked back toward the house. She would miss Mama's chairs, but she could sit on the floor if she had to. Better the furniture go than the land.

She dug Michael's note from her apron and read it again. "You will come back to me, won't you?" she whispered. "You must come back." She didn't know if they could live with each other or not—even if he did return. But she wanted to try.

Meanwhile, she must find a way to manage on her own. For the first time in her life, she wasn't a dependent daughter or wife who must be sheltered and protected. She had a mind, and she wanted to prove that she was as capable as any man of making the plantation pay.

She hoped that when—*if* Michael did come back, he'd bring most of their race winnings with him. They'd need it.

George's thirteen hundred dollars, added to what the livestock and the other furnishings had brought, came to $3,965. She was still far short of the $5,000 that her creditors demanded on the first day of October.

On Wednesday she would drive into Oxford and see Great-Aunt Maude. Aunt Maude's granddaughter Violet was soon to be married in Chestertown. Violet had always liked the Irish hunt table. Perhaps she could persuade the old lady to purchase it for Violet as a wedding gift. On the way home, she would stop at Swan's Nest and tell Mr. Swan that she had decided to part with the heifers and Papa's best carriage.

The remains of breakfast, slightly scorched oat porridge and fried fish, sat on the table. Grace was useless in the kitchen, and

Anne had been forced to do the cooking herself. Perhaps her attempts had been what drove George back to Philadelphia.

Anne wrinkled her nose as she gathered the bowls of cold porridge. The fish was a total loss, but the porridge would do for the pigs or the chickens. Nothing could be wasted now. Before Papa's death, she'd given little thought to the cost of food. Many things would never be the same, even if her fortune improved.

With Michael and the slaves had gone the remainder of the meat in the smokehouse, all of the molasses, and most of the flour and cornmeal. True, she had fewer people to feed. In the house were only Grace and her twelve-year-old sister, Charity, who had come to help with the guests.

Outside, there were free blacks who worked for day wages, and several young bondservants. She had barely enough help to do the daily farm chores, let alone tend the tobacco fields.

Always there had been an army of maids, cooks, and washerwomen in the manor house. If Anne had needed help with her hair or her gown, she'd called for one of the girls. At mealtime, food appeared on the table. And when she'd finished eating, someone had taken away the dishes and washed them.

Managing the household after Aunt Kessie's departure had been a challenge. Nothing ran as smoothly as it once had. Anne hadn't always been sure of how much to order from town or what to ask Toby to cook. Without trained help, Anne knew that her directing of the household was a disaster.

Grace, though a sweet and willing worker, was young and inexperienced. Her sister Charity was hardly more than a child. Neither knew the first thing about caring for a lady's fine clothing or about cooking and serving. Anne had a vague knowledge of housewifery. Without a staff, day-to-day chores took forever.

Simply preparing daily meals for the three of them was

difficult. That morning, Anne had asked Grace to kill a chicken for dinner. The maid managed to chop the head off a hen, dip it in boiling water, and strip off the feathers. But she'd balked at the final step. "Pulling out all that stuff would make me sick, Miss Anne," she whined.

In the end, Anne did the unpleasant job herself. By the time she was done cleaning the chicken, she wondered if she'd ever be able to eat poultry again.

Meanwhile, Charity had finished scrubbing the hall steps so Anne sent her to gather eggs from the henhouse. Three-quarters of an hour later, the girl came back with half the usual number of eggs. The ones she'd found were cracked and smeared with chicken manure.

"Why do they look like that?" Anne asked her, trying hard not to be impatient. If she lost her temper, Charity would burst into tears. If she was too pleasant, Charity would sit down and watch Anne and her sister do the work. "Why are the eggs broken?"

Charity stared at her bare feet. "The hens bite. I tried to get the eggs out of the nests, but the danged chickens kept pecking at me—and then—and then . . . They broke the eggs."

Anne eyed her suspiciously. "So you are telling me that these dirty eggs came out of the chicken house?"

Charity studied a ragged fingernail, then bit at an invisible fragment. One orange pigtail had come undone; the other was tied with a scrap of Irish lace. Anne didn't want to ask where that had come from or why Charity's starched white mobcap was missing.

"Where did you get those eggs?"

"Offen the ground."

Anne looked at the smeared and oozing eggs and shuddered. "We can't eat these. Wash them and stir what you can salvage into the buttermilk. Then take that out to the pigpen. Do you think you can do that?"

Charity scratched her nose. "Don't like pigs. Mam says pigs will eat ya if ya give 'em a chance. Gobble you right up."

"Those little pigs won't eat anything but soft mush. I don't like paying foolish girls who are useless in my house. What should I do? Send you home without your wages?"

"No, ma'am." The bare toes curled. "Guess I could dump the milk over the fence into the trough."

"Good. That sounds like a plan. Do it."

"Yes'm."

"Now, Charity. Before anything else ends up on the kitchen floor." Anne rubbed at the small of her back. She'd just carried in a mountain of wood for the hearth, and she'd gotten a splinter in her thumb. Hauling wood was easier than contending with Charity.

Perhaps it would be better to pay Charity not to work. Anne and Grace had spent the better part of three hours heating water and washing bed linens only to have them end up on the ground when Charity hung them carelessly. "If you want wages from me," Anne threatened, "you'll have to learn new skills. Otherwise, you go home to your mother, and I'll find a new maid."

"Yes, Miss Anne," Charity promised. "I'll do better tomorrow."

"She will. I'll teach her," Grace said cheerfully.

Anne wondered who would teach Grace.

At dusk, Anne sent Grace and Charity home to their mother with the raw chicken and a bag of oatmeal. "Come back in the morning," she instructed. "And ask your mother to make the porridge."

Alone in the big house, Anne locked all the doors and windows. Then she washed her hair and went up to bed without waiting for it to dry completely. Her back ached, and she had blisters on both hands from digging potatoes in the garden.

But safely under her bed was the box containing all the money she'd accumulated.

"I can do this," she said as she slid the bolt on the bedroom door.

The house seemed to echo with small creaks and sighs.

She wasn't the nervous type, but never in her entire life had she slept without someone in the house. Uneasy thoughts flitted in her mind, and she almost wished she'd not been so hasty in packing Mary and her family back to Philadelphia.

The ridiculousness of that idea made her smile. She pushed a heavy chest of drawers in front of the door, laid Papa's pistol on the table, and climbed into bed.

Shannon stood on her hind feet and scratched at the coverlet.

Anne surrendered gracefully. "Come on." She patted the mattress, and the puppy scrambled up to snuggle against her.

Anne sunk into an exhausted slumber.

"Anne."

O'Ryan called her name in that Irish way of his. She laughed and hid, burrowing into the mounds of sweet-smelling straw.

"Where are you?"

She laughed again as he found her hiding place.

"What do I have here?" he asked. "A dairymaid?" His arms went around her, and she raised her face to meet a rain of kisses.

Grasping her at the waist, he rolled onto his back, pulling her with him. His lips were warm and sweet. The taste of him made her giddy and sent delicious sensations spiraling through her. "Ah, Annie," he crooned as he fumbled at the laces of her bodice. "What lovely breasts you have."

Rain.

It was raining. She could hear the patter of raindrops on the cedar shake roof. But she didn't care. She was warm and safe in the circle of O'Ryan's embrace, and he was touching her body, making her feel alive . . . making her want to touch him.

"Annie."

A scraping sound teased at the corner of her dream, but she tried to ignore it. All that was important was O'Ryan and what he was doing to her . . . what she knew their loving would lead to.

He laid a broad palm on her face. "Annie. Wake up."

She opened her eyes, saw the form of a man looming over her, and screamed.

"Anne, it's me!" He caught her shoulders. "Michael O'Ryan."

"Michael?" She stared at him. His face was hidden in the shadows, but there was no mistaking his voice. "Michael, is it really you?"

"Yes. It's me. God almighty, woman. I didn't mean to scare you half to death. The house was locked and barred. I—"

"You're lucky I didn't shoot you!" She scrambled back across the bed. "Haven't you ever heard of knocking?"

"On my own door?" He laughed.

"You disappear with my boat and all my slaves. You're gone for . . . for what seems like forever. Then come back and sneak into the house like a—"

"Shh, shh, shhh," he warned. "You'll have the servants up in arms."

"Servants? What servants? You took them all. I'm the only servant here!"

"Annie, be reasonable."

"Reasonable? When I was worried half to death? When you couldn't tell me what you were going to do? I'll show you reason!" She hurled a pillow at his head and retreated until she had backed against the headboard and could go no farther. "You took my race money. How did I know you were really coming back?" She stopped long enough to take a breath. "And just how did you get in here?"

"The window, sweet."

"Sneak in through an open window like a . . . like a stray tomcat."

He reached for her, and she slapped at his hand. "No! Don't you touch me! Don't you dare touch me until you apologize for leaving without an explanation. Why didn't you tell me you were—?"

"You found the letter, didn't you? I promised I'd be back. I had—"

"Oh yes. I found your note. 'Trust me,' you said. Why in Hades would a reasonable woman trust you when you'd vanished with everything of value you could get your hands on?"

"I brought back your money," he said. "I needed a stake. I knew if I went to Philadelphia, I could talk my way into a card—"

"You took our winnings to gamble at cards?"

"Peace, woman! I didn't lose your precious money, I doubled it."

"You risked our money in a game of chance? What if you'd lost?"

He scoffed. "I told you, Annie. I never lose at cards. I'm unlucky in love, not gambling. At least, I don't lose often."

"You're telling me that you have what—seven thousand dollars?"

"No, not exactly, more like three. I had to give some to Abraham."

This made no sense. Had she been dreaming before or was she dreaming now? "You gave money to Abraham?"

"Some, yes. I gave something to all of them. They'd need it to make a start. Not as much as I'd like, but—"

"Where's the sloop? Did you bring that back?"

"No, I didn't."

"You didn't."

"No. I gave that to Abraham as well."

"Oh. You gave him the boat." She shook her head in disbelief. "Are they safe? All of them?"

"I can explain—"

"None of your honeyed words," she said. "Where are my people, Michael? Did you take them north?"

"Annie, Annie," he replied. "Calm yourself, and give us a kiss. All's well that ends well." He reached for her. "I did what we both wanted. I gave them all their freedom."

Chapter 19

O'Ryan moved to the table and lit a candle. "I suppose I deserve the thrashing. But I didn't want to expose you to any more danger than I already had."

"Not knowing what you were doing was . . . You told me that my father treated me like a child. You do the same."

He shook his head. "No, Annie. I never thought you a child. You are more woman than any female I've ever known before."

"Then why all the secrecy? Why can't you be honest with me?"

He removed his coat and hung it carefully over the back of a chair. "Have I given you so much reason to doubt me?"

"You have." Anne got out of bed and threw a lacy mantle around her shoulders. "From the first it's been one falsehood upon another. I doubt if O'Ryan is even your real name."

"If I've kept certain things from you, it's been for your own good."

"Damn you, Michael!" She folded her arms over her breasts and paced restlessly. "Do you have any idea how many times my father told me that? Did you ever think that I might have helped you get our people safely north?"

He shrugged. "If I'm such a worthless blackguard, I'd have thought you glad to be rid of me."

"With every cent I owned?"

"If I'd told you what I meant to do, you might have tried to stop me." He took a step toward her and her heart thumped.

"I wouldn't have." Lord help her, she found him desirable even now. Was she so weak that she'd forgive any wrong? "Tell me the truth. If I'd had the five thousand dollars to give you, would you be long gone?"

He shrugged. "Maybe."

"So where do we go from here? Either we're a team or we're not." She sank into a straight-backed chair, still shaken by his sudden return. "Tell me everything. Where are Abraham and his wife now?"

"They dropped me on a sandbar off the southern coast of New Jersey, near Barnegat Bay."

"You offered to let them take the boat?"

"Actually, I sold it to Abraham for one hundred dollars, and I gave him a bill of sale."

Gooseflesh rose on Anne's arms. "Abraham couldn't possibly have that much money."

"In a manner of speaking, he did. I paid him for work he did here on the plantation for the past few years. Not enough, but something. He's a good sailor. If his luck holds, he'll be in Canada in a few weeks. I signed papers of freedom for them all."

She sighed. "I'm glad you did it."

He began to untie the elegant lace stock at his throat. "But? I sense a *but* coming."

Anne made a small sound of distress. "I am relieved that they're safely away. But what do we do without workers? Our tobacco crop is promised. If we can't harvest, how will we pay that debt? Between us, we have enough for the first payment to Rawlings and Rawlings, but much more will be due next year. When our creditors find out that our slaves are gone, they will be certain that we sold them and kept the money."

"Probably." He draped the white lace over the arm of the chair and began to undo his cuff links.

"This is serious, Michael. I cannot rely on the generosity of our friends, and I have no money to hire labor." She bit her lower lip. "Even if we had the cash to take on free men, there are few available. Most work their own land."

"Is that all that concerns you?"

She fought back tears as silence stretched between them. With one bold act Michael had deprived Gentleman's Folly of more money than she would see in a lifetime. But what he had done was morally right.

"Is it just the money that troubles you, or is there something more?" He removed his shirt and stretched. Muscles rippled beneath the light dusting of golden hair on his chest, and she felt her pulse quicken.

She couldn't take her eyes off him. How beautiful he was, she thought, all sleek and graceful, a man such as Eve must have discovered in the Garden of Eden. In another moment, she'd forget all her doubts—forget tomorrow—and lose herself in his hot embrace.

"No," she stammered. "It's not just the money."

"Our bargain?" He pulled off his boots, one at a time, and stood them beside the chair, then carelessly pushed a wayward section of hair off his forehead.

Heat leaped between them in a glance. She had missed him every day, but not as much as she had missed him here in her bed . . . had dreamed of him being here.

"What do you want me to say, Annie?"

Say you love me, she thought desperately. *Say that you want us to be together, not in an arrangement, but for always.* But pride kept her from speaking the words that might drive him completely away.

"Papa believed that slavery would come to an end in his

lifetime, but he felt that the government should pay the price of freeing the slaves."

"Yes, I know he did. He said as much to me once. But Abraham couldn't wait. I had to act." Michael crossed the room, stopping an arm's length away, clad only in his riding breeches and stockings.

"What now?"

He stroked her bare shoulder, a feather-light caress that sent shivers under the surface of her skin. "Now we try to save your plantation without slave labor."

"Yes." She swallowed. "I agree." She moistened her dry lips. "But I want you to admit that you were wrong in not telling me what you were going to do before you ran off. You want trust, but you can't give it."

"There's truth."

His scent, his nearness, made her knees weak and her chest tight. "Tell me, Michael. Is it just business, or is there any chance for us?"

His eyes held hers for what seemed an eternity. "Ah, you're one for the hard questions, aren't you?"

"Do you care for me at all—in the way a man does a woman? Or is it just the money and what we have between the sheets?"

He inhaled softly. "Aye, colleen, I do care for you. And I mean to see you through this mess you've found yourself in. But as for what happens when we've finished, I can't tell you. I don't know myself."

"All right." The hollow ache inside swelled until she thought it would swallow her. All she could think of was how much she wanted to hear his loving lies and feel his arms around her.

"It's not you, Anne, it's me."

"No." She shook her head. "I asked for the truth. Don't try and soften it."

He wanted to tell her what she wanted to hear. But that

path was strewn with boulders. He swallowed hard. How the hell had he gotten himself into this? Love and marriage didn't go together. He'd learned the lesson all too well at his mother's knee—and later from a false sweetheart.

Lucky at cards, unlucky at love. It had been his motto for more years than he cared to count.

He should have laughed and carried her to the bed. He should have replied that she couldn't pretend theirs had been anything other than a business agreement from the start. He was fond of her, he might have said, but nothing more.

But it was too late for those lies.

Instead, he slipped his hand under her heavy mane of red-gold hair, caressing the nape of her neck. "Do you understand anything about Ireland?" he asked her.

"A little. England holds your country in an iron fist."

"True enough, and it's true also that there is a war there. It has gone on since long before my great-grandfather was weaned and will go on so long as English redcoats march on Irish lanes." He brushed her sweet mouth with his and felt her tremble in his arms.

"You're a rebel?" she asked, when they paused long enough to draw breath.

"Patriot." He kissed her again. "A soldier . . . in the cause . . ." Another kiss. "For . . . Irish freedom." He lowered his head to nuzzle her silken breasts.

Her fingers teased and stroked the curves of his upper arms and shoulders. "Annie," he rasped, beginning to unbutton the front of her sleeping gown. Her nails scraped lightly in tantalizing circles over his skin.

How had this woman slipped so deep behind his lines of defense? When he was with her, it felt to him as though they weren't two separate souls, but one. He dropped to his knees, the better to manage the tiny pearl buttons without losing contact with her warm, sweet flesh.

"Michael." She sighed as he drew one swollen nipple between his lips.

He fumbled with the buttons, then gave up and yanked the fragile garment asunder. Buttons flew across the room and hit the floor, but he didn't care. He clasped her narrow waist and slid his hands over her shapely buttocks as he trailed hot kisses over her flat belly and lower still.

"I am a wanted man on Irish soil," he whispered. Auburn curls made his blood race and his mind spin, intoxicated by the woman-scent of her.

He rained kisses over the soft nest, then glanced up into her wide-eyed gaze to add, "I escaped prison there on the day before I was to hang."

She arched her back and groaned, tangling her fingers in his hair and pressing his face deeper into the apex of her thighs. "Ah—ah . . ."

He slipped two fingers inside, savoring the wet, delicious feel of her. She bucked against him, and he heard her gasp. "I can't wait," she cried. "Please!"

He tore off his breeches and pulled her down to the floor, covering her with his body. "Annie, Annie." He moved quickly between her thighs and slid slowly inside, feeling her tight sheath contracting around his throbbing shaft.

"Yes, yes," she moaned.

He plunged deeper, and then the intensity of his desire drove him beyond control. She rose to meet him, wrapping her legs around him, crying with joy as they sought rapture together.

Later, breathing heavily, lightly sheened with sweat, they lay in the tangle of his breeches and her ruined gown. "Darling, darling," he murmured.

She nestled in the crook of his arm as he wound a length of her hair around his finger. "Have I shared my bed with a murderer?" she whispered.

"A hard bed," he teased.

Her dark eyes narrowed, and he saw that she wanted an answer.

"You're asking me if I've killed men? Or if I've broken the Ten Commandments?"

"You're good with words, Michael." She stroked the line of his jaw. "Are you a murderer?"

"Nay." He kissed her bottom lip. "Nor a thief." He chuckled. "I've relieved a few landlords of their ill-gotten gains, but I've turned everything I ever acquired back to the people."

She traced the outline of his mouth with her forefinger. "Will you tell me your real name?" she begged.

He smiled and kissed her again. "I gave that to a lady, once," he admitted. "We were to be wed. Hell, we lived together as man and wife. But she sold me to an English captain and near cost me my neck."

"You must have loved her very much."

"I thought I did then. But that's the way of love, is it not? It deceives a man, makes him think day is night, and pain pleasure."

"Is that woman Kathleen?"

He laughed softly. "Nay. I've told you what Kathleen is to me." He sat up, pulling her with him. "This floor is getting harder by the minute."

"Do you mean to return to Ireland?"

"Nay." He rose to his feet and helped her up. "I'm weary of that fight, darling. It's time others took up the struggle."

She tilted her head and looked at him strangely. "You are bitter."

"Bitterness is bred into an Irishman's bones. If I gave that up, what would I have left? I've thrown away an inheritance large enough to buy Gentleman's Folly three times over. I've given my youth and my family to the ongoing war with the

English tyrants. I've been shot, beaten, and almost sent to the gallows. That tends to stay with a man."

"I think I could love you, O'Ryan," she said. "I think I do, in spite of everything. You could start over, here. We could start over."

Her words sucked the breath from his chest and made his bones turn to water. "On my father's grave, I tell you that you mean more to me than any man or woman ever has," he admitted. "But I'm trouble. I'd bring naught to you but unhappiness. In the end, I'd break your heart . . . or you'd break mine."

"Supposing you had a heart left to break."

"Ah, Annie." He pulled her to him and kissed her lightly on the forehead. "You do make me laugh."

She pressed him gently away. "None of that," she said lightly. "What now? How do we find workmen when you've sent mine off to Canada?"

"Am I forgiven for that?"

She went to the high bed and climbed up into it. "Probably. But I won't forget the way you went about it." She beckoned to him. "Put out the light and come to bed. We can talk about that tomorrow."

He chuckled. "You're not sending me to sleep in the barn?" He wanted her again already. They might go to bed, but he doubted that either would get much rest this night. He wanted to feel her against him, to make her his for a little while, at least.

She laughed. "I should send you to the stables, but if I did, I'd follow you there."

He joined her, leaning lazily back against the heaped pillows. "I've given you enough of my heart's blood to send me back to Ireland in chains."

"No more talk," she said as she put her arms around his

neck. "Tomorrow we'll worry about the plantation and your wicked past."

"Not tonight," he teased, kissing her soundly.

"No," she answered softly. "Not tonight."

The following morning, Anne and O'Ryan shared a lovers' breakfast of scrambled eggs, biscuits, and fresh-caught fish, all of which he cooked and served. As they ate, Anne told him how much money she'd gotten from selling off the livestock and household goods.

They decided to travel to Annapolis together and pay off the first installment to Rawlings and Rawlings before going on to Baltimore to look for Sean Cleary and his family.

"I've been thinking," Anne said. "You told me that there are a lot of Irish immigrants in Baltimore. And if your friend Sean is such a good worker, perhaps we might find other laborers there, Irishmen who would be willing to come here and—"

"Do our farm labor."

"Exactly," she said.

"That would be a brilliant idea if we had the money to pay their hire. We've a little extra, after we pay your creditors, but remember, no merchant will give you anything without cash payment. If we took on ten, perhaps twelve workmen, we'd have to support them through the winter."

"I know, but what if . . ." She placed her cup on the table and continued in a rush. "What if we promised them land?"

"What?"

"Land of their own? So many acres for working for, say, five years."

"Most of these men are desperate. They'd trade their right arms for an acre of land. But are you willing to give up part of Gentleman's Folly for—"

"I can give up a little to save the rest. Besides, Papa has

some scattered holdings, good land, on the water, that aren't part of the main parcel. I think we can work something out that I can live with."

"You're serious," he said.

"Absolutely. Without laborers, we can't get our crops planted or harvested."

"You know some of these men will have families, wives, children, perhaps elderly relatives. They won't leave them in Baltimore."

"They will be welcome here if the men are willing to work. I'll put up with no drunkards or slackers. I'll expect fair exchange for what I'm offering."

"It's worth a try, Mrs. O'Ryan. But pack sensible shoes, a plain dress, and an old bonnet."

"You don't like my blue taffeta?" she asked, glancing down at the dress she had on.

"You're as pretty as a picture," he replied. "But where we're going, you'd be as out of place as an ox in a horse race."

After completing their business in Annapolis, O'Ryan and Anne took passage with a merchant delivering imported china and cheese to Baltimore. They had supper at a busy inn near the wharf, so that Anne's arriving garbed as a fine lady and leaving as a country farmer's wife caused barely a ripple of gossip among the servants.

She wasn't the only one who had changed her appearance. When she emerged from the ladies' necessary in her new persona, she found that O'Ryan had altered his station as well. He had traded his fine wool trousers for tight-fitting buckskin breeches, his sky-blue English riding coat for a well-worn, double-breasted tailcoat of indeterminate color, and his Irish lace stock for a tradesman's linen one. His leather boots remained, but instead of the elegant, low-crowned top hat, he wore a green felt tricorne.

"I don't understand," Anne persisted as O'Ryan led her out into the twilight. "Why the masquerade?"

"Where we're going, that garb would brand us as gentlefolk. Such clothing would keep a starving family in food for months. 'Tis easier to shed it than for me to spend needless energy to prevent a pack of predators from slitting our throats."

Anne noticed the thick oaken walking stick that O'Ryan had acquired in her absence. "Thieves? You want me to go back into the sort of area that almost got me killed in Philadelphia?"

He caught her arm and pulled her back as a team of horses trotted past, drawing a heavily loaded wagon. "Careful, sweet," he warned.

They were walking through a newly constructed commercial area of the town. Shops and businesses rose on either side of the narrow street, and the air was heavy with the scents of new lumber and smoke. Tradesmen hurried past, dodging ox-drawn vehicles and farmers on horseback. Anne saw no other women but plenty of barking dogs, chickens, and even a stray pig. Obviously, this section of emerging Baltimore was nothing like the gracious port town of Annapolis.

"Why, O'Ryan? Why come here if it is so unsafe?" She didn't see anyone she thought was particularly dangerous. True, many of the passersby were unshaved or roughly dressed, but all seemed honest enough. And most seemed to be workmen on their way home.

Her husband chuckled. "How is it that I am Michael when you are happy with me, and O'Ryan when you're not?"

"I'm certain neither is your true name," she replied. "I may as well call you Bill or Patrick." She lifted her skirts to avoid a puddle.

"Rest easy, Annie. Michael was the name given me at my christening."

She studied his expression to see if he was telling the truth. "You swear it?" she asked.

"On my mother's soul."

"All right." Anne walked on for a while and then asked, "If this doesn't work, what do we do then? Depend on your skill at gambling?"

He tugged his hat down low on his forehead. "It might come to that. But our neighbors are becoming wary of sitting down to a friendly game of cards with me. And furthermore, I want to put you on your feet. If I leave, I want you to be able to survive without my help."

"If?" She arched a dark brow. "When you leave, you mean."

"Don't, Annie. I've told you before: you're far better off without me. Nothing but heartbreak could come of a forever after. Heads and hearts don't mix in marriage."

"So say you," she answered softly. "But you don't know everything about women. Sometimes, I think you don't know anything at all."

"There's truth. A woman's one of God's mysteries. I can't decide if he gave Eve to Adam as a reward or as a punishment."

He tucked his arm in hers and led them down an alley and onto a narrow lane. There were houses here, a few with fences around the small front yards, but most with bare earth or patches of ragged grass. Candlelight glowed through windows, and Anne could hear a screaming newborn.

"Have you been in Baltimore before?" she asked him. "Do you have any idea where you're going?"

"No, I've not been here, but I asked directions at the inn."

They walked until they came to a wagon shed, then followed another lane where the houses seemed to lean against each other for support. They weren't old as much as poorly constructed, and they sat directly on the street without any front yards at all.

It was nearly dark, and there was much less traffic here. Instead of raw wood, Anne smelled rotting fish. They circled around a huge sow lying in the gutter and nearly collided with a man bursting out of a shadowed doorway.

"Come home stinking of rum without a coin in your pocket!" A fat woman pounded after him. "Good for nothing!" she bellowed as she tossed the contents of a bucket at his receding back. "How do you expect me to feed these children if—?"

Anne's mouth dropped open as the formidable female stopped and whirled on her and O'Ryan.

"What you staring at?" the fishwife demanded. "Nosy busybodies!" She herded a bevy of wailing children back inside, delivered a final curse, and slammed the door, nearly taking the tail off a fleeing tabby cat.

On the far side of the street, the faithless head of the household shook cabbage leaves and potato peels off his coat and delivered an equally sacrilegious retort. Digging a bottle from his pocket, he uncorked it and drained the last drops. "Ungrateful trull," he muttered before collapsing against a rain barrel. "No respect . . . no damned respect." His head sagged against his chest and he began to snore loudly.

Anne dissolved in laughter. "Here? You expect to find honest farmworkers here?"

"Oh ye of little faith," he teased.

At the end of the road was an empty lot filled with refuse. Beyond that, O'Ryan turned down another alley that led close to the bay. Anne could smell the water and see the thick mist rolling in.

"I don't like this," she said. "It was foggy the night—"

Abruptly, the pealing of church bells cut short her complaint.

"Just ahead," O'Ryan said. "There."

Anne could barely make out a squat building ahead.

"That should be Our Lady of Sorrows. Father Joseph is the priest here. He is the guardian of the Irish community.

Through him, I hope to find Sean. He'll know where to find likely men to hire."

"But what if we can't find Sean?"

"In County Clare the old people have a saying: 'The only way to cross a bog is one step at a time.' You're among my kind now. Watch and listen. Stay close, and try to keep out of trouble."

"And trust you?"

"Aye, darling. Devil or not, I'm the only hope you've got."

Chapter 20

"Well, Annie, what do you think?" O'Ryan leaned close to make himself heard above the wild swirl of Celtic music and the stamp of heavy leather boots against the wide plank flooring.

She didn't attempt an answer. Hornpipe, flute, pennywhistle, drum, and violin spun a fiery tapestry of nearly deafening enchantment that echoed off the massive rafters of the old barn and enveloped them in sound and motion.

Earlier, at the Catholic church, she and O'Ryan had found Father Joseph and a few parishioners gathered for an evening worship service. The jovial priest had explained that most of his flock would likely be at this barn on the edge of town for a *ceilidhe*, a night of Irish dancing and music.

Anne decided that half the population of Ireland must be here, dancing, standing along the walls, tapping toes in worn leather shoes, gossiping, eating, drinking, and singing along with the musicians. Old people, toddlers, and youngsters joined in the merriment. Children darted in and out of the sets of dancers, some keeping time to the beat, others twirling and stomping to their own rhythms.

All her life, Anne had attended musical get-togethers on the Eastern Shore, but she'd never experienced anything like this. Reel followed reel, interspersed with jigs, and an occasional ballad, sung a cappella in a language Anne guessed was Celtic.

Sometimes, O'Ryan would tell her the names of the pieces: "Sligo Daughter," "The Soldier's Farewell," "Thrush at My Window," and "Foggy Island Road." Tunes began almost before the last notes of the previous one faded. Some pieces were joyous, but others so sad that they brought tears to Anne's eyes, even though she could not understand a word.

The bows and fingers of the musicians moved so quickly that it seemed some of the smoke hovering overhead was from the instruments rather than the long clay pipes favored equally by men and women. Anne marveled at the stamina of the assembly, rawboned men and women clad in little more than rags, who laughed and danced for hours without rest.

Despite the open doors at either end, the big barn was very warm. The scents of boiled cabbage, baked apples, sausages, and mashed turnips vied with unwashed sweating bodies, babies' soiled nappies, tobacco, ale, and *poteen*, a potent homemade whiskey.

Men outnumbered the females three times over, so that the ladies were much sought out for dance partners. But when there was no woman available, male volunteers willingly tied a kerchief around their necks and leaped into the breach.

"When will you ask if any want work?" Anne asked O'Ryan in the seconds between the end of one reel and the start of another.

"In good time," he replied. "Tonight is for thoughts of home and family. Here for a few hours they can forget defeat and hungry bellies."

Halfway through the evening, Sean Cleary shouldered through the crowd and flung himself at O'Ryan. The two hugged one another like lost brothers before Sean remembered his manners and snatched off his cloth cap to pay his respects.

"Missus," he said warmly. "Sure and it's fine as paint you're looking."

She returned his greetings and asked after his wife.

"My Nora's here," he answered. "Over by the food tables with the young ones. They heard that there would be sweet cakes, although where the likes of us would find the makings, I'm sure I don't know. Glued to those tables they've been, with eyes as big as a Boyne *curragh*."

"Curragh?" Anne asked.

O'Ryan chuckled. "A round wicker boat covered with ox-hide. Trust the Irish to build a boat without bow or stern."

"Ah, but they be seaworthy enough," Sean said. "I've seen men cross the Devil's own seas in them, waves as high as those rafters. And come to land without a hair harmed."

O'Ryan settled an arm around Anne's shoulders, and she thrilled at his touch. She kept reminding herself that he couldn't be trusted, that he was an utter rascal, but nothing could prevent her pulse from racing when he brushed against her.

"Pay no attention to Sean," O'Ryan teased. "He's a champion liar among a race of liars. When Sean tells a story, bait-fish turn to whales, and ha'pence to guineas."

"And you don't?" Anne laughed. "If I didn't know better, I'd think you were speaking of yourself, Mr. O'Ryan."

"Ahhh." He moaned dramatically and clutched his chest. "The woman wounds me to the heart. See what I must put up with? She's a hard one, I tell you."

Sean grinned and gave O'Ryan a friendly punch in the shoulder. "What's a man to do?" the Irish craftsman asked. "It's a man's fate to love the colleens with tongues like thorn hedges."

"For shame," Anne said. "To speak so of your gentle wife."

Sean grinned at her. "My Nora? Sweet Nora could out-scream a banshee." He nodded. "And she often does just that."

"Nora came through her lying-in all right?" O'Ryan asked. "She and the babe? You've said nothing of—"

Sean's plain face creased with pain. "Nay, the mite 'twas stillborn, God rest his little soul." Hastily, he made the sign of the cross over his chest. "Took it hard, she did."

"I'm sorry," O'Ryan said.

" 'Tis not for us to question His plans. The baby was prayed over and buried in holy ground, and there's an end to it." Sean looked over his shoulder to see that no one was close enough to hear him, then stepped closer to O'Ryan. "If you're here tonight, friend, you got my message—the one I sent from Philadelphia."

"Yes," O'Ryan said. "I did."

Sean glanced apprehensively at Anne.

"It's all right," O'Ryan assured him. "Anne knows what happened aboard ship."

"I was afraid to stay in that town any longer, folks knowing that you lived with us."

"Coming here was a wise move. There was no sense in endangering Nora and the children."

Sean nodded in agreement. "So I thought."

"Have you had any luck finding work here?"

"Nah, a day here and there. Nothing steady a man can put bread on the table with. If it weren't for Father Joseph, there'd be more than one Cleary in the churchyard."

"With that at least I can help you." O'Ryan squeezed Anne's shoulders. "We want you to come and work for us. At my wife's plantation."

Sean's eyes widened. "For you? Have you room for Nora and the—"

"For your whole family," Anne said. "Michael has a cottage ready for you. It isn't much, but—"

"That's news that will bring the roses to my Nora's cheeks. I warn you, though, our young ones are a lively lot. I hope—"

"Your children are welcome." Anne swallowed the constriction in her throat. "And we need other workers as well."

"Can you find us eight, perhaps ten men?" O'Ryan asked. "I'd prefer farmers, fishermen, craftsmen. They need to be honest and in good health."

"They can bring their wives and babes?" Sean's fists knotted and unknotted, and his chest heaved with excitement. "Sweet wounds of Christ, but that's good fortune. I can think of four—no, five already. Father Joseph may know other dependable men. One lad, Owen Conway—just eighteen, he is—has no wife, but he's walking out with Darby Gilmore's Pegeen. You'll want Darby and his brother Patty. Farmers both, and Darby is a mason as well."

"Good," O'Ryan said. "Why don't we meet at the church at ten tomorrow morning? You bring the men you think I'd want, and we'll discuss wages then."

"I've got to tell Nora," Sean replied eagerly. "I can share the news with her, can't I?"

"Wait until you leave. There's many a good man here this night," O'Ryan said. "And we can only take on a few."

"Aye. If she let a word slip that there were jobs, it would start a riot. Desperate men are dangerous, and drink makes them worse. Some has already had a nip too many. You may have seen the boys escorting Jack Murphy outside. A blowhard is Jack, and too ready with his fists. None you'd want on your land."

O'Ryan exchanged a few final words with his friend, then Sean returned to his family. O'Ryan looked down at Anne. "You'll never regret hiring him. His wife Nora is sensible and easy to get along with. She'll be a help to you in the house. She's an excellent plain cook and a skilled dairywoman."

"How is it that you know these common people so well? You're Irish, true enough, but you're not of the same class at all. How does a gentleman's son come to understand poor men?"

"Ah, Anne, always the questions. I left off being a gentleman's son when I joined the fight against British occupation of our land. Poor folk like these hid me and fed me many a time. They die for freedom easier than the rich do, because they have so little to lose but their own blood. It opened my eyes, and made me value a person—wench or lad—for what they do, not what they wear or how they talk."

"That's what gave you sympathy for the slaves."

"Aye, I suppose it did."

She looked thoughtful. "Will they be willing to learn new ways, your Irish? Growing tobacco is different than potatoes."

"We'll not be raising tobacco after this crop is in. I mean to sow winter wheat. We'll send beef, potatoes, and salt-cured cabbage here to Baltimore for the ship trade. These men know cattle and grain. Their wives can milk the herd of cows I mean to purchase, and they can make butter and cheese. Your father said it, Annie. Tobacco is a dying crop here on the Tidewater. The sot weed has bled the soil and drained the strength from too many fieldworkers. If you want to save Gentleman's Folly, you've got to adapt to new times and new crops."

"And where did you acquire such advanced knowledge of farming?"

"Some from books, some from other planters like Nate Greensboro. But believe it or not, Abraham gave me most of those ideas."

"I don't know," she hedged. "It's taking a big chance."

"Isn't that what you did when you accepted my offer of marriage?"

"You're full of glib answers."

"Smile, Annie. You're the prettiest woman here, you know."

Before she could answer, the music stopped and one of the violinists called out to O'Ryan.

"You there, fine gentleman! Cleary says you've a fair hand with a bow." He held out his instrument.

"Aye!" shouted a chorus of voices.

"Show us what you can do!"

"Sea!" cried an old woman in the Gaelic tongue.

O'Ryan glanced at Anne.

"Go ahead, Michael," she murmured.

The throng parted to let him through to the crude platform where the musicians waited. A burly redhead offered O'Ryan a hand up, and he took the offered violin and cradled it against his chest.

"What can you play?" demanded a gray-haired crone in a homespun shawl and men's boots. "Know you the 'Black-water Lament'?"

O'Ryan drew the bow across the instrument so softly that it was almost a caress, then paused to tighten the D-string. The assembly hushed as he tucked the scroll under his chin and began to play.

As the first clear notes sounded, Anne shivered. The music poured out, more magic than sound. Michael might be a rogue, but he played the violin like one of God's angels.

Anne closed her eyes as the sweet, sorrowful melody swept over her. The sheer beauty of the tune touched a chord bone-deep. The dance floor faded, and in its place she could see Michael's green island in the mist and taste the fairy dew on her lips. And as the final notes died away, she could not prevent her tears from spilling any more than she could stop loving Michael O'Ryan.

"Missus?"

Anne's eyes flew open. "Oh. I'm sorry," she murmured. It was hard to shake off the enchantment and give her attention to Sean and the gaunt woman standing beside him.

"Missus." the Irishman said, "I want you to meet my Nora."

"You great cabbage-head! You might tell the lady that I'm your wife," Nora urged.

"I know who you are," Anne said. O'Ryan's golden notes still eddied through her mind, and she searched for the right words to make Nora feel at ease. "I'm greatly indebted to you, I understand. Michael tells me that you saved his life during the ocean crossing."

"And he mine. A blessing that we made his acquaintance. He saved me from worse than death and suffered greatly for the deed."

"No need to make light of what you did," Sean said. "Nora's a saint, for all her trying to seem otherwise. I was all for minding our own business and leaving Michael to his punishment. It was her what insisted . . ." He chattered on, repeating the story O'Ryan had told her about his ordeal on the ship.

Anne was all too willing to let the Irishman do the talking until her husband rejoined them. "That was wonderful," she said to Michael. "What was that piece you played?"

"Ah, the 'Lament.' " Sean sighed. " 'Tis an old tune and a sad one."

"And none can play it like our Michael," Nora said.

A thin child with the face of an angel wiggled through the press of dancers and onlookers. "Mam, Johnny's filching sweets off the table. I tried to make him stop but—"

"Hush, Daniel. Can't you see that your da's talking with someone?" Nora frowned and wiped the boy's mouth with the corner of her apron. "And what is this I see on your lips, Daniel, angel wings?" She took a firm grasp of the boy's hand. "If you'll excuse me, Mrs. O'Ryan, I must see to my greedy *spalpeens*."

Mortified, the child stared at the floor.

Sean laughed. "And you never stole a sweet either, wife?" He brushed back the lad's unruly dark hair. "I'll come along to help," he offered.

"And probably steal more than all the younglings put together," Nora retorted. The three of them moved away as the musicians began another spirited reel.

Michael smiled down at Anne. Taking her hand in his, he raised it to his lips. "Will you do me the honor, Mrs. O'Ryan?"

"I'm not sure I know how to do these dances—"

"I'll teach you," he said as he swept her out onto the floor.

She was light on her feet and quick to learn the steps as they clapped and whirled and stomped with the best of them. After the better part of an hour, she begged him for rest.

"Worn out, are you?" he teased. "Naturally, a woman of your advanced age—"

"My age? You're one to talk!" Anne protested. "And I'm only thinking about you."

Laughing like schoolchildren, they braved the hordes around the refreshment table to procure two mugs of warm stout and retreated to a quiet corner to drink them. "If I didn't know better, I'd think you one of these colleens," he said to her.

Anne's hat hung down her back by the ribbons. Her hairpins had come loose in the dancing, and lantern light glinted off the coppery strands in her tousled auburn tresses. Damp tendrils curled around her glowing face, and O'Ryan thought she looked good enough to eat.

"What do you think of my countrymen?" he asked.

"They seem good people," she replied. "And they know how to throw a fine party!"

He chuckled and drew her back into the thick of the rollicking, heart-stirring celebration. Midnight came and went, and still they danced.

Babies and small children were tucked into nests of coats and blankets in one section of the barn. The musicians shed their coats, downed gallons of brew, and the jigs and reels grew faster until the dancers' breasts heaved and sweat ran down their faces.

Then, abruptly, the music stopped.

"Ellen Moloney," O'Ryan heard someone say.

"Ellen!" cried another man.

Hands began to clap.

"Aye, Ellen Moloney!"

A green-eyed, brown-haired girl stepped to the center of the floor and began to sing a plaintive love song.

Anne rested in the circle of O'Ryan's arms. He whispered in her ear. "Come away, love." Obediently, she put her hand in his and followed him out of the light and into the shadows.

He led her through a wide doorway to a dusty alcove.

"Where are we going?" she asked.

"Shhh." He drew her close, and kissed her full on the mouth. Once, when he'd been running from the redcoats in the Mourne Mountains and hadn't eaten in two days, he'd come across an abandoned house and a small patch of red strawberries.

Anne tasted as sweet as that ripe fruit.

He'd feasted on those berries—savored them—devoured them . . . as he wanted to do with her.

She quivered in his embrace, but her lips parted to deepen the caress. Their tongues touched, and she trembled with raw need.

He could feel the heat of her soft body through her clothes, sense the racing fever in her blood. Hot . . . burning . . . but no more than his own.

"Anne, Anne," he murmured between urgent kisses. "You're enough to drive a man half out of his mind." His hands moved over her, skimming her bare throat, cupping her full, firm breasts, laying claim to her until her faint sighs turned to whimpers of desire.

She leaned into him, molding her body to his hard thighs and swollen cock. "Love me, Michael," she murmured. "I want you to love me."

All night, the men had passed jugs of *poteen* around. But O'Ryan hadn't wanted any of the homemade whiskey, hadn't wanted to risk getting drunk for fear of not being able to protect Anne. But now, he knew he was intoxicated, smashed out of his head, not by raw alcohol, but by the scent and feel of this woman in his arms.

He couldn't get enough of her.

Only a few feet away, behind a thin partition of planks, the dancing had begun again. The music and the thud of a hundred feet shook the floor, but they might as well have been an ocean away.

"Annie, Annie," he groaned as she tugged at his shirt and slid her fingers over his stomach and up across his chest. The ache in his loins intensified. He wanted her now, all of her, but he couldn't take his own pleasure without making certain she found hers.

His hands were all over her, caressing, touching, and her breath came in quick gasps. He kissed her again and again until she clung to him shamelessly, head thrown back, moaning, heedless of discovery.

But he couldn't stop kissing her, couldn't tear himself out of her embrace . . . until her fingers brushed the source of his desire.

He groaned as she clasped his swollen sex, lightly stroking its length and sensitive head. Blood pounded in his veins. The pleasure-pain was agony . . . wonderful.

He wanted nothing more than to yank up her skirt and thrust into her warm, wet cleft, to have her here and now. He knew he'd die if he couldn't satisfy this searing hunger.

But he couldn't . . .

If they were caught, her reputation, her honor, even her

life might be at risk. Swearing under his breath, he tore himself away.

"Michael?" Her eyes widened. "Why—?"

"Not here," he rasped. "Too dangerous." He tried to think. "Up the ladder. Behind you." He guided her hand to a rung. "Hurry."

"The loft?"

"Yes." Perspiration dripped down his face and soaked his shirt beneath his coat. His hand was trembling as he helped her up into the hayloft. "Yes, hurry. Careful," he warned. "Don't fall."

He followed her up the ladder and moved away from the gaping hole in the floor. Dim light filtered up through cracks between the planks, and the swirl of pipes and strum of strings permeated the heaps of golden straw. Overhead, he could hear the coo of pigeons and the rustle of wings.

"Is this private enough for you, husband?" Anne's voice was taut, breathless, as full of passion as any man's dream.

He ripped off his coat and spread it on a mound of straw. "Private enough," he answered hoarsely.

Then they were kissing and fumbling with buttons and ties. Somehow, her skirt was off, her shift above her hips, and he was between her sweet, shapely thighs, thrusting deep.

"Forgive me now for going off without explaining?" he demanded.

"Not yet." She arched beneath him, raking his back with her nails.

"Annie . . ." He freed a pink-tipped breast from its binding and suckled fervently as he raised up and slid into her silken folds again. She was tight and hot. The pleasure was beyond words, beyond reason.

Her excited moans drove him on.

"Are you ready?" He was fuller and harder than he had

ever been. His muscles clenched as they moved together in perfect harmony.

She was Eve to his Adam, not simply a woman, but the only woman, created for him alone. And he felt the power and glory of their union as if it were the first time, not just for them, but for any man and woman.

And while the fiddlers played on, O'Ryan forgot the world and everything in it, content with Anne, and this precious gift she had given him.

Later, he cradled her and stroked her hair, murmured words he had never said to another woman. His body tingled with rolling chords of music, aftershocks of shared rapture. But even sweeter was the feel of Anne in his arms, as if they would stay this way forever.

Questions rose in his mind, but he pushed them back. He would not think about the future, not tonight. Tonight he would take this joy and hold it in his heart as he held her.

Below, he could hear the farewells exchanged and the shuffle of feet as the gathering below broke up. One by one, the lanterns winked out, until there was silence below and the only light came from the stars shining through an open loft window.

"You will be my undoing," Anne said, stroking his chest with feathery caresses.

"And you mine, woman."

"I think you brought me up here like some dairy wench to save the cost of a room for the night."

He chuckled. "Aye. If it were up to you, we might have rolled on the floor in the middle of the *ceilidhe*."

She giggled. "The thought did pass my mind."

"Wicked woman."

She sighed, and after a time, she asked, "Do you think it will work? Hiring these Irishmen?"

"It will."

"You're always so certain of yourself. I wish I was."

"I've had to be," he answered, kissing the tip of her nose. "There were few others I could look to for help. And fewer I could trust."

She murmured sleepily, "Umm, so you say. But you once talked of your mother as though you loved her. You trusted her, didn't you?"

He kissed both her eyelids and the point of her chin. "My mother, God rest her soul, was a law unto herself." He kissed her bottom lip. "I did love her, but I knew better than to trust her."

"But she was a good mother to you?"

He sighed. "Can you not be still, wife? I'm trying to make love to you."

"And who's stopping you?" She kissed him back, teasing his lips with her tongue. Her stroking of his chest distracted him further, especially when she began to lightly pinch his nipples.

"Oh, have pity on a man, will you?"

She made a small sound of amusement and laved his nipple with a warm, satin tongue.

And his heart skipped a beat. "When I was young, yes." He couldn't help it if his breathing came harder or if he seemed to feel the blood racing through his veins. "I remember my mother reading to me, singing, tending me when I was sick. But . . ." He groaned again. "Have mercy, Annie. I'm trying to answer your questions."

"And I'm listening."

"My mother valued her creature comforts more than her marriage vows." He pushed away, his mood becoming somber. "She took a rich and powerful lover. I surprised them together in the orangery when I was twelve, but she begged me not to tell my father. I never did."

Anne's touch turned to one of compassion. "Oh, Michael, it must have been a terrible shock to you."

He pushed back a wave of regret. "Not so much as the shock the following year of finding that she had left both me and my father for him."

"But if she loved him . . . " Anne squeezed his forearm tightly. "If she truly—"

"She didn't. She left him for a richer prize, and died giving birth to that man's bastard son." He swallowed the lump in his throat. "My mother, for all her noble blood, was nothing but a very high priced strumpet."

"You mustn't say that. Not about your—"

"I forgave her a long time ago, Annie. Forgave, not forgot. One thing I promised myself was that I'd learn from my father's mistake."

"I'm not your mother, O'Ryan." Anne put her arms around his neck and kissed him tenderly. "You can't go on judging all women by what she did. You're too intelligent for that."

"Am I?" he asked. "Sometimes I wonder."

Chapter 21

It was two days before Michael was able to make the arrangements to hire all the men he wanted, provide transportation for them and their families, and purchase seed and supplies for the coming year. "It will be good to get home," he said. "Gentleman's Folly has dulled my appreciation for town life."

"I agree," Anne replied. "I felt the same way about Philadelphia. I'm afraid I'm just a farmer's daughter."

"Aye." He winked at her. "And you know what they say about farmers' daughters."

"No. What do they say?"

"Shrewd in making a bargain, but oh, so easy in the hayloft."

"Not a bad description." Anne joined in his laughter, but she hadn't missed the word "home" when he spoke of the plantation.

With each passing day, Michael's ties to her and the Eastern Shore became stronger. She didn't believe that he could walk away from what they'd shared that night in the loft. It wasn't simply physical pleasure they gave each other; it was something more. And sooner or later, he had to realize that he loved her.

What troubled her most was whether or not love would be enough to make their marriage real. If she couldn't trust him, their wedding vows would always be a farce. And sooner or later they would break each other's hearts, just as Michael had predicted.

The journey back to the Eastern Shore was uneventful. Sean, his wife and children, and two other families came back on the same sloop. The rest of the Irish would arrive within the week.

To Anne's surprise her sister's maid Gerda was waiting for her when they reached the manor house. Anne dropped her bundles in a chair and glanced around the immaculate entrance hall.

The banister and wainscoting gleamed with beeswax. Not a single cobweb or dust mote marred the floor or ceiling. A quick glance through the open door into the dining room revealed an equal transformation. A bouquet of early autumn flowers stood in the center of the table. And the curtains, which had hung limply when Anne left for Annapolis, had been washed and starched as well.

"Gerda? Is Miss Mary with you?" Anne asked.

Grace, splendid in starched mobcap and white apron, bobbed a curtsy. "Welcome home, Miss Anne." Charity was nowhere to be seen.

Anne returned the greeting and looked back at the German woman. "If Mary isn't here, then how did you—?"

"The lady send me," Gerda replied. "And good t'ing. These girls you hav' is dumpling heads both. The house vas a shame."

Anne stared at her. "Mary sent you by yourself. But why?"

Gerda made a shooing motion with her hands. "Vhy you stand here, Grace? Take the mistress's t'ings upstairs. Go. Go. Vhat I hav' to say is for the lady's ears only."

Grace gathered up Anne's packages.

"That and that are for the kitchen larder. And the thread is to go—" Anne hesitated, remembered what Michael had said about thrift. "Put that in my room as well," she ordered. Then she motioned Gerda into the small parlor and closed the door behind them.

"Nothing's wrong with Mary? Is her pregnancy—?"

"Miss Mary is fine. She send me to help you." Gerda reached into the pocket of her voluminous apron. "And she also send this money and a letter. She vorries about you, her sister. She cannot go against the master, but she vants me to tell you that she loves you and prays for you every day."

"Mary sent me money?" Anne opened the envelope. Inside were two hundred dollars in small bills.

"Yes, Miss. Your mother's jewelry she takes to the pawn-shop, so the master vill not know. Take it and velcome, Miss Mary says. She is sorry, I t'ink, for the hard feeling vhen she vas here."

Anne's eyes clouded with moisture. "Thank you, Gerda. It was very good of you to come. But I'm afraid—"

"Not to vorry about vages," the sturdy maid replied. "A year Miss Mary has promised me. And I like it here. I like this country place. Of my home it reminds me. Fresh air, good milk, and vegetables."

"I think I have you to thank for the condition of the house. Grace has a good heart but she—"

"Is young and needs haus keeper to tell her vhat to do." Gerda pursed her lips. "And that odder one, that Charity. A dumkin, she is. Lazy, but I vill not stand for lazy girl."

"I need a housekeeper very badly, Gerda," Anne said. "Do you think you could do that for me, at least for a little while?"

Gerda beamed. "You see. Vhat did I say? A good place. Two days here, and already I am promoted to haus keeper." She curtsied. "If you vill excuse me, Miss Anne, I must see to dinner. A roast I have on the spit and—"

"You cook as well? Praise God," Anne said. She waited

until she was alone, then walked to a window where the light was better and unfolded the single page of parchment that had been tucked in with the money.

Dearest Anne,

I take pen in hand to tell you that I fear we failed you when we were at Gentleman's Folly. I am sending a little money. I hope it will help. We must remember that with Papa and Mama gone, we have only each other. Please do not let anything drive us apart. If you need anything, do not hesitate to ask. I must be loyal to George, but sometimes he can be difficult.

I must tell you something unpleasant that may make Mr. O'Ryan's desertion easier to bear. An Irishman here in the city contacted George with information regarding your husband. He demanded money, which I fear George paid. The rascal's claim is that he came to Philadelphia aboard the same ship as your Mr. O'Ryan.

But the informer claims that Mr. O'Ryan is really Cormac Payne, a stowaway and thief who is wanted for committing a murder aboard the ship Providence, *September last.*

If the accusation is true, we can thank fate that you have only lost property and not your life. If you hear of Mr. O'Ryan's whereabouts, do contact the authorities at once. On no account allow him back into the house, on peril of your own safety.

I remain, your devoted sister,
Mary

Anne read the note twice, folded it, and tucked it back inside the envelope. It seemed to her that the air had suddenly become cooler in the parlor, despite the sunshine streaming through the windows. She rubbed her arms and tried to put Mary's message into perspective.

O'Ryan had told her the truth of what had happened aboard the *Providence*, hadn't he? He'd explained that the bosun's death was an accident, a result of the brute's attack on Nora Cleary.

But what if that wasn't what had really taken place? Was Cormac Payne Michael's real name? Why had someone gone to the trouble of seeking out George and selling him information about her husband?

The thought that Michael might have deceived her totally was shattering. She'd seen evidence of his creative way with words and his ability to persuade her creditors that he was someone other than who he really was. He'd made no secret of the fact that he was a fortune hunter. Was she so head-over-heels for him that she would ignore the possibility that he was a liar and a rogue? That she would accept O'Ryan's explanations for what had happened aboard the *Providence* without question or proof?

In her heart of hearts, she truly believed him to be a good man. He'd not harmed her or anyone since he'd been in Maryland. And he'd shown real compassion for Abraham, Ivy, and the other slaves. But what if this unknown informer's tale was true? If Michael had killed the sailor deliberately, she wasn't sure she wanted to face it.

If she confronted him with Mary's letter, O'Ryan might run. That would mean losing him and probably the plantation.

Not yet, she thought. She'd wait and think about what Mary had said. What harm could come of delaying long enough to harvest the tobacco and put in a crop of winter wheat? After all, if Michael wanted to be rid of her, he'd had plenty of chances already.

Besides, how could she be certain if George was genuinely concerned about her safety or if this was a ploy to gain control of Gentleman's Folly? If she had to trust someone, she'd rather it be her husband than her greedy brother-in-law.

"Miss Anne?" The parlor door opened and Shannon came bounding in. "Miss Anne," Charity repeated. "The master wants you to come outside. He needs to ask you . . . somethin' . . . somethin' . . ."

"All right, Charity. Tell him I'll be right there." She bent to hug the frisking pup, all legs and paws and licking tongue. "Good Shannon," she murmured. "Good dog." Shannon had grown too big to pick up anymore, but she was dearer to Anne than ever.

"Anne!" O'Ryan shouted from outside. "Can you come and . . ."

She couldn't make out the rest of what he was saying, but it didn't matter. Her questions and fears would have to wait. There was simply too much to be done. Thirteen immigrants were waiting in her barnyard. There were babies and old people, as well as able-bodied men and women. She'd have to find shelter for them, arrange for their noon meal, and start to assign duties. And next week, when the others came, she'd have to do it all over again.

"You'd best not be lying to me, Michael O'Ryan," she muttered. "If you are, you won't need a judge and jury to hang you, I'll finish you off myself." And then she took a deep breath and went out to do what had to be done.

Anne knew when it was time to cut the tobacco. She might not remember everything about cultivation and curing times, but she'd followed her father through the fields every September since she was old enough to walk.

Cutting the precious tobacco had to be done at exactly the right stage. Some of this year's crop had already been choked by weeds or had gone to flower before it had been topped, but what was there looked good to Anne. The leaves had to be ripe, not too green, or they would never dry properly. And if an early frost struck, the cold could destroy the plants before harvest.

Anne allowed O'Ryan to direct the laborers. She let him instruct his Irish to build a hog barn and pen in the south pasture. She even permitted him to trade some of their remaining riding horses for mules. But she would not listen to him or to Nate when it came to making a decision about the right day for cutting tobacco.

On the whole, the new arrivals were proving to be dependable laborers. There were normal disputes between the new employees and the old, and some of the immigrants didn't understand the difference between free blacks and slaves. Women argued over chores and where to string their clotheslines, and some children wandered into mischief while their parents were at work. One family spoke no English at all, and Anne required an interpreter to communicate with them.

Today, every hand, young and old, had been pressed into service to bring in the tobacco crop. Anne, astride her little bay mare—the one she'd spent a solid hour the day before to talk her husband out of selling—rode up and down the fields giving instructions. Her hired black workers knew their tasks well; they could swing machetes from early morning until the noon break without stopping. The Irish were not only slower, they tired more quickly.

"We aren't getting enough of the field done," Anne protested to O'Ryan. "At this rate, it will take us days to finish. You must get them to work faster."

O'Ryan had stripped to the waist and joined the lines of sweating men moving slowly down the rows. Muscles rippled along his chest, arms, and broad shoulders, making it hard for Anne to keep her eyes off him.

A few had stared at Michael's scarred back and whispered among themselves when he joined the cutters. "Do you think that's wise?" she'd asked him. "If the sheriff comes looking for you . . ."

She hadn't been able to keep Mary's letter a secret. After much thought, she'd shown it to Michael the night before. She was fully committed to him. No matter what he'd done in the past, she was prepared to stand by him, even if it meant breaking the law.

"If the authorities come, we'll deal with them," O'Ryan had answered. "They'd have to prove I'm Cormac Payne and not Michael O'Ryan before they could arrest me. For now, I'll be damned if I'll try to chop tobacco in a shirt."

Women, white and free black, followed the men with the long knives. Their hair tied up in kerchiefs, skirts girded, the wives and daughters of the field hands cradled the leafy stalks as gently as babies and laid them in the beds of horse-drawn wagons.

Once a wagonbed was full, a driver delivered the leaves to a curing barn, where still more men hung them from the rafters to cure. Later, when the tobacco was dry, workers had to strip the leaves from the stalks and remove the biggest stem fibers. Next they would pack the cured leaves into wooden barrels to be pressed tightly before shipping to market.

At any point in the process, something could go very wrong. Anne knew she couldn't afford to lose a single hogs-head of leaf. And with clouds hanging low over the bay and a brisk wind blowing, she had a real fear that the weather would turn against them before they could complete the harvest.

At noon, men and women stopped to eat cold bread and meat. No one went back to their quarters or to the house for dinner. Anne and O'Ryan ate in the fields with their help, washing down the simple meal with water from the well.

If she'd had her way, Anne would have gone immediately back to work, but O'Ryan shook his head. "Many of these men have gone without proper food for months. They need an hour of rest, and we have to give it to them." He wiped the sweat from his brow and tied a red handkerchief around his hair in pirate fashion to keep it out of his eyes.

"I'm going to drive one of the wagons," she said. "That will free Dave to join the cutters." She tied the ribbons of one of Kessie's old straw hats under her chin and pulled on a pair of leather gloves.

"You're trying to do the work of two," he said. "You'll wear yourself out."

"And you don't?" She touched his shoulder affectionately. "You cut twice as much tobacco as any of the others."

"We'd have none cut at all if it wasn't for your idea to bring in the immigrants." He smiled and rubbed the small of his back. "These Irish of mine prize land above all else. Ten acres for every grown man and woman who will stay five years, twenty-five acres if the family has children old enough to work. It's more than fair."

"Now we have to make certain we don't fail to pay off the mortgage. We can't let them down after I gave my word," Anne said.

"Don't worry. This new strategy will work. Baltimore is a growing market. Our beef and wheat will bring top prices. In five years you'll have your land free of the mortgage. I told my countrymen the risk, but they're willing to take it."

"I thought of the Irish, but changing Gentleman's Folly to a beef and grain farm is your idea. I would have gone on growing tobacco and falling further behind every year."

He grinned at her. "Are you saying that we make a good team?"

Her dark eyes sparkled. "Maybe we do."

It was something that he couldn't get out of his mind. The thoughts of staying here, of making Gentleman's Folly his true home, of someday having children with Anne seemed like heaven. But always his other concerns crowded in to shadow that dream. His responsibility for Kathleen and her child. And there were the charges of murder against him in Philadelphia.

He'd assured Anne that he could manage, but there was only one way to protect her home from his past—to run, to change his name and identity again. He could never go to trial, never face the inquiries into his past. And he cared too much for Anne to drag her down with him. Her reputation would recover from being abandoned by an Irish scoundrel, but not from being the widow of a hanged criminal.

In time, Anne would get over his leaving. She might hate him, but she would eventually find someone else, someone without a haunted past, someone worthy of her. If anyone deserved happiness, she did.

He'd not abandon her now. First he'd save her home and security. Then he'd give Annie the greatest gift he could—setting her free.

Chapter 22

Anne, Michael, and their crew cut and hung tobacco until it was too dark to see. In fourteen hours they had finished three-quarters of the smaller field. Michael estimated that it would take another whole day and most of the next to finish the harvest.

When they got back to the house, they found that Gerda, Grace, and two of the Irish women who were too old for heavy labor had prepared kettles of oyster chowder, pitchers of cool buttermilk, and fresh-baked bread for everyone.

Anne was too exhausted to eat. The leather reins had left blisters on both hands. She'd been bitten by mosquitoes, and she'd fallen while getting down from the wagon and scraped her knee. She could barely keep her eyes open long enough to strip off her dirty clothes and wash in cold water before falling into bed. She never stirred when Michael crawled between the sheets nearly an hour later.

In the darkest hour between dusk and dawn, the urgent clanging of the plantation bell pealed an alarm. Michael leaped up and ran to the window, pistol cocked and ready. "Anne!" he called. "Wake up!"

Her heart pounded in her chest as she fought her way out of a mist-cloaked stupor. "What is it?" she cried. "What's wrong?"

A woman's scream turned Anne's blood cold.

Michael thrust the weapon into her hands. "It looks like the tobacco field is on fire. Take this gun, and stay in the house." He reached for the coarse trousers he'd worn the day before.

"Fire? How?" She laid the pistol on the table, barrel turned toward the wall, and fumbled for the lamp.

"No! No light."

"Why? If there's a fire—"

"If there's someone outside who means us ill, the light will make you a target. No lamps and no candles."

"But the tobacco. How could the field catch fire?" She ripped off her nightgown and felt her way to her dressing closet. There she donned the first dress and shoes she could find.

"Stay in the house!" Michael insisted. "And lock the door behind me."

"I can help put out the fire. We'll need every pair of hands. We can't lose—"

"For once do as I say, woman!" He broke into a run, and she heard his footsteps fade away.

"Blast that man," she muttered under her breath. Did he believe her useless in a crisis?

She found her way back to the table, eased the hammer down on the pistol, and shoved it under the mattress. She didn't particularly like guns, and she didn't think she needed one now.

Shannon followed close behind as she entered the passageway. "No," she told the dog. "You stay here." She pushed Shannon back inside and shut the door.

The pup's anxious yips followed Anne as she hurried down the upstairs hall to the front staircase. Below, at the bottom of the steps, stood a small weeping wraith in a white shift.

"Oh, miss, it's awful," Grace cried.

"Where's your sister? And Gerda?"

"Charity's at Ma's. Gerda ran outside. I heard her yellin' for buckets. What should I do, Miss Anne? The master told me to stay here with you. He said to—"

Without warning, a heavy thud sounded from the door opposite the front entrance, the back door leading into the garden. Before Anne could react, that blow was followed by the crack of splintering wood.

Grace screamed and fled up the stairs past Anne as a man brandishing a torch shouldered his way through what was left of the door. In an instant, Anne glimpsed two wild-eyed, bearded strangers, one with an ax in his hand.

Pirates!

Anne didn't stop to reason with them. Twisting around, she pounded up the steps behind the shrieking Grace.

At the top landing, the terrified girl stopped short. Anne seized her by the hair and dragged her along toward her own bedchamber. She snatched open her door, shoved Grace inside, and slammed home the iron bolt behind them.

The maid sank to the floor sobbing. "Devils." She moaned. "Devils. I saw fire and pitchforks."

Smoke, more screams, and the sound of gunshots drifted through the open window. Downstairs, Anne could hear furniture overturning and the crash of glassware. Shannon began barking furiously.

"Oh God. Oh God, help us," Grace whimpered.

"Stop that!" Anne ordered. "Help me move this chest in front of the door." Loud male voices and the scrape of feet echoed down the hall. "Now!" Anne warned. "Or I'll make you wish the devils had you."

"I'm scared."

Anne threw all her weight against the heavy piece of furniture. Something shattered in the adjoining room, and a drunken voice laughed.

Anne was so frightened that she was afraid she might

throw up. She clenched her teeth to keep them from chattering as Grace threw her shoulder against the dresser and it slid, inch by inch, to block the door.

Anne's mouth tasted like ashes. Robbers were looting her house. Any second they might burst in. She didn't want to think what could happen to her and Grace if they got through the door. But worse was not knowing what had happened to Michael.

What if he'd been shot? What if he was lying in the field bleeding to death?

The doorknob rattled furiously. "This one's locked!" a man shouted.

White-hot anger burned away Anne's panic. "Grace, go into the dressing room," she whispered. "In the end wall is a loose panel. Move it aside. There's a ladder that leads to the attic. Go up there and hide. Quick now."

"You come, too. You know what they did to Palmer's slave girl. They'll ravish us. Then they'll cut our—"

"Grace, stop that talk. You do as I say." Anne retrieved Michael's pistol from under the mattress. This was her house, her bedchamber. She wasn't running anymore. "Go on!" she hissed at the girl. "Do you want the devils to eat you?"

Grace gave a squeak of pure fright and ran.

The knob turned, but the lock held fast.

"You gonna let that stop you?" asked a harsh voice on the far side of the door.

The marauder's words were heavily slurred, difficult for her to understand, but she recognized the accent: bay islanders. A wicked bunch, Papa had called them. Descended from redcoat deserters, criminals, and wreckers, they paid no taxes, knew no religion, and heeded no laws but their own. Even sheriffs and tax collectors gave the marshy islands a wide berth.

"Open up, little birds!"

Anne backed away from the door. The wood creaked as an intruder threw his weight against it.

" 'Twill go worse for thee, do we have to smash this door!"

"I'm warning you, get out of my house!" Anne shouted.

Her answer was a burst of coarse laughter.

"I have a gun," she called. "I'll shoot."

A man swore. "Will ye now?"

"Maybe she'd change her mind, if she got a look at Jock's pizzle!"

"Stand away from that door!" Anne said as she cocked the hammer on the pistol. She extending her pistol arm and steadied her wrist with her free hand.

Another blow struck the door, and Anne squeezed the trigger. Fire flashed in the darkened room as the bullet tore through the wooden panel. A man howled.

"Shit!"

"Tup me, Jock, the bitch has killed me."

Anne lowered the smoking pistol and crouched on the floor. Shannon whined and crept out from under the bed, then burrowed into the circle of Anne's arms.

A rifle blast smashed through the upper door, and window glass shattered. Shocked into action, Anne crawled across the floor, keeping her head low. She thought briefly of trying to escape up to the attic, but she couldn't leave Shannon to be murdered.

Directly below the windows facing the bay grew large boxwood. If she dropped the dog onto the bushes, perhaps—

Another shot rang out, this one from downstairs. Suddenly, the voices outside her door retreated, thuds and curses growing fainter as commotion grew on the bottom floors of the house.

Anne waited, heart pounding, unsure whether it was wiser

to wait or to try to jump out the window. Then she heard Michael calling her name.

"Anne! Anne! Are you all right?"

"In here!" she shouted. "Wait until I unlock the door." Somehow, she managed to move the chest of drawers and ease back the bolt.

"Stand away," Michael warned.

The door shuddered and creaked, and then he was in the room and holding her. "Are you all right?" he asked as he crushed her against him and showered her face with kisses. "Are you hurt?"

Shannon frisked around them, yipping and barking. Michael paid no attention. "Annie, Annie," he whispered into her hair.

"You're breaking my ribs," she protested.

Instantly he let her go. "You gave me a fright, woman." The thought of those men putting their filthy hands on her had shaken him to the core. Even now, with her in arm's reach, he couldn't stop thinking how much he loved her and how close he had come to losing her.

"The tobacco?" she asked. "How much—"

"We lost some," he answered brusquely. "But the fools didn't reckon with the ditch that cuts across that end of the field. The fire burned out there on its own."

It crossed his mind that if she'd died during the attack, Gentleman's Folly would have been his. The thought was sickening. He didn't care about the tobacco or about the damned plantation. Compared to Anne, they were worthless.

"Is anyone hurt?"

"Nora Cleary put a pitchfork through one of the swine. I winged one with a rifle bullet, but his companions carried him off. Some of our people are roughed up, but the only one seriously hurt is Darby Gilmore. He has a broken arm. The fire must have been a decoy to get us out of the house so that they could sack it. Silver, slaves, money. It's what they've been stealing along the Virginia shore."

"Are you certain they've gone? Is it safe—"

Michael nodded. "They're away, more's the pity. The scum landed at our dock, bold as brass. Two open boats. And not nearly so tough as I expected them to be. You're sure you aren't hurt?" He knew he should be outside calming his people, but he couldn't bear to let Anne out of his sight.

"I'm fine, Michael." She tried to sound brave, but her voice was thin and thready. She located the fire kit on the bedside table and lit a whale oil lamp. "I think I shot one of them, too."

"Do you, now?" He took the light and went out into the hall. Dark spots stained the floorboards.

"So you did," he said grimly, inspecting the blood trail that led down the hall. One dead, two wounded. It wasn't enough.

The outlaws, witless as they seemed to be, had come here, to his wife's house—to her bedroom—the one place she should have been safe. Cold rage simmered in his gut, but he forced himself to speak calmly. "Be glad you listened to me and stayed locked in here," he said to her. "If you'd have been downstairs—"

"You were right, of course," Anne replied. "But if I'd shot straighter—"

"You did fine. No man or woman could have done better." He swallowed, nearly overcome with pride at how strong she'd been. "You did exactly the right thing." He returned the lamp to the table.

She sank onto the bed with her hands in her lap. Her face was pale and her lower lip quivered. "Will they be back, do you think?"

"Not tonight. We bloodied their noses for them. They

won't be so anxious to repeat the experience." Absently, he rubbed the aching bruise on his chin. His hand came away smeared with red.

"You've been hurt," Anne gasped and leaped up.

"It's nothing. But Nate's right. We have to put an end to them."

"Let the authorities handle these criminals," she said as she found a cloth and poured water from the pitcher into the washbowl. "We can file a report and—"

"No." He shook his head. He'd seen what happened when honest people waited for the law to protect them from predators. There was only one way to end this threat against Anne and the other families on the bay shore. "This time, the pirates came with a dozen men," he said. "Next time— Ouch."

She wiped gently at the cut on his face. "Don't fuss. If I don't clean this up, it could get badly infected."

"They may be stupid, but they could come back with too many for us to handle. We'll have to form an expedition to go after them, scour their island hideout, and destroy them once and for all."

"I don't want you to," she replied. "You don't know how dangerous they are. Papa said they were bad before the last war, but they've gotten much worse since the redcoats came up the bay and burned Washington when I was a girl. Rumor is that English deserters joined the wreckers and thieves that already hid out there. Whenever the authorities go after them, they find nothing but empty shacks. The night-raiders hide in the marsh or sail to another island.

"Honest mainlanders who go onto those islands vanish. There are stories of murdered fishermen, bodies washed up on the Eastern Shore half-eaten by crabs. Those bay islands are a morass of mudflats, marsh, and swamp. There aren't any maps. If you don't know where to go, you'll never catch them."

"They're flesh-and-blood men," he answered softly. "We've proved that tonight. And they seem to have no leadership. They could have done far more damage here with less effort. But fools or not, no household on the bay can sleep easy until they are wiped out." He knew all too well how hard it was to hunt down dangerous men in their own territory. He'd been one of them for years, and he and his comrades had led the English a merry chase through the Mountains of Mourne and the streets of Belfast.

"But my fields, they're not half cut."

"We'll get in your tobacco, Annie. Then I'll make certain that you're never threatened by these outlaws again."

On the afternoon of the third day, they hauled the last load of tobacco leaf to the drying barn. The morning of the next day, Michael, Nathaniel, six other planters, and two score of armed men set out by boat to find the pirates' settlement.

Nate had been difficult. Getting him to organize a militia to pursue the robbers hadn't been as hard as persuading him not to punch Michael in the jaw. Nate was still angry over O'Ryan's departure with Anne's slaves. And he couldn't begin to understand why he'd thrown away all that money by freeing them.

But in the end, the immediate problem of the island pirates had been more important than his ire, so long as it was perfectly clear that he, Nate, would be the leader of the avenging party.

Most of the Irish workers remained on Gentleman's Folly. They were farmers and laborers who had never learned to use a gun. "It's better if they stay here with you," Michael had said.

Anne suspected that he was right, but she still didn't understand why Michael felt he had to go after the thieves at once. "At least wait until Sheriff Clough gets back from Annapolis," she'd argued. Nate had sent a rider for the Talbot County sheriff, but John Clough's wife sent word that he was across the bay on business.

"You wanted your tobacco in the barn. It's there," Michael answered. "It's past time this matter was settled."

"You're a stubborn man, Michael," she said. "Stubborn and foolish. You won't be happy until you get yourself killed!"

"They're free to try. They'll not be the first, or likely the last."

She waited for him to utter the words that she was certain he'd been close to saying the night before in their bedroom. He loved her. She knew he did.

Instead, he bent to kiss her.

For an instant, their lips met, and then she turned her face away. "Don't do this, Michael. I'm afraid of what will happen to you."

He smiled and touched his hat brim with a forefinger in salute. "Take care of yourself, Annie. And don't wander off alone."

"Go on, then. Get yourself killed playing hero. But don't expect me to go down to the landing to wave good-bye!"

Rifle in hand, he'd turned and strode away down the hill without looking back. She mounted her waiting mare and rode through the barnyard and out to the field to give orders to the workmen.

She hadn't cried, she wouldn't give in to the threatening tears, but nothing could take away the dread she felt inside. Suddenly, having Michael safe beside her was more important than anything else in the world.

Sean Cleary, Owen Conway, and Joseph Magee were waiting to begin plowing. Each man snatched off his cap and wished Anne a good morning as she rode up.

She pointed out over the field. "We're putting all this ground into winter wheat," she explained. "We need to get the seed in the ground as soon as possible. Spread out. You start here," she indicated to Sean. "You take the middle, Owen, and you, Joseph, the far end."

Sean nodded and clicked to his team of mules. The big animals strained against the harness, and the iron-tipped plow dug into the earth, cutting a dark furrow in what had been a tobacco field until a few days before.

As if by magic, seagulls appeared overhead. The shrill cries of the birds filled the air as they swooped to snatch worms and insects from the damp soil behind the plows.

The rich, familiar scent of newly turned humus filled Anne's head and took her back to memories of her childhood. How simple life had been then. How happy she'd been, and how much she'd taken for granted.

Papa had planted grain, but not in these fields, and never so many acres. She only hoped that soil that was worn out from growing tobacco might produce a good crop of wheat. They'd know that in early summer when they harvested. As soon as the field was ready, she would go out with the women to sow the grain.

She pursed her lips and made a small clicking sound with her tongue. She wondered what her father would say if he could see her, dressed in men's breeches with a coarse skirt over it for decency, wearing clothing he'd not have tolerated on his household servants.

"Different times, Papa," she murmured softly.

She shielded her eyes from the sun and stood in the stirrups to stare toward the bay. A few white sails were still visible in the distance. "Come back to me, Michael," she murmured. "Please, come back to me."

Then she straightened her shoulders and reined the mare

around. There was other work to be done, and no one else to give the orders. Somehow, despite the hollow ache inside, she must find the strength to do what was needed.

Chapter 23

All that day, Anne kept busy. She dreaded the night, when she'd have to retire alone to her bedchamber. She knew it would be hard to sleep, not because she was afraid of the pirates coming back, but because she didn't know if Michael and the others were safe.

At dusk, just as she was preparing to go upstairs, Sean's wife came to the kitchen door. Anne welcomed her in. "Nora, is there anything wrong?"

The Irishwoman slid her homespun shawl off her hair onto her shoulder. "Nay, Missus." A calico cat slipped inside and strolled lazily toward the bowl of milk on the hearth.

"Is the water still hot? Could we have a pot of tea?" Anne said to Gerda as she waved Nora to a bench at the plain oak kitchen table.

"I didn't think to take liberty," Nora replied in her lilting Irish tones. "I only came to bring some soda bread." She held out a small bundle wrapped in faded checkered cloth. "My oldest girl, she made it whilst we were in the fields."

Anne smiled. "Thank you. And I can't tell you how grateful I am that you and Mr. Cleary have come to help us."

Stiffly, Gerda set cups and saucers for two on the table.

"Four cups, Gerda," Anne corrected her. "Cups and saucers for you and Grace as well." She turned to Nora and placed a hand over her rough one. "You must call me Anne," she said. "We need each other too much to stand on formality."

Clucking in disapproval, Gerda poured hot water over tea leaves and carried the earthenware teapot to the table before she brushed her spotless apron and perched on a bench opposite Nora. "In Mistress Mary's house, this vould never do," she muttered.

Anne smiled. "You're right, Gerda. In my sister's home, it wouldn't do. But I'm no longer a wealthy woman. It's silly for me to put on airs."

"A household must have standards," the German woman answered.

"I agree. I cannot run the manor house without you," Anne said. "I want you to stay on as my housekeeper."

"I vill," Gerda agreed firmly. "You cannot manage vit'out me." Gerda reached for the sugar. "But I vill call you Miss Anne as I alvays have. Miss Anne you are to me, and Miss Anne you stay."

"Nora, I was hoping you would take on the responsibility of the dairy," Anne said.

Nora sat up a little straighter as Anne poured the tea. "I would be happy to be your dairywoman."

"It's settled then," Anne said.

"My Sean said you wanted to pack cheese and butter for the ship trade," Nora replied. "We would need . . ."

They chatted on about the logistics of setting up the dairy as the cat curled up on the warm hearth and a cricket chirped on the closed back staircase.

Anne and Nora did most of the talking. Gerda said little; Grace said nothing. But when the pot had been filled a second time and that finished, Anne was sure that more than business had been conducted here. The four of them, different in so many ways, had taken the first shaky steps to what she suspected might grow into lasting friendship.

* * *

As she was taking her leave, Nora paused and touched Anne's shoulder. "You must not worry. The men are taking shifts guarding the house and barns."

"I wish Michael hadn't gone," Anne said.

"He will do as he wants, that one."

Anne walked a little way with Nora, back toward the cottage. Shannon gamboled after them, pausing to sniff at leaves and twigs and to bark at the barn cats and crickets.

"Do you know him well, my Michael?" Anne asked. She sensed, rather than saw, Nora stiffen.

"Well enough to advise you to hold him close. If you can . . ."

"He told me about what happened on the ship."

"Aye."

"But much of his life is a secret."

"Sometimes, 'tis best for a wife not to know everything about her man."

"Would you tell me if Michael had done anything—?" Anne stopped, searching for the right words. "It was an accident, wasn't it? He didn't intend to throw that bosun's mate into the sea, did he?"

"That troubles you, that a good man would take a bad one's life? I am a woman who hates violence, but I stabbed one of those pirates with a pitchfork. He broke into my house, threatened my children. A man like that is no man at all, but a rat. And a woman who cannot kill vermin in her kitchen will soon see her family die of hunger."

Anne nodded. "I shot one of them myself. And I'm not sorry, either."

"Aye." Nora sighed. "The Church would say we are unrepentant sinners, but I would do it again if I had to."

"But the charges against my husband are . . . You can't blame me for wondering. It's difficult to know what is real about his past and—"

"This I will tell you, but if you tell another, I will swear you lie. I do not think his name is Michael O'Ryan, and I do not think it is Cormac Payne. But whatever it is, it is no name to be ashamed of. And he must have good reason for hiding it."

"Would you trust him, if you were me?"

"With my daughter's honor. The name is not important. What's in his heart is all that counts."

"Thank you, Nora, and good night. Thank your daughter for the bread. Perhaps someday she can teach me how she makes it."

Nora said her own good-bye, and Anne left her by the edge of the orchard. She had gone perhaps a hundred feet when Shannon began to bark. "Come on," Anne called. "Come on, girl. Leave that rabbit until morning."

"Miss Anne."

A man-size shadow emerged from the orchard.

Fear made her freeze where she stood. She stared toward the nearest apple tree, heart pounding.

"It's me, Miss Anne."

She took a few steps toward the familiar voice. "Abraham?"

"Shhh, miss, don't let that Irish watchman with the musket know you're talking to me. They'll shoot first and sort out who I am when I'm dead."

"Abraham?" She walked closer, then crouched and called Shannon. "Why are you here?"

"I brought back your boat."

"My sloop?"

"Yes, ma'am. Mr. O'Ryan, he gave me a paper that said it was mine. But that wasn't right. It was your daddy's boat. It wasn't Mr. O'Ryan's to give away. The boat is anchored in the river."

"I thought you and the others were in Canada."

"Got as far as Maine. Most of them people, they were afraid to go so far north, afraid of the Indians, and the snow. They say the winters are powerful bad in Canada. Some went ashore in Massachusetts, some in Maine. Big Sam, he didn't go no farther north than New York."

"And Ivy? Is she with you?"

"Can't say. Got to ask you some questions first. Mr. O'Ryan, he gave us papers that said we're free. Are they for real? Am I free, Miss Anne, or am I just another runaway slave?"

"You're free. All of you. And if the papers aren't legal, I'll make them that way. You have my word on it."

"Good. Ivy said we could trust you. It was for her that we came back, other than bringing your sloop. She missed her sisters and her auntie. They're free women. Seems my Ivy didn't want to go to Canada. Said it was my dream, not hers."

"And you, Abraham? Will you be content to live here in Maryland?"

"As long as my son is born free, I can live anywhere."

"What about the baby? Ivy hasn't—"

"Not yet. She's a stubborn woman. She wanted her sisters and her auntie with her when the baby comes."

"Do you want to stay here? Come back to Gentleman's Folly to work?"

"No, I don't want that. No disrespect, but I mean to make my own way. I figure to start my own business with the money Mr. O'Ryan gave us. In Baltimore. That's where Ivy's auntie has a little shop. I just came to bring back your boat, and to see if we had to go on hiding."

"No more hiding. Send word to me in a few months and give me Ivy's aunt's name and where to send it, I'll see you get your properly drawn up papers."

"Thank you, Miss Anne. You've been fair with me, more than fair. And one more thing."

"Yes?"

"If it's not too much trouble, could you have that lawyer draw papers for Old Henry? He's with us. He said he didn't like the North, either. Too much salt water, and not enough dry land."

"You know he's welcome here. This was his home for so many years. I'll give him his cabin back, and he won't have to do any chores at all."

"No, I don't think that would suit him. He's got his eye on Ivy's auntie. He says he's lived single long enough, and he thinks he'll look for a young wife." Abraham chuckled. "Old Henry says he'd like to be a town man for a few years before he dies. Don't worry about Old Henry. Ivy and me, we'll look out for him."

"Do you need anything? I don't have much money, but—"

"There's something else, Miss Anne, something I heard about that you should know."

"What's that?"

"Maybe you already heard, and that's why you got strangers with guns watching the house."

"Tell me, what is it? What do you know?"

"I can't say whether it's true or not, but a sailor in Chestertown told me where some easy money was to be had. He said that an Irishman was hiring a crew to come down on the Eastern Shore and put the fear of God into some lady. They said nobody would get hurt bad, but we could make believe we were pirates and take whatever we could carry off. He wanted us to burn a barn or two and frighten off the hired help."

"When? When did you hear this?" Fear knotted in Anne's stomach.

"A week ago. I don't know if they meant you, Miss Anne. But the sailor told me that the coin came straight from some rich nob in Philadelphia. It worried me. Ivy was having pains, or I would have gotten here sooner."

"That's all right," she whispered. Her chest felt tight and

her mouth dry. She took a deep breath. "What makes you think he was talking about Gentleman's Folly?"

"Didn't know for sure. But the sailor said a lady, alone. And he claimed the house was on the bay. There's lots of houses fit that, and lots of lone women, but I don't know of any white lady living by herself on a big plantation. Maybe down in Virginia, but not around here."

"You were right to tell me, Abraham."

"But you already knew, right, Miss Anne? You wouldn't have people—"

"They already hit us. Four nights ago. They burned part of the tobacco field, broke into the manor, and wrecked furniture."

"I'm sorry. I'm so sorry. I should have come—"

"It doesn't matter. We drove them off. But we thought they were pirates. Mr. O'Ryan, Mr. Greensboro, and a lot of our neighbors went after them to put a stop to the raiding."

"They won't find them, not on those islands."

"That's what I tried to tell them." She shivered in the cool October air. "But this—this is crazy. Who would want to pay men to frighten off my workforce?"

"It's not for me to say, Miss Anne."

"Tell me what you think. Papa trusted you. He said you were smart."

"For a black man?" Bitterness crept into Abraham's voice. "If I was smart, I'd know that it's best to keep my mouth shut. It would be worth my life to speak out against a white man."

"I can't change what's happened in the past, and neither can you," she said softly. " We can only change what's ahead of us. Between us, I'm asking what you believe. Who . . . except—?"

"Mr. O'Ryan or Mr. Whitfield."

"You think one of them would commit such a wicked act? Why?"

"What all men do bad for. Money. Land."

"You think my husband could betray me that way?"

"Mr. O'Ryan gave me something I've wanted all my life: freedom for me and mine. It's hard for me to think he might do something bad to you."

"Me either." But Michael had told her to stay in her room. And the thugs had almost broken in there. The thought that Michael might have betrayed her was sickening. She couldn't accept it—wouldn't. If she hadn't had the pistol, things might have gone differently. But it had been Michael who had put the weapon in her hand.

"No, not Michael. It isn't in him to want to hurt me. Besides, as my husband, it's too easy for him to profit from what's mine."

"That leaves Mr. Whitfield. He wants Gentleman's Folly. He's always wanted it. Master James once told me he didn't trust Mr. Whitfield any further than he'd trust a Yankee running for sheriff of Talbot County."

Shannon licked Anne's chin and wiggled, eager to get to Abraham. "Shh, be still," she soothed the dog.

"I best be off. I don't know anything more. I've got to catch a ride back—back to the other shore before daybreak. I need to get back to my Ivy."

"Thank you . . . for everything."

"I be obliged for those freedom papers."

"You'll have them. I promise you."

Twigs crunched as a shadow slipped off between the trees. "Abraham?" Anne murmured. Her only answer was the rustle of salt wind through the falling apple leaves.

She slept a few hours, then rose just after dawn, still mulling over what Abraham had told her. Was it possible that George had tried to have her murdered? She knew he was selfish, but it was hard to believe that he could hate her so much.

If only Michael would get back. He would know what to do about George. Together they would face this threat and find a way to protect themselves against Mary's husband.

After breakfast, Anne saddled her mare and rode along the river road that led toward Greensboro Hall. Shannon trotted after her, eyes bright, nose sniffing the crisp morning air.

The lane ran through a thick grove of old beech trees before dipping into a low spot bordered by cattails and marsh grass. When Anne reached the small sandy beach, she saw her father's sloop anchored in five feet of water.

"Thank you, Abraham!" she said, reining in her mare to look at the boat. It looked none the worse for wear, and having it back would simplify her life. With roads being what they were for most of the year, travel by water was the life's blood of an Eastern Shore plantation. "See that, Shannon?" Anne called to the pup. "See our boat? That's our boat."

At least she wasn't losing her mind. When she'd awakened, her first thought had been to wonder if she'd dreamed Abraham's return. But if the sloop was here, he'd really come home. And if that was true, his accusations against George were probably—

Anne's reverie was broken by the sound of wagon wheels. She clicked to her mount, urging the animal back onto the dirt path.

"Hallo, Mistress Anne!" A white-haired black man waved to her from the seat of a farm wagon pulled by a team of gray ponies.

Anne recognized him as one of Nate's grooms. "Charles! Good morning!" Shannon barked excitedly as the vehicle came toward them.

Charles took off his cap. "Good day to you, mistress. I was on my way to your house."

"Is there word of Mr. O'Ryan? Of Mr. Greensboro and the others? Are they back?" she called.

He pulled the team to a halt. "No, ma'am, not so I knows. Mistress Susannah, she asked me to carry these folks along to Gentleman's Folly. They come a far piece, and they's tired. Sorry I couldn't bring them in the carriage, but Vernon drove Miss Sibyl to Talbot Courthouse and Johnny's fixing the wheel on the dogcart."

For the first time, Anne realized that there were people sitting in the back of the wagon on the floor: two women, and a small child with porcelain skin, huge brown eyes, and a head of dark ringlets. "Visitors?" she asked.

Charles nodded. "Yes, ma'am. Relatives, Mistress Susannah said."

Curious, Anne guided her mare closer. "I'm Anne O'Ryan. Were you looking for me?"

" 'Tis Mr. . . . Michael O'Ryan we've come to see." A round-cheeked Irishwoman in her late thirties shifted the squirming boy on her lap and smiled at Anne. "I hope he's to home, for as this lovely man has told you, we have come a very long way to find him."

"Want to get down!" the two-year-old insisted. "Want a drink!"

"Hush, darling. Be good for mama. Do not forget your manners. What will Mrs. O'Ryan think of us?" The second woman, her features nearly hidden by the wide brim of a straw bonnet, raised her head, revealing an oval-shaped face and hair as dark and shining as that of the child.

"You must forgive our appearance," the first lady said. "Travel is very hard on one's attire, and—"

"She is Blanche Tully, my dearest friend and companion," continued the dark-haired beauty. "And this is my son Conall."

"And you?" Anne said, knowing the answer before it came. "You are?"

"Oh, I am so sorry," the stranger replied. "I thought you knew. Michael said . . . Oh dear, now I am embarrassed. I'm Kathleen, Kathleen Brady."

Chapter 24

Gerda and Grace came out of the house to stare at the new arrivals as Nathaniel's groom reined in his team near the front entrance to the manor house. Shannon frisked back and forth, running in circles and wagging her shaggy tail.

"Please, get down," Anne said to her guests, covering her distress with Eastern Shore courtesy. "You must come in. Michael isn't here, but we expect him back at any time."

Nora's son Daniel ran to take Anne's mare.

Blanche Tully got out of the wagon and lifted small Conall in her arms. Instantly, he reached for Shannon. "Doggie!" he cried.

Anne couldn't take her eyes off the boy. As petite and fragile as his mother, he was a fairy of a child, so exquisite that he hardly seemed real. Blanche set him carefully on his feet, and, keeping a firm grip on the child's hand, glanced around as if to ask for assistance.

Anne nodded to Grace.

"I can take him, ma'am," the maid said. "I've got lots of little brothers and sisters." She squatted down so that her head was nearly level with the boy's. "Would you like something good to eat?" she asked. "Gerda has hot gingerbread in the kitchen." She looked up at Blanche. "If you don't mind, missus."

"No, that would be lovely." Blanche beamed. "Would you

like gingerbread, Conall?" She chuckled. "Might as well ask a frog if he likes to hop. Our Conall is always ready to eat, aren't you, me wee bobbin?"

Grace took the boy's other hand, and the child regarded her cautiously. "Do you like kitties?" the girl asked him. "There's a kitty in the kitchen, and if you're nice, she'll let you pet her."

Conall's Irish green eyes twinkled with mischief. "I like doggies." He pointed at Shannon. "Like that doggie!"

"Me too," Grace agreed. "Would you like the doggie to come with us?" The boy nodded, and Grace called to Shannon. Anne heard the child giggling merrily as the three disappeared through the open front door.

The groom got down off the wagon seat, and came around to the back of the vehicle. "Let me help you down, miss," he said to Kathleen.

Michael's foster sister raised her head and smiled. Again Anne was struck by the stunning beauty of her dark Irish features. If her husband's heart belonged to this woman, she didn't stand a chance.

Kathleen's attire, like Blanche's, was of expensive cloth and stylish, if somewhat out of date. But it was obvious to Anne that both women's traveling dresses had seen years of use and had been mended more than once. Kathleen's woolen cloak looked to have been cut and sewn from a man's garment, and her leather boots were worn thin.

They're educated and genteel, Anne decided, but extremely frugal or poverty-stricken. Yet, Kathleen wore pearl earrings that were worth the cost of Nate's team and wagon, and the child was dressed well indeed. It was puzzling to her.

Kathleen murmured her gratitude to Charles and extended her hand for his assistance. She missed contact with his hand by inches. Anne's mouth went dry. She stared at Kathleen as Blanche took her arm.

"Here we go," Blanche said. "A long step, Katie. There. That's it."

"We're finally here," Kathleen said smoothly. "It was so long, over the sea. Sometimes, I wondered if we'd ever find this place. Your America is very large."

Her eyes were the same sparkling hue as those of her son. But there was something different about Kathleen's sensual, almond-shaped eyes, fringed in thick dark lashes, something that made Anne's breath catch in her throat.

Kathleen Brady was blind.

"Mrs. O'Ryan?"

Anne hurried forward. "I—"

"It's all right," Kathleen said gently. "Michael didn't tell you, did he? I'm certain it's quite a surprise to you. Please don't concern yourself. I'll be right as rain as soon as I learn the layout of the house."

"She's quite self-sufficient," Blanche added.

Anne felt her cheeks grow warm. "I'm so sorry. And please, you must call me Anne. We are . . . related."

"Don't feel sorry for me." Kathleen's bright voice was as lovely as her face and figure. "I fell from a barn roof when I was seven and lost my eyesight. It was a long time ago, and I've learned to cope."

"We've no intentions of imposing on you, Mrs. O'Ryan," Blanche said. "It was Michael's idea that we should come to America, but we've only come to visit. We'll be making our home in—"

"If I know my husband, he'll want to have some say about where you settle," Anne replied. She had to keep talking, saying anything to cover her confusion—her fears.

What if Michael had lied to her about his relationship with Kathleen? What if this beautiful child was his son? "Now, please," Anne continued, "do come inside. Gerda will make you comfortable. Would you prefer that the little boy have his own bedroom, or—?"

Kathleen shook her head. "Please, put the three of us together. We've lived so close for so long that I know Conall would be terrified to sleep alone. I need dear Blanche. She's my eyes, you see."

"You must be hungry and weary from your journey," Anne said. "Would you like—?"

"Tea would be heavenly," Blanche answered. "We've not had a decent cup since we left Galway."

"Of course," Anne said. "Gerda, ask Grace to put a kettle on the fire." Heart racing and knees weak, Anne followed the others into the house and tried to welcome her guests as Maryland hospitality demanded.

In Philadelphia, in the grand townhouse on Spruce Street, the early-morning decorum of the household was shattered when Mary hurled her Chinese porcelain teapot against the wall.

"Blast you!" she cried. "Rot your greedy bowels!"

Two maids came running.

"Get out of here!" Mary snapped. A cup and cream pitcher followed the teapot. She flung them with unerring accuracy, striking the large gilt mirror and splintering that as well.

The wide-eyed cook peered in through the kitchen door.

Mary threw the matching saucer. It smashed inches above the German's head. "Out!" she shouted. "Go back to your duties!" The door closed as quickly as it had opened.

George removed his spectacles with his left hand. "Are you through with your little tantrum?" He stood and gathered the documents he'd been inspecting. "Really, Mary, this is a bit . . . too dramatic. I realize that women in your advanced condition—" He brushed an invisible spot off his lapel.

"How dare you?" She swept the sugar bowl off the table. It

broke into four pieces, spilling sugar and shards of porcelain onto the rich Aubusson carpet. "I've put up with your constant neglect of our daughters and your coming home at all hours smelling of cheap perfume. I've ignored your uncharitable remarks about my appearance and my friends. But I will not let you rob my sister of her birthright."

His eyes narrowed. "Calm yourself. You may do injury to my son."

"Your son? That's all you can think of," she raged. "Your son! Suppose I'm carrying another daughter? Will you ignore her as you ignore little Margaret and Lucy?"

George frowned. "After the luxuries I've provided for you, the least you could do is to bear me a healthy male heir."

"And if this one is a daughter? What then?" Her fingers itched to smack the smug expression off his face. But George had a temper to match her own. The one thing George had never done was physically abuse her. No matter how angry she got, she was afraid to tempt him into crossing that line.

"Then we will have another child, and we will keep having them until you die or you give me the son you promised when I married you."

"What do you suppose I am? A broodmare?"

"You betray your country lineage, my dear, when you bring the barnyard into our house."

"You insufferable prig! How dare you insult my family? We are gentry, landowners for hundreds of years! You, whose grandfather was a common butcher?"

George ignored her challenge. He stepped away from the table and eyed the broken shards that littered the floor. "Be careful, dear. Harm my son by your hysterics, and I'll be forced to take steps to protect you from yourself. Robert Twinning's wife lost her reason, and he placed her in a nunnery in upstate New York. They do wonders with the poor creature, I understand."

"I promised you a son. What did I know? I was an ignorant girl, little more than a child myself when we wed. You promised to love and honor me, husband. And little honor I've found in this house." She put her balled fists on her hips and blocked his escape. "When did you buy Rawlings and Rawlings, George? When did you assume Papa's mortgage?"

His lips twisted into a crooked smile. "I didn't. I've always owned the mortgage. The Rawlings brothers work for me. And if you hadn't been snooping through my papers where you have no business looking, this wouldn't be troubling you this morning."

"You're going there to try and take Gentleman's Folly away from Anne and her husband," she accused.

"O'Ryan's real name is Cormac Payne. He is a common stowaway, a fortune hunter, and a murderer."

"I don't believe you!"

"It's the truth. I had it from the lips of an eyewitness, a man who was present when Payne knocked an unarmed seaman over the head and threw him overboard."

"Who told you that? That no-account Mick I've seen creeping around to your office door?"

"Hold your tongue, Mary. You're too ignorant to realize that I'm doing your precious Anne a favor by assuming control of the plantation." George glared at her. "I've recently learned that this Payne hired thugs to attack the house and burn the fields. If I don't take control, he will. And your sister is more valuable to him dead than alive. Would you prefer me to take the matter in hand, or would you rather he murder Anne?"

"If you're telling the truth, you'll let me come with you." She wasn't convinced that O'Ryan was this Cormac Payne. He certainly didn't seem like a killer to her. She'd heard enough of George's lies to know when he was trying to conceal something, but she hoped that she could be of help to

Anne if she was there. "Please, George. Forgive my outburst. I was upset. Take me with you."

He took hold of her shoulders and moved her firmly aside. "You are deranged," he said. "In your condition? A decent woman wouldn't consider setting foot out of the house, let alone taking a sea journey. You'll remain here with our children. Doubtless Anne will want to come back with me, once she sees how she's been betrayed by this scoundrel. You'll see her then."

"Not likely," Mary muttered as her husband stalked from the room. "Anne would sooner go to hell than go one step with you." She sank into a mahogany chair. "And sometimes I feel exactly the same."

Michael and his neighbors arrived home that afternoon. They'd found and burned a few cabins, rescued three free blacks who claimed that they were about to be sold south into slavery, and cared for a white woman, ill with fever, who seemed to be of limited intelligence.

There had been a single shooting incident. None of the Eastern Shore planters had been injured, but they killed one pirate outright and brought two more back for trial at Talbot Courthouse. Nate's opinion was that the thieves would be convicted and hanged before the month was out.

Anne walked hand in hand with Michael back from the dock. His eyes were bloodshot, his face streaked with sweat and dust, but other than insect bites, he didn't have a scratch on him.

"We need to talk," Anne said. She felt as though a weight of uncertainty were crushing her chest. When Michael had stepped off the sloop, he swept her up, lifted her in the air, then wrapped his arms around her and kissed her passionately. But her joy at having him home safely was tempered by her fear of what he would do once he found out who was waiting at the house. Did Kathleen's presence mean an end to all Anne's hopes for their marriage?

"You've had no trouble while I was gone, have you?" he asked her. He pulled off his hat and let the breeze blow through his hair. "I want something to eat, and then I intend to sleep until—"

"Kathleen is here," Anne said bluntly.

"Here? Now?" An expression of amazement spread over his face. "How? She wouldn't have had time to get the money I sent for passage."

"Apparently they'd saved up what you sent earlier. Blanche said they came steerage into New York, then traveled down the coast, first on a cattle boat, then a fishing schooner. They came from Lewis to Oxford by coach."

His step quickened. "How is she? And the baby, Conall, is he well?"

Anne stopped short, still holding his hand. "I want the truth, Michael. I can live with the truth. Is Conall your son? If he is, we'll annul our marriage so that you can—"

"Annie, Annie. Is that what you think? That I've brought my lover and illegitimate child to your house?"

"I don't know," she whispered. "I—I have to know." She swallowed. "I love you, Michael. I don't care if you're a rebel or a mutineer . . . or even a fortune hunter. I love you, but I won't stand between you and your son."

He took her other hand. Holding both, he looked into her eyes. "Kathleen is my sister," he said. "I love her, and I feel responsible for her. I would do anything in the world for her . . . anything but be what I can't. You've seen her. You know how vulnerable she is."

"I know she's blind." Her own vision clouded with tears.

"Conall's father was an English officer who befriended Kathleen, took advantage of her innocence, and then abandoned them both. She told me of her condition and begged me to marry her and give her unborn child a name. It is the only thing I've ever refused her, and she suffered terribly for it. Townspeople—friends she'd known for years—threatened her with tar and feathering, terrorized her, and burned the house where she was living."

Pain twisted Michael's features. "Even the village priest called her a whore and a traitor for sleeping with an Englishman. All she was, was lonely."

He paused, and then went on, his voice heavy with emotion. "I could have saved her honor if I'd been willing to go to her bed. But I couldn't. We don't share the same blood, but in every way that counts, Kathleen is my sister. That's why I've tried to protect her, to see that she and Conall didn't go without."

Anne closed her eyes and listened, trying to imagine how hard it must have been for a blind woman to bear a child out of wedlock.

"In many ways, I failed them," Michael said. "I was too busy trying to drive out the British army to look after her properly. And then, when I was arrested, I put her life in danger." He paused for a long breath. "I'd been financially supporting the three of them with English gold. Somehow, she learned that I'd been arrested and came to visit me just before I was supposed to be executed. It would have been only be a matter of time before the authorities questioned her about my escape. They could have charged her with aiding a rebel and imprisoned her and Blanche as well."

"Did she help you?"

"No, they weren't even in Belfast. They were in County Clare. But that wouldn't have mattered. She was on record as being an acquaintance of mine. And I was an enemy of the Crown."

She opened her eyes again. "Does Kathleen think of you as a brother?"

"I'd be lying to you if I didn't admit that she hasn't always seen our relationship the way I have. But I owe her just the same. It was my fault that she was on the barn roof that day she fell. I'd been teasing her and—"

"She said that she was seven years old, Michael."

"Yes, but I was older. I should have realized what—"

"You were a boy. A boy teasing his sister. You can't blame yourself for Kathleen's blindness, and you certainly can't blame yourself for not taking her to wife." She flung her arms around his neck. "You great Irish fool!" She kissed him so hard that the stone on her chest turned to fairy dust. "I do love you," she murmured between sobs of relief. "I hate you for doing this to me—but I love you just the same."

"Michael! Michael! Is that you?"

Anne broke away from his embrace to see Blanche and Kathleen hurrying down the hill toward them. "Go to them," she said, giving Michael a little nudge.

His eyes met hers, and she read the hesitancy there. "Go on. What are you waiting for?" she cried. "I'd gladly share you with a hundred sisters."

That evening, shortly after ten o'clock, an elegant carriage stopped at the corner of an alley that ran down to the Philadelphia waterfront. A gentleman in a black coat and tall beaver hat stepped down onto the water-slicked street. "Wait here," he ordered.

The coachman nodded and reached under the seat for his pistol. "Be careful, sir," he warned. "This is a bad part of town."

His master walked away without replying. He kept to the center of the lane, avoiding shadowy doorways and the even darker gaps between sagging buildings.

A drunken sailor clinging facedown to a flight of steps sang the chorus of an obscene sea ditty loudly and off-key. The man in the beaver hat ignored him as he had the coachman.

At the end of the street, someone had extinguished the lamp that the watch had lit earlier in the evening. The gentleman turned left and took the first wharf extending over the harbor.

Odors of tar, sewage, and rotting fish fouled the night air. There was no moon, and clouds hung low over the city. On either side of the sagging wooden dock, ghostly sloops bobbed on their moorings.

Halfway down the walkway, another man waited.

"Cove?"

"Yes, sir."

"Were you successful?"

"I did what you wanted. Did you bring the other half of my money."

"How successful?"

"We burned some stuff, shot up the place."

"And the lady? Did she suffer an unfortunate accident?"

"I had to hire what I could find down there on the Chesapeake. Some was more talk than fight when bullets started flying."

"In other words, you failed in your assignment."

"I've done plenty for you," Cove said. "I told that sheriff where to find Payne, and I risked my neck while you sat up here snug and warm. I would have killed her, if I'd got the chance. But it didn't work out that way. You want the bitch dead, you do it."

"That's always best, isn't it?"

Cove stuck out his hand. "You owe me. Pay up, or I might be talking to the law again. And this time, it might be your name I drop."

"Very well. I will consider our business concluded." He clasped the Irishman's hand firmly with his gloved right hand

and used his left to drive a Damascus steel blade deep into Cove's belly.

Cove groaned and clutched at his midsection. George yanked the knife free and plunged it into the dying man's chest. And as he fell, George kicked him over the edge of the dock.

The body hardly made a splash.

Chapter 25

The week that followed Michael's homecoming was a joyous time for Anne. The two of them walked and rode over the plantation, sailed the river and bay, and planned the future of Gentleman's Folly. He said nothing of leaving, and she was afraid to ask. It was almost the honeymoon she'd never really had.

Michael was warm, laughing, and attentive. And the presence of his foster sister, her son, and Blanche Tully seemed to add to the sense of real family. Anne found that she genuinely liked both women and adored small, mischievous Conall. Michael's behavior around Kathleen was so obviously that of a concerned brother that Anne felt foolish and mean-spirited to have ever doubted the nature of their relationship.

And if secret fears lurked in the corners of her mind, Anne was able to forget them each night when they closed their bedroom door against the world. Their lovemaking was both passionate and tender. Sometimes, Michael brought her grandfather's violin upstairs and sang and played just for her. Once, he even shared an original composition he had written. It was so beautiful, so haunting, that it brought tears to her eyes.

"What is it called?" she asked.

He smiled and rested the bow across his knee. " 'Annie's Song.' "

Michael returned the violin to its case and slid into bed beside her. Tenderly he kissed her eyelids, her brow, and finally her lips. "You make me happy," he admitted as he looked deeply into her eyes. "I've never felt this way before. Never . . ."

"Can I ask you something?" she'd murmured between caresses.

"Anything."

"What is your real name?"

For long seconds he didn't answer, and the only sounds in the room were the rise and fall of their breathing and the crackle of wood burning in the fireplace. Applewood, she realized. Only apple could smell so sweet.

"You ask hard questions, woman."

"Please, I want to know. I think I have a right to know." She didn't tell him—couldn't—that her monthly time was late, and she suspected she might have good reason to know.

If they'd made a child of their love, she wanted to be able to tell that child what his or her father's name was. It was important, vital. She could recite her family lineage back four hundred years on the Davis side to one Owen Davis from a wild holding in the Welsh mountains.

"I'm not sure," Michael answered, so faintly that she wasn't certain she'd heard. "When my mother left my father the first time, she took me aside and told me that he couldn't have children."

"Oh, Michael, how cruel of her," she'd said, pulling him tight against her and feeling his muscles tense with an ancient pain.

"I loved him as much as I loved her. I didn't believe her, so I went to Father and demanded to know. He told me that in every way that mattered, I was his son."

"It was true?"

"True . . . and false. Whoever sired me, she never said. I

was angry, called her names that should never have come from a boy's mouth."

"She should have left well enough alone."

"Aye, so I think now. But then—ah, then, Annie. I was young and sure of so many things. I didn't believe I had a right to her husband's name. That's why I took Ryan Collins when I joined the 'moonlight boys.' "

"And was it Ryan Collins who was arrested and nearly hanged?" she demanded. He laid his head against her breast, and she stroked his soft, thick hair.

He caught her hand and raised it to his lips. One by one he kissed her knuckles, and then turned her palm so that he could kiss the pulse at her wrist. "When I reached America, I'd had time to think. If the only father I'd ever known had claimed me, who was I to reject him?" Michael's breath exhaled slowly. "In his memory, I took his name back again."

"O'Ryan?"

"Aye. Michael O'Ryan, as I was christened."

She chuckled and shoved him away playfully. "Michael O'Ryan of Belfast?"

"And Shannon," he admitted. "And a few other places I'd rather not mention."

"You scoundrel," she teased. "You tricked me into thinking that O'Ryan was an assumed name when all the while—"

Laughing, he sat up and enveloped her in a heated embrace. Pressing her back against the heaped pillows he began to kiss her in earnest, all the while trailing exploring fingers over her breasts. "I told you the truth," he murmured, nibbling at her lower lip. "If you chose to think me a liar . . ."

And then they were concerned with other matters than his name and never quite got back to the subject until breakfast the following morning. There, Kathleen and Blanche joined in the conversation.

"I once visited a Ryan Collins in prison," Kathleen said

with a barely suppressed giggle. "Poor fellow. Quite homely, he was."

"Ghastly," Blanche agreed. "But he was an enemy of the Crown and a ruthless rascal."

"What came of this rascal?" Anne asked as she passed the honey.

Kathleen shrugged. "Hanged, I believe."

"He was not hanged," Michael insisted, blue eyes twinkling. "Being a fellow of stout heart and wit, he escaped in the very shadow of the gallows."

"I suppose he took ship for the colonies?" Anne suggested.

"Alas, no," her husband said. "Gallant lad that he was, he dove into the river and drowned. Seems he'd forgotten that he couldn't swim a stroke."

"He drowned," Anne said.

"Oh yes. A tragedy," Michael went on. "And the tide was so swift that they never found his body."

Kathleen chuckled. "You are insufferable. Don't believe a word of what he says, Anne. He's always been like this. If you keep on, he'll convince you that you are a Collins."

"He drowned, I tell you," Michael insisted. "There was even a witness."

Anne lowered her head in mock exasperation and covered her face with her hands. "Cormac Payne?"

"It might have been," Michael agreed. "Now there was another stout fellow of courage. He—"

"Enough!" cried Kathleen. She tossed a biscuit and struck him full in the forehead, and they all laughed and laughed until Gerda came into the dining room to see what the commotion was all about.

"You explain it," Michael said. He kissed Anne and bid the others a good day. "I'm off to Swan's Nest to buy a bull," he said. "Sean's coming with me. And I'll be home in time for the evening meal." He turned and winked at Gerda. "Cook something good, and don't let my bride anywhere near the kitchen."

Later that morning, Anne, Kathleen, Blanche, and Conall joined a group of women and children in the orchard. Blanche spread a blanket on the grass for Kathleen and tied a rope around Conall's waist. Kathleen attached the other end to her wrist so that she could keep tabs on her son while Blanche helped with the apple picking.

It was a glorious autumn day, with white fluffy clouds above and the smell of ripe fruit in the air. Since she couldn't see to assist in the harvest, Michael's sister made herself useful by sorting apples, dividing the perfect fruit from the bruised or insect-damaged.

Two older Irishwomen cut away the soft spots and tossed apples into separate baskets, some to be ground and pressed into cider, others to be peeled for applesauce. Gerda and her assistants prepared and carried the midday meal outdoors so the workers could take their dinner in the orchard.

By afternoon, more than half the apples had been picked, and the laborers had lost all shyness with one another as Kathleen led them in singing round after round of ballads and riddle songs. Her voice was a clear, flawless soprano that rose above the rustle of the wind and the faint cry of the shore birds.

> *. . . What is whiter than the milk?*
> *Sing ninety-nine and ninety,*
> *And what is softer than the silk?*
> *And I am my true love's bonny.*

The women and youngsters, Irish and Marylanders, black and white, joined in lustily for the chorus.

Oh, you must answer questions nine,
Sing ninety-nine and ninety,
Or you're not his, but one of mine,
And you'll n'er be your lover's bonny.

Anne clung to a ladder, her feet on the next-to-highest rung, and reached for a shining red apple. Her hair was braided in a single plait and covered with a handkerchief; her skirts were rucked up. Her blouse was torn and smeared with rotten fruit, and yellowjackets buzzed around her head. She couldn't remember ever working so hard or having such a good time at apple picking.

"Miss Anne!" Charity came running. "Miss Anne. You gotta come right now. The sheriff and Mr. Whitfield and Miss Mary are at the landing. I think Sheriff Clough, he's come to arrest Mr. O'Ryan!"

Anne smoothed her hair and her skirt and petticoats as she ran toward the dock. She dashed through the sheepyard and past the strawberry patch. Just before she ducked through the hedgerow and onto the bay path, she stopped, took a deep breath, and tried to regain her dignity.

Sheriff John Clough, Anne's sister, and her brother-in-law were only a few yards away, striding toward the house. A half-dozen somber men, strangers all, followed closely on their heels.

"Miss Anne," the sheriff said as she stepped out in front of them. He was a big man, and she had to look up at him. Graying and severe in appearance, John Clough was impeccably dressed, as always.

"Good afternoon, John. Mary." She stepped forward and kissed her sister on the cheek. Mary, her pregnancy now obvious, seemed ill at ease. Her eyes were red and puffy, as if she'd been weeping. "It is good to see you, sister," Anne said.

Then she glanced at George. "You catch me at a disadvantage. We were just getting in the last of our apple crop. I wasn't expecting company."

"Is your husband at home?" Clough asked sternly.

"We know he's been here. You may as well give him up," George said.

"Mr. O'Ryan?" Anne tried to look unconcerned. "If he'd known you were coming, I'm certain he would have stayed at home. Can I help you with something?"

The sheriff frowned. "I'm afraid this is quite serious. It would be best if we spoke directly with Mr. O'Ryan."

She glanced at Mary. "I don't understand. How does this matter concern George?"

"This is hardly the place for this conversation. Can't we go to the house—?" Clough began.

"You and my sister are always welcome at Gentleman's Folly," Anne said, cutting him off. "But my brother-in-law isn't. I would appreciate it if you'd tell me what this is all about."

"Your husband Michael O'Ryan is an imposter," George said. "His real name is Cormac Payne, and he's wanted on a charge of murder on the high seas."

"Absolutely ridiculous," she replied. "I don't know who this Mr. Payne is, but Michael is a well-known gentleman. I believe this is more of your nonsense, George." She glanced back at the sheriff. "George wants to control this plantation and—"

"I do control this land," George corrected. "I hold the mortgage on it, and I demand my money immediately."

"You're lying," Anne flung back. "He's lying. Sheriff, you know that Obediah and Stoddard Rawlings—"

"Rawlings and Rawlings belongs to me," George retorted. "I've owned the establishment for some years."

"Mary, is that true?" Anne demanded.

Mary nodded as tears rolled down her cheeks, smearing the light dusting of face powder.

"The debt is mine," George insisted. "It's obvious to me that my wife's sister is totally unsuited to manage my property." He pointed at her. "I have serious doubts about her mental condition, since she's clearly under the influence of this criminal."

"Unfortunately, Miss Anne, it is my duty to arrest Mr. O'Ryan and turn him over to the authorities in Philadelphia for trial."

"He's not Cormac Payne!" Anne argued.

"I hope not," Clough replied. "In that case, he should be able to clear himself of these accusations. If not—"

"This is all a mistake!"

"Yes." George smiled unpleasantly. "It is a mistake, and you've made it."

Anne looked out her bedroom window for the hundredth time. Below, in the garden, she saw one of George's hired men leaning against a piece of marble statuary.

So much for her idea of jumping out the window and going to warn Michael that the sheriff was waiting for him.

She hugged her arms against her chest and paced the floor. She'd been furious when George had ordered both her and her sister up to her room and locked them in, but she couldn't waste energy fuming over that. She had to think of a way to stop Michael from walking into a trap.

Mary lifted her head from the pillow and sat up on the bed. "Oh, Anne, I'm so sorry about this," she said. "This is all wrong."

"Wrong? Of course, it's wrong! It's craziness. George is doing this for money."

"Have you considered that he might be right?" Mary asked

gently. "That Mr. O'Ryan might be this Cormac Payne—this murderer?"

"He's not!" Anne seized Mary's hand. "Can't you see? It doesn't matter if he is or not, not to me. I love him!"

"You thought you were in love with Mr. Preston and he was—"

"It isn't the same, Mary. O'Ryan—Michael's not the same. He's really a good person. He cares about me. And no matter what he's done, I won't let them arrest him and take him away."

Mary grimaced, and Anne released her hand. She was sorry to have hurt her. Mary didn't look well at all.

"Men can be very difficult at times," Mary said. "Even George."

"Even George? Especially George. He's a greedy, ill-tempered—"

"Don't, please don't." Mary wiped away an invisible tear. "Don't you think I know his shortcomings? I live with him every day . . . It's not easy. But he is my husband and the father of my children. I owe him a certain . . . respect—even gratitude."

"Not love?"

"Don't be childish. A woman marries because she must. How else would she have a family, a social position?"

"The two of you seemed as though you were in love when he courted you. Papa didn't like him, you know."

"Papa liked George's money well enough." Mary sighed. "And yes, I'll admit I found him handsome . . . in a gentle sort of way. Best of all, he could take me off this isolated plantation."

"You've always seemed happy to me."

"A woman makes her own happiness, Anne. Only a fool looks to someone else, least of all a man, to give it to her."

"But you are here with him," Anne pointed out. "It looks very much as though you approve of what George is doing."

"That's ridiculous. He didn't want me to come down here. We had a terrible quarrel. He left Philadelphia without me, but I defied him and followed on my own. I took a coach to Head of Elk and had the bad luck to meet George there. He was livid, but he was afraid to send me back home without an escort. So here I am." She grimaced. "He's still very, very angry."

"George has always been angry with me," Anne said. "He's never liked me, not from the first day."

"Perhaps it would be best if Mr. O'Ryan answers their charges."

"No, it wouldn't be," Anne said vehemently. "Think! Philadelphia is George's town. His money can buy any verdict he desires, and he wants to be rid of Michael."

She stopped short of telling her sister that Nora Cleary was the only witness to what really happened aboard the *Providence*. Anne seriously doubted that a jury would put faith in the testimony of an Irish female who happened to be friend, employee, and countrywoman of the accused.

She was so worried about Michael that George's threat to take Gentleman's Folly didn't matter. Without Michael . . .

He'd promised he'd be back from Swan's Nest in time for supper, and by the sun, it was already after five. Anne decided she could wait no longer.

"Can I trust you?" she asked Mary. "I have to do something. Will you stay here and stall them from finding out that I'm gone?"

"You're going out through the panel in the dressing room?"

Anne nodded. "If you don't help me, I don't stand a chance."

"What do I say if George asks for you?" Mary folded her

arms across her ample breasts and rocked back and forth. "I don't know. I just don't know."

"Tell him I'm on the closestool. Tell him anything. Just give me a little time. Please, Mary. You're my sister. You can't betray me."

"All right," she agreed. "But you're only going to make this worse."

"I'll have to chance it." Quickly, Anne changed into a dark dress and sensible shoes. Then she removed the panel and climbed the hidden stair to the attic, as Grace had done when the pirates attacked the house.

When she reached the top, she paused and listened. Below, she heard the scrape and click of wood against wood as Mary fitted the hatch back into place. "Good girl," Anne whispered.

Stepping as carefully as she could, she moved from the attic of the main house into the one over the winter kitchen. She crawled through another hatch into Grace's room and took the girl's hooded cloak from a nail. She tied a scarf around her head to cover her hair, smeared ashes on her cheeks, and donned the cape.

Anne took the narrow back steps to the kitchen and pressed her ear to the door. When she heard nothing, she pushed the door open a crack. Gerda looked up from the table and opened her mouth in surprise. Anne put a finger to her lips.

Seated with his back to the staircase was one of the men who had come with George and the sheriff. He was drinking a cup of coffee and devouring one of Gerda's apple turnovers.

Anne's heart was beating so hard that she wondered why he couldn't hear it rattling against her chest. Gritting her teeth, she stepped into the kitchen and started for the back door.

"Take that basket and fetch me some eggs from the hen-house, Nan," Gerda ordered. "And take care not to crack any of them."

"Yes'm," Anne mumbled. She snatched up the basket and went out onto the porch. Keeping her head down, she walked swiftly toward the chicken run. The man in the garden didn't even glance in her direction.

When she reached the grape arbor, she changed direction and made her way to the barn. She opened a side door and slipped inside. It took only a few moments to throw a saddle and bridle on the nearest horse. Then she scrambled up into the saddle and rode boldly into the barnyard.

"Hey, you!" someone cried.

Anne dug her heels into the gelding's side, leaned low in the saddle, and thundered away at a full gallop.

Chapter 26

The bay wasn't one of the fastest horses in Anne's stable, but he jumped the split-rail pasture fence with ease. Ignoring the shouts behind her, Anne urged him on. They galloped through an open gate and turned onto the rutted path that led toward the river and Greensboro Hall on the far side.

Two field hands stopped digging holes for the new cow pasture fence to watch her ride by, but she paid them no mind. Then, a short distance ahead, where trees closed in on either side of the road, she saw John Clough and several of his companions.

"Stop right there!" The sheriff stepped into the center of the lane and tried to wave her down.

Anne reined the gelding in hard, turned his head left, and urged him through a meadow of freshly cut hay toward the river. She glanced back over her shoulder and saw that two men had mounted up and were following her on horseback.

"Get up! Go!" she yelled to the bay. She slapped the ends of the reins across his withers, and the animal flattened out into a dead run, leaping heaps of hay and splashing through low spots in the field. A covey of quail burst out of the grass, exploding into the air, but the gelding didn't falter.

They crashed through a stand of cattails, and the horse shied when he saw the river dead ahead. He tried to turn away, but she pulled hard on the reins and held him straight on course. The gelding half leaped, half slid into the tributary, went under, and came up swimming with Anne still in the saddle.

She was in midstream when a shot whistled over her head. She gasped in astonishment and pressed her face into the animal's mane. Seconds later, her mount lurched sideways as a second bullet plowed into his hindquarters.

The terrified horse threw his head back and whinnied in pain. "No!" Anne cried. "Don't shoot!"

Assuming that the fire came from Clough's deputies, she twisted around to get a glimpse of them. In that instant, she caught sight of a black sloop, sail billowing, bearing down on her. The deck was crowded with grim-faced brigands. One terrifying figure standing in the bow held a smoking rifle.

Her gelding's shrill, agonized neighing deafened Anne as the animal thrashed wildly. Blood poured from the gaping wound, turning the water crimson around her. Anne struggled to kick free of her stirrups, but her wet skirts tangled around her legs, trapping her right foot.

Another bullet tore through the horse's neck. With a final gurgling scream, he twisted and went under in a frenzy of churning hooves.

Black terror seized Anne as bloody water closed over her head. The weight of the dying beast pulled her down. Unable to see, she held her breath, and tried frantically to loosen her right shoe.

She was beyond prayer, beyond reason. Her nails tore as she ripped at the laces. Her lungs burned. Then, abruptly, her foot came loose. Hope surged as she pushed away from the horse—and hit muddy bottom.

She knew that she had to reach the surface, had to get air. But blackness deeper than the river channel clouded her mind and weakened her determination.

An odd soothing voice told her that she didn't have to fight anymore. She could lay here, rocked by the current, with the cold water around her, safe, beyond fear and hurting, where nothing could harm her again.

She was bone tired . . . so tired.

And then Michael's image rose in her mind. What was it about Michael that troubled her . . . nagged at her complacency?

"I need you, Annie," he seemed to say in his deep, musical Irish voice.

The circle of darkness was closing, the brilliant amber-green aura of light growing smaller and smaller, flickering silver-gold and fading . . . fading.

"Annie." Michael's voice was insistent. "You must try."

Fiercely, she lashed out against the water, kicking, driving her weary body up toward the surface. Her head broke through, and she sucked in precious gulps of air. Coughing and gasping, she tried to swim with arms that held no strength, legs that would not obey.

And sank under again.

Sheer will drove her up one final time.

She took another breath, choked, and fought for the shore. But her reserves were gone, and the crimson water closed over her.

Something seized her hair and yanked her head back. Hard fingers dug into her shoulder. "Not gonna drown on us, gal. Not after we kilt that horse to stop ye."

Coarse hands tugged at her, dragging her over the side of a boat. Bay island voices jeered and a ruffian kicked her hip. She lay in the bottom of the sloop, retching, eyes clamped shut, unable to lift herself even to a sitting position.

. . . Until a musket blasted over her head.

Anne's eyes flew open. She tried to push herself up, but a heavy boot slammed her against the deck.

"Keep yer head down, woman! You want it blown clear off?"

Two more guns roared from the far shore. Splinters flew from the single mast, showering Anne with bits of white oak. She covered her face with her hands as the marauders gave an answering volley.

When the shooting ceased, she peered up between her fingers at the ragged sailor kneeling beside her. Bearded, hair long and unkempt beneath a dirty, cocked hat, he whistled between broken, green-scummed teeth as he reloaded a flint-lock musket. Behind him, a second pirate, head shaved but for a single braid that hung down over one ear, waved a Spanish cutlass and let out a high, almost girlish peal of laughter.

Then the stench of the men around her hit, and she clamped her eyes shut and curled into a ball, trying to keep from gagging. Her throat burned raw; her mouth tasted of death. She almost wished they'd let the river take her.

"On yer feet, trull!" a ruffian ordered. "Less you want old Tom to swive ye there in plain sight o' the rest." Anne scrambled to her feet as several of the other men jeered, offering lewd suggestions.

She looked around her, counting. There must be nine, ten—no, eleven raiders on the sloop. All wore various mixtures of ragged, filthy clothing that had lost all color and such newer garments as a plum silk vest and good leather boots.

The man who had spoken to her pointed to a pile of rope, and she sat on it and removed her single remaining shoe and soaking stockings. She crouched, trying to make herself small and invisible.

Then, her racing heart skipped a beat as she saw a big man in a blue coat near the bow. She knew that coat. Grace had sewn a button on it yesterday. It belonged to Michael. He had worn it this morning when he'd left for Swan's Nest.

Anne's stomach clenched and she grew light-headed. Hopelessly, she stared at the pirate. And then he turned away. Her lips moved in silent prayer as she saw the bullet hole in the back of the garment and knew that Michael was already dead.

Minutes later, Anne felt the sloop shudder as the keel scraped over the shallows. The pirates leaped over the side, splashing up the sandy bar and climbing the riverbank in the gathering dusk.

"You too," the bald man said. "Old Tom, he wants to keep you close."

"Why?" she demanded. Her voice sounded flat and emotionless to her ear. "Why are you here?" Why have you killed my husband, she wanted to ask, the only man I'll ever truly love. But she couldn't speak Michael's name to this scum . . . couldn't utter the words that would make him really dead.

" 'Twere a bad thing to go t' Tom's island and burn his house," the raider answered, grabbing her around the waist and leaning close to hiss foul breath into her face. "Kilt one o' Tom's brothers, yer menfolk did. Got to teach you a lesson, Tom says. Stay offen our islands. Out of our marsh."

Anne hit the water, sank to her waist, and waded ashore. There, in the gathering dusk, other men waited with horses. The bearded man tied her hands together and threw her up on a dapple gray. Someone took the mount's reins, and the whole party started off toward the house and barns at a hard canter.

Ahead, she could hear shots and the sound of the alarm bell. The smell of smoke was strong in the air, and flames shot from the unfinished cow barn. They were all going to die, Anne thought. Mary, Kathleen and Conall, Gerda . . . Nora's Daniel. Michael was forever lost to her, and soon . . .

Not by hell, if she could help it. Cold fury burned away the total despair that had numbed her mind and body. If she was going to leave this earth, she'd take some of them with her.

Staying in the saddle with her wrists bound wasn't easy, but that was the least of her worries. She raised her hands and began to gnaw at the knotted rope with her teeth. She'd felt one loop loosen when the horse slowed to a trot as they clattered into the barnyard.

Everywhere was pandemonium. Men cursed and groaned as they fought hand to hand with knives and fists. Pistols cracked. Women shrieked. Here a frightened horse galloped by without a rider; there a pig ran squealing. A single chicken ran in circles amid the havoc.

Anne slipped out of the stirrups, grabbed hold of the dapple gray's mane, and threw herself off the saddle and onto the ground. She fell to her knees and rolled, nearly being trampled by another horse in the process. But she reached the corner of the pound fence and scooted underneath.

The enclosure was empty. Anne got to her feet, worked the free end of the rope back to gain more slack, then wiggled out of her bonds. Behind the barn, in the flickering firelight, a wild-eyed stranger chased a calf with an ax. She ran the other way, across the pound, under the bottom rail, and toward the turkey pen.

She'd almost reached the safety of the next building when she tripped over a fallen body and fell flat. Stunned, breath knocked out of her, she used her hands to regain her balance. Her right hand hit something warm and sticky, and the fingers of her left closed on a hard object. Gritting her teeth to keep from crying out, Anne pulled back from the repulsive sensation gripping a length of steel that could only be the barrel of a pistol.

Shaking, clutching the weapon, she got to her feet in time to see a shadowy figure lunge at her from the darkness. She whirled, facing him, and leveled the pistol. Her finger tightened on the trigger.

The firing pin clicked dully on a spent load.

Her assailant sneered and grabbed her arm. Anne fought to wrench away, and she swung the heavy handgun at his head. She felt the clunk and heard him groan. His iron grip bit into her flesh, and hair rose on the back of her neck as she heard the hiss of a knife sliding out of a leather sheath. Screaming as loud as she could, she struck at him again and again with the pistol.

"Ye foul bitch! I'll cut ye bow from stern."

A rifle spit fire and lead, and the pirate dropped like a stone.

"Annie!"

She turned toward the voice. "Michael?"

"Anne! Anne!"

Then she was in his arms, burying her face in his chest, shutting out the blood and the clash of steel and the scent of death. "I thought you were dead!" She sobbed tears of joy. "You're not dead! You're not dead!"

"Come," he said urgently. "No time. I've got to get you somewhere safe." He took her hand and ran with her toward the back of the house. "Into the cellar! Kathleen's there, and your sister."

He banged on the cellar door and shouted to the women. "Open up! I've got Anne!"

"Don't go back!" she begged him, knowing she was asking the impossible. "Please! I don't care about anything else. I can't stand to lose you twice!"

"Praise be!" Nora said as she opened the cellarway hatch wide enough to let Anne in. "Quick, now!"

O'Ryan tore himself out of Anne's arms. "Next time use a loaded pistol," he said, thrusting his own into her hand. Then he shoved her down into Nora's arms and slammed the door. Anne heard the rasp of the iron lock as her husband snapped it shut.

"Go with God," she whispered.

Nora tugged at her hand, and Anne let Sean's wife lead her to the feeble circle of candlelight. Mary burst from the group of keening women and children and threw her arms around her.

"You're safe," Mary said, over and over. "We didn't know where you were. O'Ryan came to the house to warn us. But he couldn't find you. We thought—"

"I'm all right," Anne said. "Are you? You're not hurt. The baby—"

"It's dark and dirty down here. I think I have a spiderweb in my hair, but otherwise . . ." Mary shook her head. "I'm fine. Better than being up there." She pointed upstairs to the main house. Then she squeezed Anne again. "And I'm so glad you're safe. I was worried about you."

Anne heard a low whine and knelt to embrace Shannon. The gangly pup licked her face and bare arms. "Good girl," Anne said. "Good girl." She held the dog and looked around, seeing Kathleen and Conall, Blanche, Grace, and two Irish girls, and a black freeman's wife. Then she noticed taller shadows, near the foot of the stairs that led up into the hall chamber.

"My Sean," Nora said. "He has a shoulder wound. They were coming home with the bull when the pirates ambushed them. Michael and Sean got away, but Michael's horse was shot out from under him. He insisted my Sean stay here. Mr. George, too. He's guarding the—"

"Your children, Nora? Are your children here?" Anne searched the faces again. Some of the young ones had their heads buried in their mother's aprons. Others sat on the hard-packed dirt floor in frightened silence.

"All but Daniel," Nora replied. "He was with the sheep. We didn't have time to . . ." She broke off, overcome with emotion. "I should have gone after him. He's headstrong, my Daniel. I—"

"No," Anne said. "You did the right thing. Your girls are here, Nora. They need you. And your little ones. He'll be all right. Daniel's smart. He'll hide until this is over."

"They'll burn the house over our heads," Grace whimpered. "I want to go home. I want my mother."

More gunshots echoed from outside. Overhead, Anne heard running feet, and the sounds of breaking glass. She glanced back at her sister. Mary was visibly shaken, her face pale and strained.

"Here," Anne said, handing her the pistol Michael had given her. "Keep this. Use it if you have to." It was terrible that Mary had to go through this ordeal in her condition— unthinkable that any of them should.

Suddenly the hall door crashed open. Two pillagers spilled down the cellar steps. "Stop right there or I'll shoot!" Sean yelled.

"Get down!" Anne warned the women.

Mothers and children scattered in the far recesses of the multiroom cellar. Grace ducked through a door into a darkened chamber that held casks of wine and vinegar.

One of the intruders raised a pistol and fired. Sean and George shot back. The first man tumbled down the stairs. The second leaped over him at Sean, and Anne recognized him as the sailor with the shaven head and pigtail.

He landed on top of Sean. The two fell to the floor, rolling over and over in the darkness, locked in combat. George scrambled to the top of the steps and pulled the door shut.

Anne ran to the edge of the stairs. In the faint light, she could see the pirate, his butcher knife inches from the Irishman's face. She looked around and saw a stack of small lard crocks lined up against the wall. Grabbing the nearest stoneware container, she smashed it down on the raider's skull. He slumped on top of the Irishman, and Anne seized his arm and tried to drag him off.

She heard footsteps behind her and glanced over her shoulder to see George coming toward her. "Help me," she said. "He's heavy. I can't—"

Her brother-in-law stopped and aimed a flintlock pistol directly at her head. "A pity, Anne," he said. "You weren't meant to survive this—"

"No! You can't—" she began.

The pistol blast rocked her back. She threw herself face-down across Sean. Seconds passed. Anne took a breath and waited for the pain.

"Anne?" It was her sister's voice.

Was it possible that the bullet had missed her at this range? "Stay back, Mary," she warned.

"George isn't going to hurt anyone, not ever again."

Anne raised her head and saw her brother-in-law sprawled on the floor. For an instant she couldn't comprehend what had happened. Then she became aware of the smoking pistol in her sister's hand. "You—didn't . . ."

Mary dropped the heavy handgun and kicked it toward the fallen pirate. "Poor George is a hero, isn't he? He died defending us from those—those villains." She wiped her hands on her gown, and looked back over her shoulder.

As far as Anne could tell, there were no witnesses. Sean was still groaning on the floor, his assailant was unconscious or dead, and the others were hiding in the recesses of the dark cellar.

"You killed him," Anne said.

"Obviously someone had to."

"But he was your husband," Anne whispered. "You saved my life."

"You were always far too dramatic," Mary answered matter-of-factly. "Yes, he is—was my husband, but you are my only sister. A resourceful woman can always find another husband."

Anne stared at her in shock.

"Surely you didn't think that I would let George kill you." Mary shrugged. "I suppose I shall have to content myself with being a rich widow now."

Trembling, Anne knelt by George's side. "He may still be alive."

"I should hope not. Papa would be ashamed. He taught me to shoot, too."

Anne touched the nape of George's neck and found it warm. But when she rolled him onto his back, one look told her that there was no need to feel for a pulse. "He's gone."

"Good." Mary helped Anne to her feet. "Nothing, sister, not my hope of heaven or my fear of eternal damnation, would keep me from choosing your life over George's. Now, let's speak no more of it. We'll say the pirate killed him."

"You don't feel any regret, do you?"

"Some, perhaps. But George brought this on himself with his greediness and his wicked plotting."

Mary pulled a folded parchment from the bosom of her gown. "This is your mortgage. And it's caused far too much upset." She marched deliberately to the single candle and slowly fed the contract to the flame until there was nothing left but drifting ashes.

Anne stood motionless, trembling, and unable to accept what had just happened until she heard Sean moan. The sound broke her from her trance. "Call Nora," she said to Mary. "Her husband's hurt. He needs her."

A dark stain covered one side of Sean's shirt. "I think he's bleeding again from his shoulder wound," Anne added.

She glanced over at the fallen pirate. He hadn't moved since she'd hit him with the crock. She was no better than Mary was, she thought. If she'd killed a man, surely she should feel some remorse. But she didn't. He would have gladly killed any of them, and she was beyond pity for his kind.

Instead, she took George's pistol and stepped back so that she had a good view of the stairs. Part of her wanted to go up into the house to try to find out if Michael was safe, but she knew she couldn't. She had to remain here and keep the women and children from harm.

"Dear God, please don't let him die," she whispered. "Bring him back to me."

Nora and one of her friends came to Sean's side. Together, they helped him back into one of the windowless rooms. Grace brought a second candle and lit it so that they could see to tend his shoulder.

"Don't let the pirates get me," Grace begged Anne. "I don't want to die."

"You're not going to die," Anne assured her with more enthusiasm than she felt. There were no more loud noises from the house, but the sound of gunfire still came faintly from the yard. "I want you and the others to hide in the back, away from the stairs," she said. "You too, Mary."

Blanche nodded and shepherded the curious children away from the main section of the cellar. Anne carried the remaining candle to a shelf near the top of the steps, then retreated to the darkness below. Now if anyone tried to get down to them, she could see better than they could.

She waited, pistol in hand, trying not to think about the two bodies lying on the floor. Suddenly, behind her, she heard a faint scrape. "Who is it?" she demanded. "Who's there?"

Suddenly, something hot sliced down her arm. Instinctively, she raised the pistol and fired. There was a grunt, and the gun flew from her hand, propelled by a powerful male fist. Then she was flat on her back, fighting for her life with the pirate on top of her.

"Bloody cow!" he swore. "I'll kill you! I'll—"

His fingers closed on her throat. She struggled, gasping for breath, striking out with knees and fists, but he was too strong. Slowly, gradually, she could feel his hold tightening, and she knew that she had only seconds to live.

Then, without warning, the awful pressure was gone. His weight flew off her chest, and she caught a glimpse of a second man's legs as he smashed the thug against the brick wall.

Anne crawled to the bottom of the stairs and staggered to her feet. She heard a heavy thump and then the scraping of cloth on stone as one of the men slid down the wall to the floor.

"Anne!"

"Michael?" She tried to scream his name, but she could only whisper. "Michael. I thought you were dead before. I . . . saw your coat . . . the bullet hole—"

"It was hot, darling. I had my coat off, tied behind my saddle. They shot my horse, but I jumped free and made it into the woods. Sean and I came to warn—" He caught her as she fell, lifting her in his arms.

"I thought—I thought . . . I'd lost you . . . forever."

"Annie, Annie, my love," he murmured hoarsely. "It's all right, I have you. I have you safe. And I'll never let you go again—not on this green earth or the golden fields of heaven."

* * *

Later, the dead pirates were laid in rows in the barnyard. Anne's own dead and wounded people were carried into the house and made comfortable or decently prepared for their next of kin.

Six had died defending Gentleman's Folly: both of the sheriff's deputies, the Irishmen Owen Conway and Patty Gilmore, a free black fisherman named Johnny Thomson, and Anne's brother-in-law George. Sheriff Clough, Sean, and four more were wounded.

But the island marauders had suffered far worse. Nine were dead, most of the fourteen prisoners wounded. And the shaven-head pirate that Michael had fought in the cellar breathed his last within two hours of the struggle.

Nora's young son Daniel was safe, as Anne had predicted. He'd seen the group of raiders on horseback and gone to Greensboro Hall for help. It was the combined force of Nate's followers and those of Swan's Nest Plantation that had turned the tide of battle.

"Not one of them got away," Nate said proudly. His face was smeared with black powder, and he bore a gash along his right cheekbone.

O'Ryan extended his arm and the two shook hands firmly. "Without your help—"

"You'd have done the same for me," Nate answered. He looked around the compound and shook his head. "You've a right mess to clean up, neighbor."

"Aye, that I do," Michael replied. "But I've all the time in the world to do it."

"Have you?" Anne asked, coming up behind him with her sister Mary. The knife wound on Anne's arm was a shallow one, but Mary had insisted on washing and bandaging it against infection. "Are you staying?" She waited, not daring to hope, but hoping just the same.

"Aye, wife." Michael blue eyes caressed her tenderly. "If you'll still have me after I've proved myself the total fool."

She nodded and reached for his hand. It was warm and strong, and the touch of him made her heart leap with joy. "I've always wanted you," she murmured. "From the first minute I laid eyes on you."

" 'Tis natural, I suppose," he teased. "For a Shannon man's a rare thing on these colonial shores." He pulled her into his arms and kissed her, oblivious to the amused audience.

"I hate to be the one to add trouble to what you've suffered here today," Sheriff Clough said. "But I came to serve papers on you, Mr. O'Ryan, and nothing that's happened changes that. As much as I hate to do it, I've still got to take you back to Annapolis to—"

"Why?" Mary demanded. "What business have you with my brother-in-law?" She'd had a good cry brought on by belated sorrow for her George's passing, and looked the proper grieving widow.

"There's been a charge, ma'am—your . . . your late husband instigated charges that Mr. O'Ryan is really a suspect named Cormac Payne. He's wanted—"

"Ridiculous," Mary answered haughtily. "He can't be Cormac Payne."

"And why not?" Clough asked.

"Because he is," Anne said, pointing to the dead pirate who had nearly killed her.

"Yes, Miss Anne, I'm sure you want to protect your husband, but—"

"No," Mary said. "That is Payne. He once worked for my husband. I know his face well. How could you miss that shaven head?" She made a sound of disgust and covered her mouth with a lace handkerchief. "He's the one who killed my dear George."

The sheriff looked doubtful. "Ma'am, I don't—"

"That's Payne, all right," Nate agreed. "I've had dealings with the rascal before. I caught him cheating at cards in Oxford."

"It is," chimed in Gerda. "It is Cormac Payne. I heard Master George call him by that name. And I vill go to court and svear to it."

"You're liars all," Clough answered. But he sighed heavily and shrugged. "You swear to the fact, each one of you? That dead man lying there is the accused, Cormac Payne?"

The verdict was unanimous. "Absolutely," Nate said. "My wife can attest to it. She was with me—"

"At Maudy's Inn while you were playing cards," Clough finished.

"Absolutely," Anne said. "I was there. So was Mrs. Brady and—"

"Enough," the sheriff said, shaking his head. "I know when I'm licked. I'll inform those that need to know that Payne's dead, killed while committing another heinous murder."

"Then it's over?" Anne said, holding tight to O'Ryan. "Michael's free?"

"As free as any married man," Clough answered.

Laughing, Anne turned in Michael's embrace and put her uninjured arm around his neck. "Welcome home, darling," she whispered.

He kissed her again. "Have I ever told you that I loved you?"

"Do you? Truly?"

"Aye, darling. I love you."

"Both of us?"

His blue eyes clouded with puzzlement.

She stood on tiptoe and whispered in his ear.

". . . a baby?"

She nodded. "In late spring, I think."

And his whoop of joy answered every question that lingered in the recesses of her heart.

Epilogue

Gentleman's Folly Plantation
April 1825

One warm afternoon in April, nearly four years after she
and Michael had wed, Anne went out to cut an armful of
lilacs for the house. She meant to take just enough blooms to
fill the silver vase in the entrance hall, but the sweet-smelling
clusters of purple flowers had run riot this spring, nearly
blocking the arch leading to the garden maze.

Shannon lay at Anne's feet, wagging her tail and burrowing her nose in the grass while a Carolina wren scolded
them both noisily from a nearby branch. Anne laughed at the
small bird's bravado and murmured to the dog, "Best be
careful, girl, or that wren will yank out a few of your hairs to
build her nest."

"Who's building a nest?" Michael called.

Anne turned to see her husband stride around the corner of
the house with a chubby-cheeked child riding on his shoulders. Golden-haired Lizzie, soon to be three, wore her father's broad-brimmed hat, no shoes, and a very dirty dress
and apron.

"Mama! Papa's a horsee!" the moppet declared. "My
horsee!" She giggled mischievously, and Anne's heart swelled
with joy.

These two, father and daughter, were all the world to her. She dropped her lilacs and the shears and hurried to meet them. "Where have you been?" Anne asked. "And how did she get so filthy? You look as though you've been planting corn with your nose, Lizzie. You promised you'd be only a little while. You know that Lizzie will be a bear at supper if she misses her naptime."

"Will she? Will she be a bear?" Michael teased, grabbing the child by the waist and lifting her high in air. Lizzie squealed with delight and growled ferociously as her father's hat tumbled off.

Michael laughed and Anne laughed with them, fooling no one with her halfhearted scolding, least of all her husband.

"Aye, that's what we were doing, wasn't it, Lizzie?" Michael said. "Planting corn with our noses." He set the bear cub lightly on the grass, and she ran to her mother.

Anne scooped her up and showered her with kisses, heedless of the smears of mud and the small dirty hands. "Someone's going to have to give you a bath, isn't he?"

"I suppose someone will," Michael agreed. "Maybe we'll both wash off in the bay."

"In April? You certainly will not take this child—" She broke off as the twitch at the corner of her big Irishman's mouth became a grin.

"It seems to me that I can remember when you didn't mind taking a dip there," he teased.

"That was when I was a foolish colleen who knew no better," she answered in as close an imitation of his Irish accent as she could manage.

"You're sassy, woman. I can see I'll have to take you in hand—as soon as I get this small Lizzie bathed and ready for her nap."

"Noo," their daughter protested, rubbing her blue eyes with two grubby fists. "Not sleepy."

"We rode out to see the wheat in the north fields. It's looking good, Annie, very good, bigger heads of grain than I've ever seen. Do you know what they're paying for wheat this year?"

She nodded. The two of them had turned out to have a knack for farming. His steers brought the best prices at market, and she was selling her cheese as far away as Philadelphia. Gentleman's Folly had flourished, so much so that it had become common for Eastern Shore planters to drop by to ask Michael for advice. And if Anne no longer lived in as grand a manner as she had before her father died, she knew that Lizzie's financial future was secure.

"A letter from Mary arrived early this afternoon," Anne said. "She and Kathleen and the children will be coming to spend a few weeks with us as soon as Conall finishes his first term at school. And Mary's new beau—"

Michael had recaptured the squirming bear cub. "You can tell me all the news as soon as I—"

"There she is!" Grace, her white mobcap only slightly awry, pushed up a downstairs window and leaned out. "I've been looking for Miss Lizzie. She's way past her naptime."

"She needs a bath," Michael warned.

"Yes, sir. I can see that," the serving girl replied good-naturedly.

"Go along with Grace," Michael urged, "and Papa will see that you get a piece of strawberry shortcake after supper." When the little girl nodded, he passed her through the open window to the maid.

"Two shortcakes," Anne heard her daughter say. "Two."

"One dessert is enough for one small girl," Anne said firmly. "I vow the two of you will spoil her beyond redemption."

"What about me? Can I have two pieces of shortcake?" Michael pleaded.

Anne smiled and knelt to gather up her fallen lilacs. Suddenly, Shannon sniffed the air, gave a sharp bark, and plunged into the maze.

"She's on the trail of another rabbit," Michael said, retrieving his hat and putting it back on.

Anne glanced up at him and went all fluttery in the pit of her stomach. *God, but I'm a lucky woman,* she thought.

The years on the land had been good to her husband. The bluest eyes on the Chesapeake were framed by rugged, sun-bronzed skin and wheat-blond hair. And his full-sleeved linen shirt still spanned shoulders that would have done justice to a blacksmith.

Michael's sleeves were rolled up, revealing muscular arms and strong, lean hands as tanned as the exposed vee of his throat and chest. A flush of heat spread through Anne as she let her gaze skim lower, over his flat belly, lean hips, and long, sinewy legs thrust into knee-high leather boots.

"And what are you looking at?" he asked. "Staring at me with bold, dark eyes that would lure a saint into temptation."

In answer, she let the blooms fall, caught up her petticoats, and dashed through the lilac archway.

"Annie?"

Laughing, heart thudding, she darted down one path, took a right and then a left. She heard his footfalls coming after her as she wound her way deeper into the green boxwood puzzle.

"I'll find you. You know I always find you," Michael called.

"Not this time!" She giggled, as lighthearted as a new bride, and she continued on, skimming down the passageways, taking one opening after another. "Where are you, Michael O'Ryan?" she teased. She stopped and listened. There was no sound now but the wren singing a clear, bright love song.

Anne took a few more steps, then doubled back and turned left. She had played here since she was Lizzie's age, and she should have known every foot of the complex. But each wall of boxwood looked exactly like the next, and in many sections the vegetation had grown together overhead.

She thought that she was somewhere in the back quarter of the labyrinth, close to the kitchen garden, but she couldn't be certain.

She took two right turns, then another left.

Ahead of her, a fountain bubbled merrily in the mossy center of the maze. Still smiling, she rounded the last corner and stepped out directly into her husband's arms.

"Caught you," he cried.

"I—" Michael swept her up into his arms and kissed her soundly. Anne put her arms around his neck, leaned her head back, and closed her eyes, wanting to capture this perfect moment of happiness.

Sunlight filtered down through the trees, frosting the green carpet with a golden aura. "Annie, Annie," he whispered into her ear. "Isn't it time we gave our Lizzie a little brother?"

"Or a sister," she murmured. "Yes, I think it is."

He kissed her throat, her mouth, and eyelids, and she returned the favor. "Do you know how much I love you?" he asked her between kisses.

"Tell me," she urged. His hands were on her, pulling her down onto the soft bed of grass, stroking and caressing, sending sweet, wild sensations through her veins.

"I love you more than heaven."

She straddled his hips, tugging his shirt up over his head so she could feel his bare skin against hers. Her skirts tangled around her waist, and her stockings slipped down to expose her bare thighs.

"Annie O'Ryan, you're not wearing drawers!" Michael exclaimed abruptly.

"I am too! Silk ones!"

"Let me see!"

"Shushh!" She put her hand over his mouth. "Do you want the whole shore to hear you?"

He wrestled her down so that he was on top and she on the bottom. "Will they guess what we're doing, do you think?"

She giggled. "How could they not?"

"Unless they think I'm still in the fields, and you're here with some mysterious stranger."

"Michael! That's a terrible thing to say."

He leaned close, pressing his naked chest against her, and kissed her. She stopped struggling and sighed. "I love you, too," she murmured.

"You're not sorry you made that bargain in Philadelphia with an Irish lad?" he teased.

"Never," she answered fervently. "Never, never, never."

"Good. Me either."

And this time when he kissed her, the flame leaped between them, and Anne forgot everything but the man in her arms, the rogue she knew she would love and cherish forever.